THE
PATHFINDERS
SOCIETY

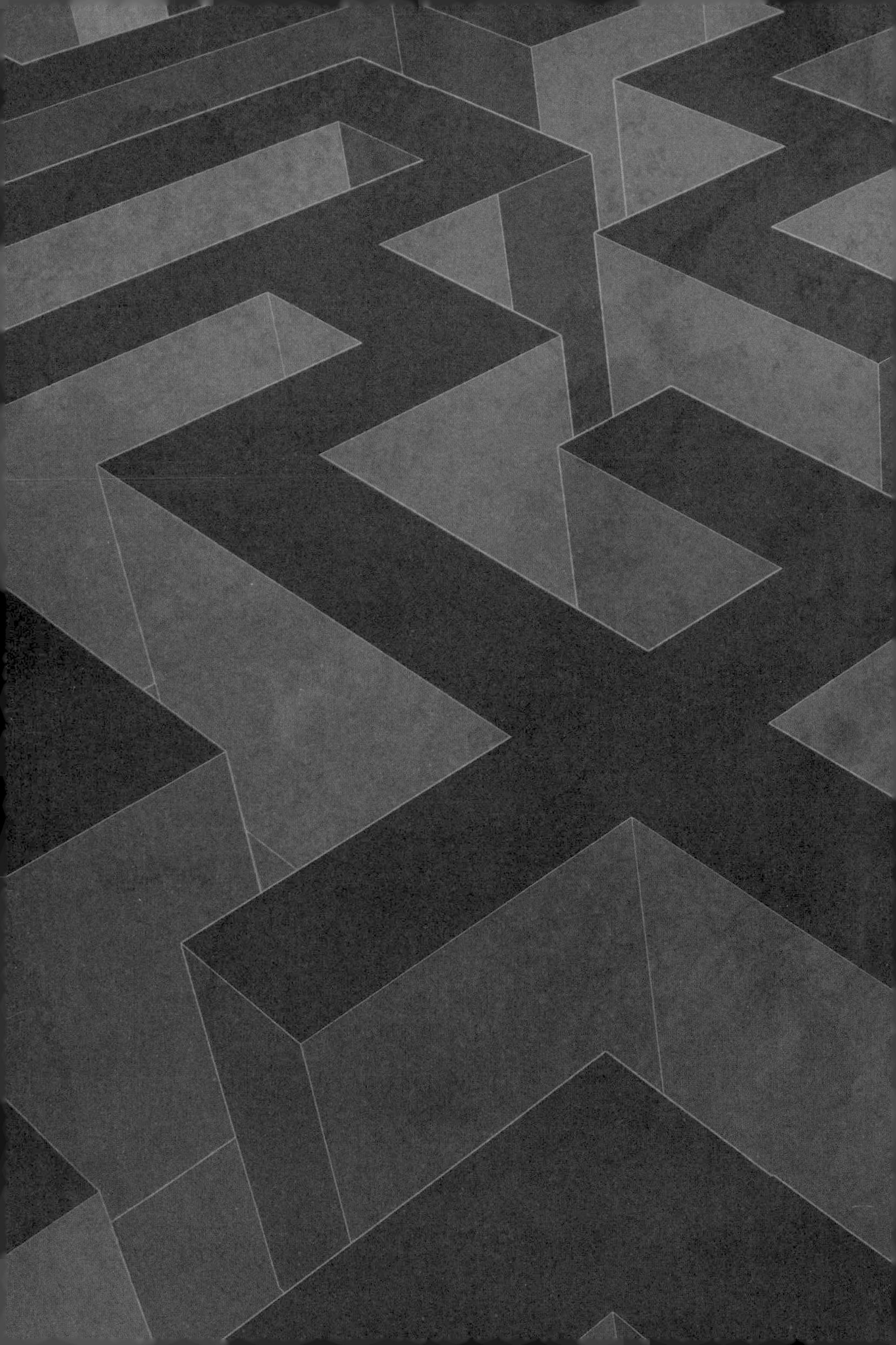

THE PATHFINDERS SOCIETY

The **Curse** of the **Crystal Cavern**

Francesco Sedita &
Prescott Seraydarian

illustrated by
Steve Hamaker

VIKING

VIKING

An imprint of Penguin Random House LLC, New York

First published in the United States of America by Viking,
an imprint of Penguin Random House LLC, 2021

Visit us online at penguinrandomhouse.com.

LIBRARY OF CONGRESS CATALOGING-IN-PUBLICATION DATA IS AVAILABLE

Manufactured in China

ISBN 9780425291894 (hardcover)
ISBN 9780425291900 (paperback)

1 3 5 7 9 10 8 6 4 2

Book design by Steve Hamaker and Jim Hoover

Dedications

For my parents, Rochelle and Danny,

for helping me find my own path.

(And making me take Latin.) —FS

To my students, for teaching me so much. —PS

To Garth Murphy,

a comics colleague and a friend. —SH

Meet the Pathfinders

KYLE is the new kid in town. He's always got a sketchbook in his pocket—and drawing is a very useful tool when you're connecting the dots on a treasure hunt!

BETH is super-organized and a bit of a history nerd. Need to go forward following a map? Or backward in time to solve a mystery? She's your girl.

HARRY is a goofball whose mouth sometimes moves faster than his brain. But his love of magic means he spots what's hidden in a tricky situation.

VICTORIA (VIC) is a popular cheerleader—and a secret math whiz. She figures out numbers and patterns along the path before anybody else even sees them.

NATE likes to invent stuff. His motto? A.B.R.: *Always Be Ready.* He's the guy you want on your team when you need solutions . . . *fast!*

The Path So Far

ON THEIR FIRST DAY at Camp Pathfinder, Kyle, Vic, Nate, Beth, and Harry quickly became friends. After learning about Henry Merriweather, a famous local adventurer from the past, their first activity was a treasure hunt that took them all over the strange town of Windrose.

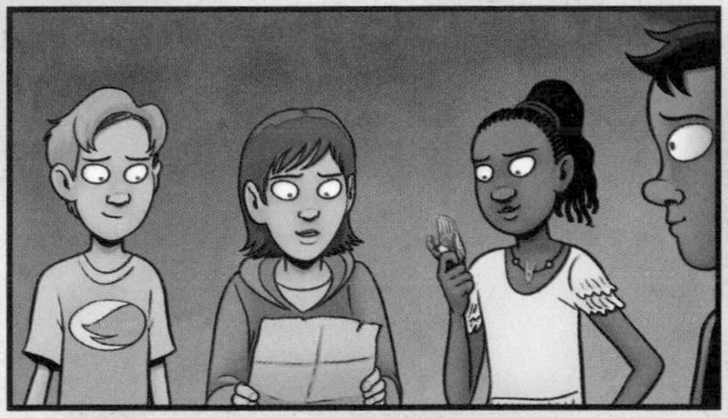
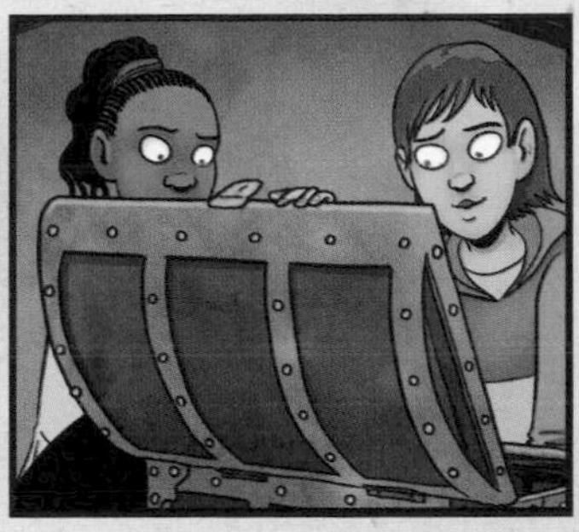

At Henry's old castle, they met Henry's great-niece Mildred, who let them explore. In a secret room, something incredible happened. The kids all saw a vision of Henry from a hundred years ago!

The Pathfinders followed Henry's trail to find a treasure he left behind—and this time, it wasn't a game! The path led them to Henry's infamous Moon Tower, where they unearthed a buried box. Inside were mysterious objects, including a jeweled hand, a guidebook, and a strange device . . .

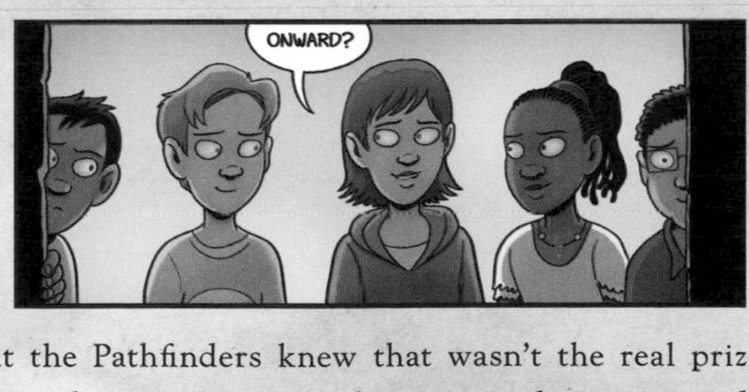
ONWARD?

But the Pathfinders knew that wasn't the real prize—they discovered a secret stairway that promised even more adventure. Now the hunt for the Treasure of Windrose continues!

Plus Ultra!

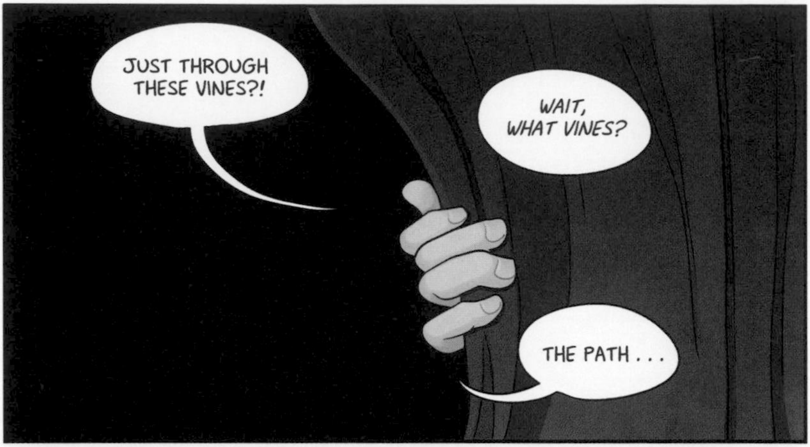
JUST THROUGH THESE VINES?!
WAIT, WHAT VINES?
THE PATH . . .

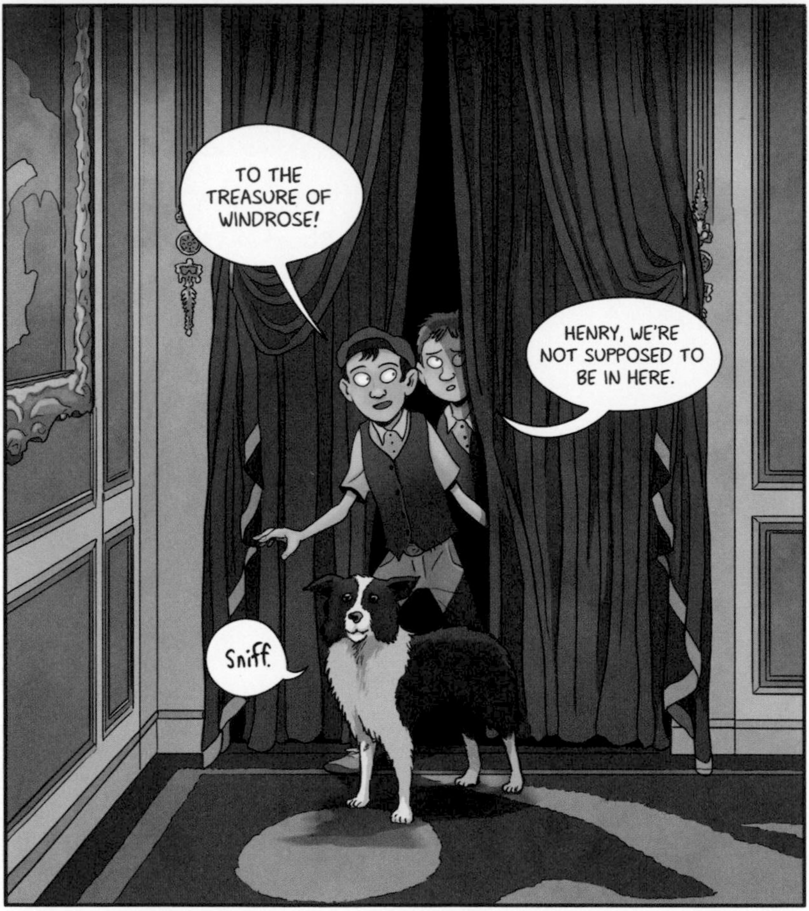
TO THE TREASURE OF WINDROSE!
HENRY, WE'RE NOT SUPPOSED TO BE IN HERE.
Sniff.

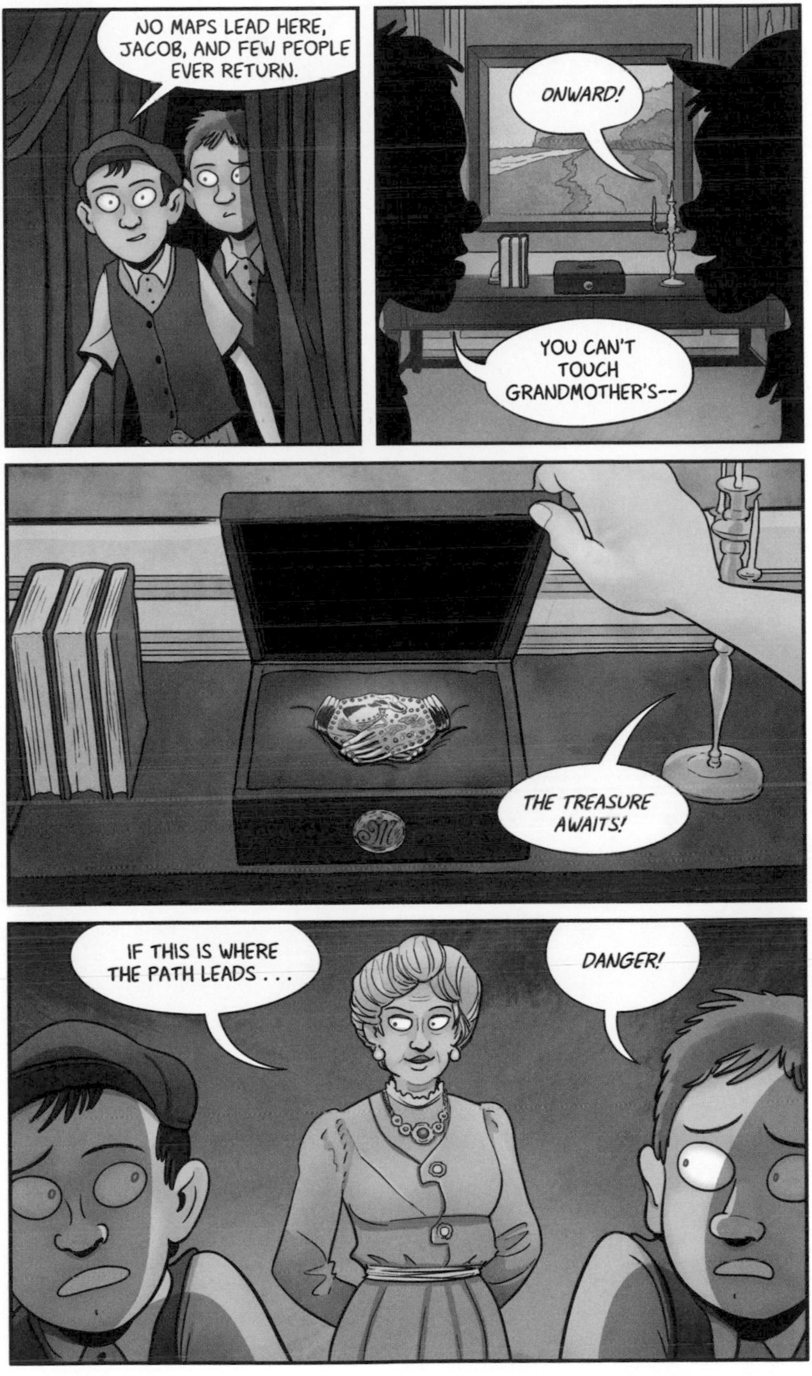
NO MAPS LEAD HERE, JACOB, AND FEW PEOPLE EVER RETURN.
ONWARD!
YOU CAN'T TOUCH GRANDMOTHER'S--
THE TREASURE AWAITS!
IF THIS IS WHERE THE PATH LEADS . . .
DANGER!

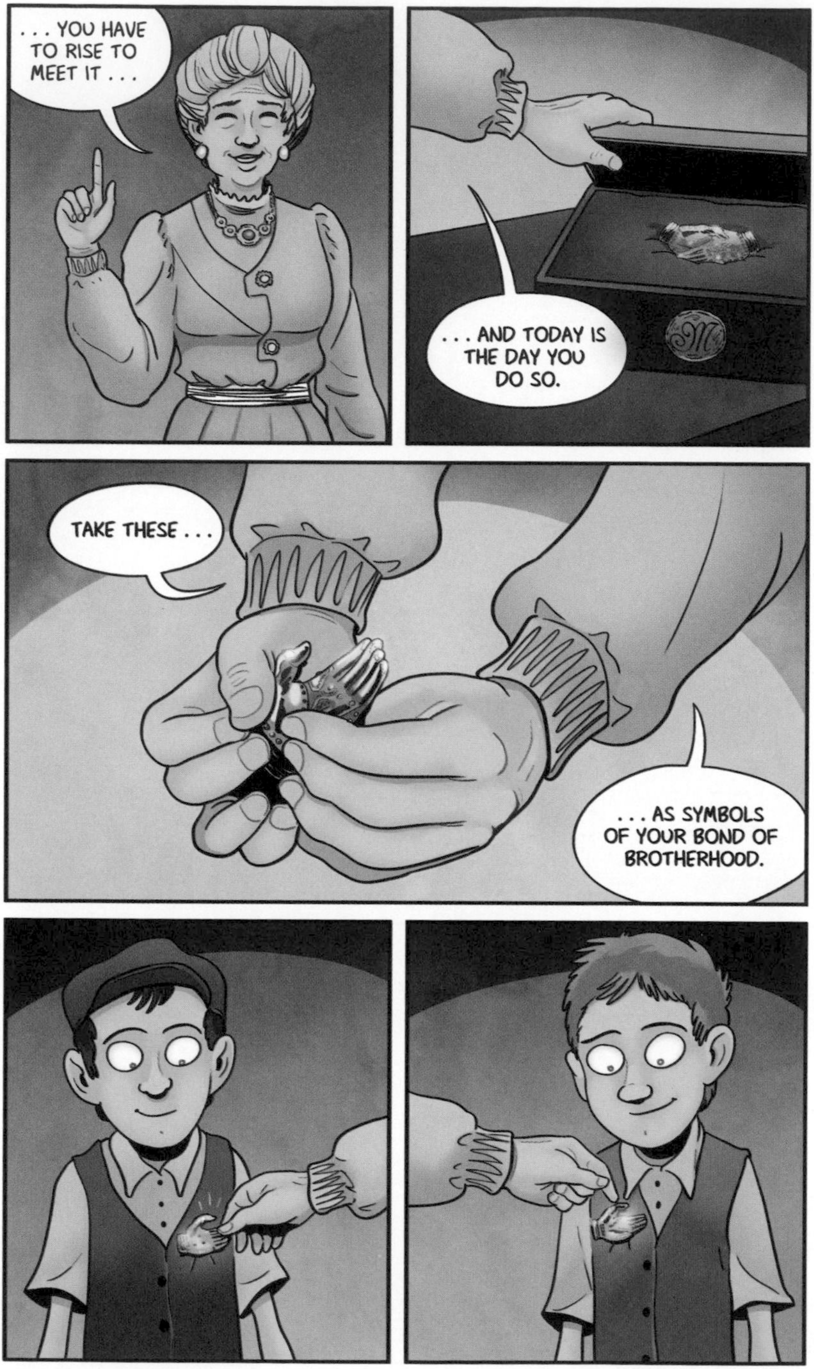
. . . YOU HAVE TO RISE TO MEET IT . . .
. . . AND TODAY IS THE DAY YOU DO SO.
TAKE THESE . . .
. . . AS SYMBOLS OF YOUR BOND OF BROTHERHOOD.

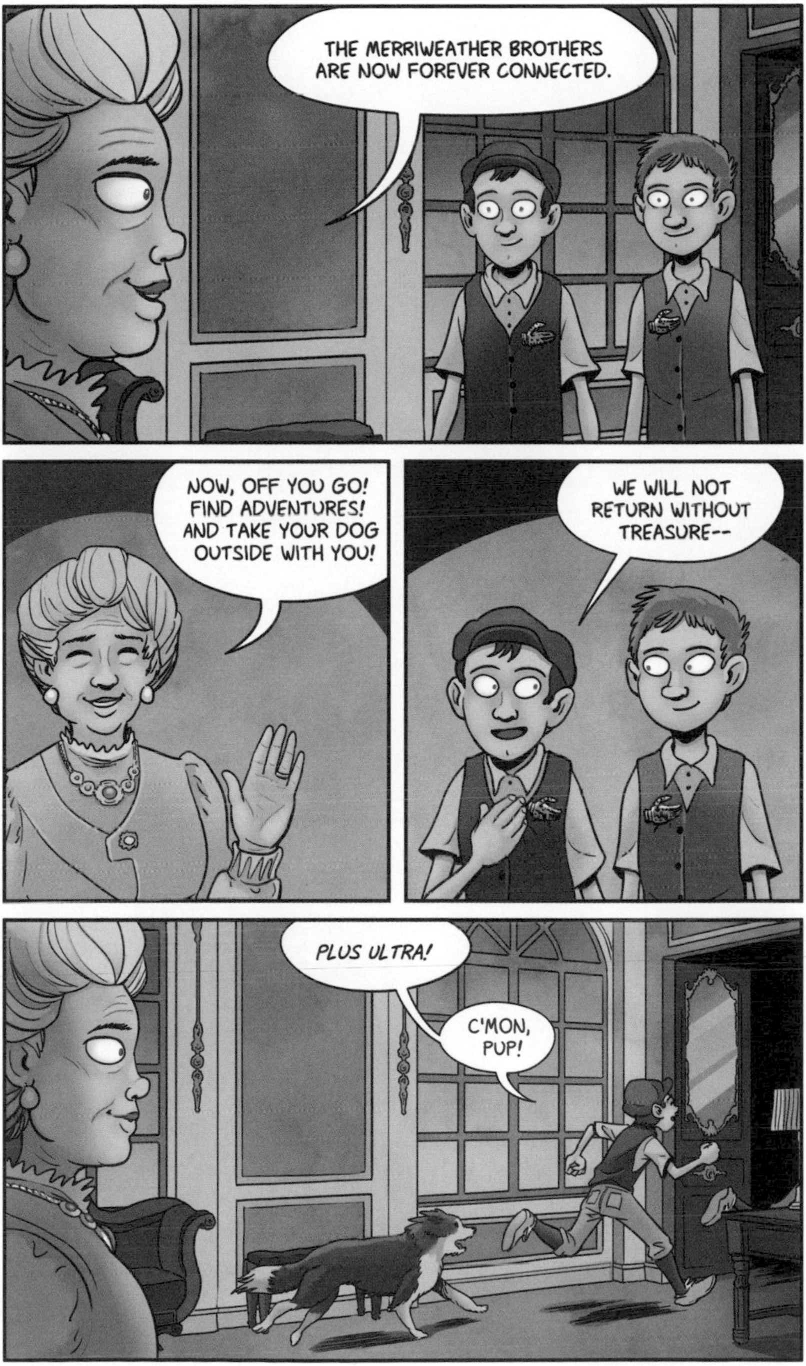
THE MERRIWEATHER BROTHERS ARE NOW FOREVER CONNECTED.
NOW, OFF YOU GO! FIND ADVENTURES! AND TAKE YOUR DOG OUTSIDE WITH YOU!
WE WILL NOT RETURN WITHOUT TREASURE--
PLUS ULTRA!
C'MON, PUP!

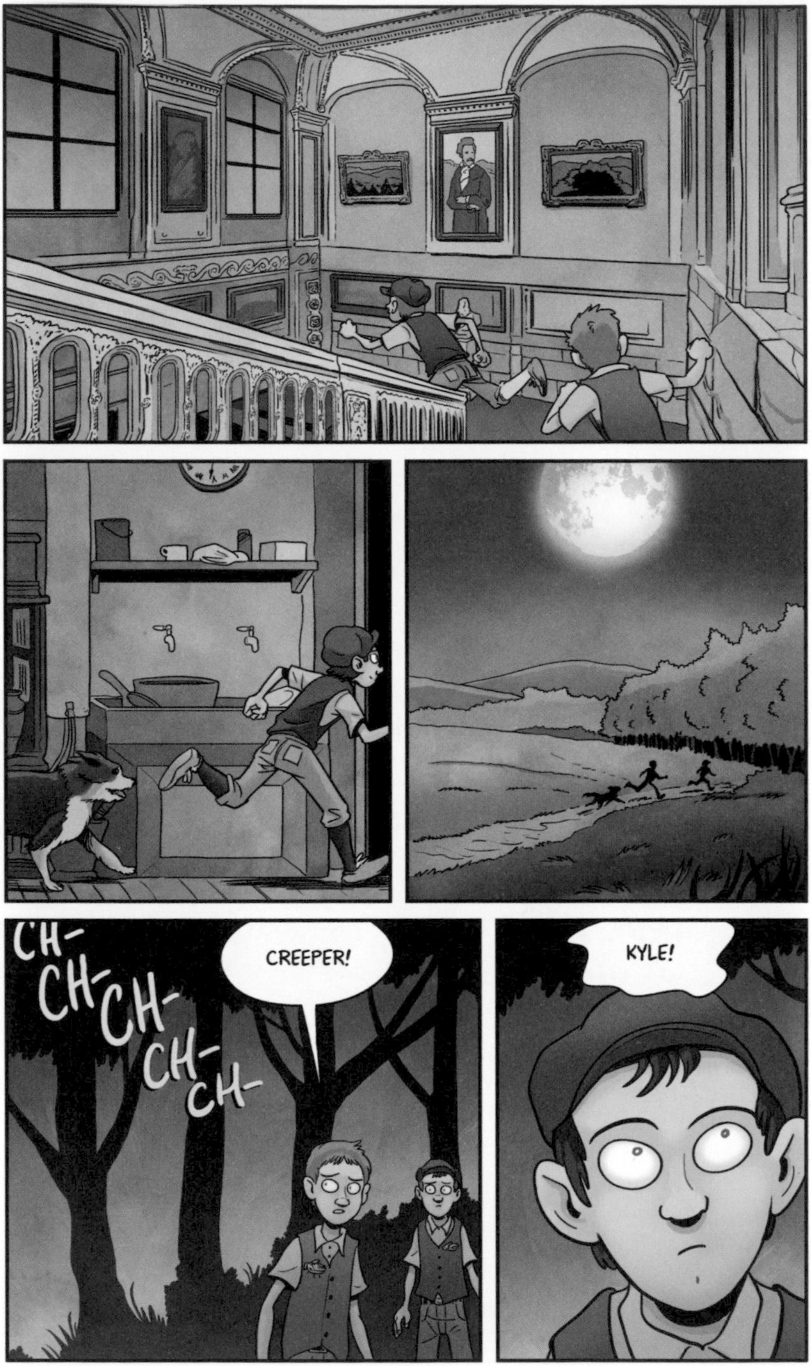
CH-
CH-CH-
CH-
CH-
CREEPER!
KYLE!

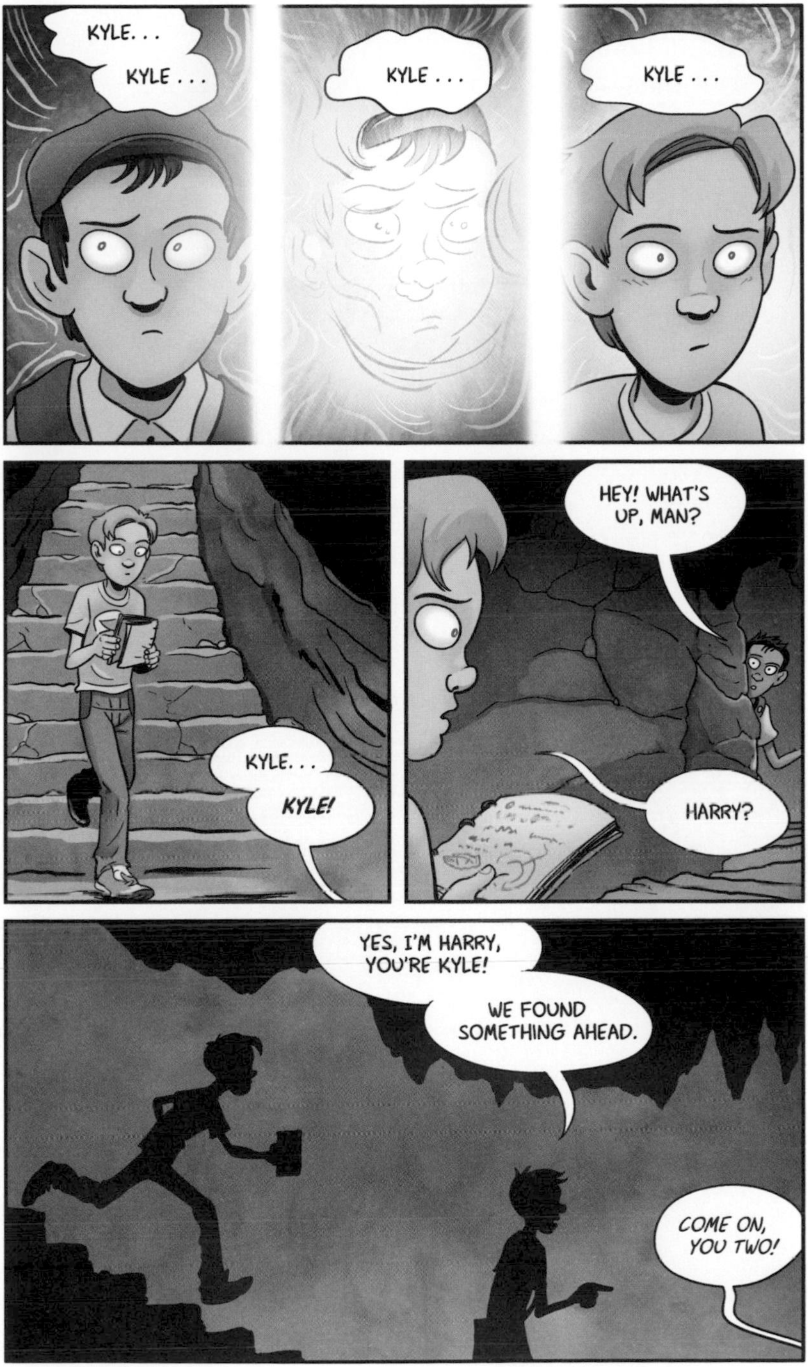
KYLE. . .
KYLE . . .
KYLE . . .
KYLE . . .
KYLE. . .
KYLE!
HEY! WHAT'S UP, MAN?
HARRY?
YES, I'M HARRY, YOU'RE KYLE!
WE FOUND SOMETHING AHEAD.
COME ON, YOU TWO!

Chapter
ONE
I FOUND KYLE!
WE FOUND THE PATH!
PLUS ULTRA
PLUS ULTRA!

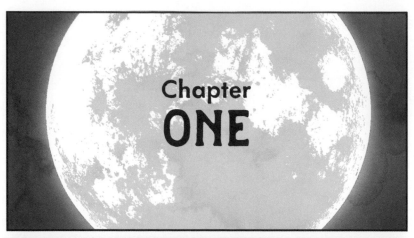

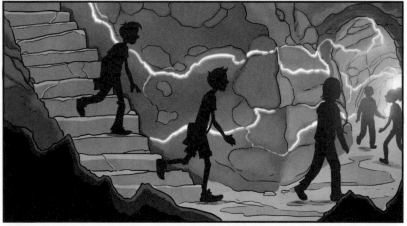

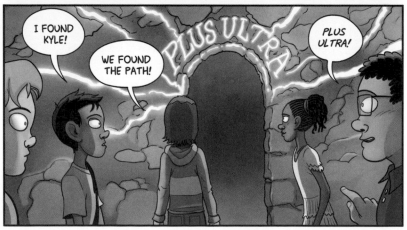

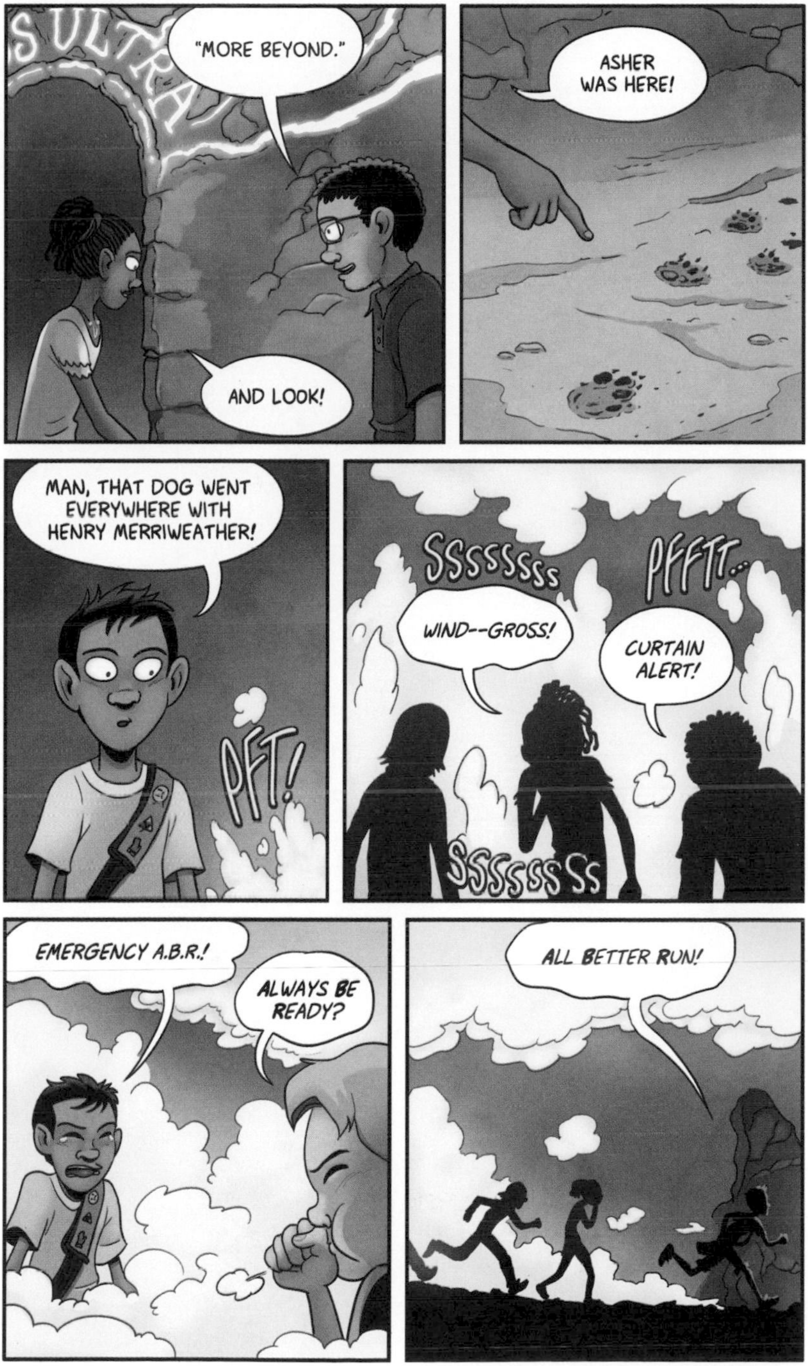
SULTRA
"MORE BEYOND."
AND LOOK!
ASHER WAS HERE!
MAN, THAT DOG WENT EVERYWHERE WITH HENRY MERRIWEATHER!
PFT!
SSSSSSSS
PFFTT...
WIND--GROSS!
CURTAIN ALERT!
SSSSSSSSS
EMERGENCY A.B.R.!
ALWAYS BE READY?
ALL BETTER RUN!

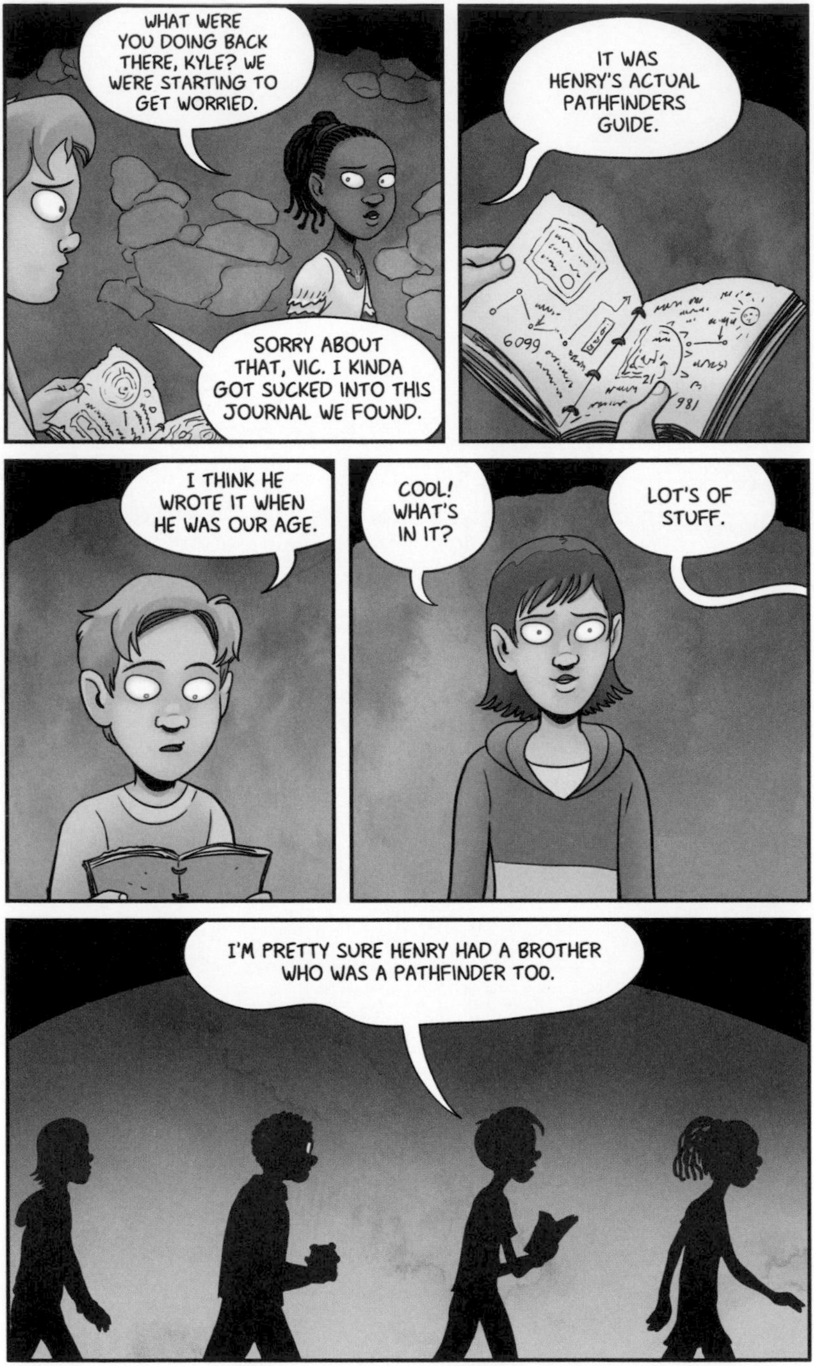
WHAT WERE YOU DOING BACK THERE, KYLE? WE WERE STARTING TO GET WORRIED.
SORRY ABOUT THAT, VIC. I KINDA GOT SUCKED INTO THIS JOURNAL WE FOUND.
IT WAS HENRY'S ACTUAL PATHFINDERS GUIDE.
I THINK HE WROTE IT WHEN HE WAS OUR AGE.
COOL! WHAT'S IN IT?
LOT'S OF STUFF.
I'M PRETTY SURE HENRY HAD A BROTHER WHO WAS A PATHFINDER TOO.

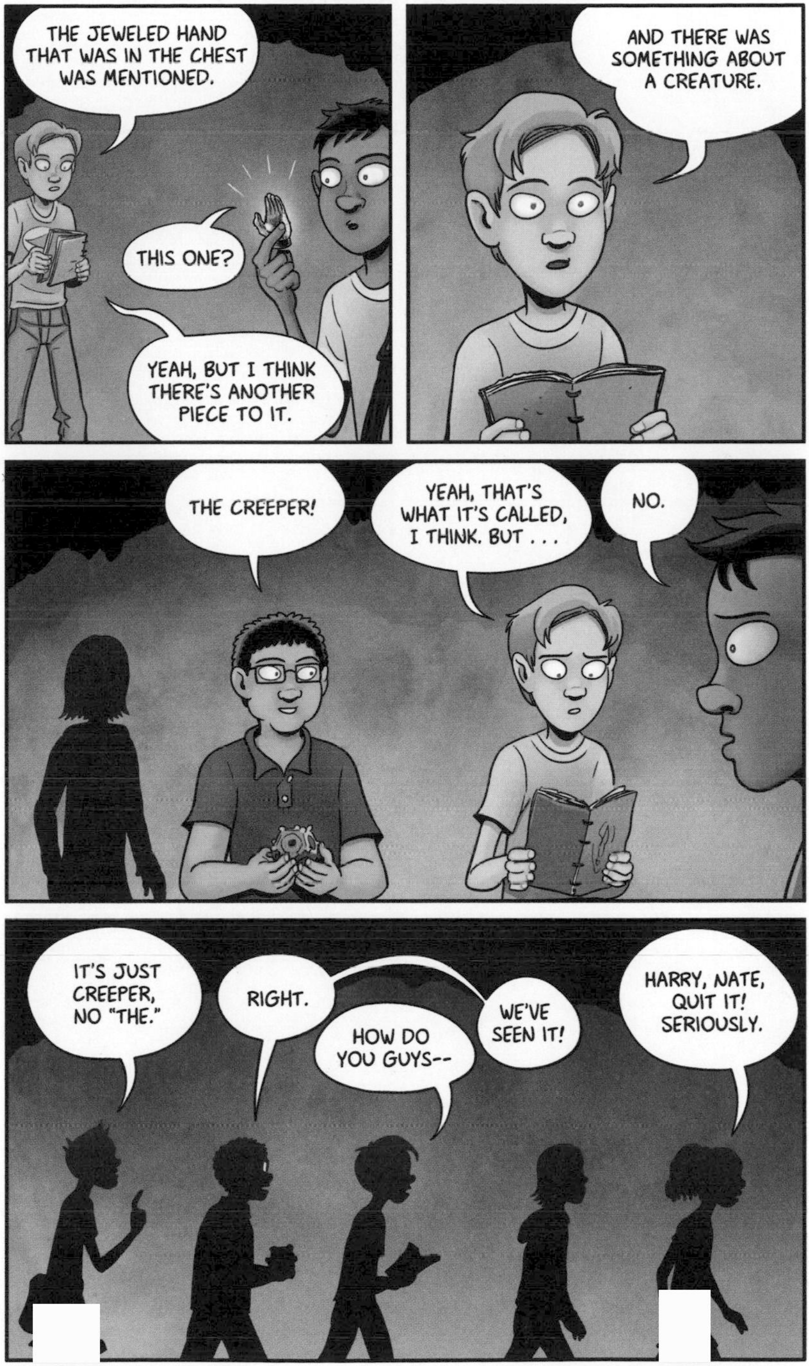
THE JEWELED HAND THAT WAS IN THE CHEST WAS MENTIONED.
THIS ONE?
YEAH, BUT I THINK THERE'S ANOTHER PIECE TO IT.
AND THERE WAS SOMETHING ABOUT A CREATURE.
THE CREEPER!
YEAH, THAT'S WHAT IT'S CALLED, I THINK. BUT . . .
NO.
IT'S JUST CREEPER, NO "THE."
RIGHT.
HOW DO YOU GUYS--
WE'VE SEEN IT!
HARRY, NATE, QUIT IT! SERIOUSLY.

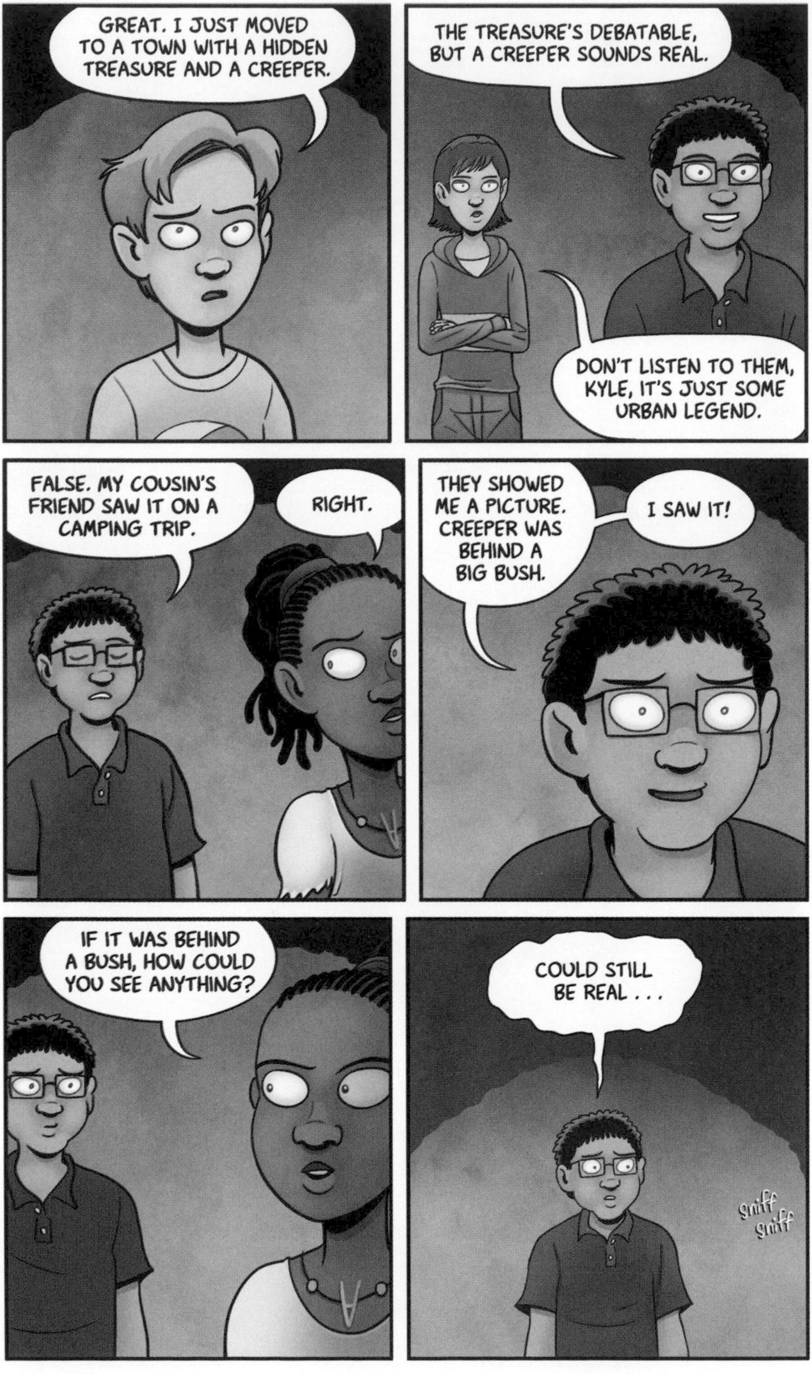
GREAT. I JUST MOVED TO A TOWN WITH A HIDDEN TREASURE AND A CREEPER.
THE TREASURE'S DEBATABLE, BUT A CREEPER SOUNDS REAL.
DON'T LISTEN TO THEM, KYLE, IT'S JUST SOME URBAN LEGEND.
FALSE. MY COUSIN'S FRIEND SAW IT ON A CAMPING TRIP.
RIGHT.
THEY SHOWED ME A PICTURE. CREEPER WAS BEHIND A BIG BUSH.
I SAW IT!
IF IT WAS BEHIND A BUSH, HOW COULD YOU SEE ANYTHING?
COULD STILL BE REAL . . .
sniff sniff

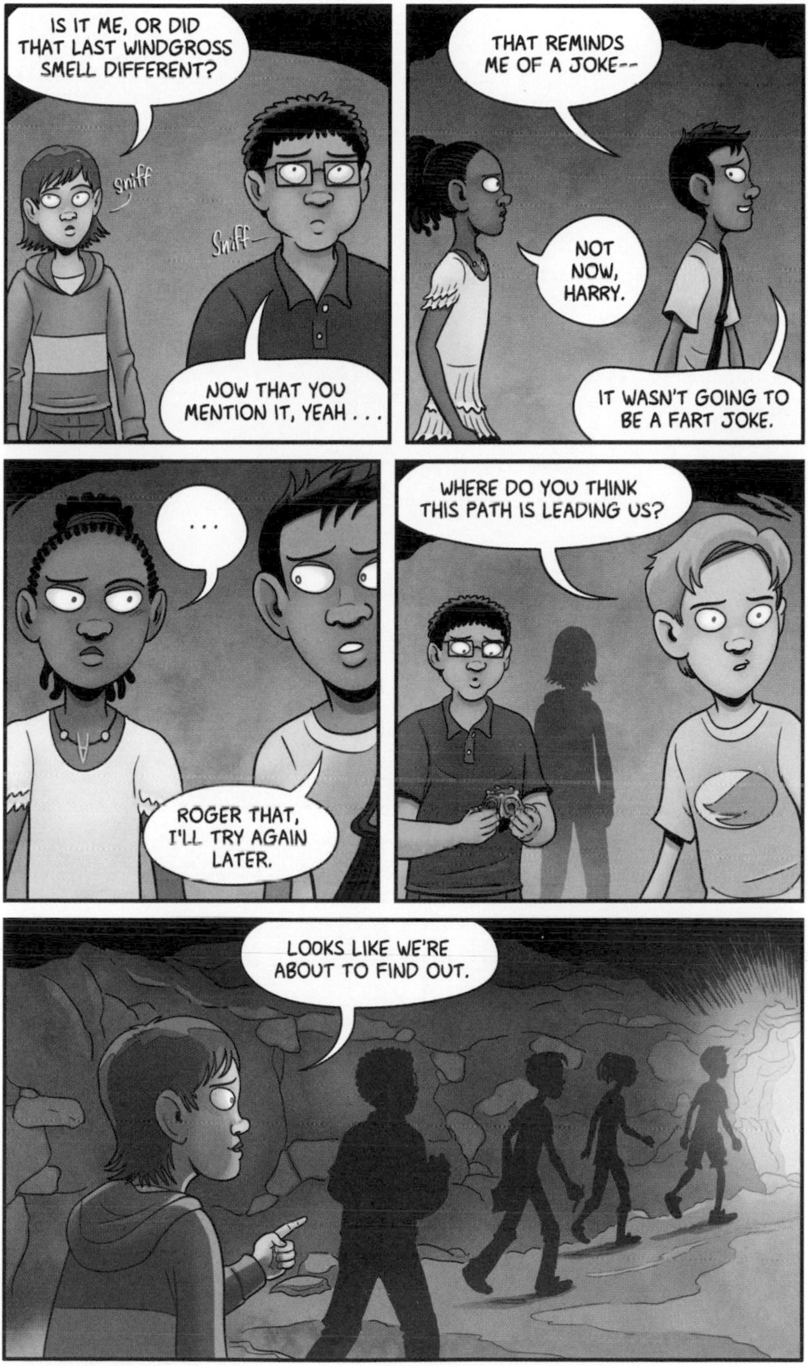
IS IT ME, OR DID THAT LAST WINDGROSS SMELL DIFFERENT?
sniff
Sniff
NOW THAT YOU MENTION IT, YEAH . . .
THAT REMINDS ME OF A JOKE--
NOT NOW, HARRY.
IT WASN'T GOING TO BE A FART JOKE.
. . .
ROGER THAT, I'LL TRY AGAIN LATER.
WHERE DO YOU THINK THIS PATH IS LEADING US?
LOOKS LIKE WE'RE ABOUT TO FIND OUT.

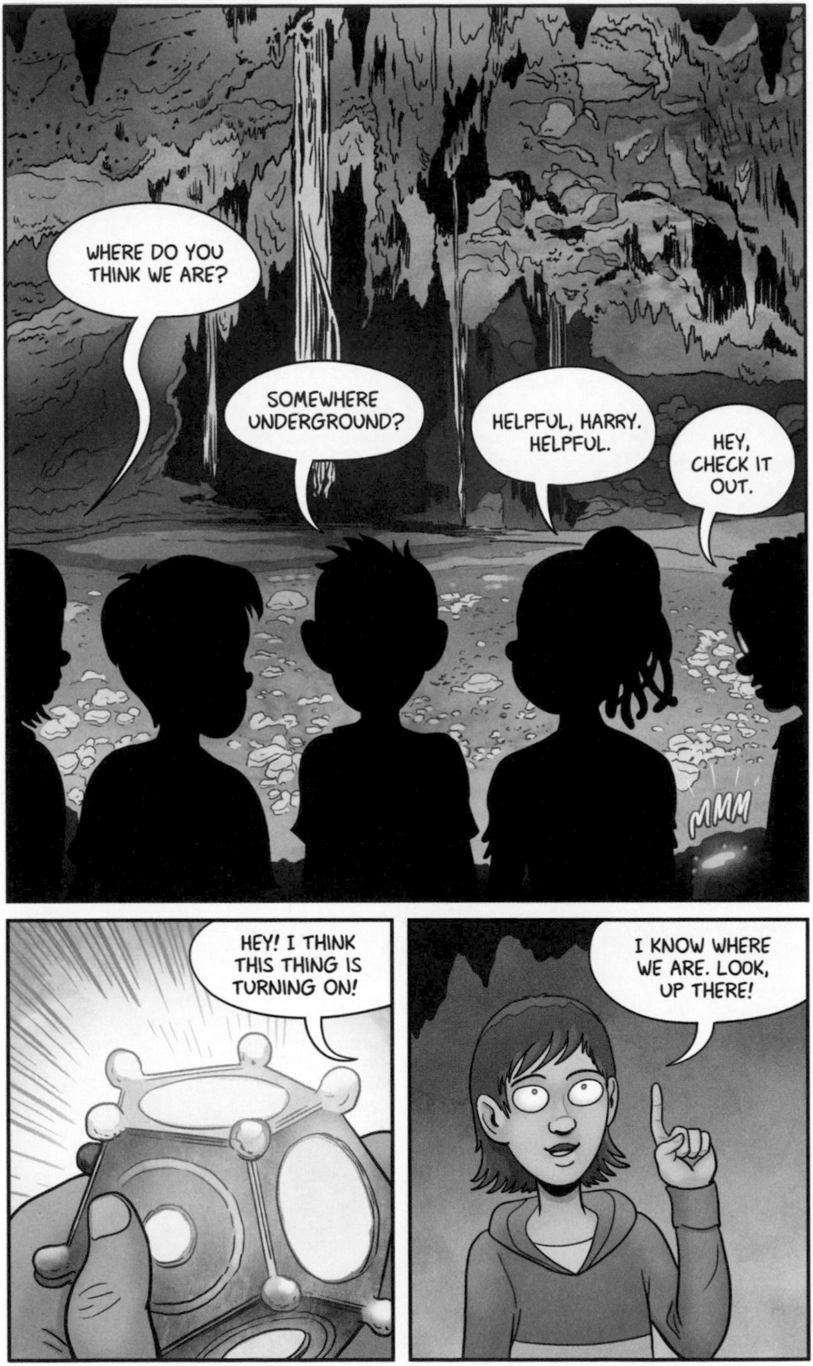
WHERE DO YOU THINK WE ARE?
SOMEWHERE UNDERGROUND?
HELPFUL, HARRY. HELPFUL.
HEY, CHECK IT OUT.
MMM
HEY! I THINK THIS THING IS TURNING ON!
I KNOW WHERE WE ARE. LOOK, UP THERE!

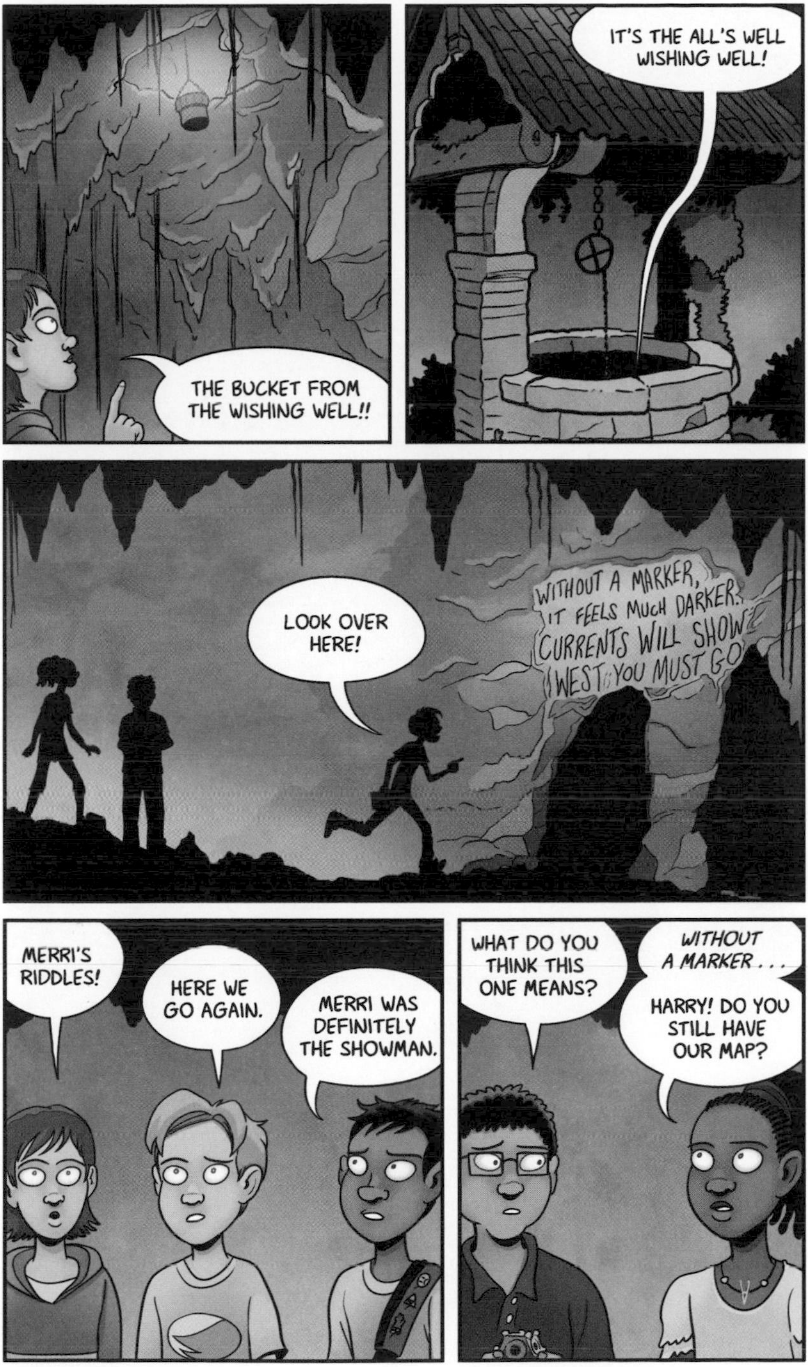
THE BUCKET FROM THE WISHING WELL!!
IT'S THE ALL'S WELL WISHING WELL!
LOOK OVER HERE!
WITHOUT A MARKER, IT FEELS MUCH DARKER. CURRENTS WILL SHOW WEST YOU MUST GO
MERRI'S RIDDLES!
HERE WE GO AGAIN.
MERRI WAS DEFINITELY THE SHOWMAN.
WHAT DO YOU THINK THIS ONE MEANS?
WITHOUT A MARKER . . .
HARRY! DO YOU STILL HAVE OUR MAP?

HERE'S THE WISHING WELL . . .

HOW DO WE KNOW WHICH WAY IS WEST? WE'RE UNDERGROUND!

THERE'S A TOOL FOR THAT!

IT LOOKS LIKE--

UH, THAT WAY'S WEST.

S MUCH DARKER.
WILL SHOW
WEST YOU MUST GO

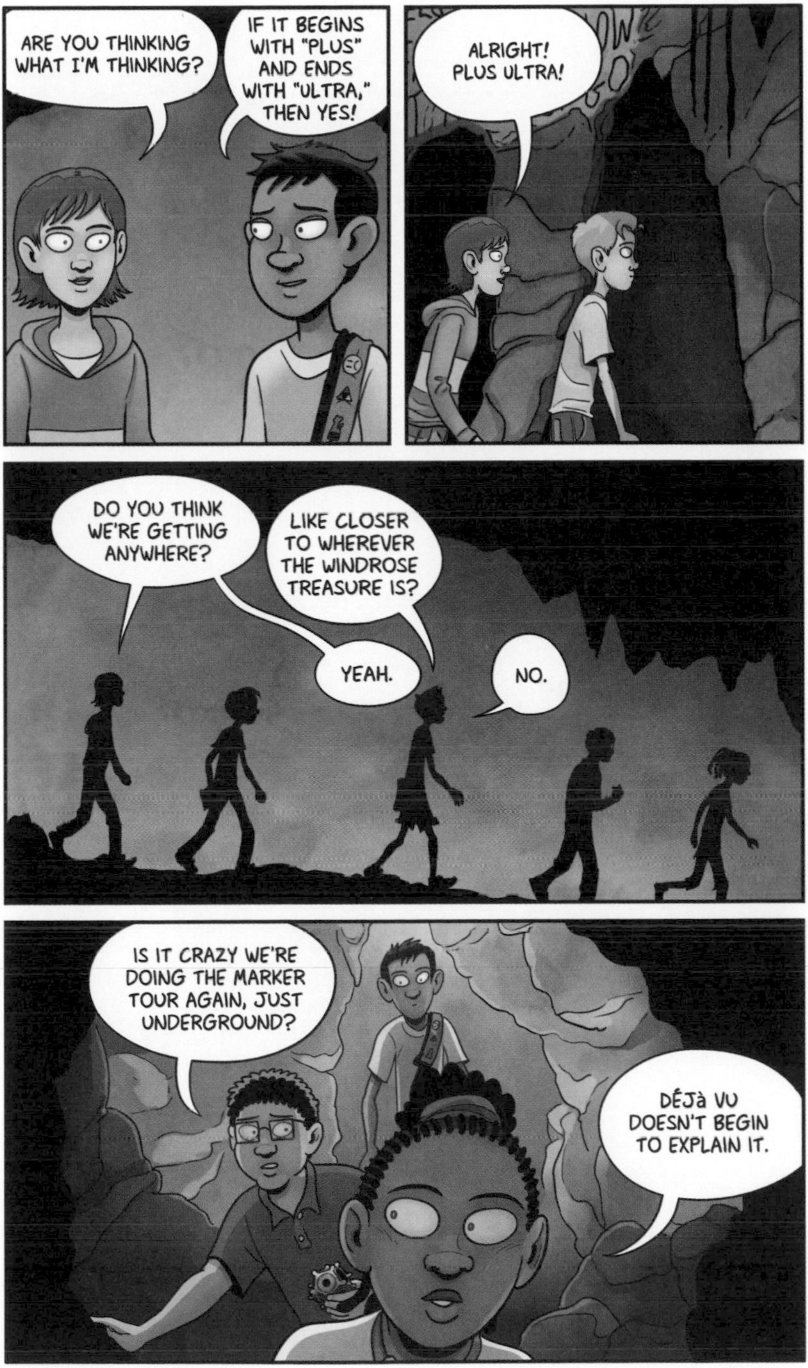
ARE YOU THINKING WHAT I'M THINKING?
IF IT BEGINS WITH "PLUS" AND ENDS WITH "ULTRA," THEN YES!
ALRIGHT! PLUS ULTRA!
DO YOU THINK WE'RE GETTING ANYWHERE?
LIKE CLOSER TO WHEREVER THE WINDROSE TREASURE IS?
YEAH.
NO.
IS IT CRAZY WE'RE DOING THE MARKER TOUR AGAIN, JUST UNDERGROUND?
DÉJà VU DOESN'T BEGIN TO EXPLAIN IT.

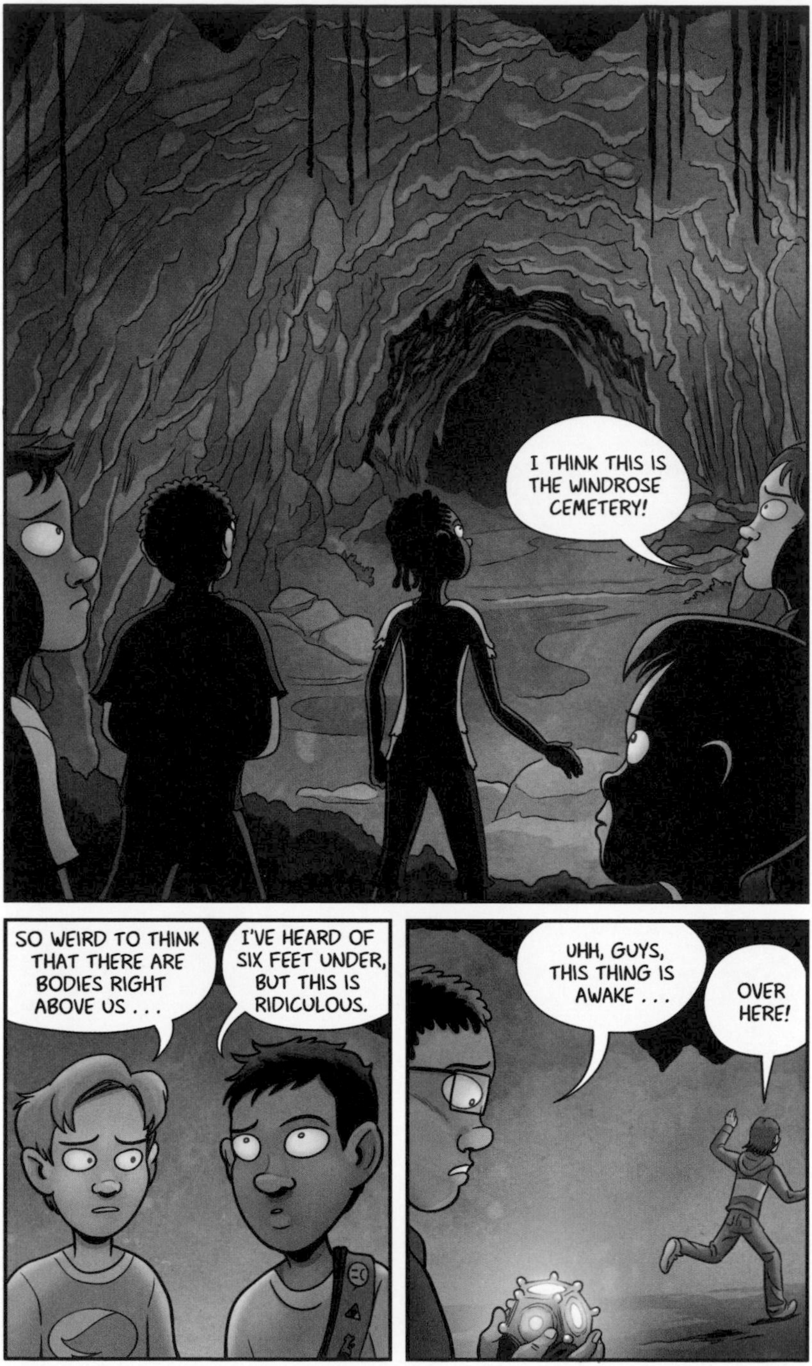
I THINK THIS IS THE WINDROSE CEMETERY!
SO WEIRD TO THINK THAT THERE ARE BODIES RIGHT ABOVE US . . .
I'VE HEARD OF SIX FEET UNDER, BUT THIS IS RIDICULOUS.
UHH, GUYS, THIS THING IS AWAKE . . .
OVER HERE!

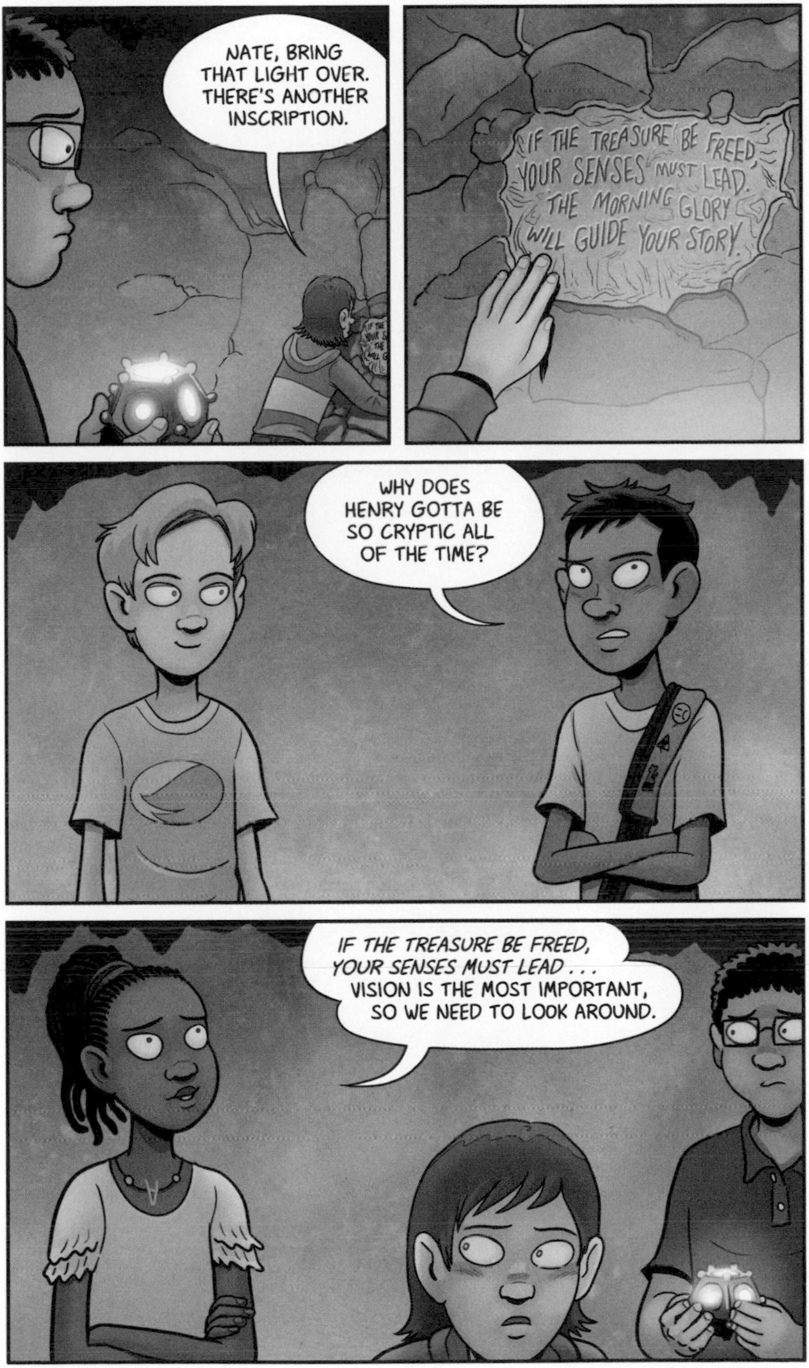

NATE, BRING THAT LIGHT OVER. THERE'S ANOTHER INSCRIPTION.
IF THE TREASURE BE FREED, YOUR SENSES MUST LEAD. THE MORNING GLORY WILL GUIDE YOUR STORY.
WHY DOES HENRY GOTTA BE SO CRYPTIC ALL OF THE TIME?
IF THE TREASURE BE FREED, YOUR SENSES MUST LEAD . . . VISION IS THE MOST IMPORTANT, SO WE NEED TO LOOK AROUND.

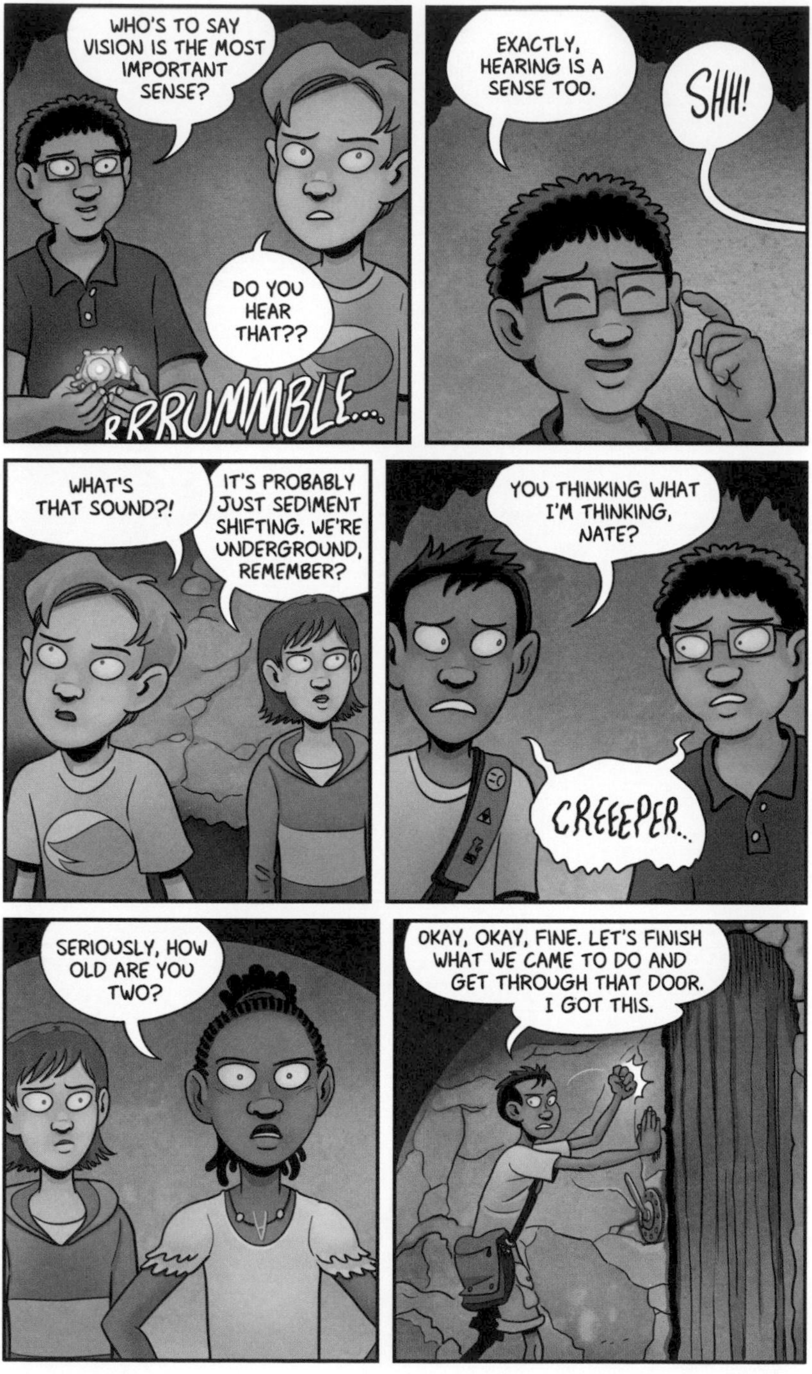
WHO'S TO SAY VISION IS THE MOST IMPORTANT SENSE?
DO YOU HEAR THAT??
RRRUMMBLE...
EXACTLY, HEARING IS A SENSE TOO.
SHH!
WHAT'S THAT SOUND?!
IT'S PROBABLY JUST SEDIMENT SHIFTING. WE'RE UNDERGROUND, REMEMBER?
YOU THINKING WHAT I'M THINKING, NATE?
CREEEPER...
SERIOUSLY, HOW OLD ARE YOU TWO?
OKAY, OKAY, FINE. LET'S FINISH WHAT WE CAME TO DO AND GET THROUGH THAT DOOR. I GOT THIS.

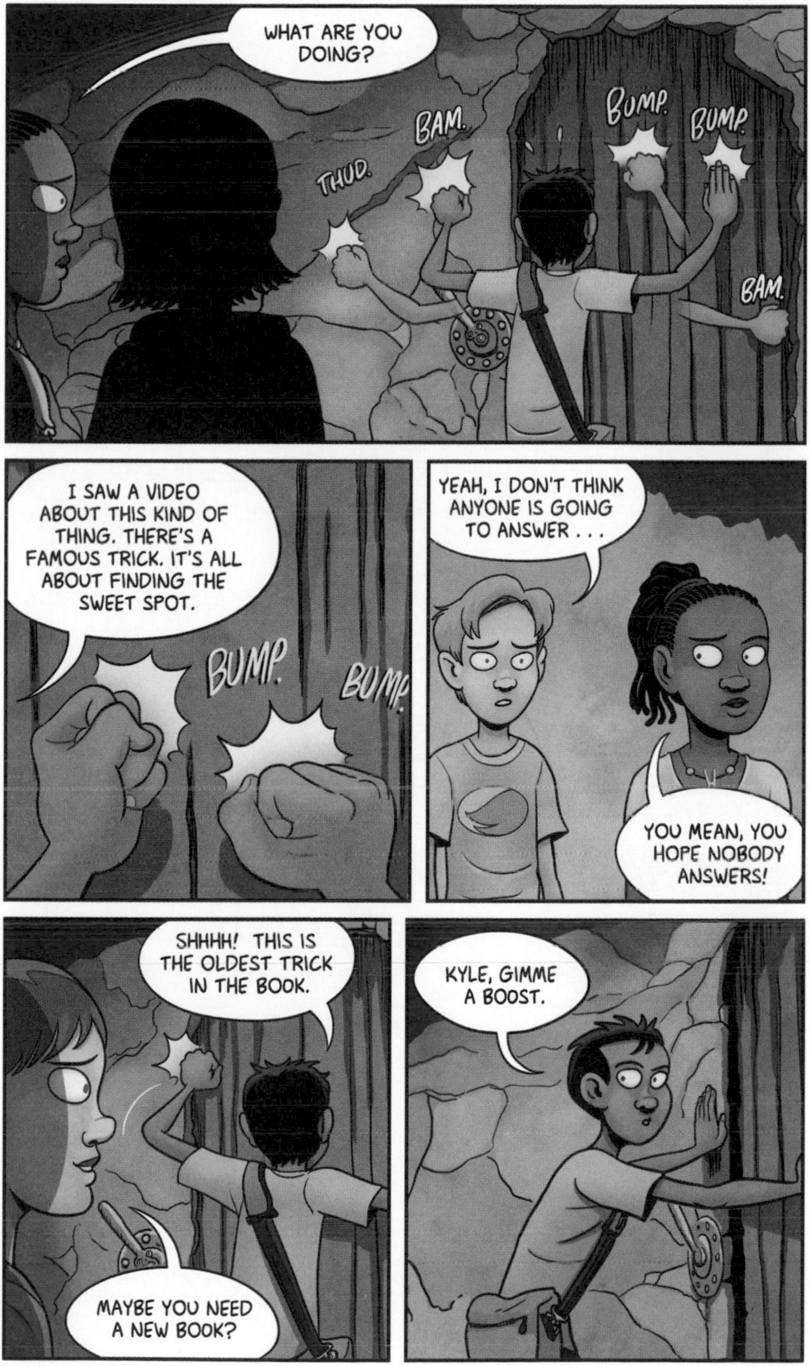
WHAT ARE YOU DOING?
THUD.
BAM.
BUMP.
BUMP.
BAM.
I SAW A VIDEO ABOUT THIS KIND OF THING. THERE'S A FAMOUS TRICK. IT'S ALL ABOUT FINDING THE SWEET SPOT.
BUMP.
BUMP.
YEAH, I DON'T THINK ANYONE IS GOING TO ANSWER . . .
YOU MEAN, YOU HOPE NOBODY ANSWERS!
SHHHH! THIS IS THE OLDEST TRICK IN THE BOOK.
MAYBE YOU NEED A NEW BOOK?
KYLE, GIMME A BOOST.

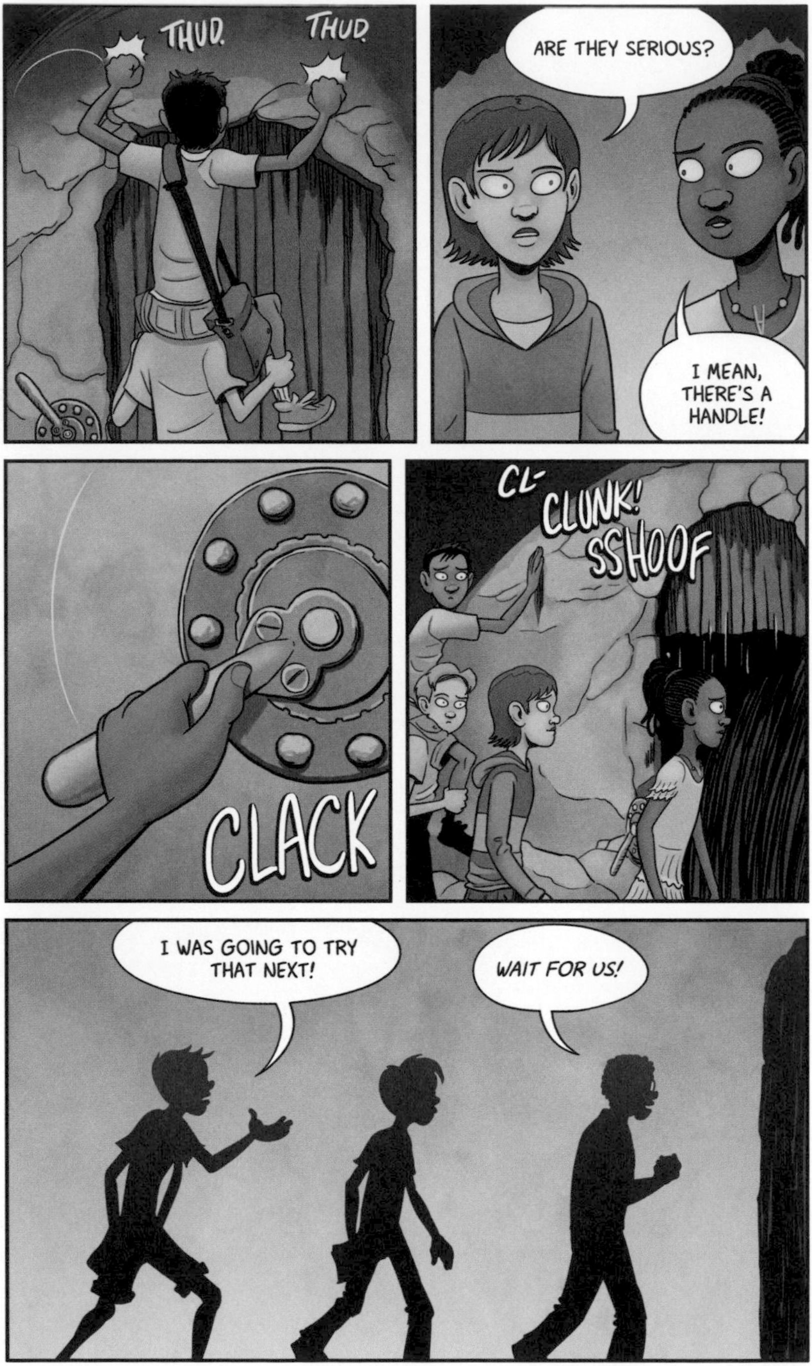
THUD.
THUD.
ARE THEY SERIOUS?
I MEAN, THERE'S A HANDLE!
CLACK
CL-
CLUNK!
SSHOOF
I WAS GOING TO TRY THAT NEXT!
WAIT FOR US!

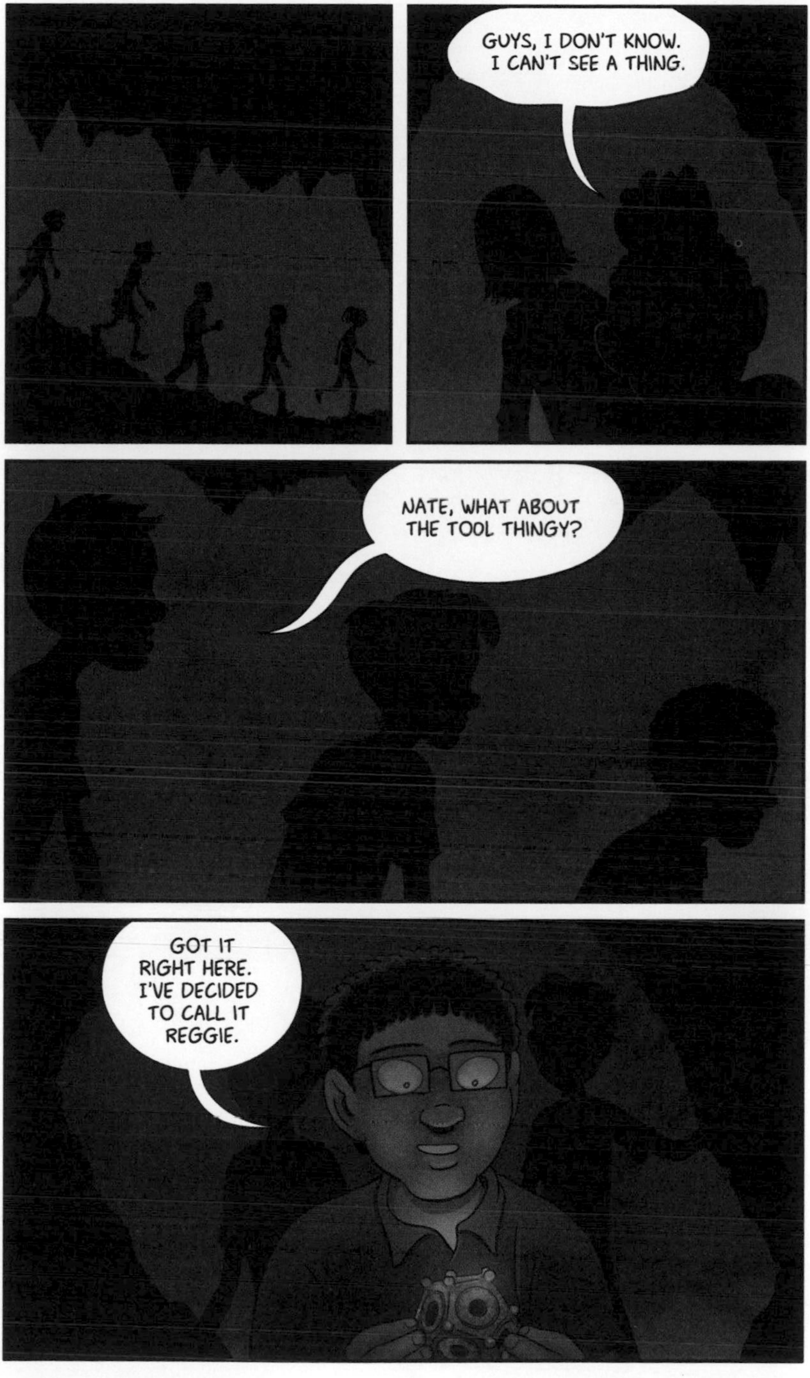
GUYS, I DON'T KNOW. I CAN'T SEE A THING.
NATE, WHAT ABOUT THE TOOL THINGY?
GOT IT RIGHT HERE. I'VE DECIDED TO CALL IT REGGIE.

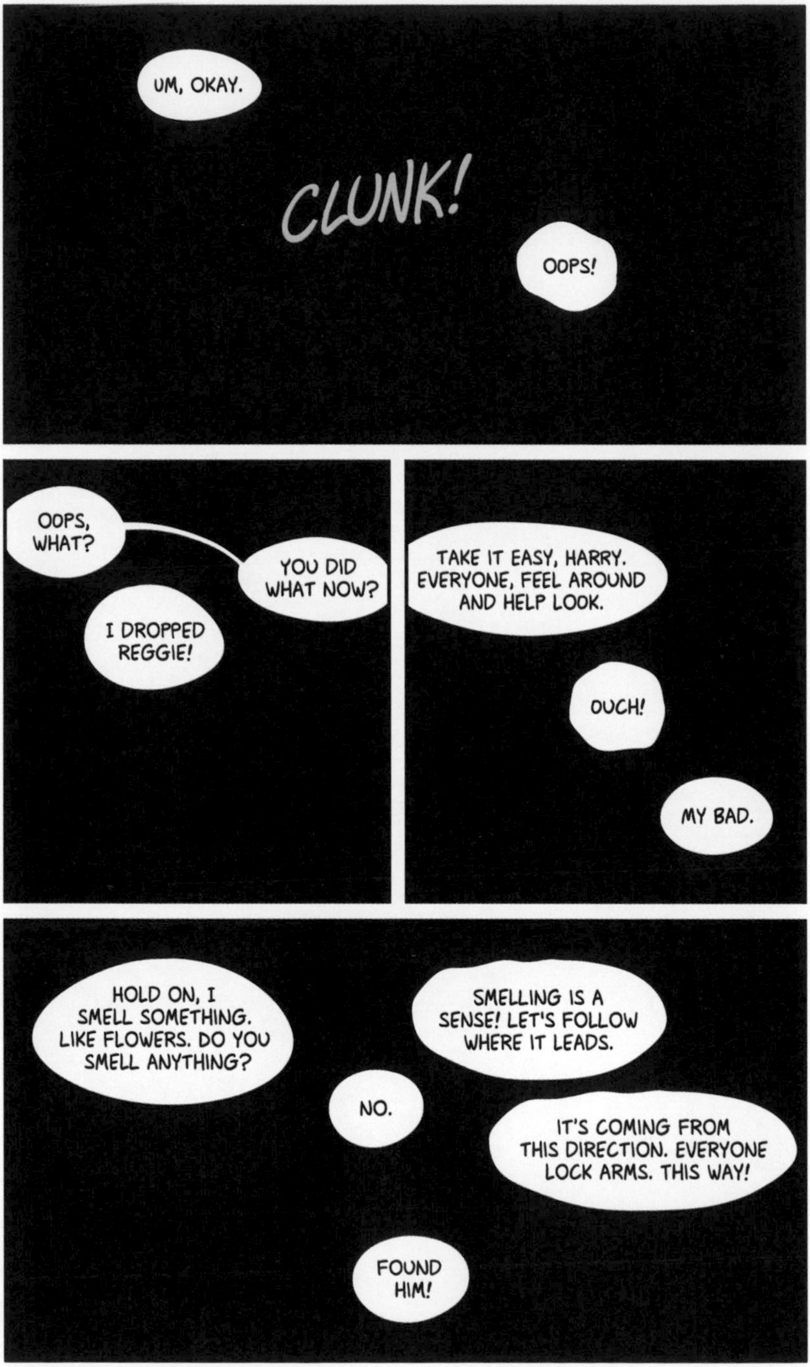
UM, OKAY.
CLUNK!
OOPS!
OOPS, WHAT?
YOU DID WHAT NOW?
I DROPPED REGGIE!
TAKE IT EASY, HARRY. EVERYONE, FEEL AROUND AND HELP LOOK.
OUCH!
MY BAD.
HOLD ON, I SMELL SOMETHING. LIKE FLOWERS. DO YOU SMELL ANYTHING?
NO.
SMELLING IS A SENSE! LET'S FOLLOW WHERE IT LEADS.
IT'S COMING FROM THIS DIRECTION. EVERYONE LOCK ARMS. THIS WAY!
FOUND HIM!

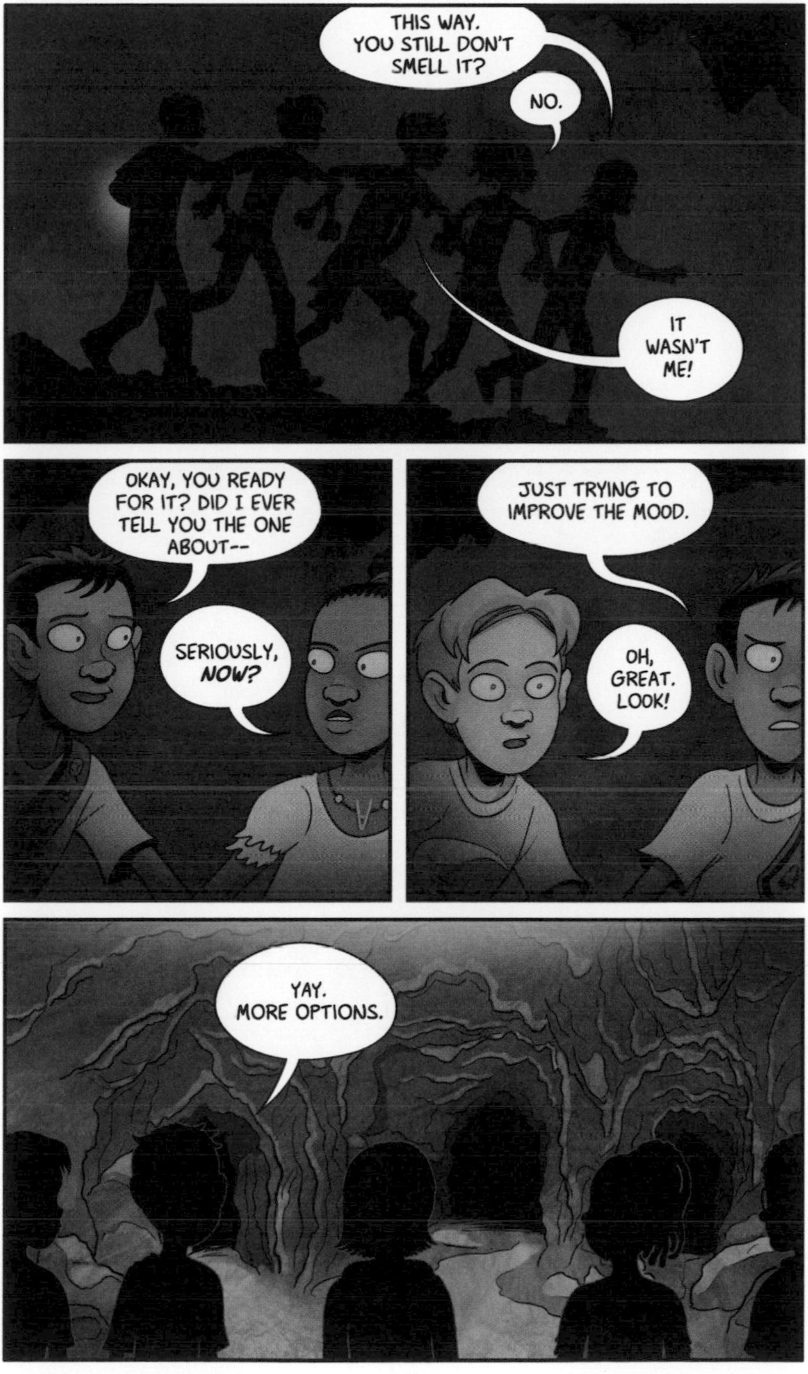
THIS WAY. YOU STILL DON'T SMELL IT?
NO.
IT WASN'T ME!
OKAY, YOU READY FOR IT? DID I EVER TELL YOU THE ONE ABOUT--
SERIOUSLY, *NOW?*
JUST TRYING TO IMPROVE THE MOOD.
OH, GREAT. LOOK!
YAY. MORE OPTIONS.

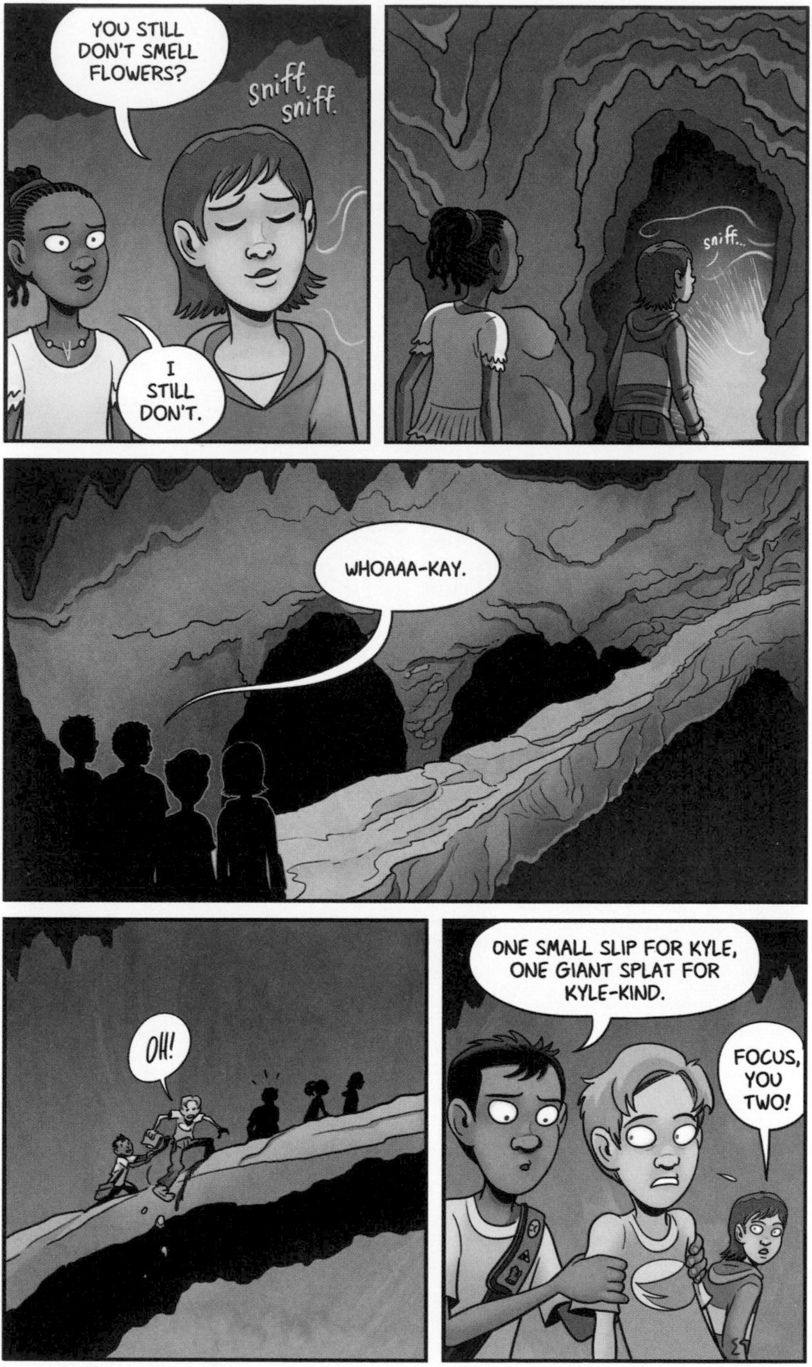
YOU STILL DON'T SMELL FLOWERS?
sniff, sniff.
I STILL DON'T.
sniff...
WHOAAA-KAY.
OH!
ONE SMALL SLIP FOR KYLE, ONE GIANT SPLAT FOR KYLE-KIND.
FOCUS, YOU TWO!

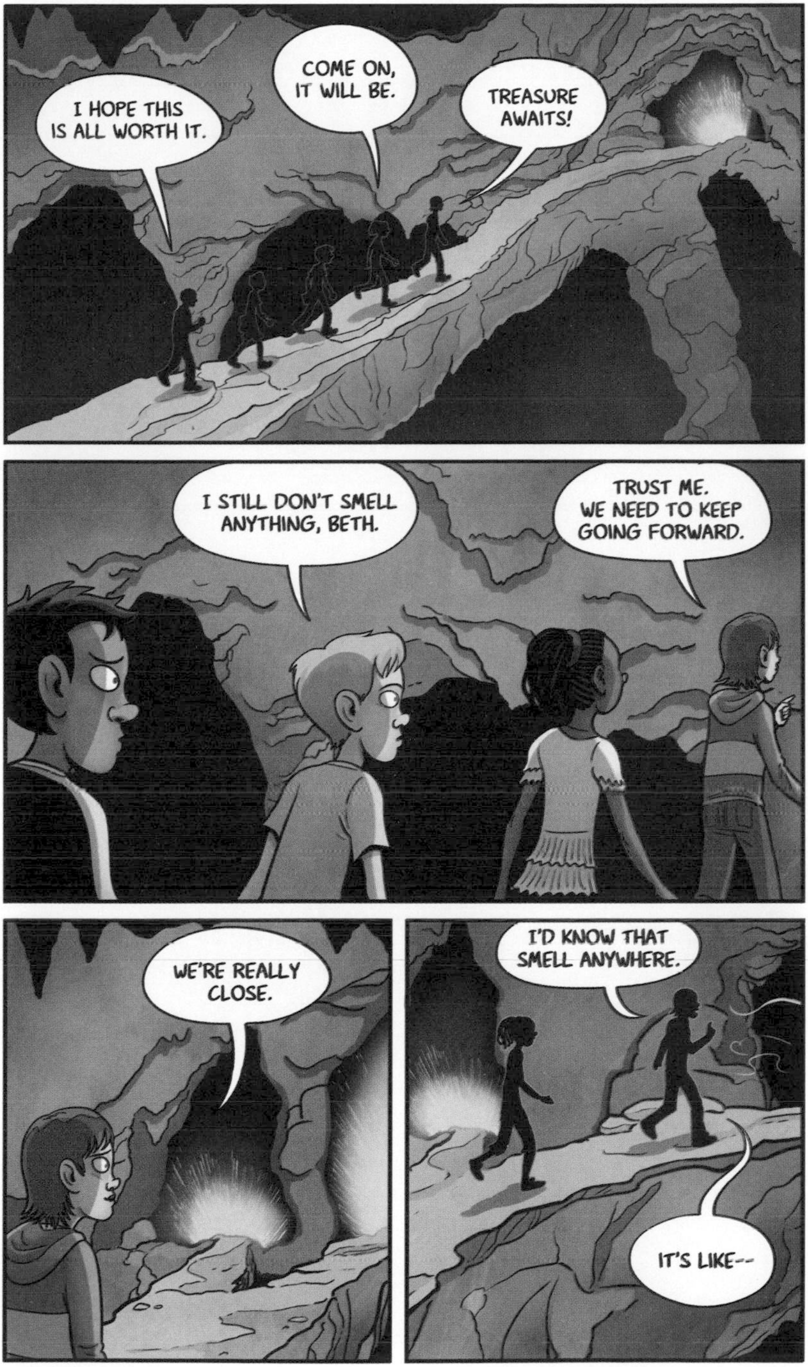
I HOPE THIS IS ALL WORTH IT.
COME ON, IT WILL BE.
TREASURE AWAITS!
I STILL DON'T SMELL ANYTHING, BETH.
TRUST ME. WE NEED TO KEEP GOING FORWARD.
WE'RE REALLY CLOSE.
I'D KNOW THAT SMELL ANYWHERE.
IT'S LIKE--

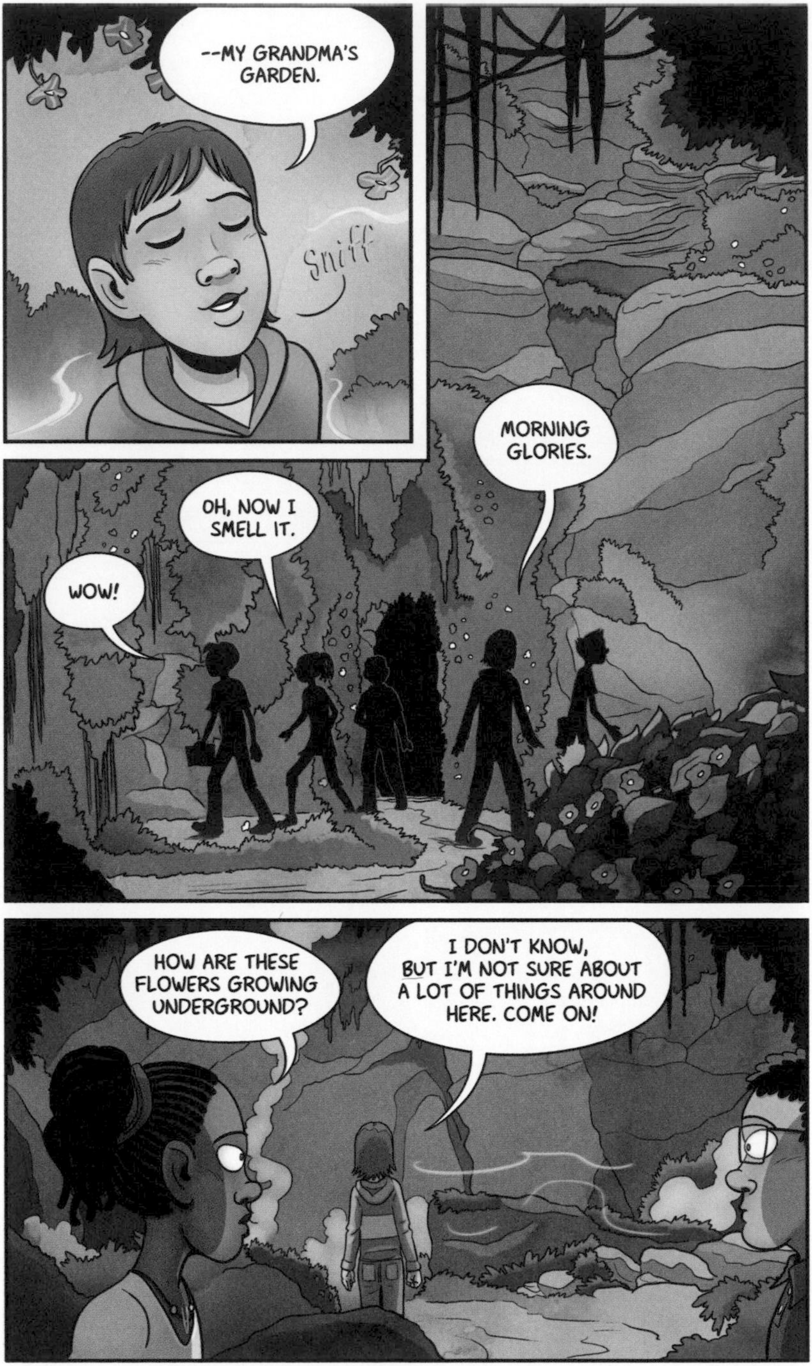
--MY GRANDMA'S GARDEN.
Sniff
MORNING GLORIES.
WOW!
OH, NOW I SMELL IT.
HOW ARE THESE FLOWERS GROWING UNDERGROUND?
I DON'T KNOW, BUT I'M NOT SURE ABOUT A LOT OF THINGS AROUND HERE. COME ON!

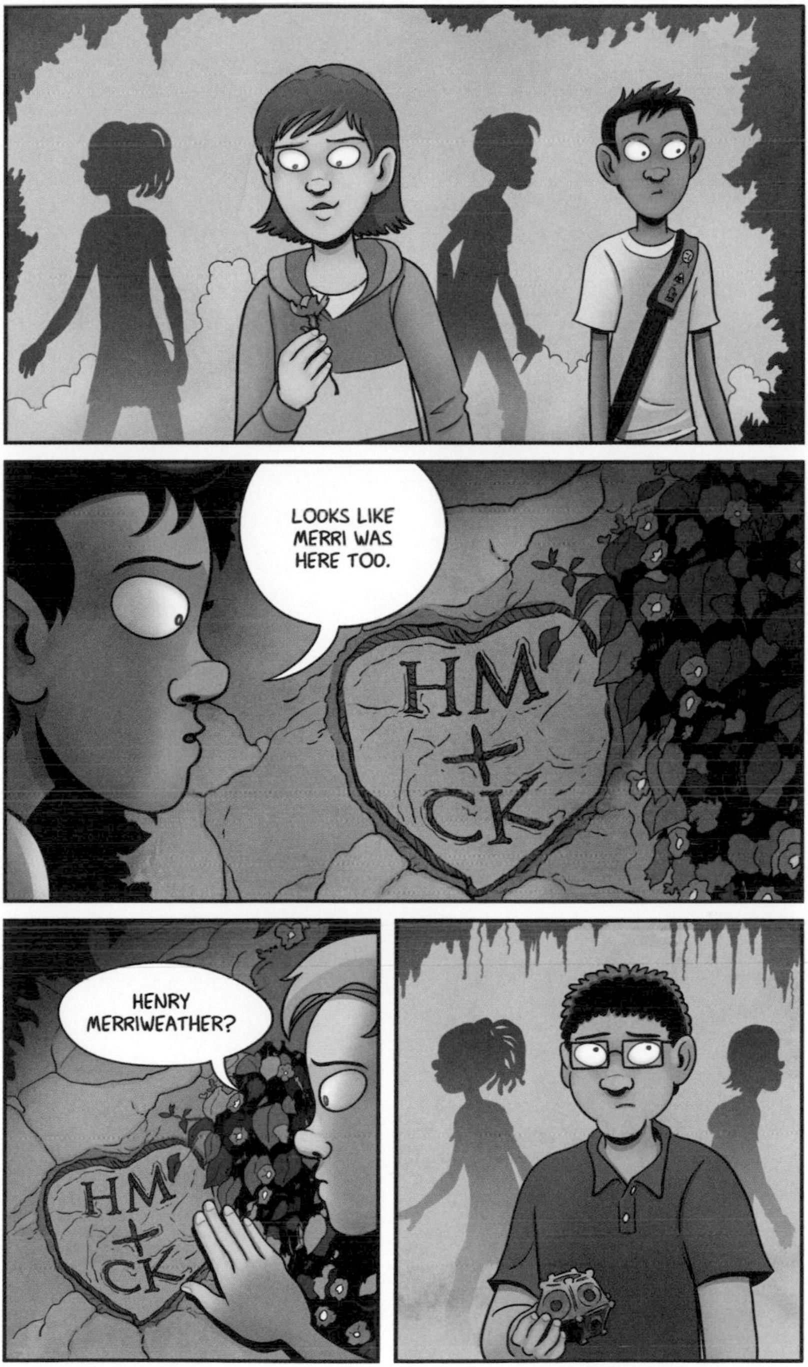
LOOKS LIKE MERRI WAS HERE TOO.
HM + CK
HENRY MERRIWEATHER?
HM + CK

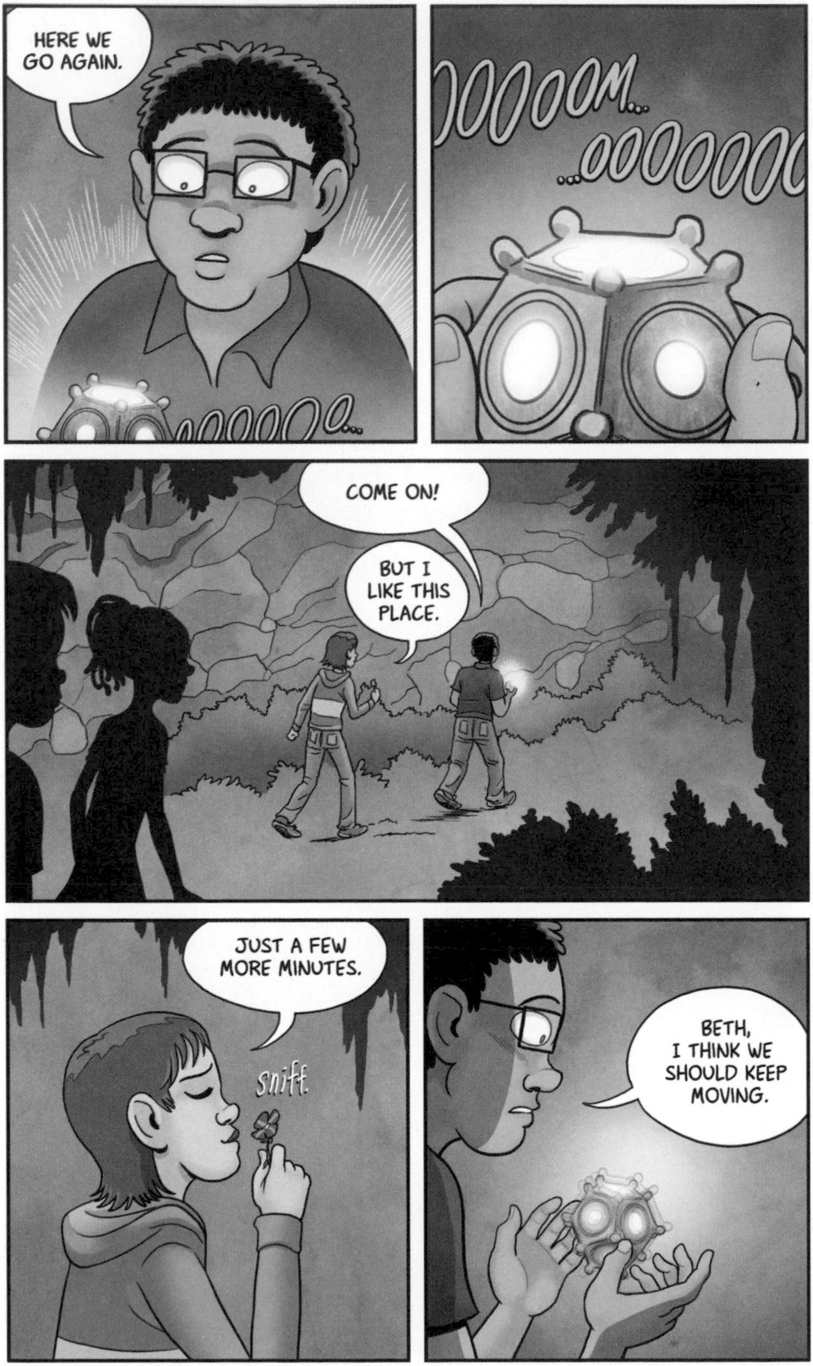
HERE WE GO AGAIN.
OOOOOO...
OOOOOM...
...OOOOOOO
COME ON!
BUT I LIKE THIS PLACE.
JUST A FEW MORE MINUTES.
SNIFF.
BETH, I THINK WE SHOULD KEEP MOVING.

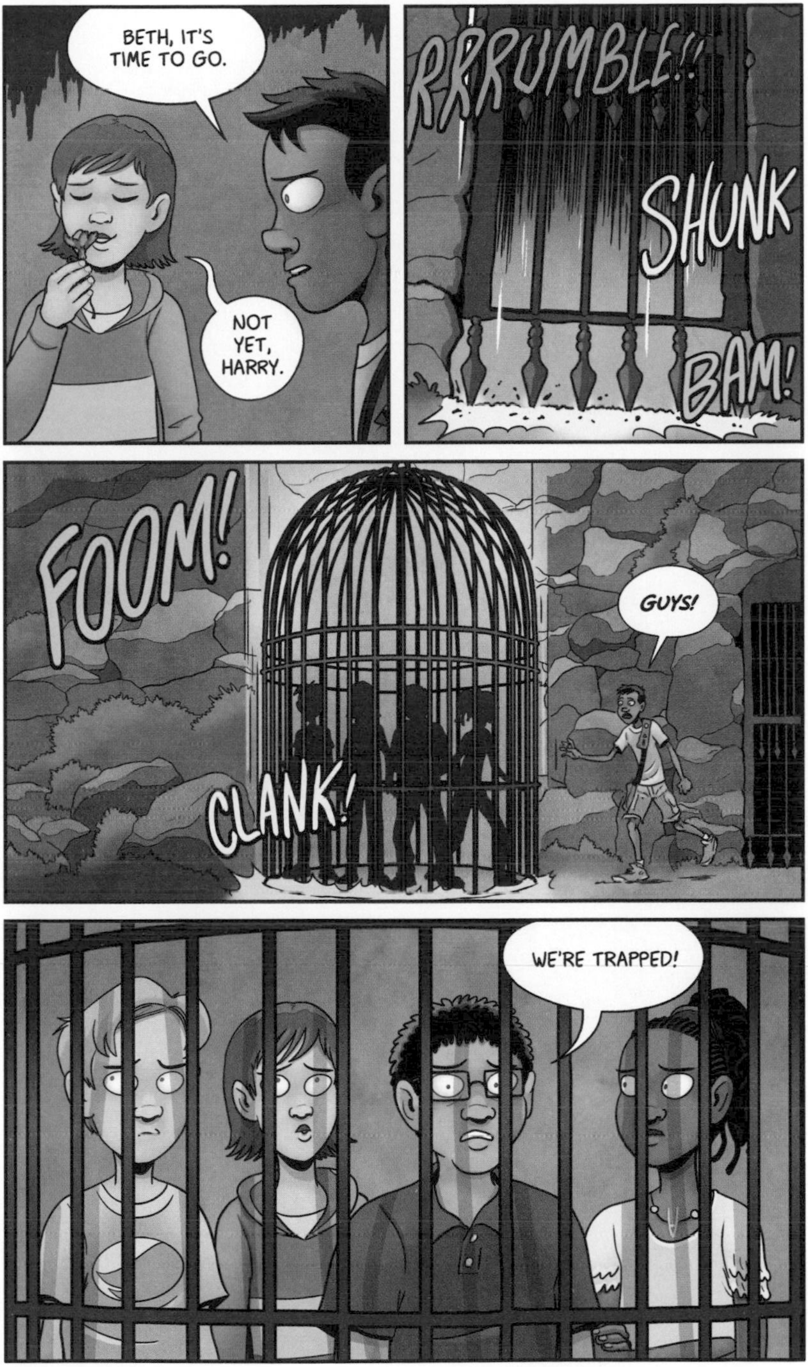
BETH, IT'S TIME TO GO.
NOT YET, HARRY.
RRRUMBLE!!
SHUNK
BAM!
FOOM!
CLANK!
GUYS!
WE'RE TRAPPED!

Chapter
TWO

GREAT!

NOW WHAT?

NO ONE KNOWS WE'RE DOWN HERE.

GRR-CH-CH

CRACK!

YOU'VE GOT TO BE KIDDING.

YOU ALL HEARD THAT THIS TIME, RIGHT?

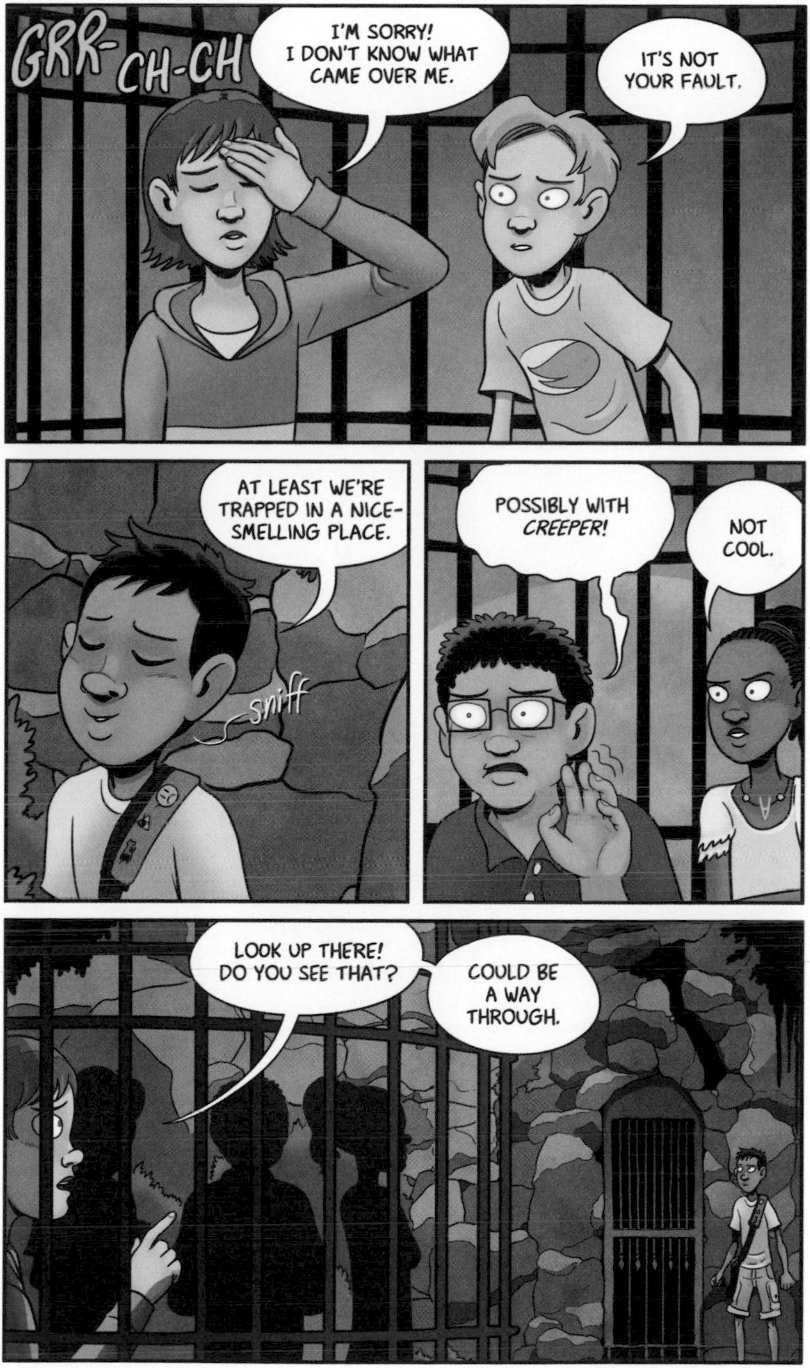
GRR-CH-CH
I'M SORRY! I DON'T KNOW WHAT CAME OVER ME.
IT'S NOT YOUR FAULT.
AT LEAST WE'RE TRAPPED IN A NICE-SMELLING PLACE.
sniff
POSSIBLY WITH *CREEPER!*
NOT COOL.
LOOK UP THERE! DO YOU SEE THAT?
COULD BE A WAY THROUGH.

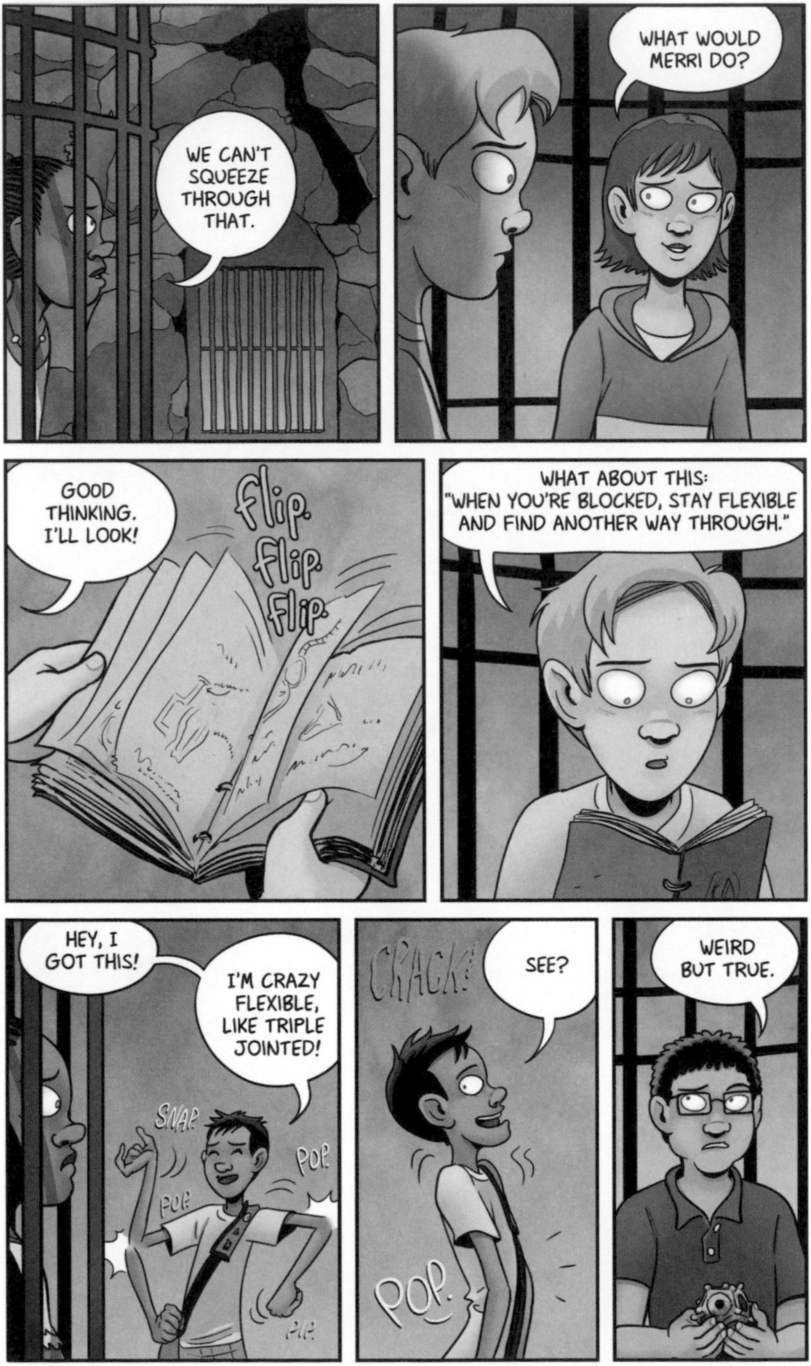
WE CAN'T SQUEEZE THROUGH THAT.
WHAT WOULD MERRI DO?
GOOD THINKING. I'LL LOOK!
flip. flip. flip.
WHAT ABOUT THIS: "WHEN YOU'RE BLOCKED, STAY FLEXIBLE AND FIND ANOTHER WAY THROUGH."
HEY, I GOT THIS!
I'M CRAZY FLEXIBLE, LIKE TRIPLE JOINTED!
SNAP
POP
POP
PIP
CRACK!
SEE?
POP.
WEIRD BUT TRUE.

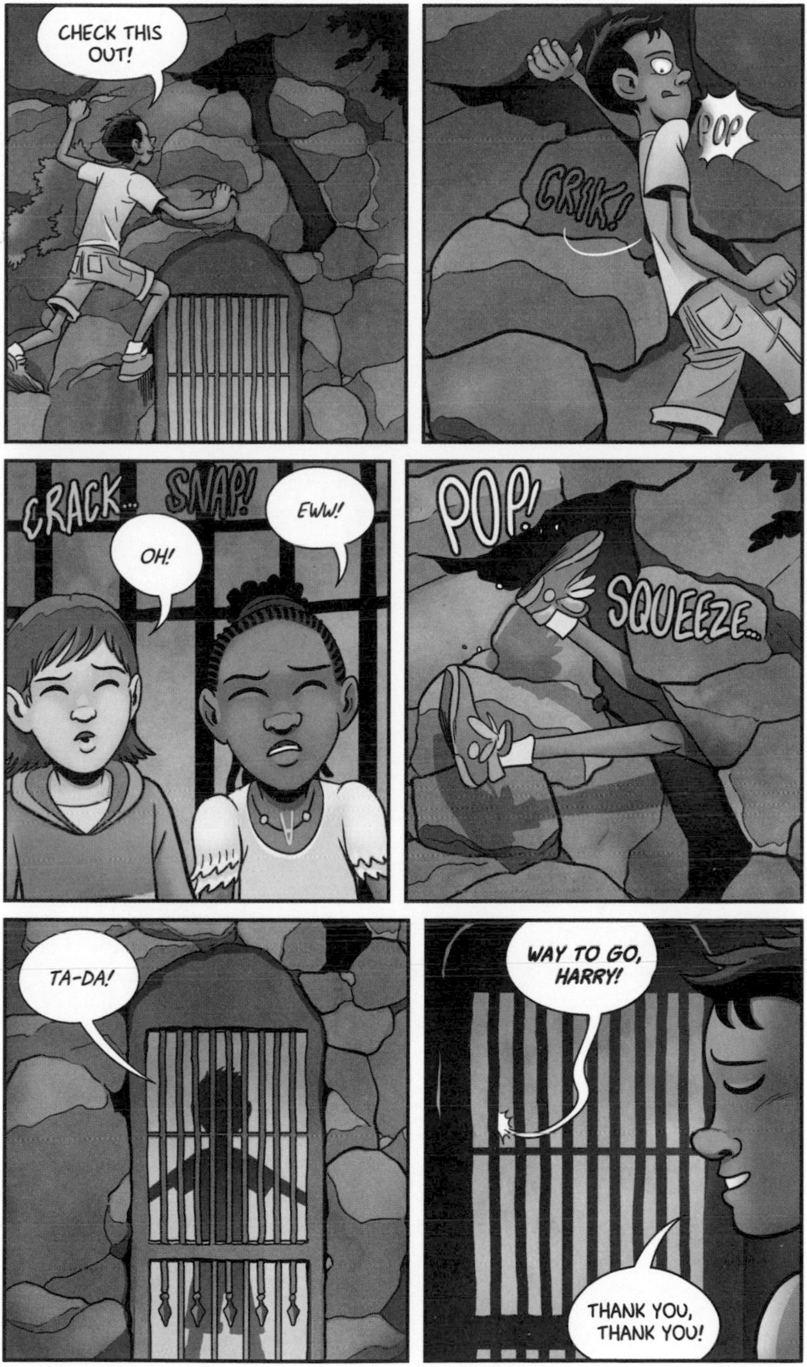
CHECK THIS OUT!
CRIK!
POP
CRACK...
SNAP!
OH!
EWW!
POP!
SQUEEZE...
TA-DA!
WAY TO GO, HARRY!
THANK YOU, THANK YOU!

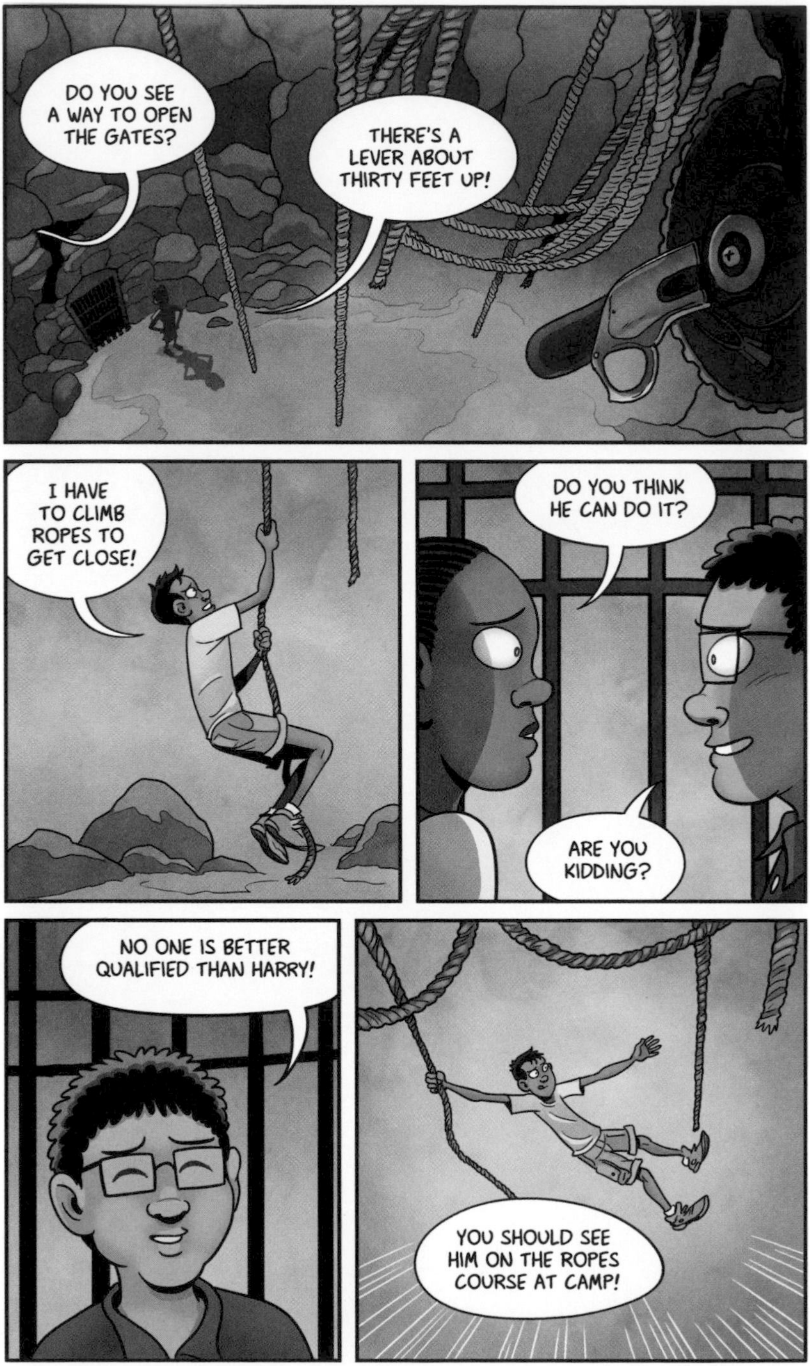
DO YOU SEE A WAY TO OPEN THE GATES?
THERE'S A LEVER ABOUT THIRTY FEET UP!
I HAVE TO CLIMB ROPES TO GET CLOSE!
DO YOU THINK HE CAN DO IT?
ARE YOU KIDDING?
NO ONE IS BETTER QUALIFIED THAN HARRY!
YOU SHOULD SEE HIM ON THE ROPES COURSE AT CAMP!

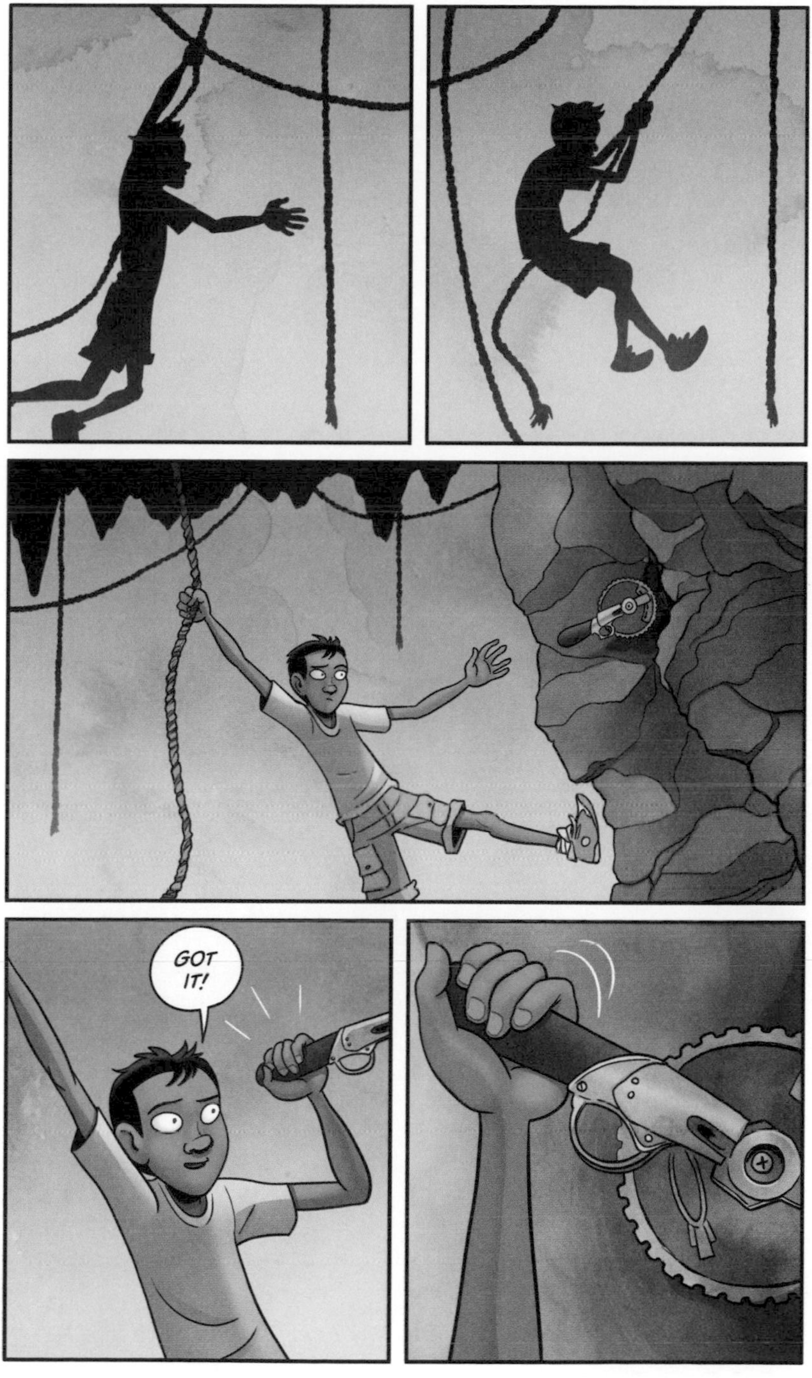
GOT IT!

CLINK CLINK CLANK

IT'S WORKING! THE CAGE IS LIFTING TOO!

RRUMBLE RUMBLE

THAT SOUNDS BAD. MAYBE IT GOES THE OTHER WAY?

CLINK

CLUNK- CLUNK- CLANK- BANG!

NO, HARRY!

RRUMBLE...

ARE YOU SURE? IT SOUNDED LIKE I STARTED AN EARTHQUAKE!

GRRA

GRRUM RRRUMBLE...

SOMETHING IS COMING! PUSH THE LEVER BACK, HARRY!

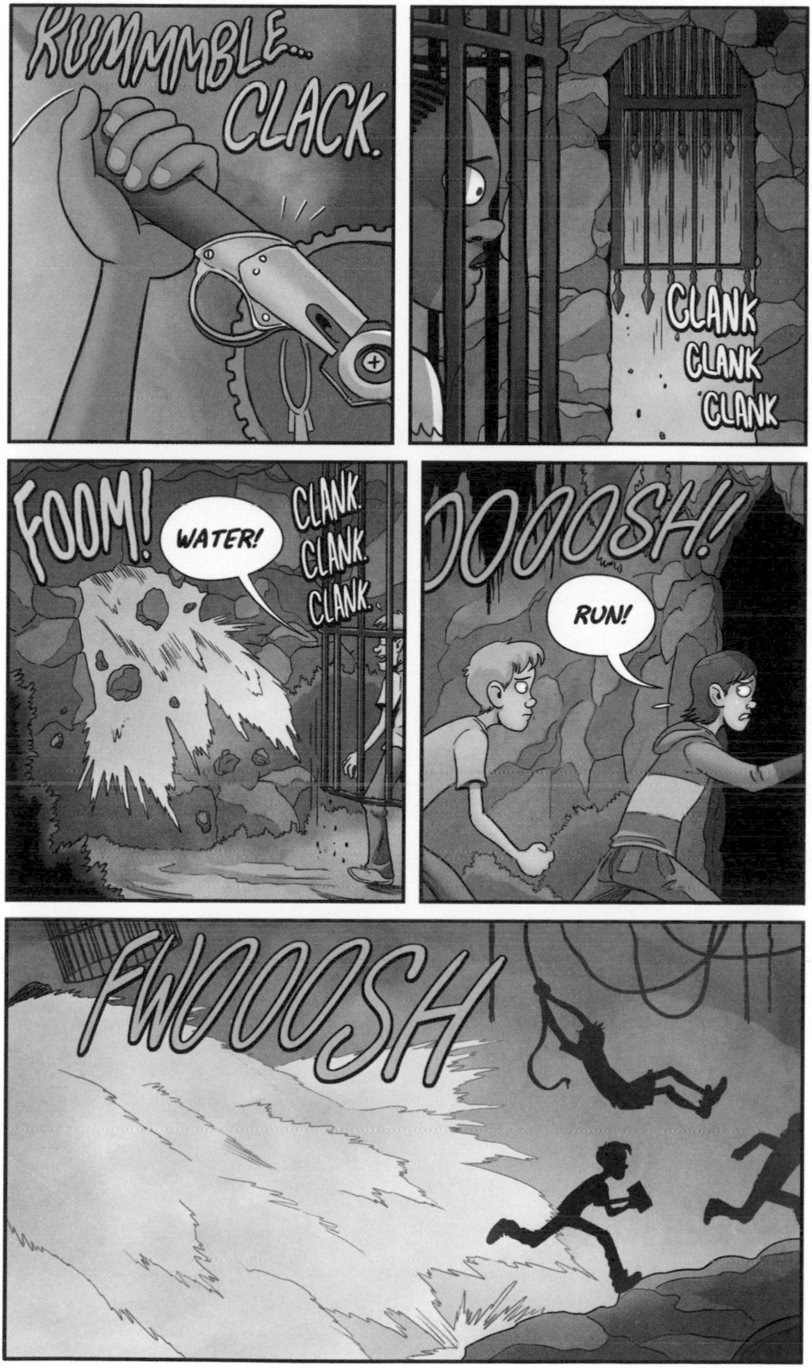
RUMMMBLE...
CLACK.
CLANK
CLANK
CLANK
FOOM!
WATER!
CLANK.
CLANK.
CLANK.
OOOOSH!
RUN!
FWOOOSH

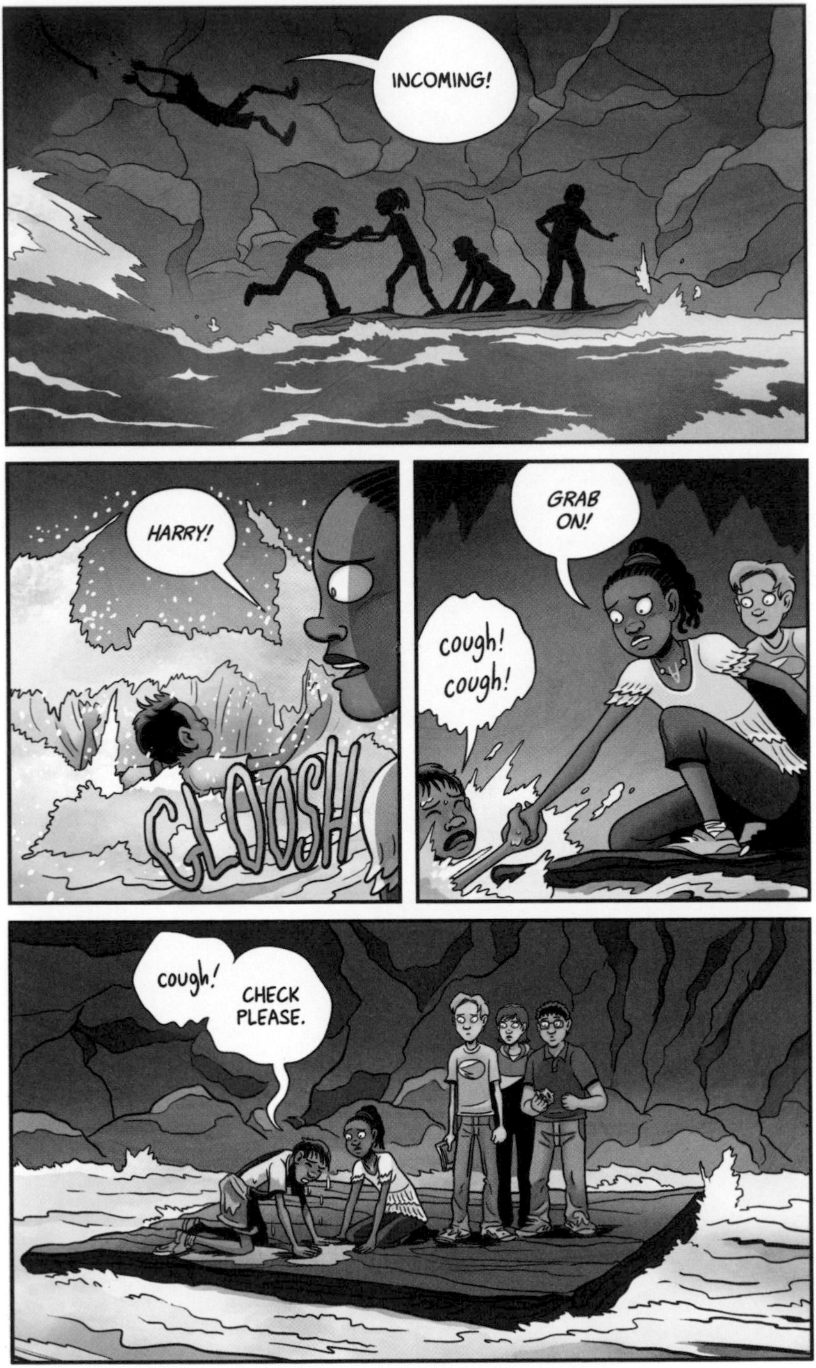
INCOMING!
HARRY!
GLOOSH
GRAB ON!
cough! cough!
cough!
CHECK PLEASE.

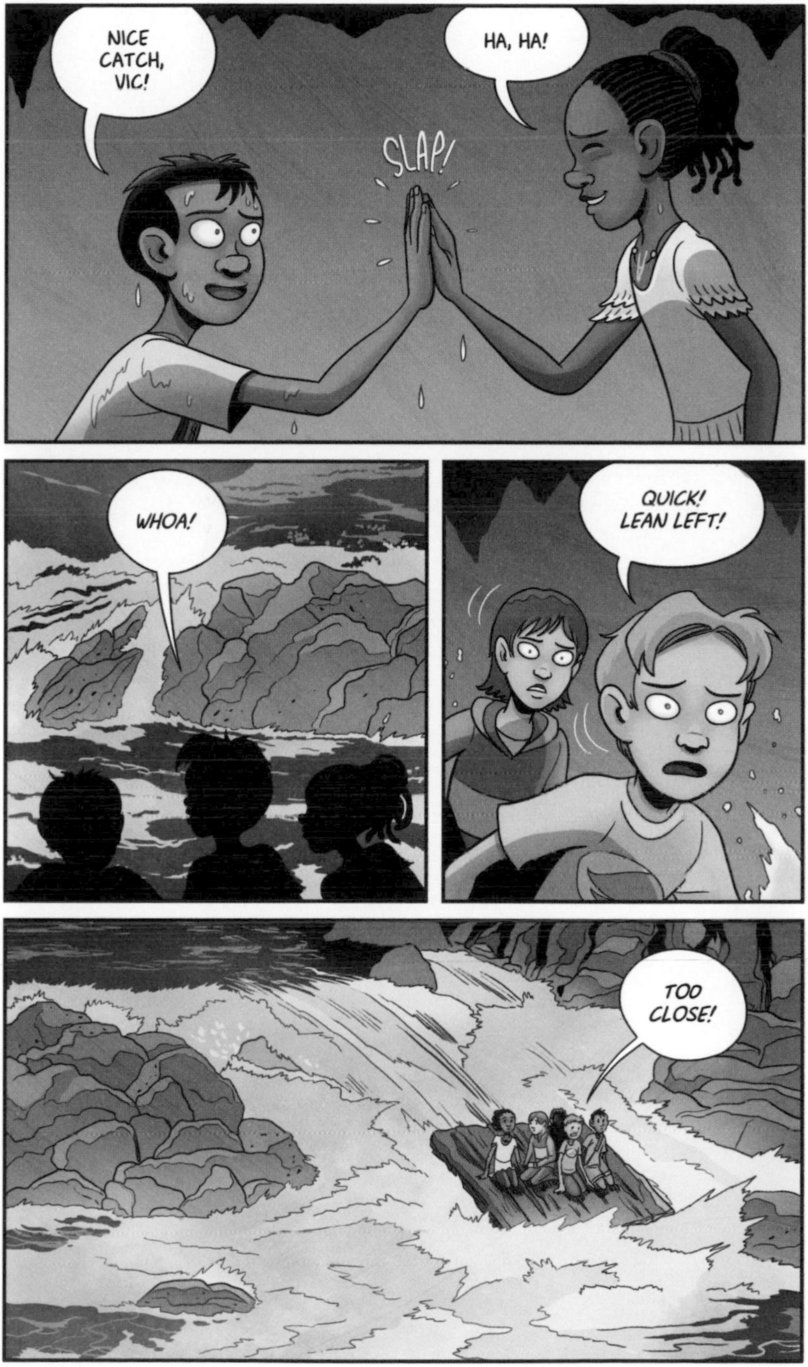
NICE CATCH, VIC!
HA, HA!
SLAP!
WHOA!
QUICK! LEAN LEFT!
TOO CLOSE!

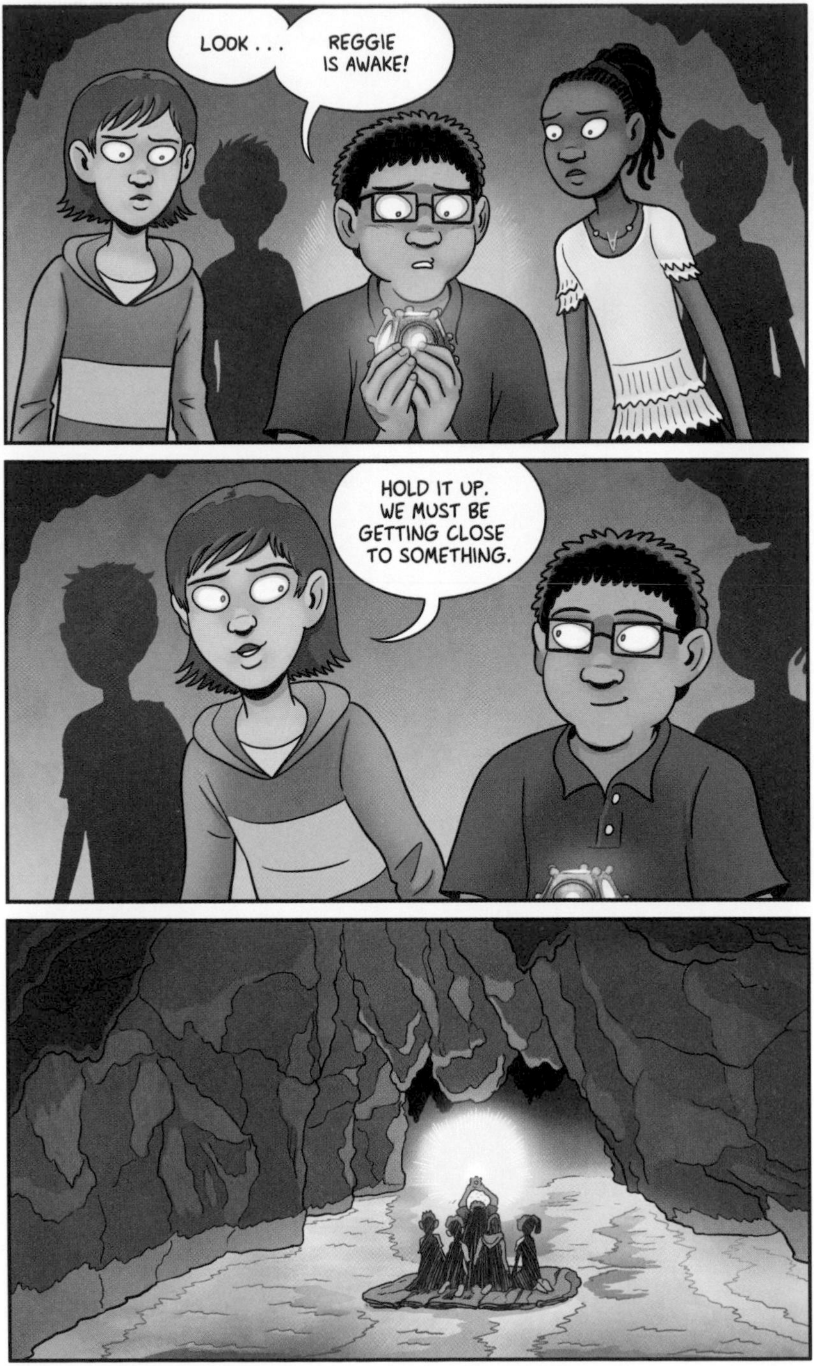
LOOK . . .
REGGIE IS AWAKE!
HOLD IT UP. WE MUST BE GETTING CLOSE TO SOMETHING.

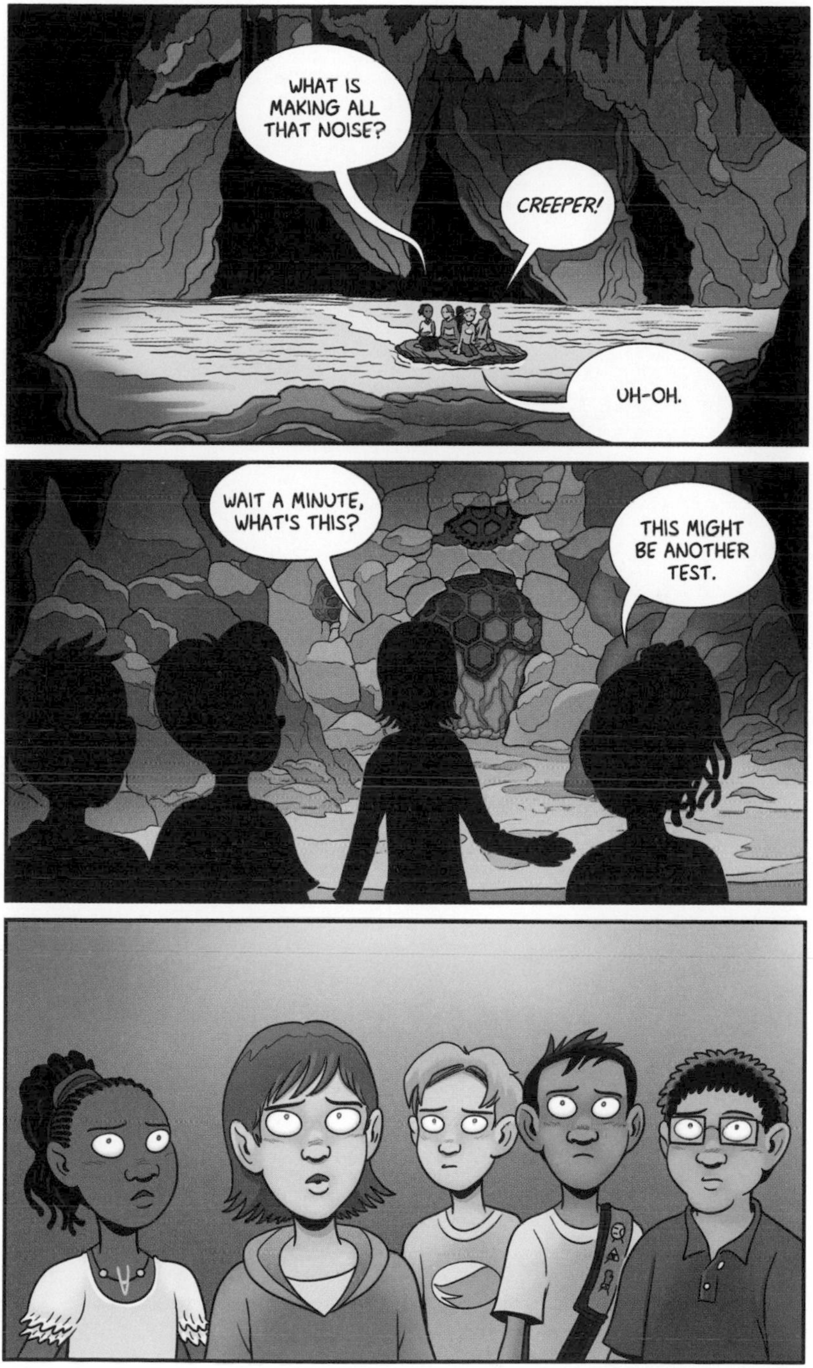
WHAT IS MAKING ALL THAT NOISE?
CREEPER!
UH-OH.
WAIT A MINUTE, WHAT'S THIS?
THIS MIGHT BE ANOTHER TEST.

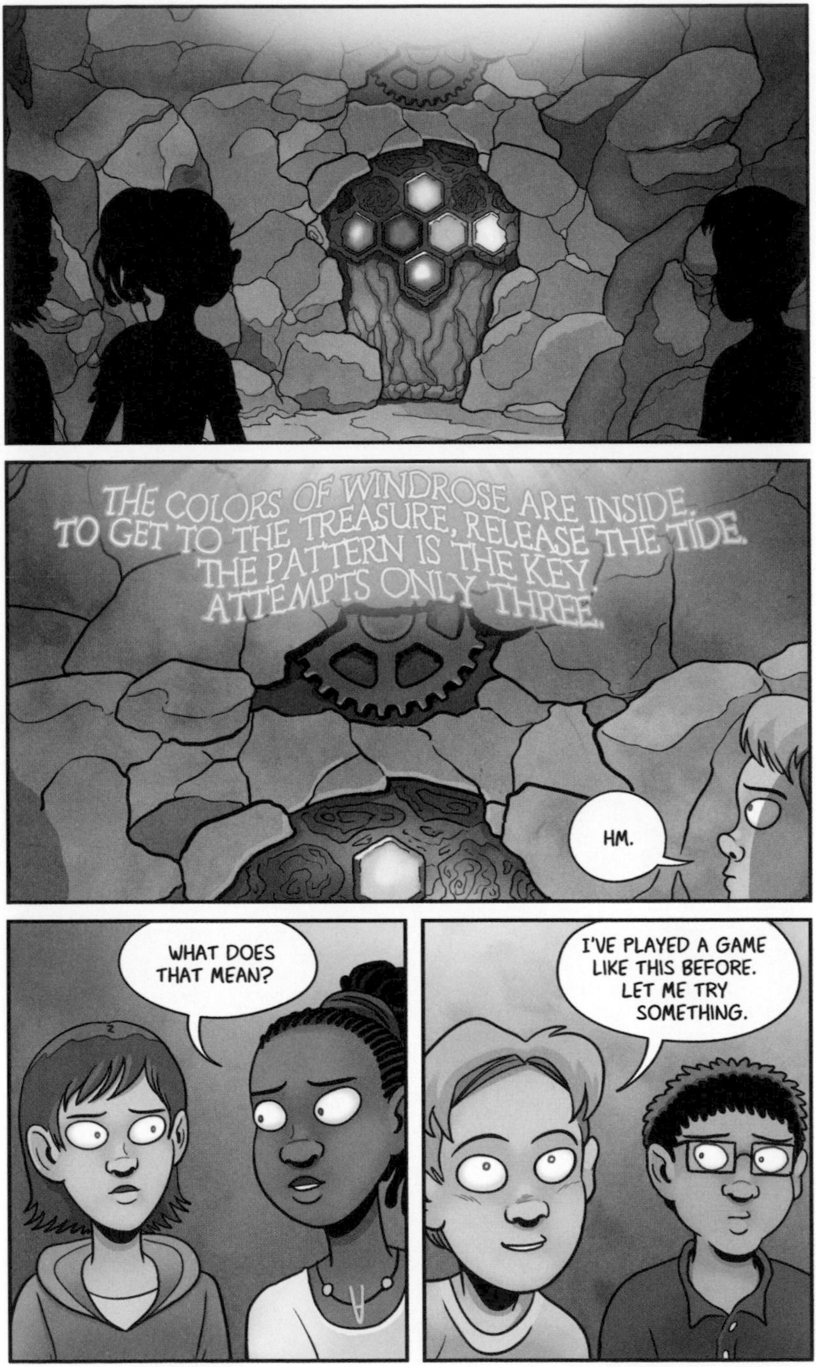
THE COLORS OF WINDROSE ARE INSIDE.
TO GET TO THE TREASURE, RELEASE THE TIDE.
THE PATTERN IS THE KEY.
ATTEMPTS ONLY THREE.
HM.
WHAT DOES THAT MEAN?
I'VE PLAYED A GAME LIKE THIS BEFORE. LET ME TRY SOMETHING.

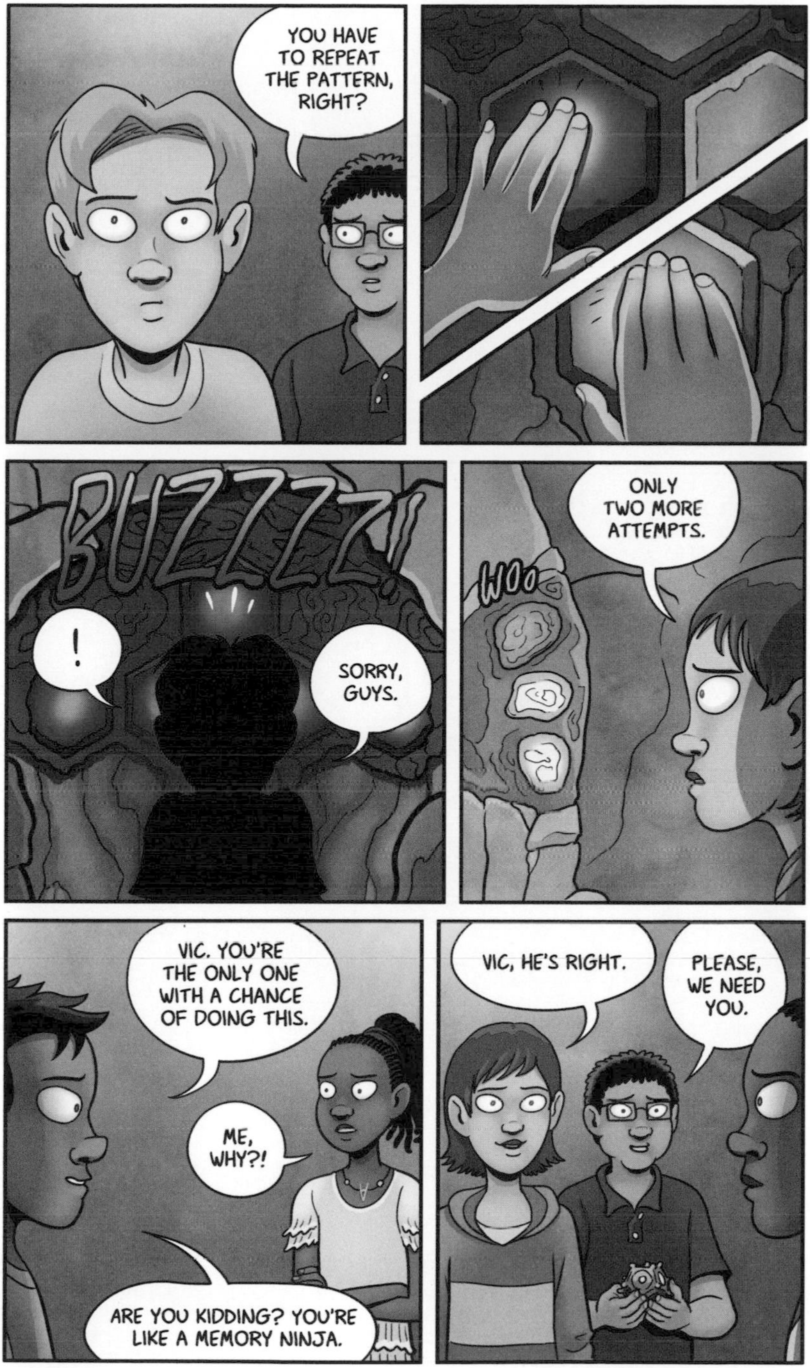

YOU HAVE TO REPEAT THE PATTERN, RIGHT?
BUZZZZ!
!
SORRY, GUYS.
WOO
ONLY TWO MORE ATTEMPTS.
VIC. YOU'RE THE ONLY ONE WITH A CHANCE OF DOING THIS.
ME, WHY?!
ARE YOU KIDDING? YOU'RE LIKE A MEMORY NINJA.
VIC, HE'S RIGHT.
PLEASE, WE NEED YOU.

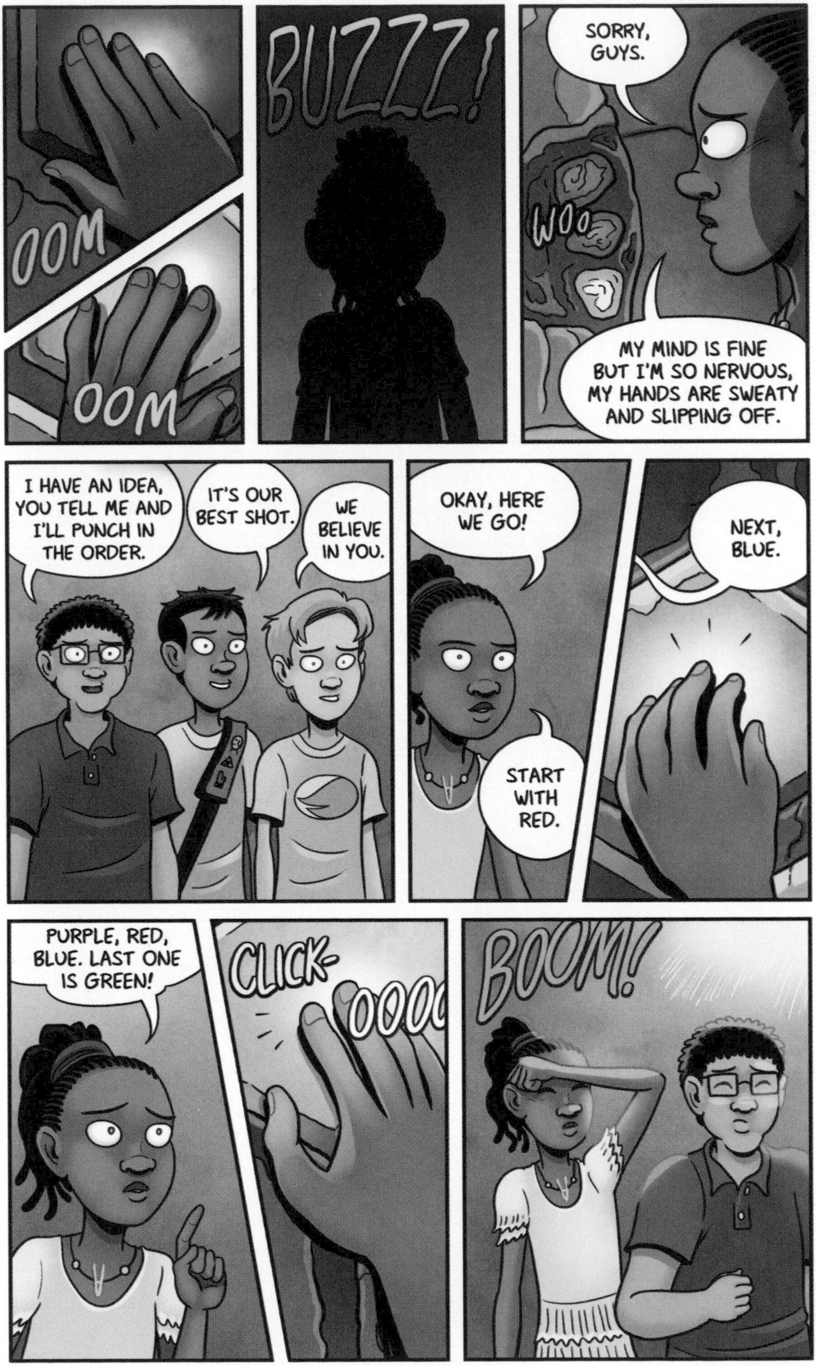
OOM
OOM
BUZZZ!
SORRY, GUYS.
WOO
MY MIND IS FINE BUT I'M SO NERVOUS, MY HANDS ARE SWEATY AND SLIPPING OFF.
I HAVE AN IDEA, YOU TELL ME AND I'LL PUNCH IN THE ORDER.
IT'S OUR BEST SHOT.
WE BELIEVE IN YOU.
OKAY, HERE WE GO!
START WITH RED.
NEXT, BLUE.
PURPLE, RED, BLUE. LAST ONE IS GREEN!
CLICK-
OOOO
BOOM!

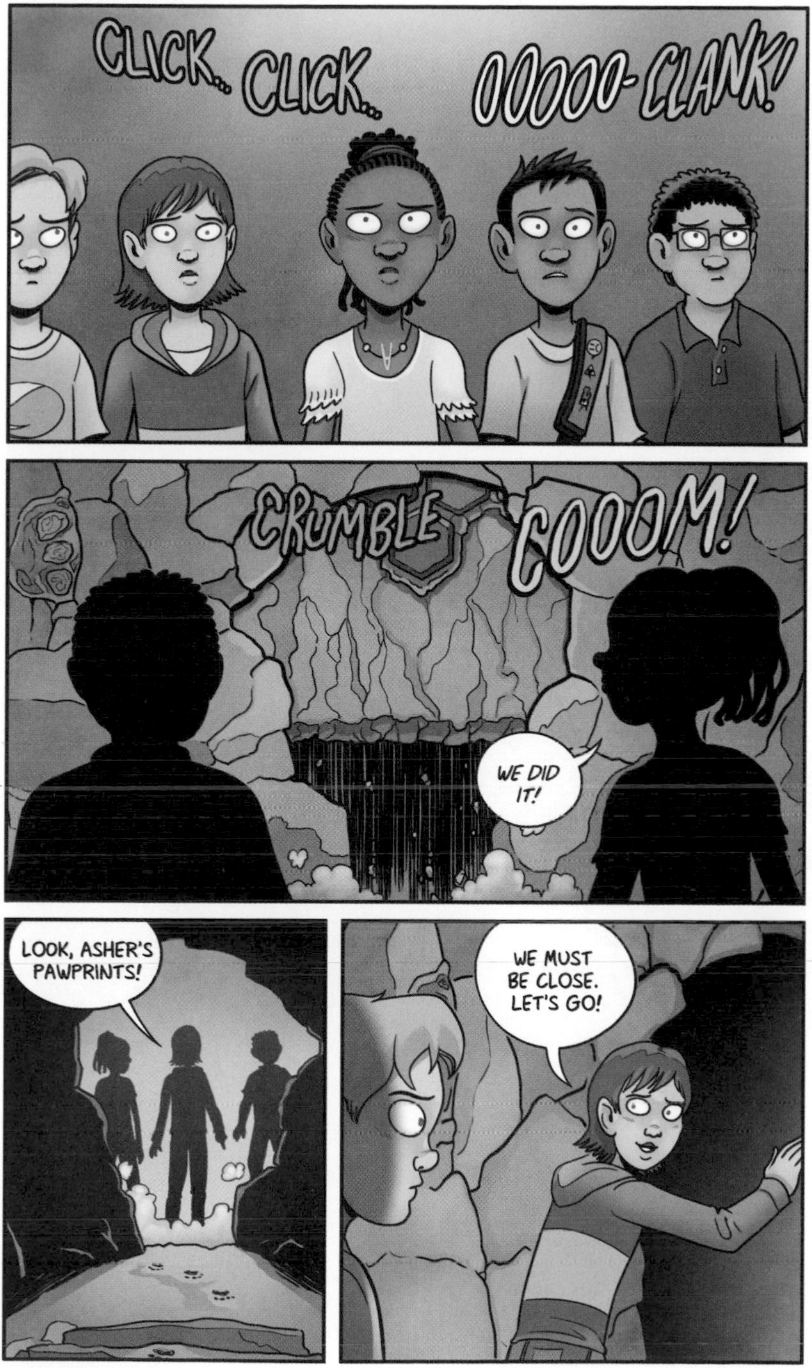
CLICK... CLICK...
OOOOO-CLANK!
CRUMBLE
COOOM!
WE DID IT!
LOOK, ASHER'S PAWPRINTS!
WE MUST BE CLOSE. LET'S GO!

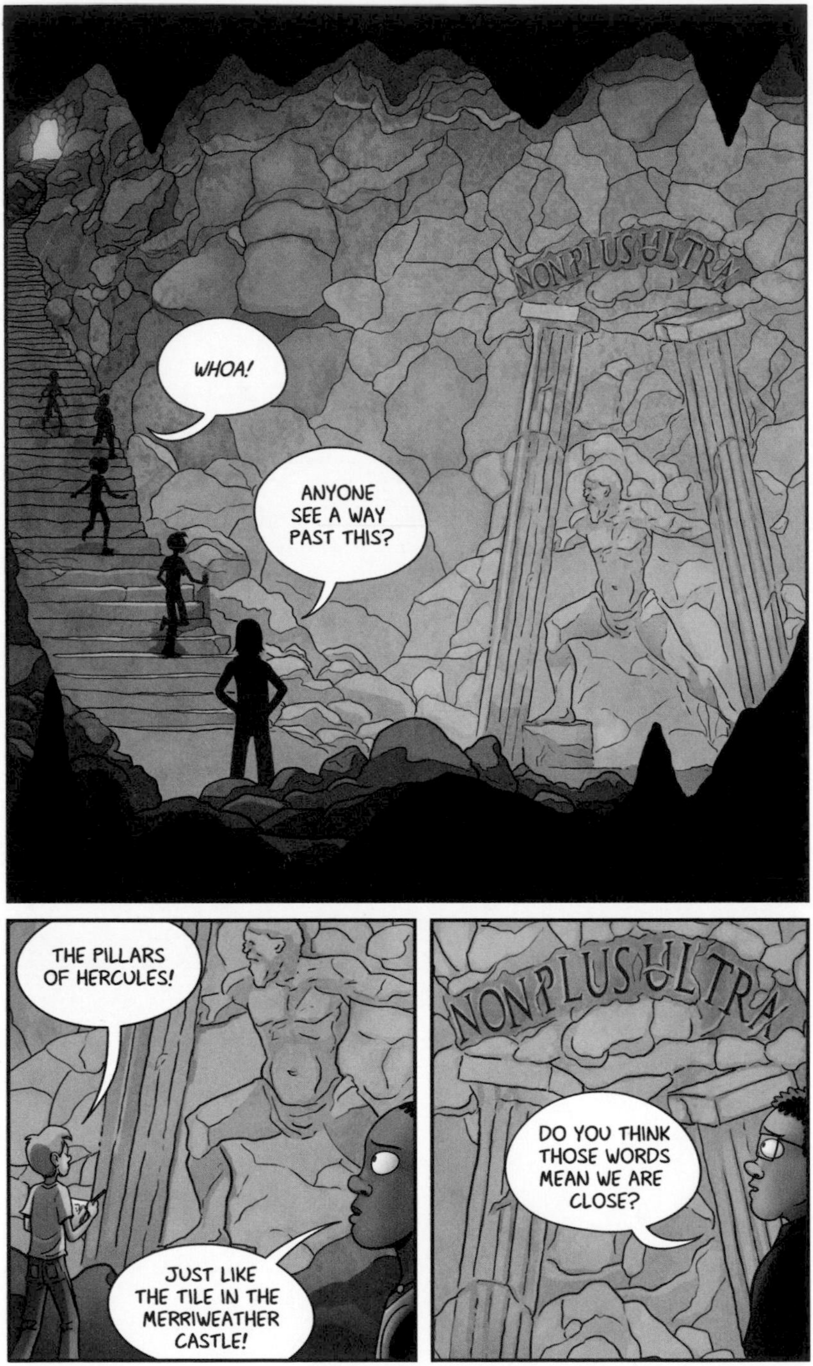
NON PLUS ULTRA
WHOA!
ANYONE SEE A WAY PAST THIS?
THE PILLARS OF HERCULES!
JUST LIKE THE TILE IN THE MERRIWEATHER CASTLE!
NON PLUS ULTRA
DO YOU THINK THOSE WORDS MEAN WE ARE CLOSE?

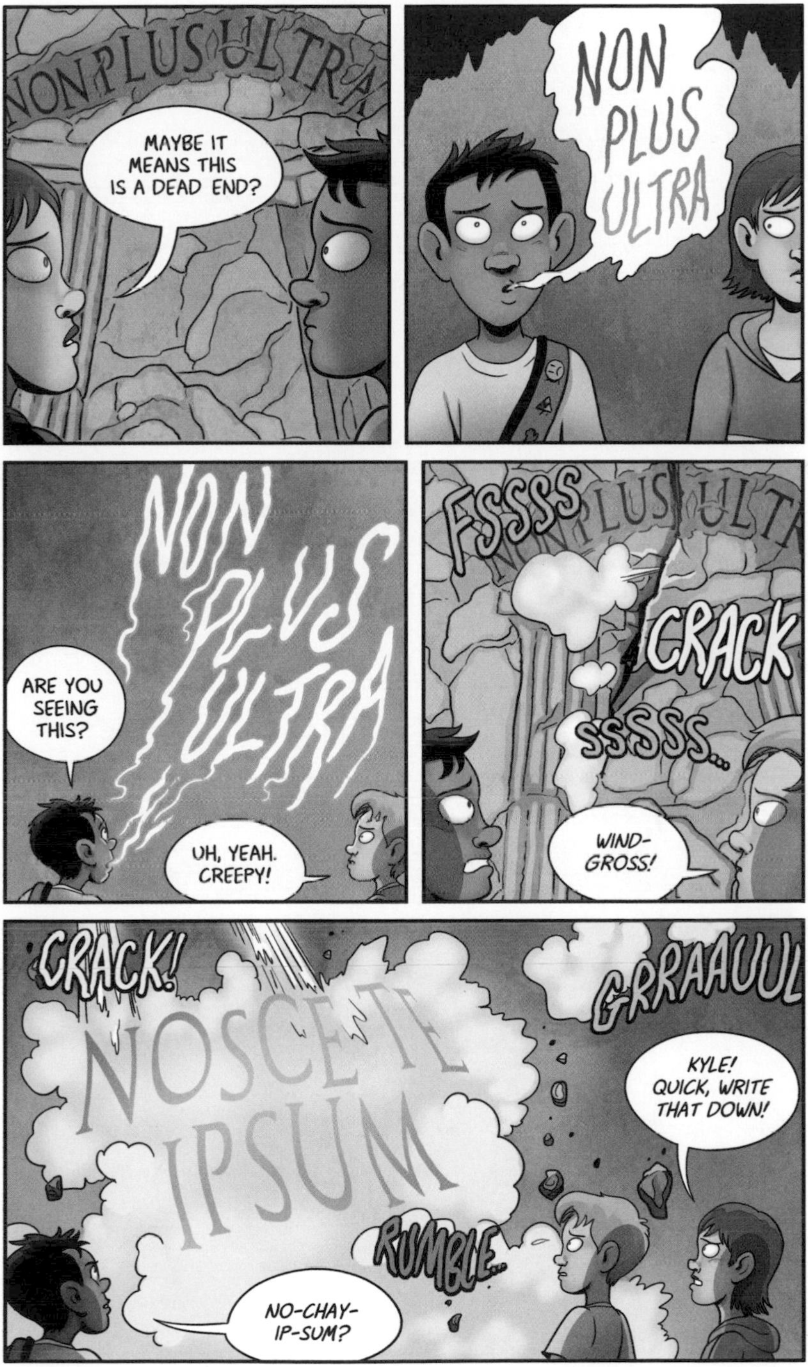
NON PLUS ULTRA
MAYBE IT MEANS THIS IS A DEAD END?
NON PLUS ULTRA
NON PLUS ULTRA
ARE YOU SEEING THIS?
UH, YEAH. CREEPY!
FSSSS
NON PLUS ULTRA
CRACK
SSSSS...
WIND-GROSS!
CRACK!
GRRAAUUL
NOSCE TE IPSUM
KYLE! QUICK, WRITE THAT DOWN!
RUMBLE...
NO-CHAY-IP-SUM?

RRUMBLE... SSSSSSS

LOOK! ON THE WALL!

FIND THE MINUTES TO WIN.
TO FIGURE IT OUT, LOOK IN.
FOLLOW THE CURRENTS
AND WATCH FOR DOOM.
HEAD FOR THE LAB NEAR
THE TOWER OF THE MOON.

LAB? LIKE A SCIENCE LAB?

KYLE, CAN YOU GET ALL OF THIS IN YOUR NOTEBOOK?

RRRRUMBLE...

UH, PEOPLE?

CRASH!

RRUUMB

ON IT! I'LL GET THOSE NUMBERS TOO.

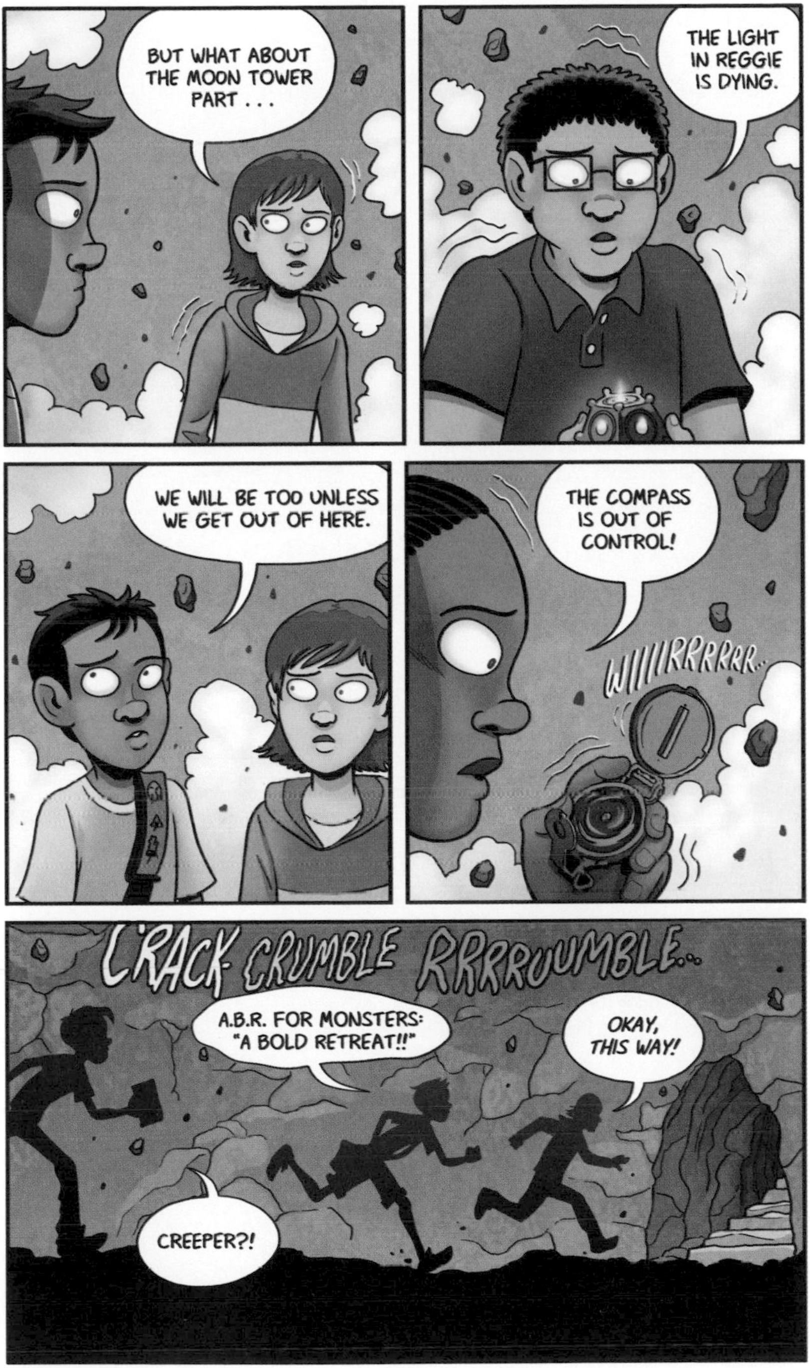
BUT WHAT ABOUT THE MOON TOWER PART . . .
THE LIGHT IN REGGIE IS DYING.
WE WILL BE TOO UNLESS WE GET OUT OF HERE.
THE COMPASS IS OUT OF CONTROL!
WIIIIRRRRRR...
CRACK CRUMBLE RRRRUUMBLE...
A.B.R. FOR MONSTERS: "A BOLD RETREAT!!"
OKAY, THIS WAY!
CREEPER?!

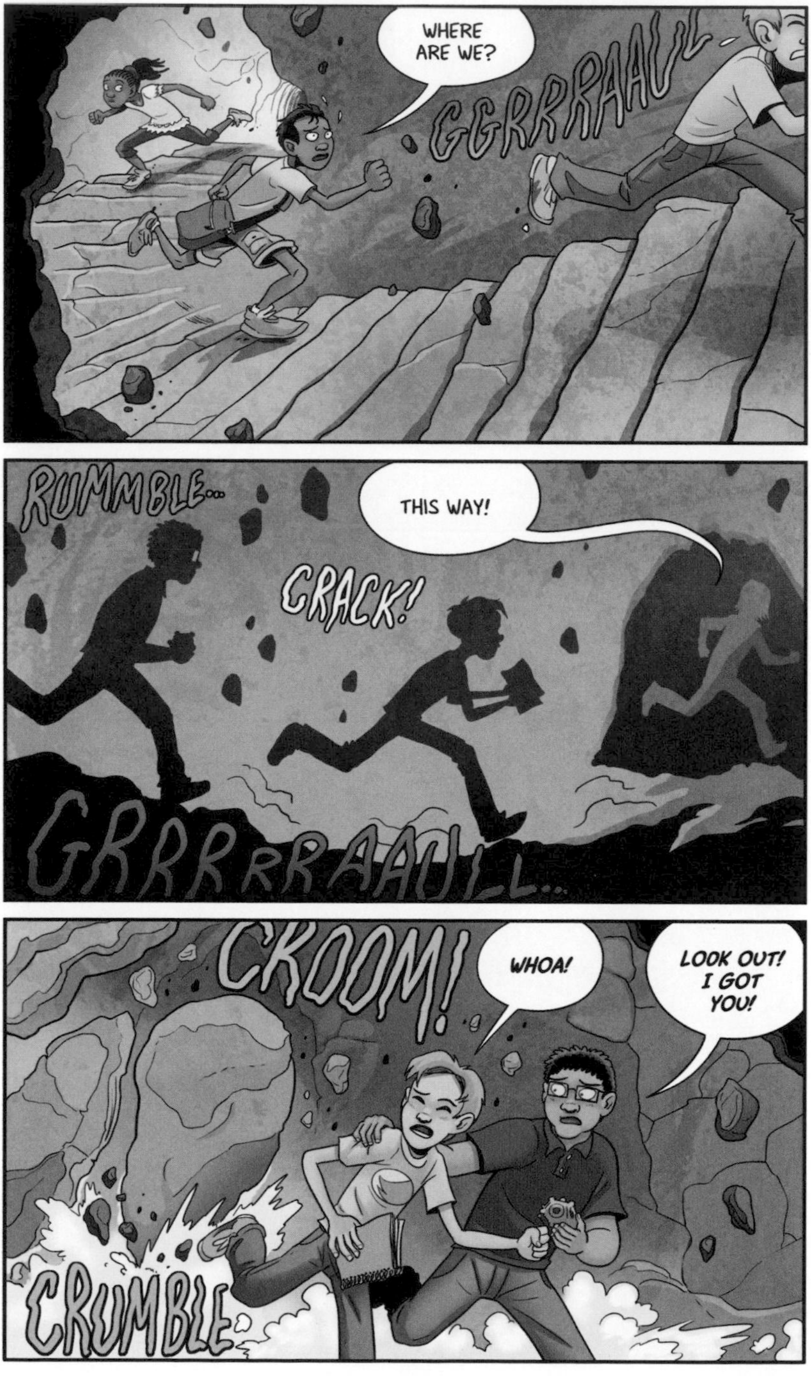
WHERE ARE WE?
GGRRRAAUL
RUMMBLE...
THIS WAY!
CRACK!
GRRRRRRAAULL...
CKOOM!
WHOA!
LOOK OUT! I GOT YOU!
CRUMBLE

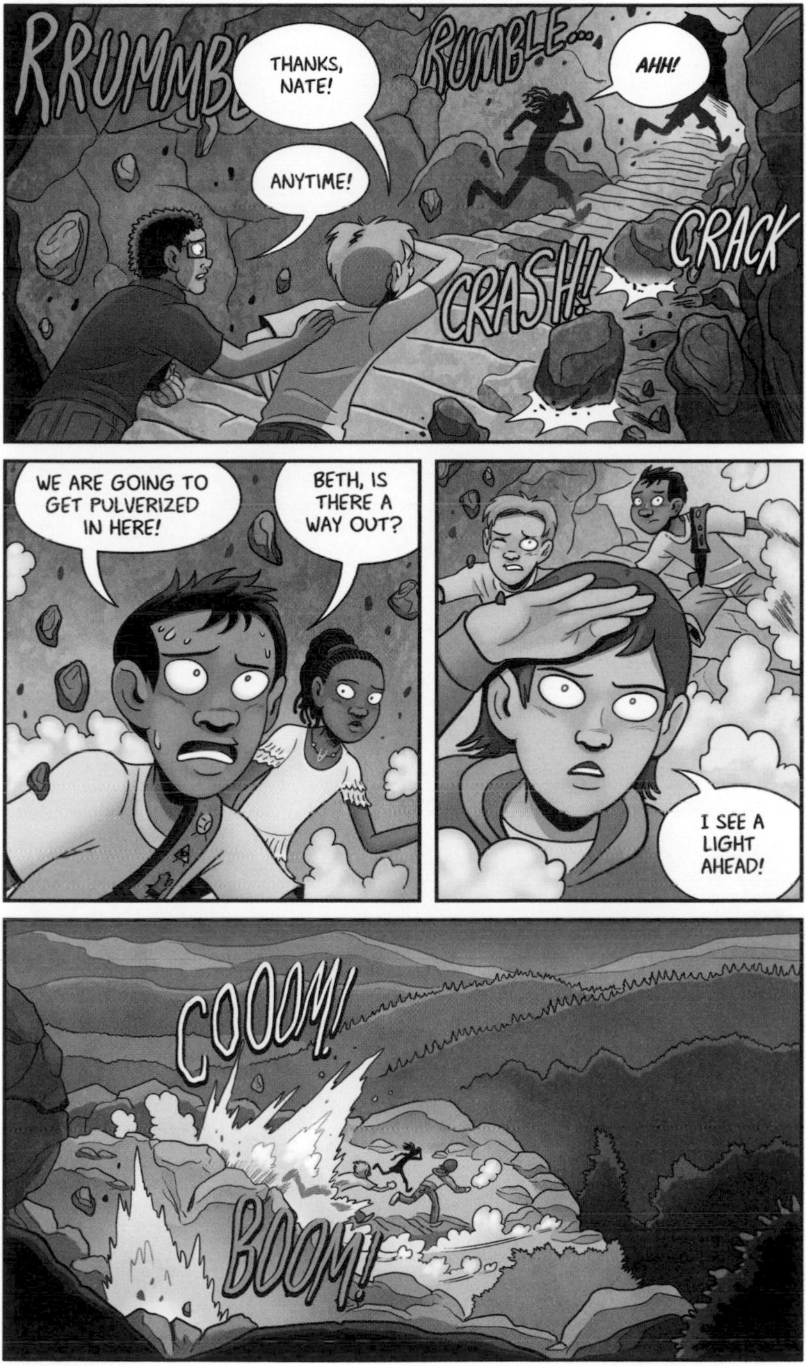
RRUMMBLE
THANKS, NATE!
ANYTIME!
RUMBLE...
AHH!
CRASH!
CRACK
WE ARE GOING TO GET PULVERIZED IN HERE!
BETH, IS THERE A WAY OUT?
I SEE A LIGHT AHEAD!
COOOM!
BOOM!

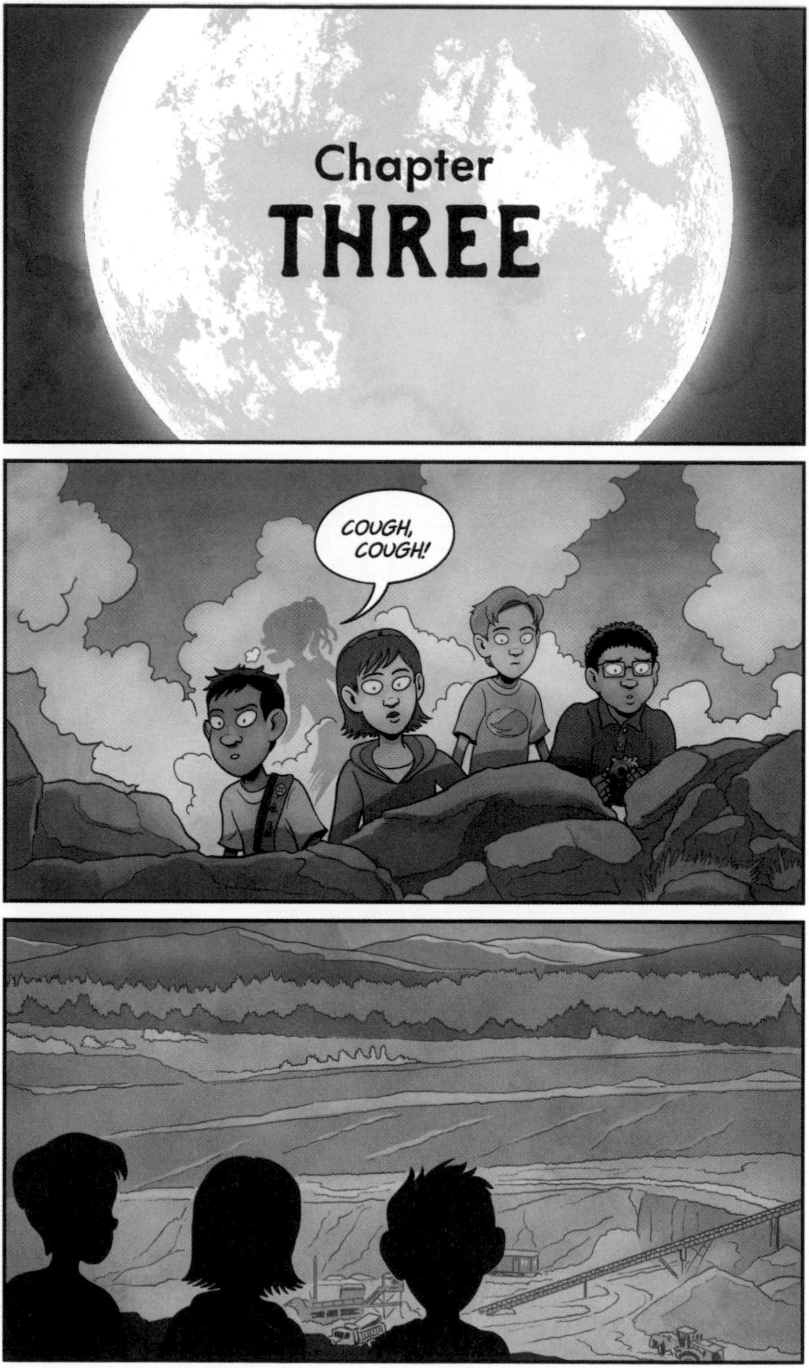
Chapter
THREE
COUGH, COUGH!

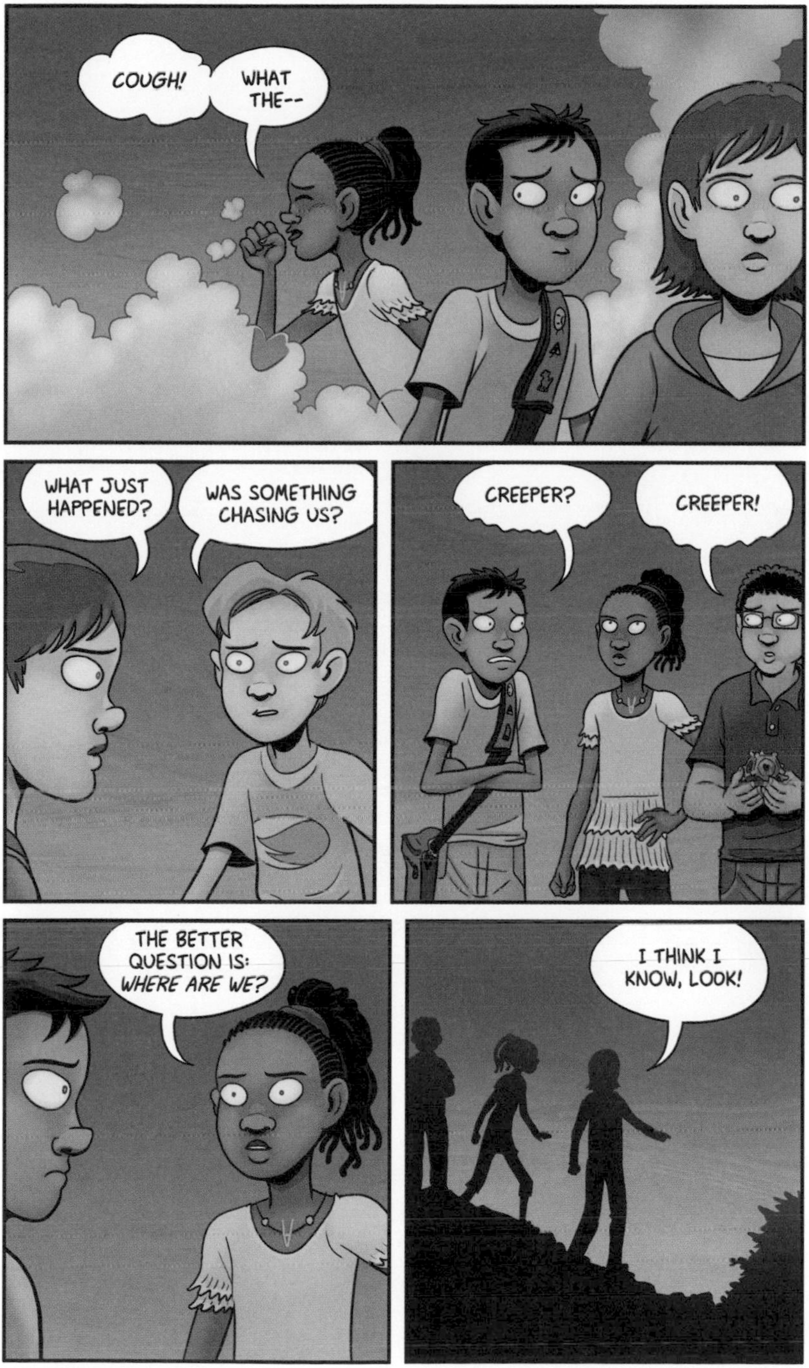
COUGH!
WHAT THE--
WHAT JUST HAPPENED?
WAS SOMETHING CHASING US?
CREEPER?
CREEPER!
THE BETTER QUESTION IS: WHERE ARE WE?
I THINK I KNOW, LOOK!

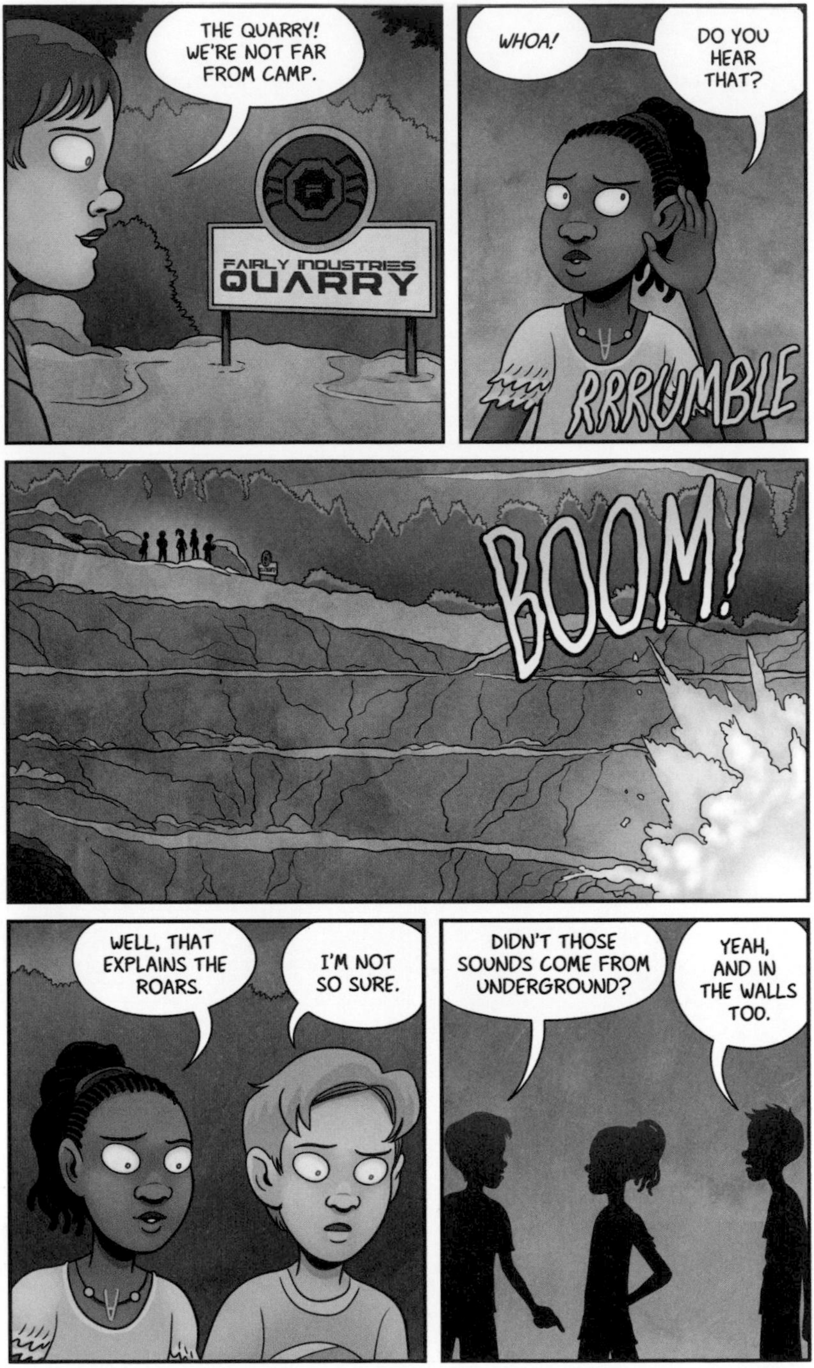
THE QUARRY! WE'RE NOT FAR FROM CAMP.
FAIRLY INDUSTRIES QUARRY
WHOA!
DO YOU HEAR THAT?
RRRUMBLE
BOOM!
WELL, THAT EXPLAINS THE ROARS.
I'M NOT SO SURE.
DIDN'T THOSE SOUNDS COME FROM UNDERGROUND?
YEAH, AND IN THE WALLS TOO.

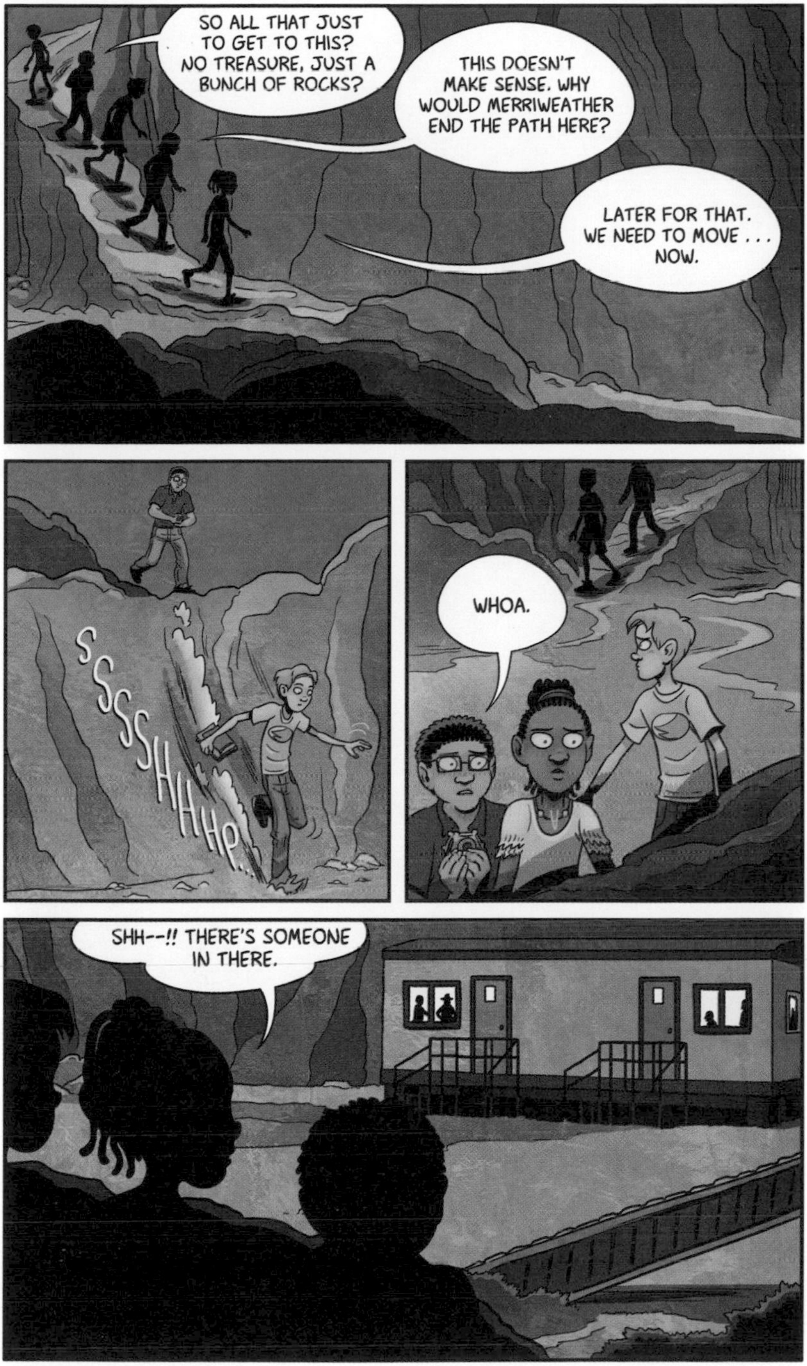
SO ALL THAT JUST TO GET TO THIS? NO TREASURE, JUST A BUNCH OF ROCKS?
THIS DOESN'T MAKE SENSE. WHY WOULD MERRIWEATHER END THE PATH HERE?
LATER FOR THAT. WE NEED TO MOVE . . . NOW.
SSSSHHHHP...
WHOA.
SHH--!! THERE'S SOMEONE IN THERE.

THEY'RE COMING OUT! RUN BEHIND THAT BULLDOZER!

CLICK CLACK.

DID HE SEE US?!

SHUT THAT THING UP!

I'M TRYING!

OOOOOo..

WHO'S THERE?

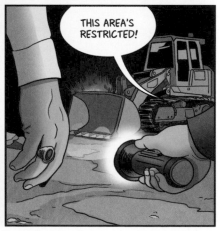

THIS AREA'S RESTRICTED!

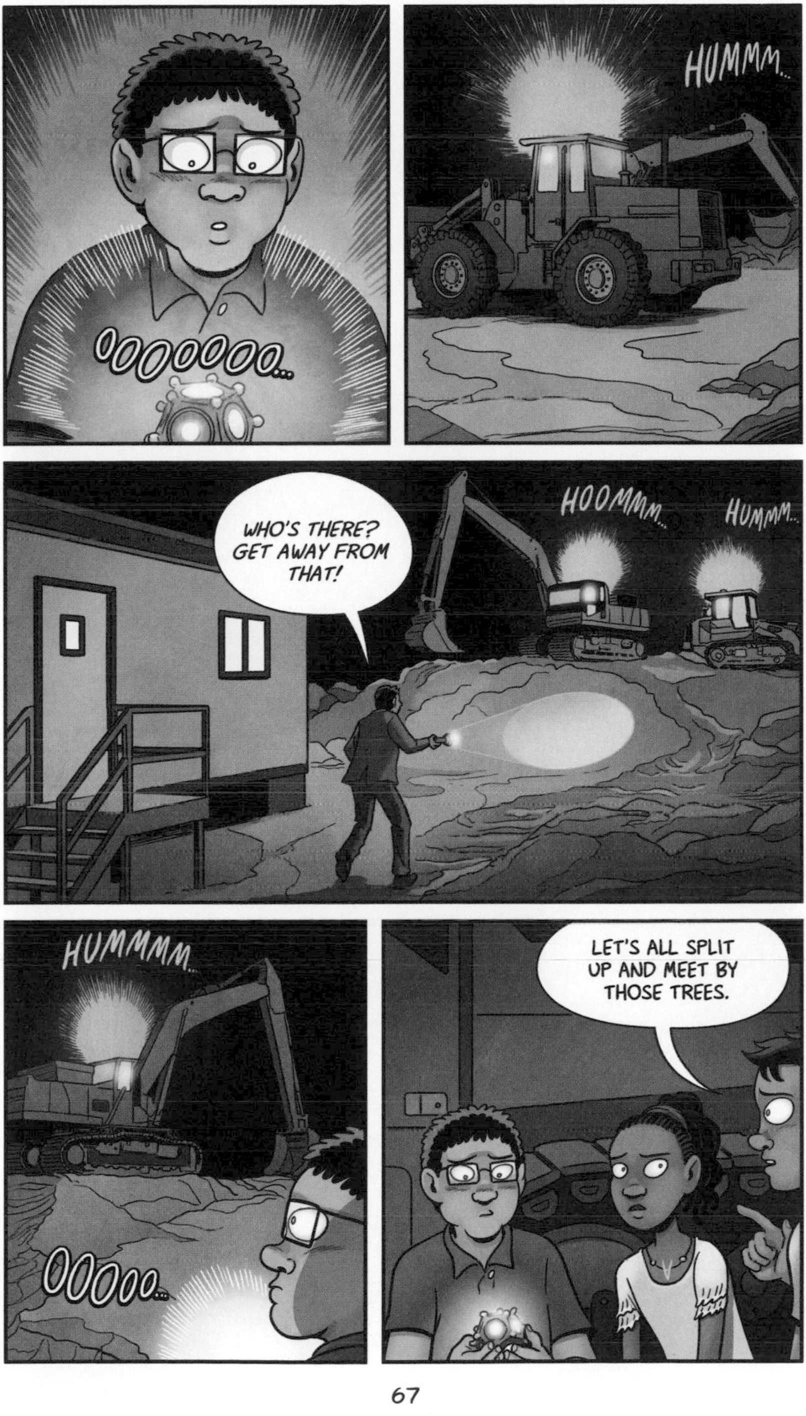
OOOOOOO...
HUMMM...
WHO'S THERE? GET AWAY FROM THAT!
HOOMMM...
HUMMM...
HUMMMM...
OOOOO...
LET'S ALL SPLIT UP AND MEET BY THOSE TREES.

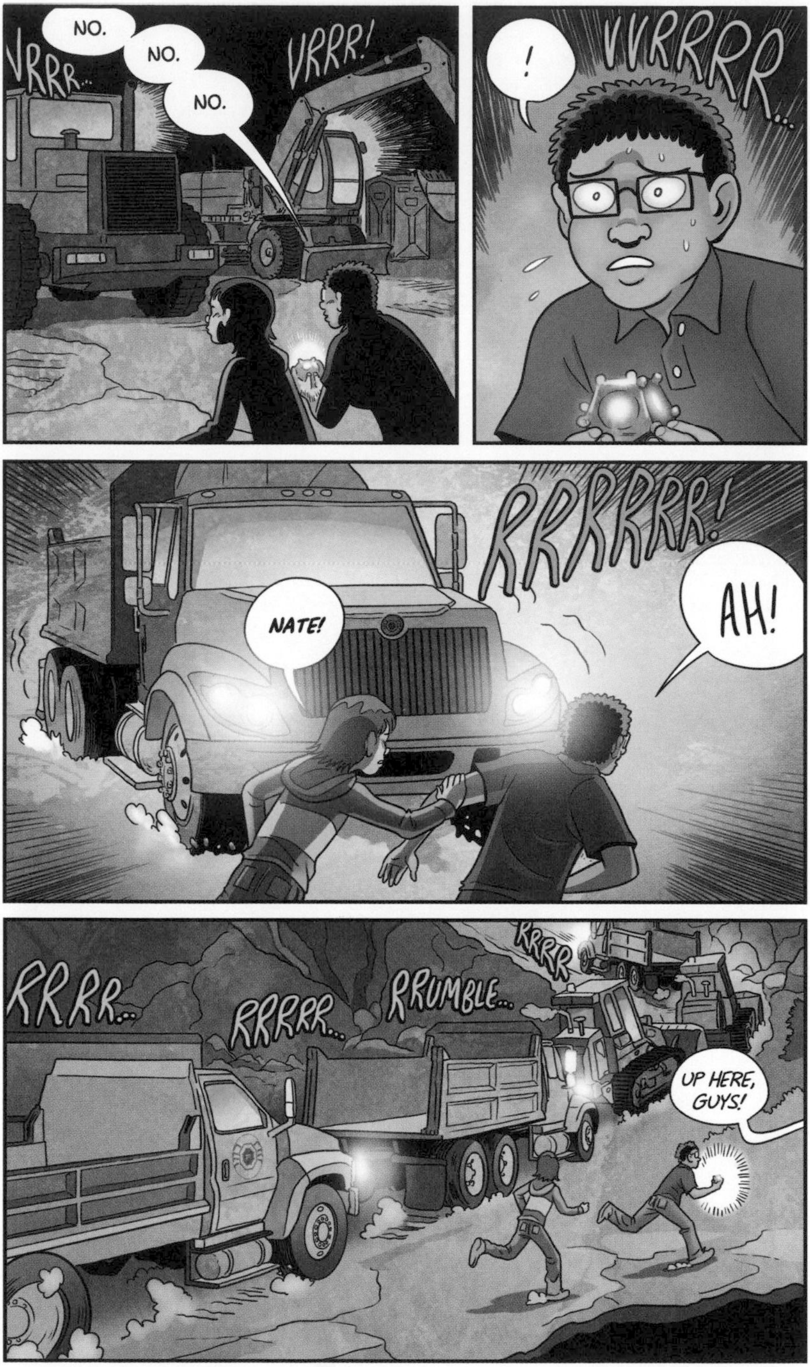
VRRR...
NO.
NO.
NO.
VRRR!
!
VVRRRRR...
RRRRRR!
NATE!
AH!
RRRR...
RRRRR...
RRUMBLE...
RRRR
UP HERE, GUYS!

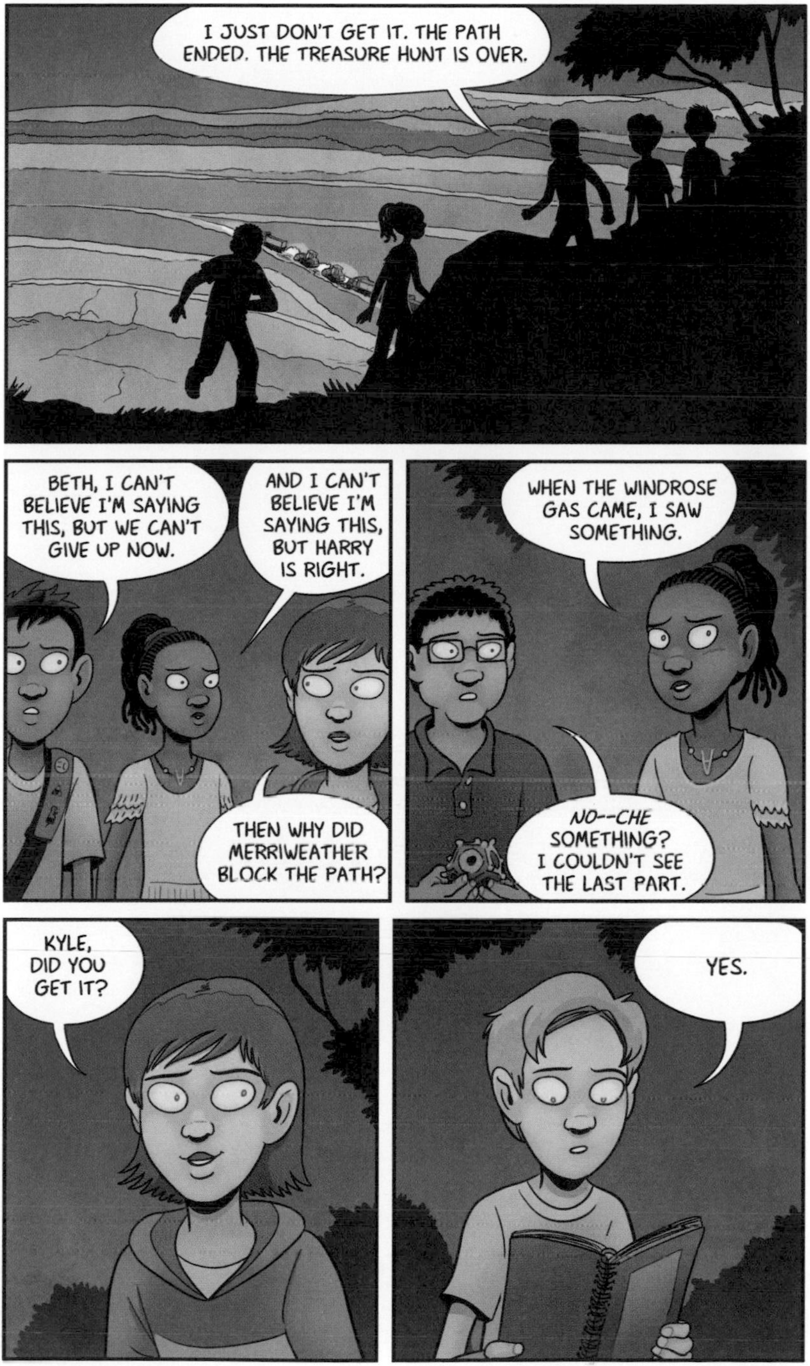

I JUST DON'T GET IT. THE PATH ENDED. THE TREASURE HUNT IS OVER.
BETH, I CAN'T BELIEVE I'M SAYING THIS, BUT WE CAN'T GIVE UP NOW.
AND I CAN'T BELIEVE I'M SAYING THIS, BUT HARRY IS RIGHT.
THEN WHY DID MERRIWEATHER BLOCK THE PATH?
WHEN THE WINDROSE GAS CAME, I SAW SOMETHING.
NO--CHE SOMETHING? I COULDN'T SEE THE LAST PART.
KYLE, DID YOU GET IT?
YES.

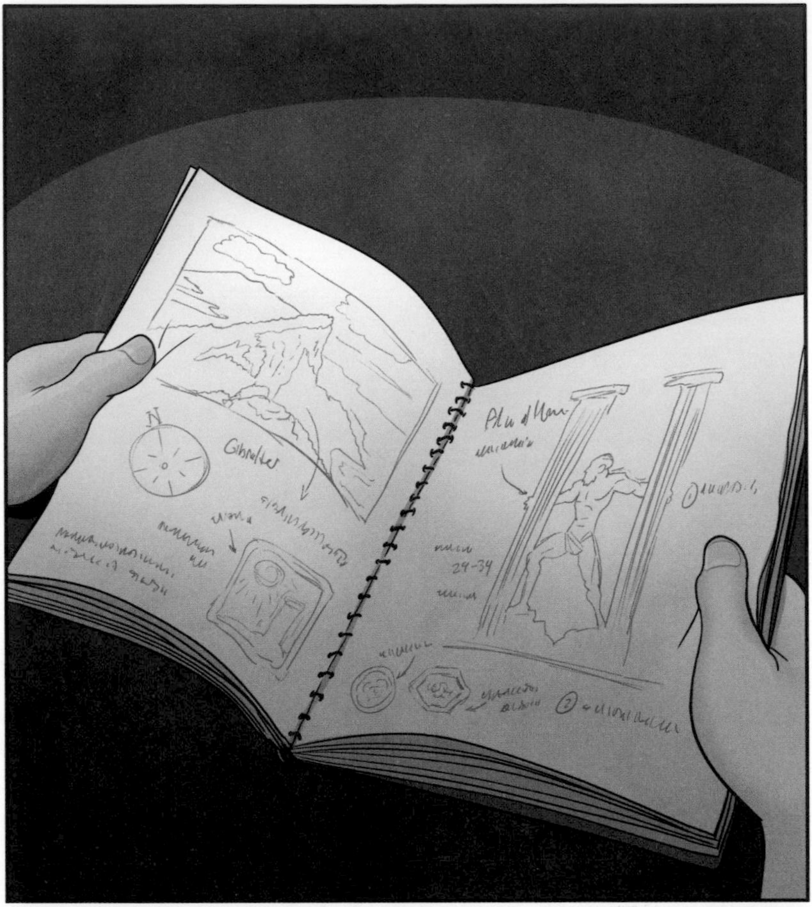

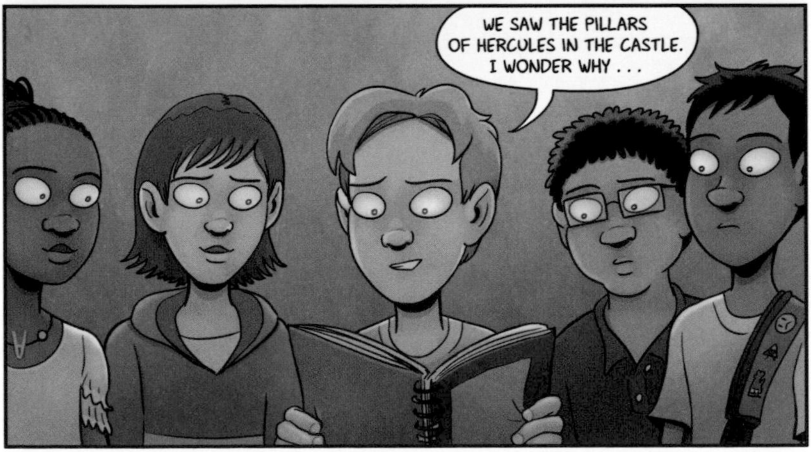
WE SAW THE PILLARS OF HERCULES IN THE CASTLE. I WONDER WHY . . .

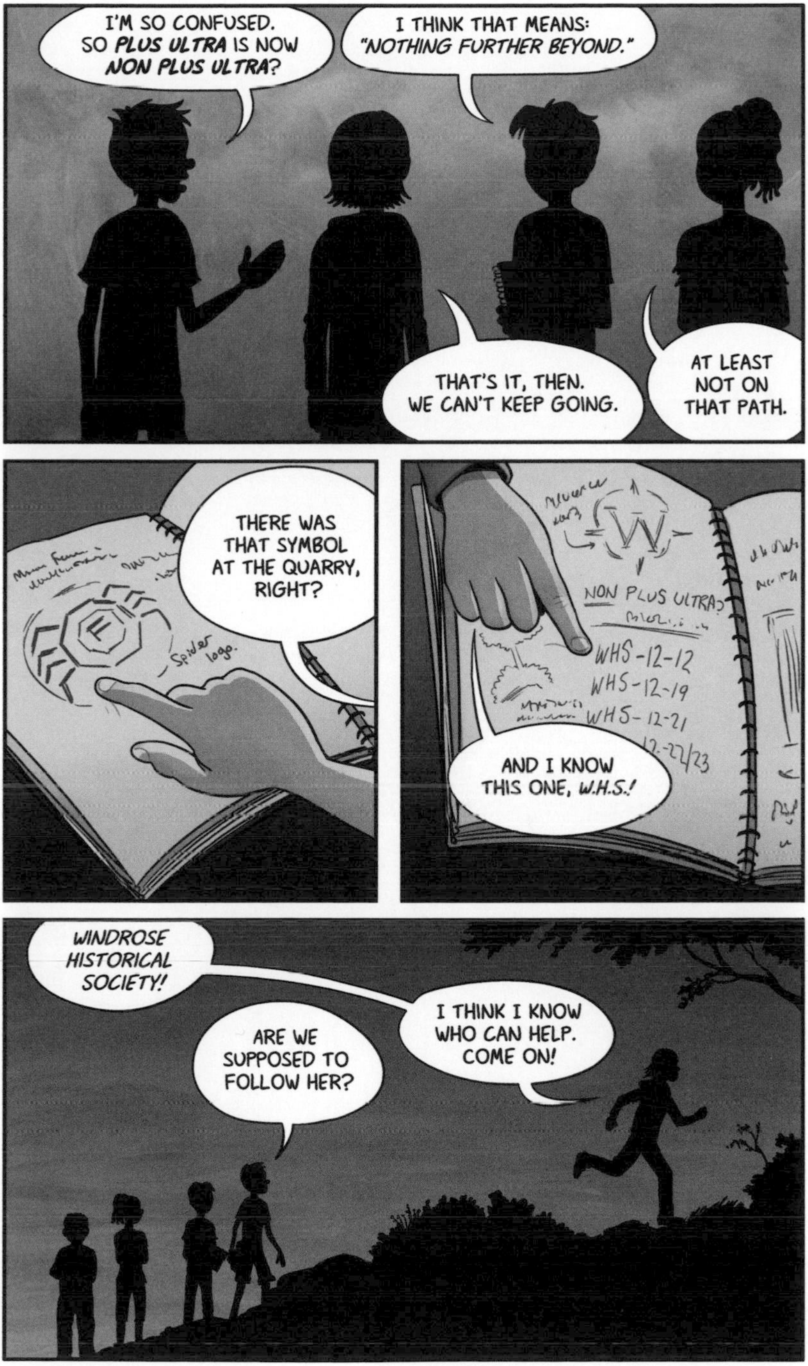
I'M SO CONFUSED. SO *PLUS ULTRA* IS NOW *NON PLUS ULTRA*?
I THINK THAT MEANS: *"NOTHING FURTHER BEYOND."*
THAT'S IT, THEN. WE CAN'T KEEP GOING.
AT LEAST NOT ON THAT PATH.
THERE WAS THAT SYMBOL AT THE QUARRY, RIGHT?
Spider logo.
NON PLUS ULTRA?
WHS-12-12
WHS-12-19
WHS-12-21
AND I KNOW THIS ONE, *W.H.S.!*
WINDROSE HISTORICAL SOCIETY!
I THINK I KNOW WHO CAN HELP. COME ON!
ARE WE SUPPOSED TO FOLLOW HER?

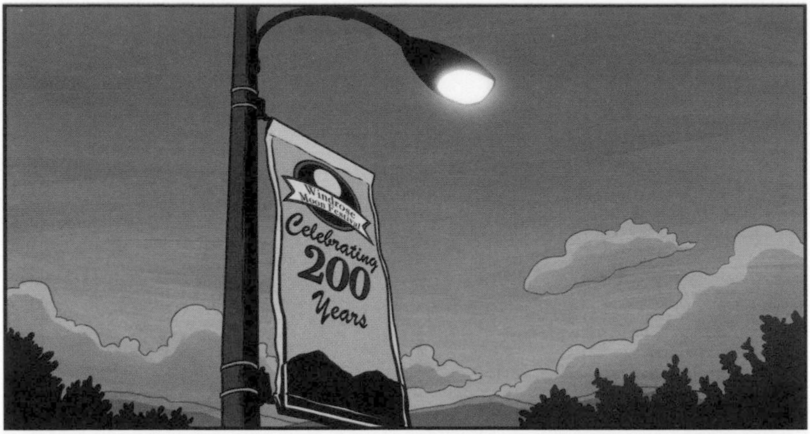
Windrose Moon Festival
Celebrating 200 Years

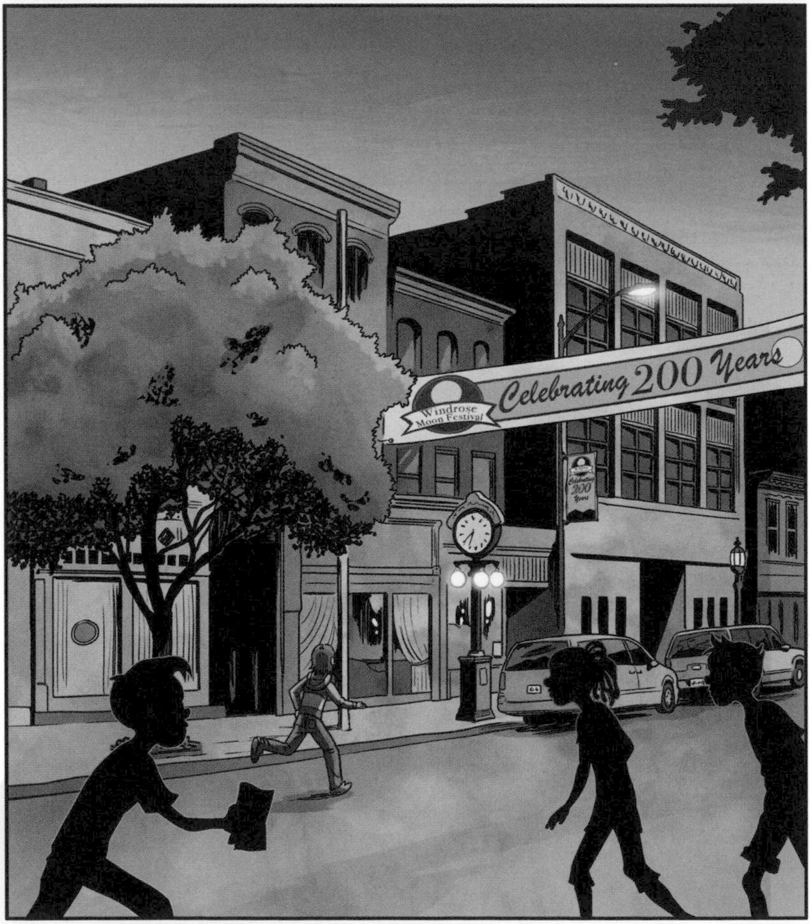
Windrose Moon Festival
Celebrating 200 Years

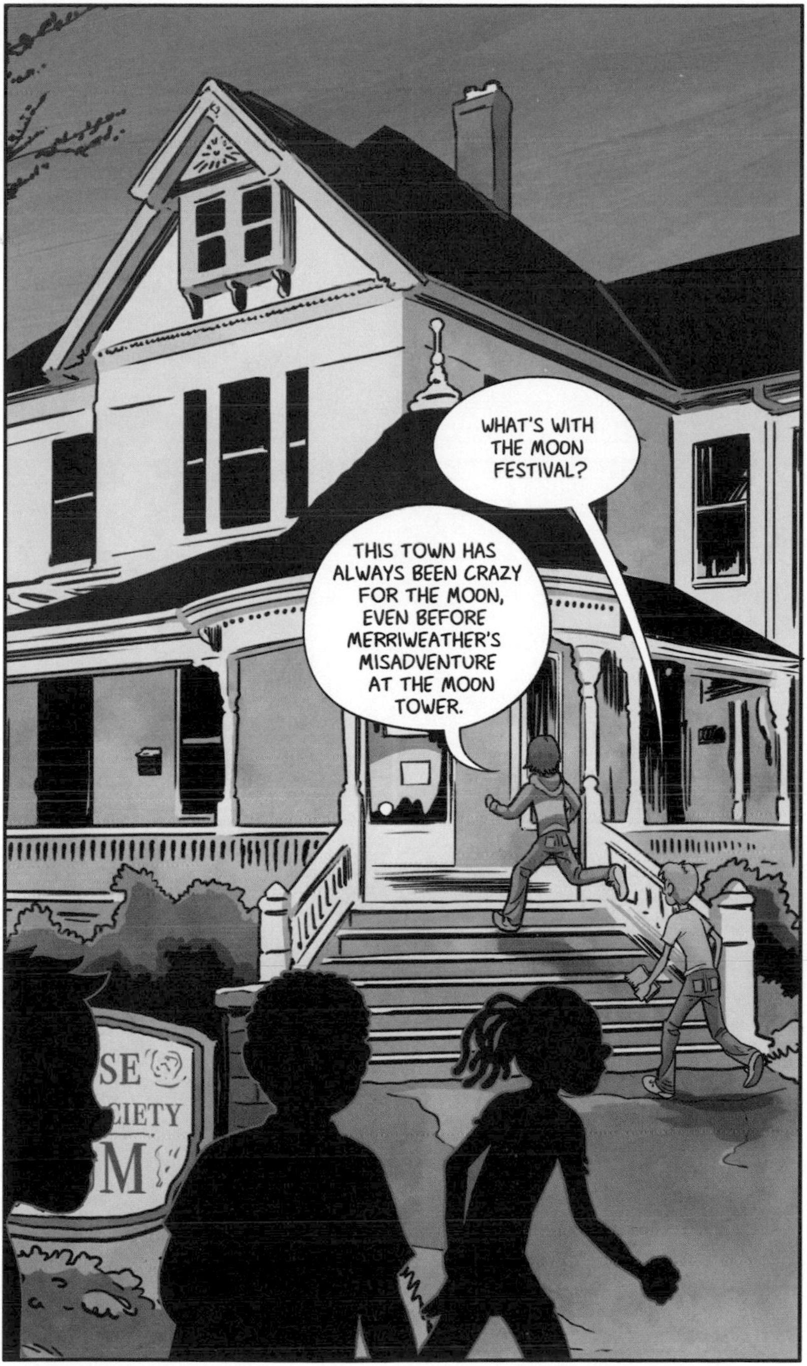
WHAT'S WITH THE MOON FESTIVAL?
THIS TOWN HAS ALWAYS BEEN CRAZY FOR THE MOON, EVEN BEFORE MERRIWEATHER'S MISADVENTURE AT THE MOON TOWER.
SE
CIETY
M

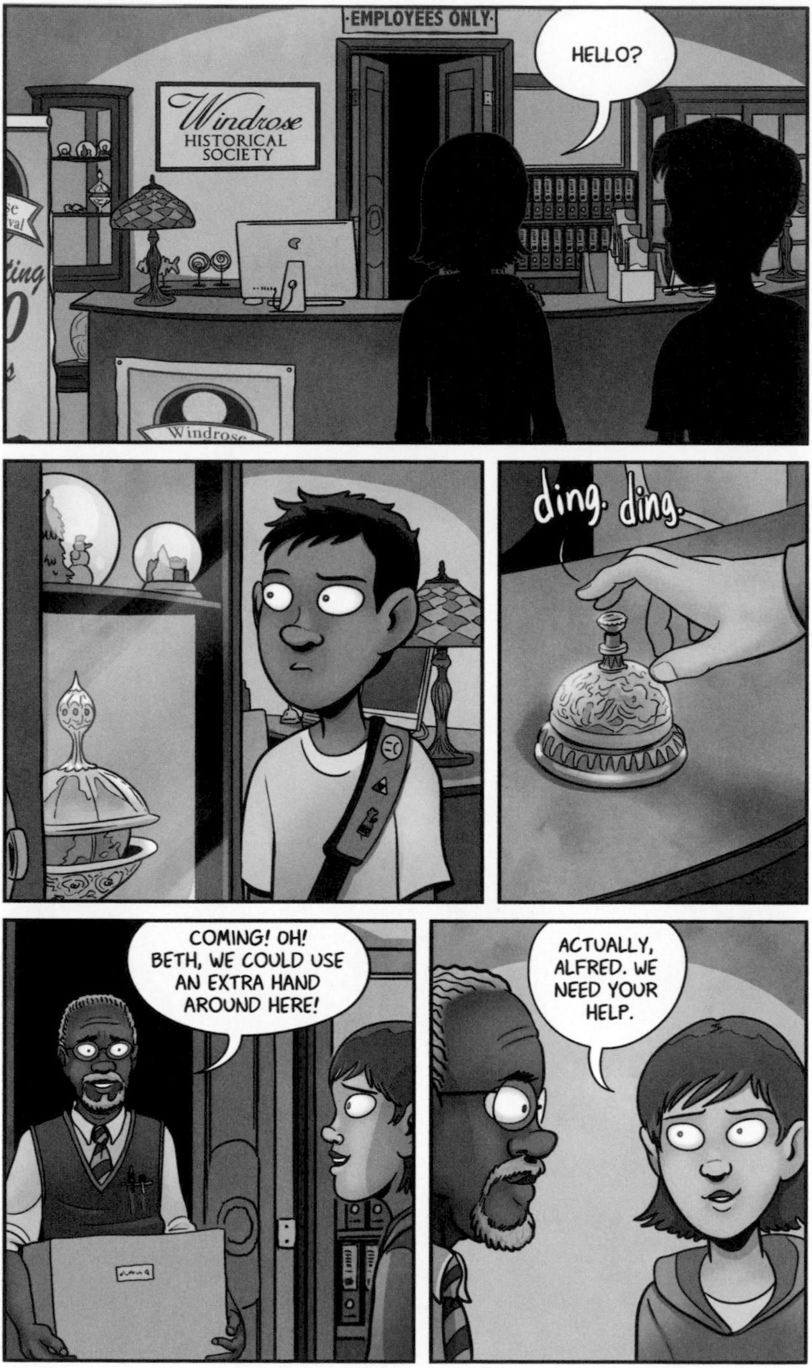
·EMPLOYEES ONLY·
Windrose HISTORICAL SOCIETY
HELLO?
ding. ding.
COMING! OH! BETH, WE COULD USE AN EXTRA HAND AROUND HERE!
ACTUALLY, ALFRED. WE NEED YOUR HELP.

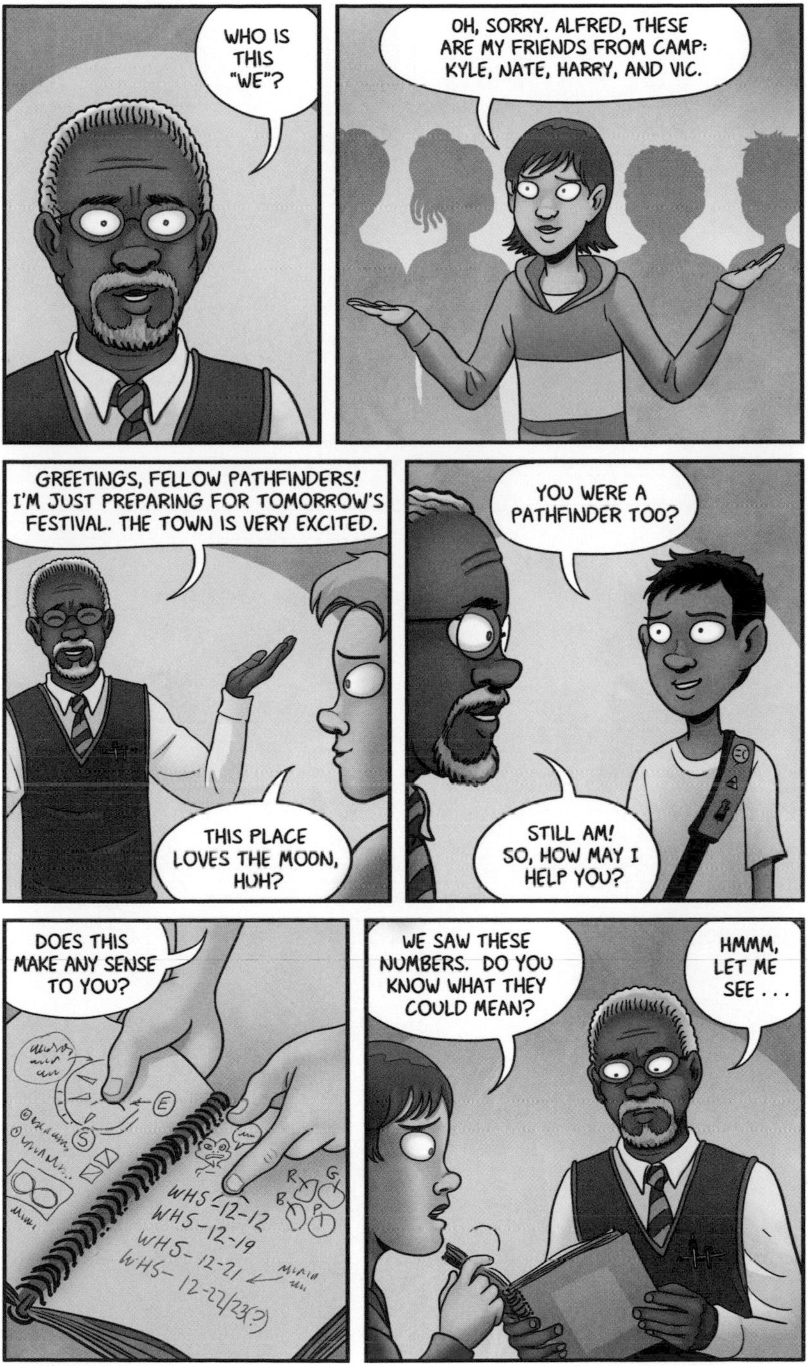
WHO IS THIS "WE"?
OH, SORRY. ALFRED, THESE ARE MY FRIENDS FROM CAMP: KYLE, NATE, HARRY, AND VIC.
GREETINGS, FELLOW PATHFINDERS! I'M JUST PREPARING FOR TOMORROW'S FESTIVAL. THE TOWN IS VERY EXCITED.
THIS PLACE LOVES THE MOON, HUH?
YOU WERE A PATHFINDER TOO?
STILL AM! SO, HOW MAY I HELP YOU?
DOES THIS MAKE ANY SENSE TO YOU?
WHS-12-12
WHS-12-19
WHS-12-21
WHS-12-22/23(?)
WE SAW THESE NUMBERS. DO YOU KNOW WHAT THEY COULD MEAN?
HMMM, LET ME SEE . . .

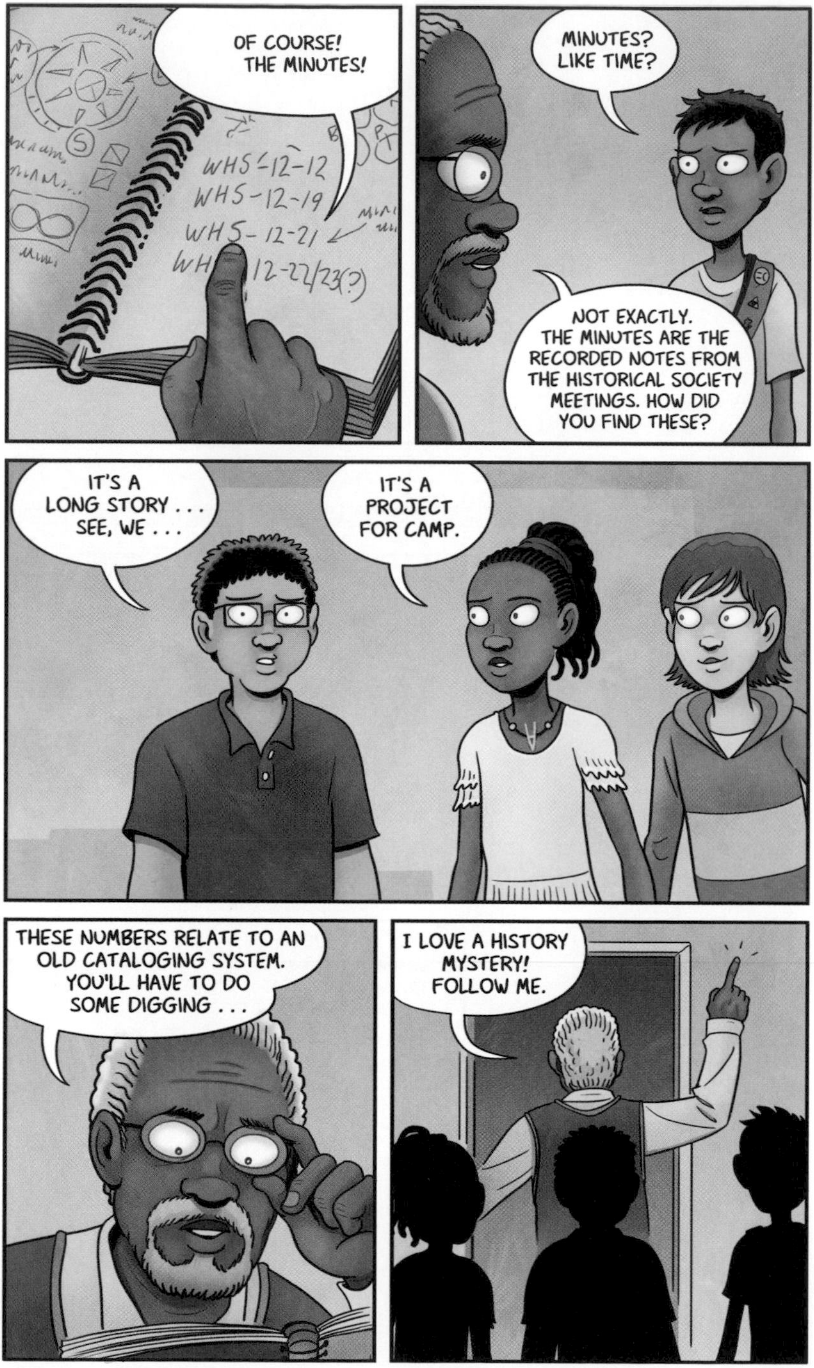
OF COURSE! THE MINUTES!
WHS-12-12
WHS-12-19
WHS-12-21
12-22/23(?)
MINUTES? LIKE TIME?
NOT EXACTLY. THE MINUTES ARE THE RECORDED NOTES FROM THE HISTORICAL SOCIETY MEETINGS. HOW DID YOU FIND THESE?
IT'S A LONG STORY . . . SEE, WE . . .
IT'S A PROJECT FOR CAMP.
THESE NUMBERS RELATE TO AN OLD CATALOGING SYSTEM. YOU'LL HAVE TO DO SOME DIGGING . . .
I LOVE A HISTORY MYSTERY! FOLLOW ME.

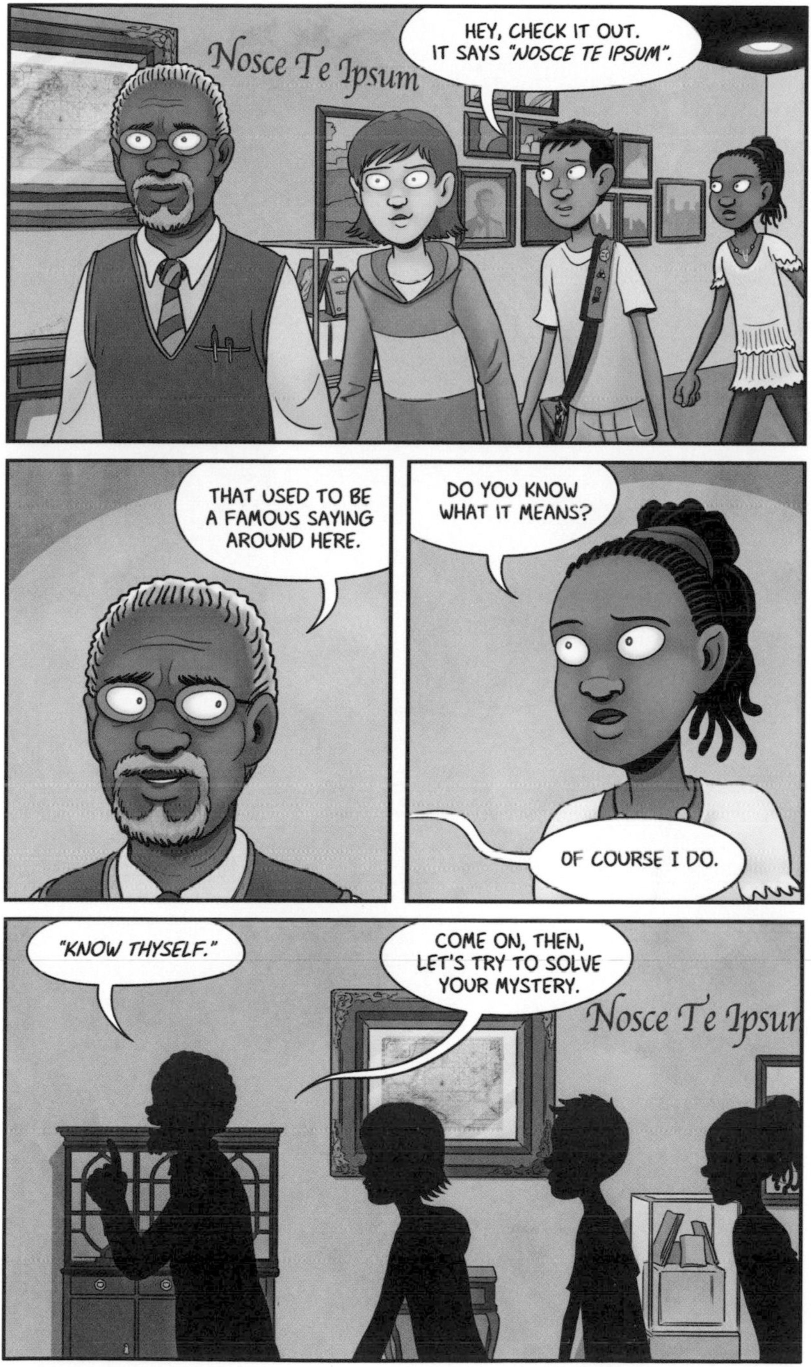
Nosce Te Ipsum
HEY, CHECK IT OUT. IT SAYS "NOSCE TE IPSUM".
THAT USED TO BE A FAMOUS SAYING AROUND HERE.
DO YOU KNOW WHAT IT MEANS?
OF COURSE I DO.
"KNOW THYSELF."
COME ON, THEN, LET'S TRY TO SOLVE YOUR MYSTERY.

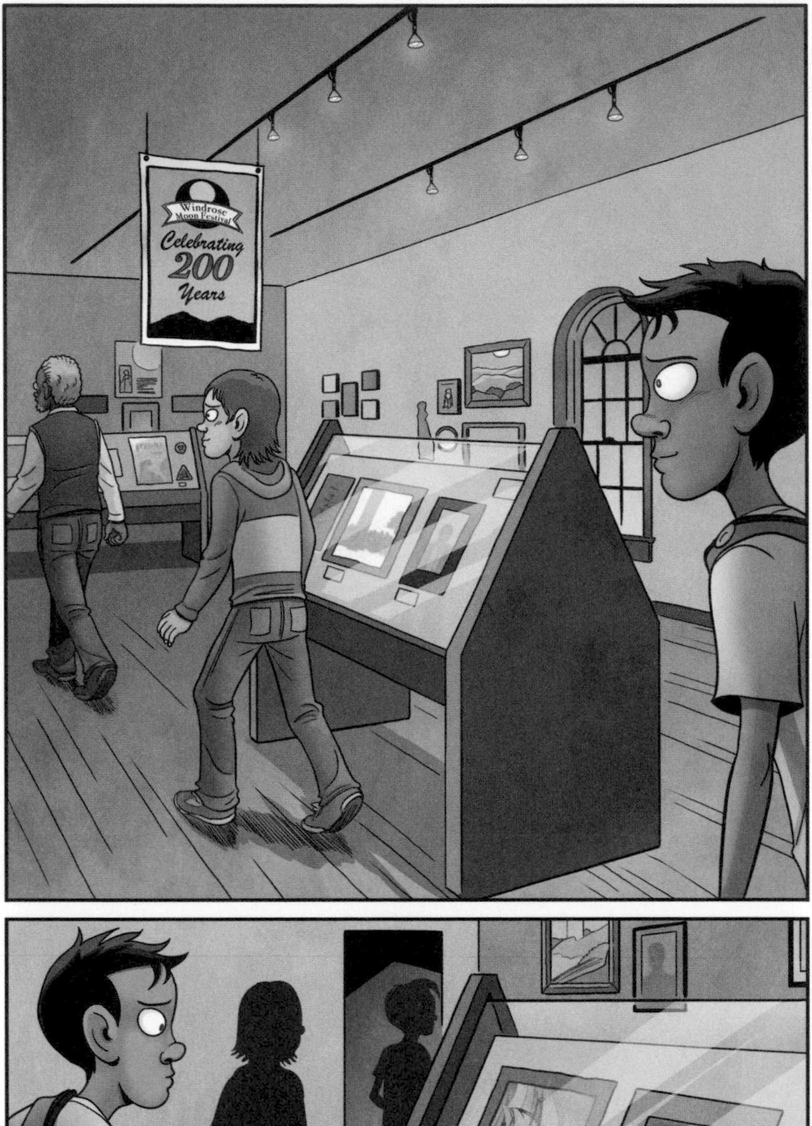
Windrose
Moon Festival
Celebrating
200
Years

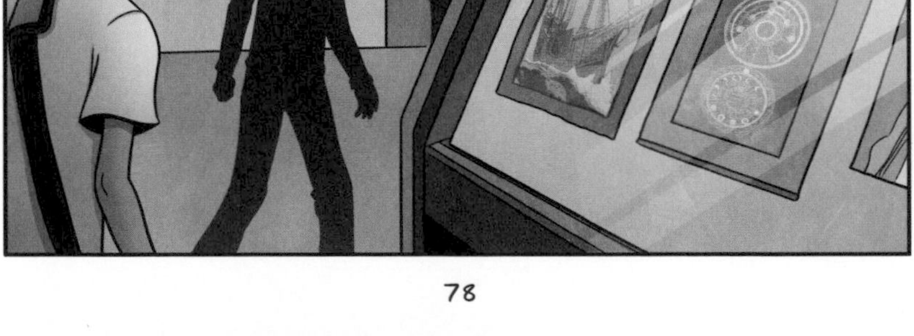

THE ORIGINAL PATHFINDERS!
Henry & Jacob Merriweather
The brothers were the founding members of the Windrose Pathfinders Chapter.
HENRY AND JACOB MERRIWEATHER!
Henry & Jacob Merriweather
The brothers were the founding members of the Windrose Pathfinders Chapter.
I LIKE TO THINK OF THEM THIS WAY. CLOSE, BROTHERLY.
CREEPER!
LOST BOY FOUND
CLAIMS TO HAVE SEEN WINDROSE BEAST

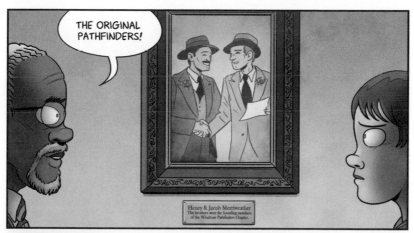

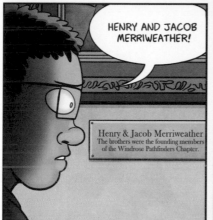

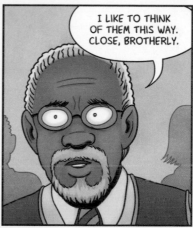

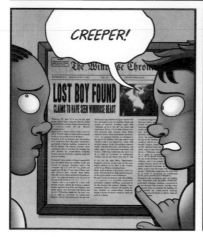

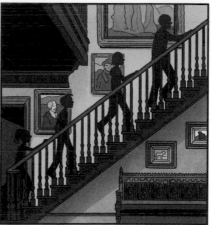

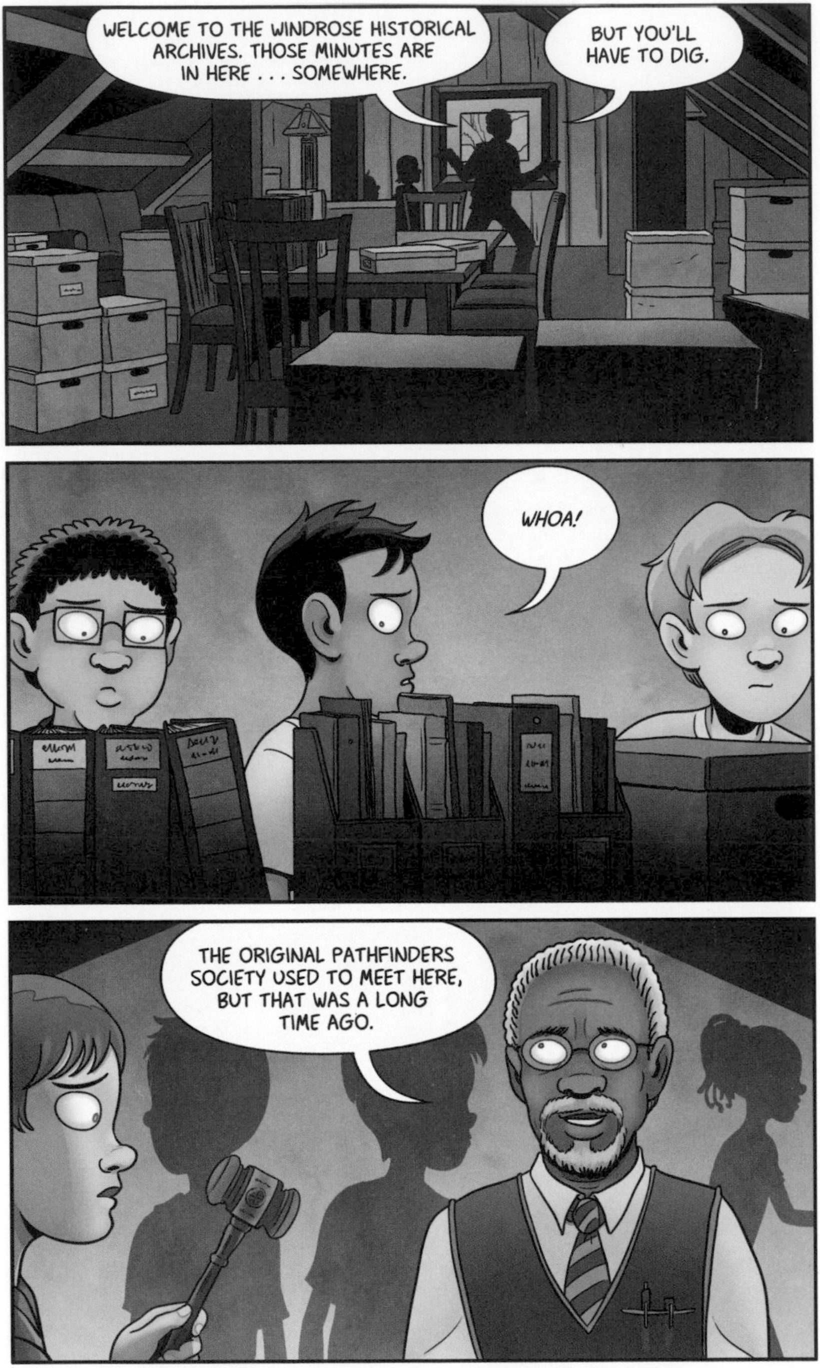
WELCOME TO THE WINDROSE HISTORICAL ARCHIVES. THOSE MINUTES ARE IN HERE . . . SOMEWHERE.
BUT YOU'LL HAVE TO DIG.
WHOA!
THE ORIGINAL PATHFINDERS SOCIETY USED TO MEET HERE, BUT THAT WAS A LONG TIME AGO.

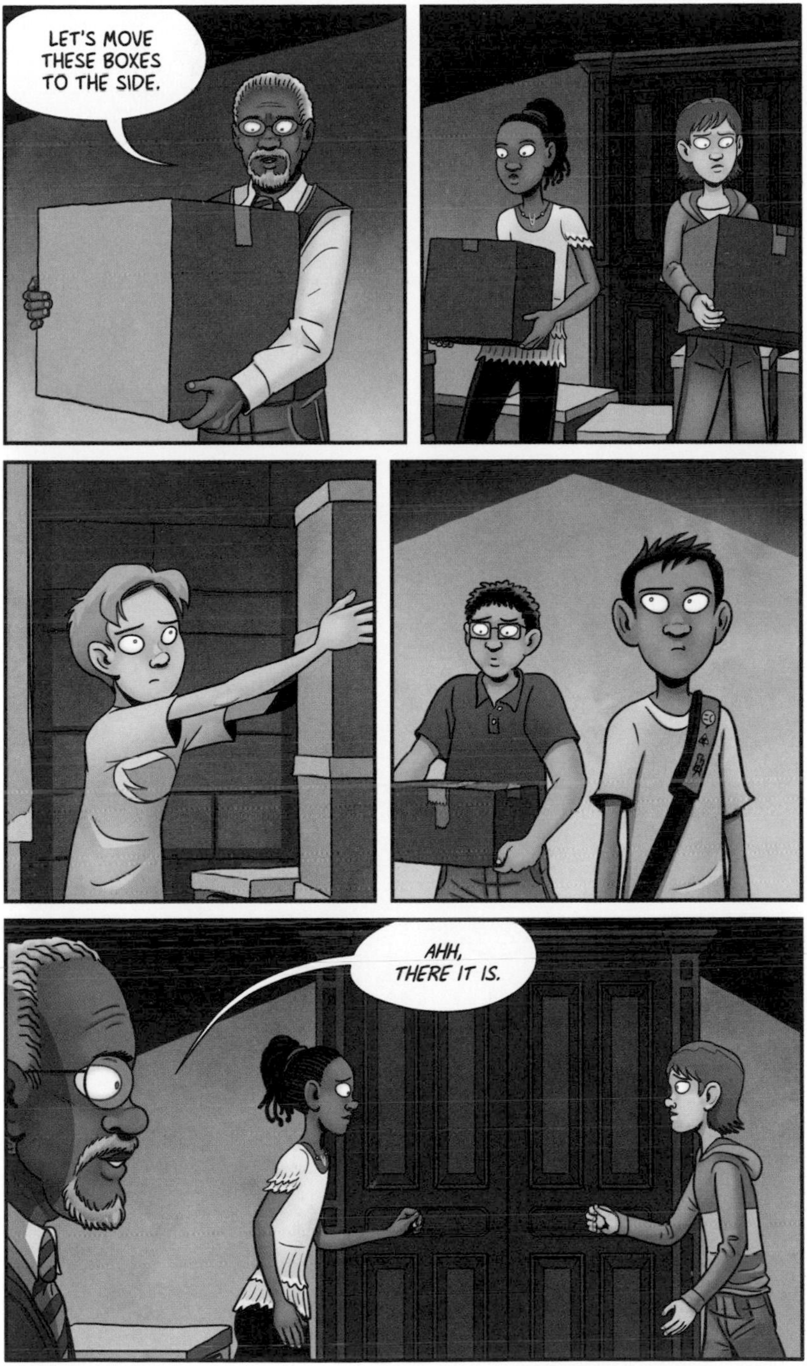
LET'S MOVE THESE BOXES TO THE SIDE.
AHH, THERE IT IS.

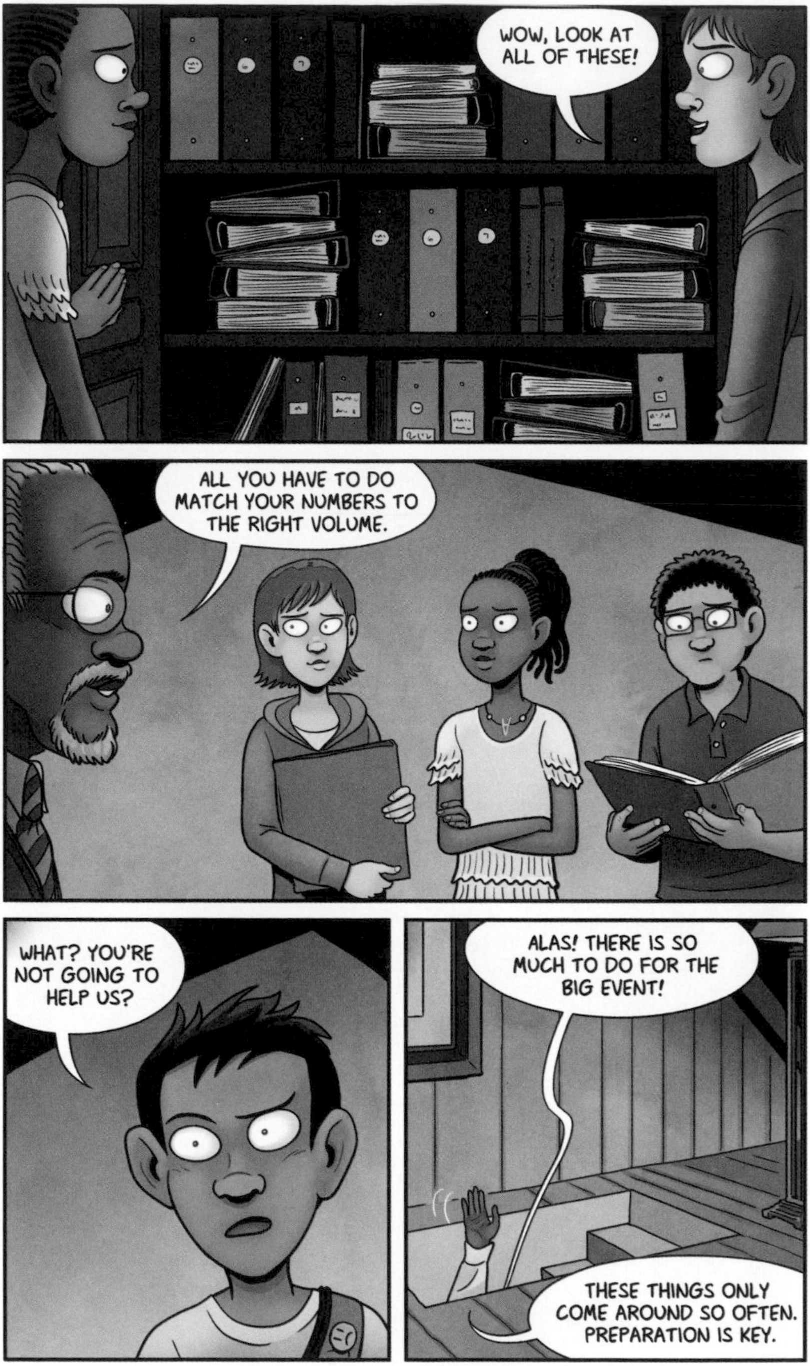
WOW, LOOK AT ALL OF THESE!
ALL YOU HAVE TO DO MATCH YOUR NUMBERS TO THE RIGHT VOLUME.
WHAT? YOU'RE NOT GOING TO HELP US?
ALAS! THERE IS SO MUCH TO DO FOR THE BIG EVENT!
THESE THINGS ONLY COME AROUND SO OFTEN. PREPARATION IS KEY.

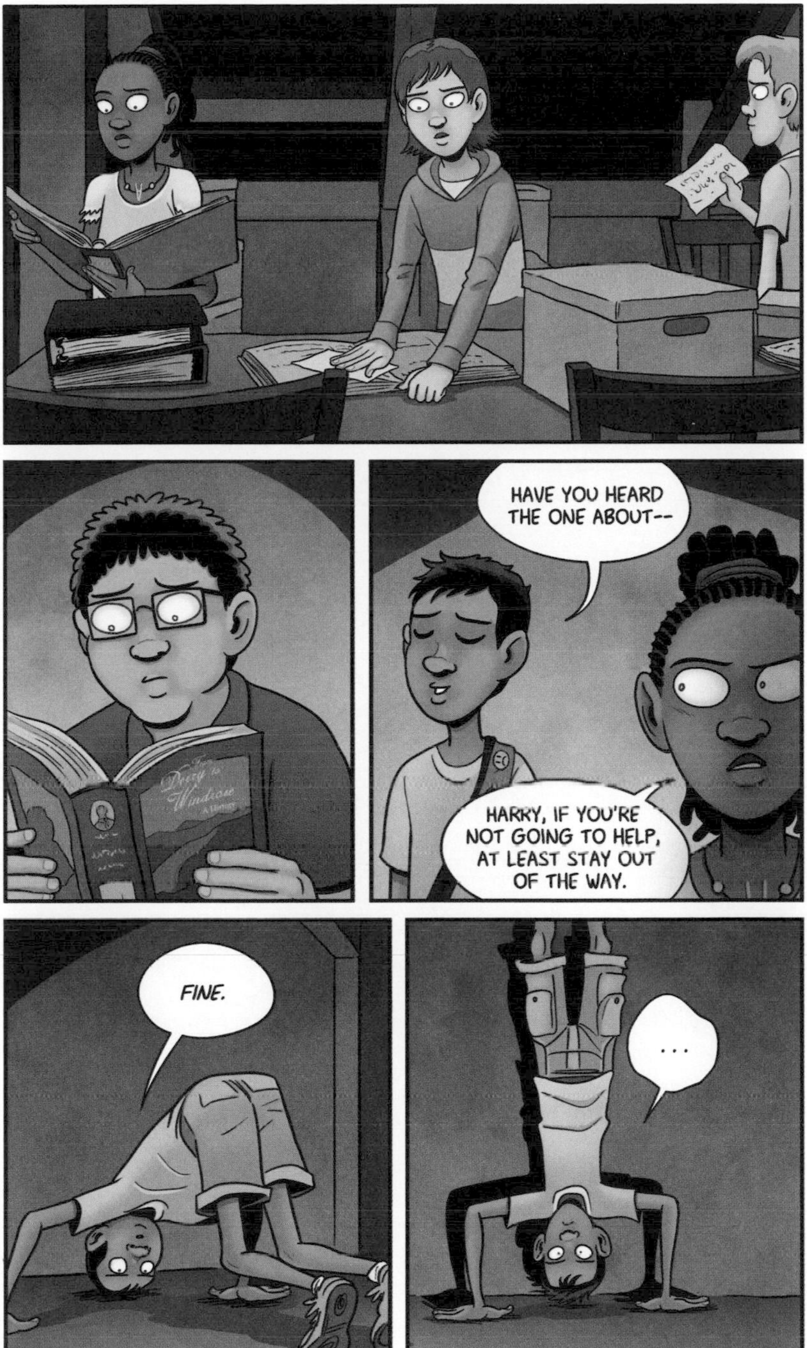
HAVE YOU HEARD THE ONE ABOUT--
HARRY, IF YOU'RE NOT GOING TO HELP, AT LEAST STAY OUT OF THE WAY.
FINE.
...

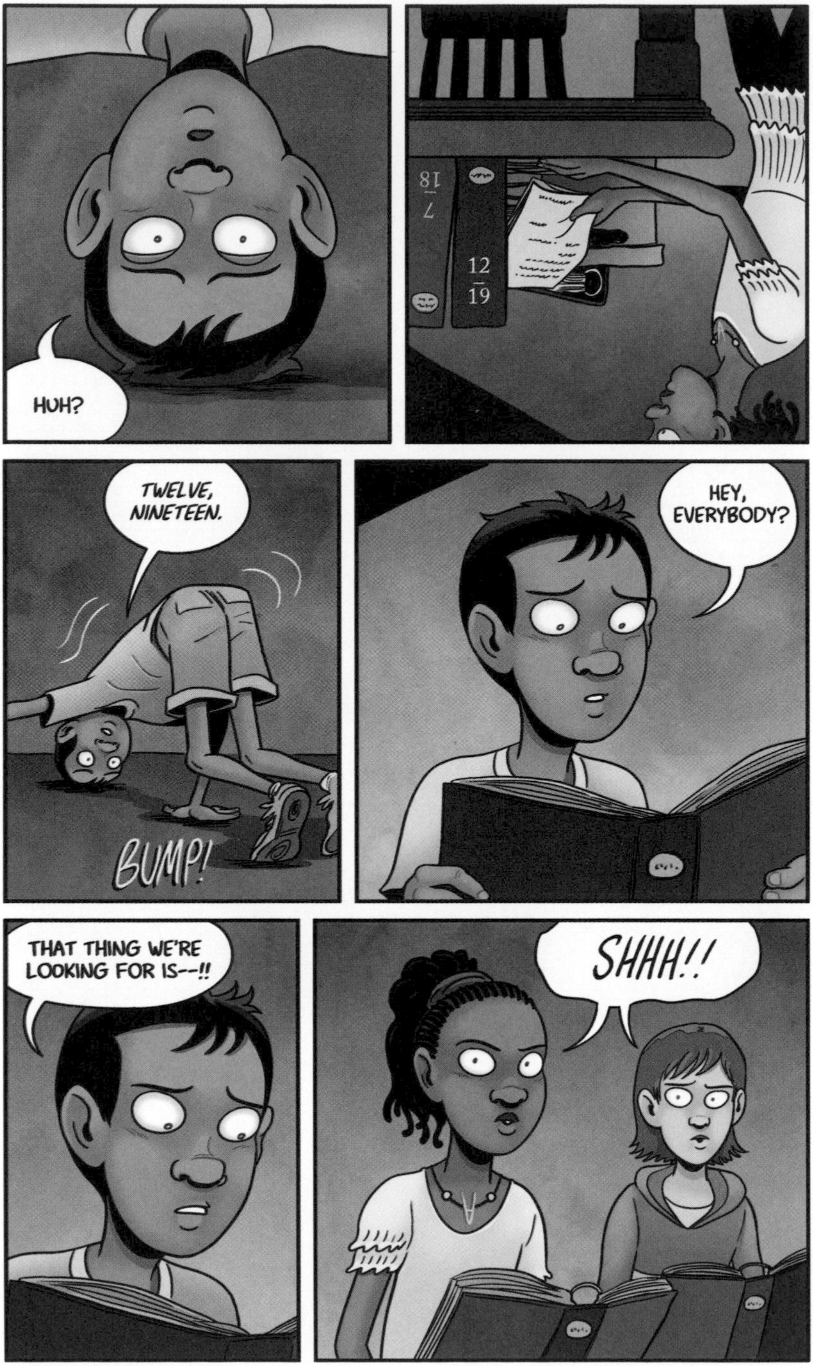
HUH?
7 18
12 19
TWELVE, NINETEEN.
BUMP!
HEY, EVERYBODY?
THAT THING WE'RE LOOKING FOR IS--!!
SHHH!!

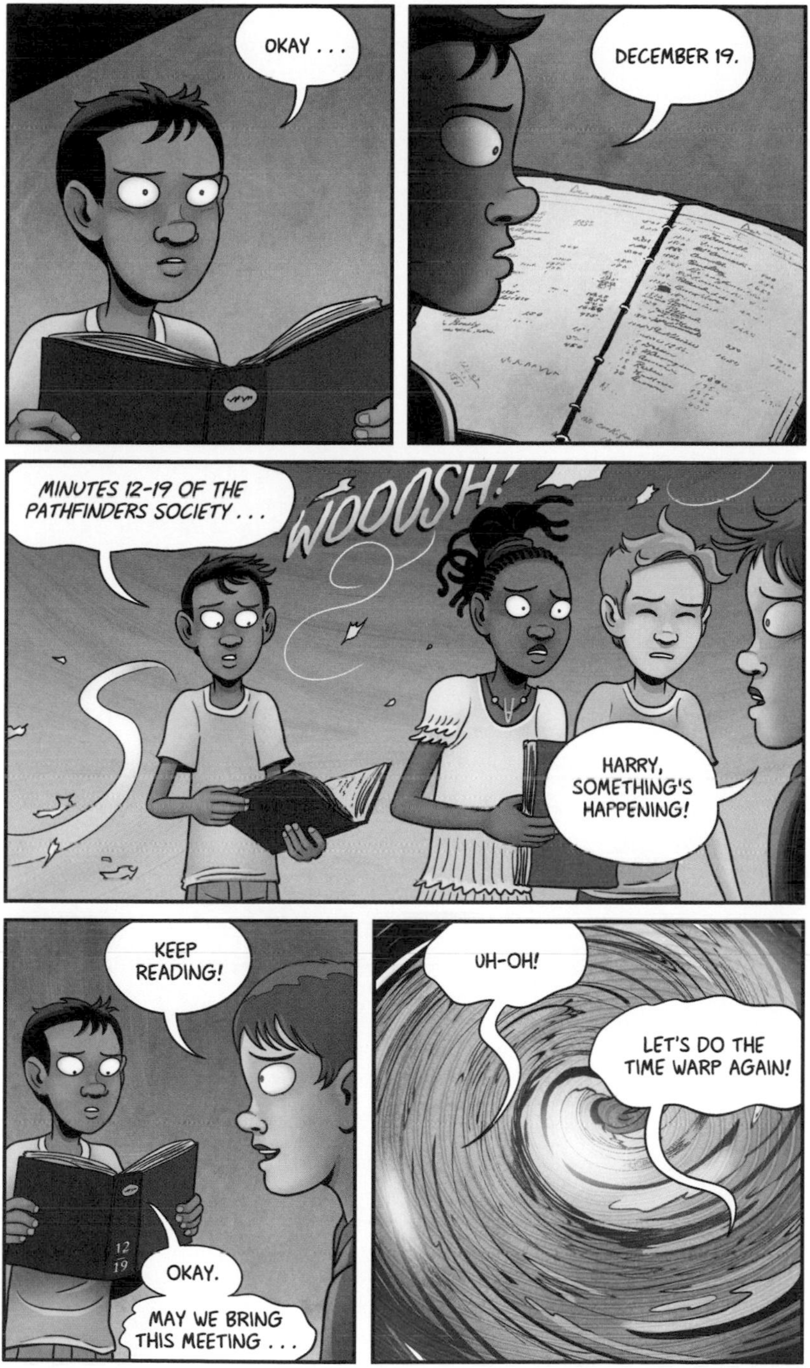
OKAY . . .
DECEMBER 19.
MINUTES 12-19 OF THE PATHFINDERS SOCIETY . . .
WOOOSH!
HARRY, SOMETHING'S HAPPENING!
KEEP READING!
12 19
OKAY.
MAY WE BRING THIS MEETING . . .
UH-OH!
LET'S DO THE TIME WARP AGAIN!

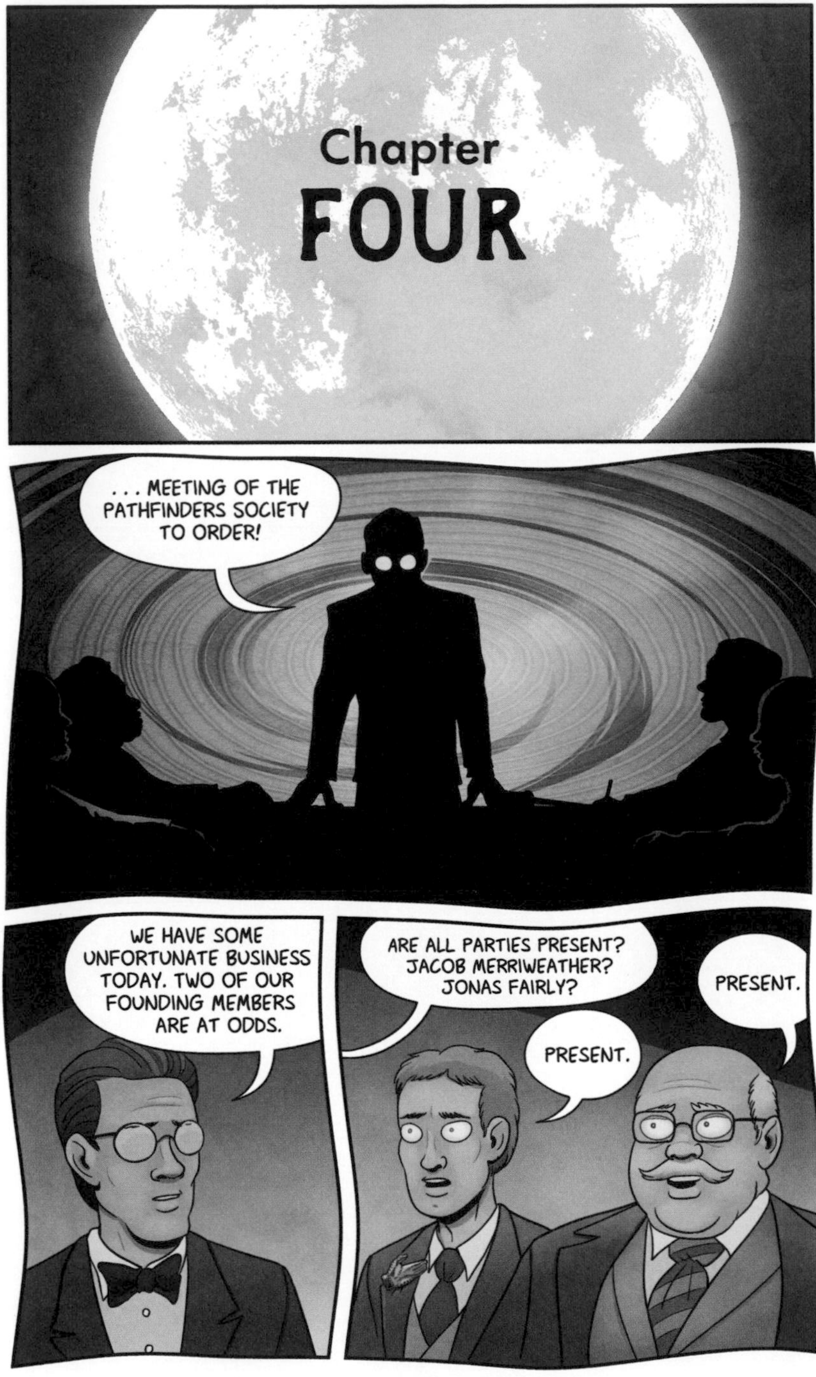
Chapter
FOUR
. . . MEETING OF THE PATHFINDERS SOCIETY TO ORDER!
WE HAVE SOME UNFORTUNATE BUSINESS TODAY. TWO OF OUR FOUNDING MEMBERS ARE AT ODDS.
ARE ALL PARTIES PRESENT? JACOB MERRIWEATHER? JONAS FAIRLY?
PRESENT.
PRESENT.

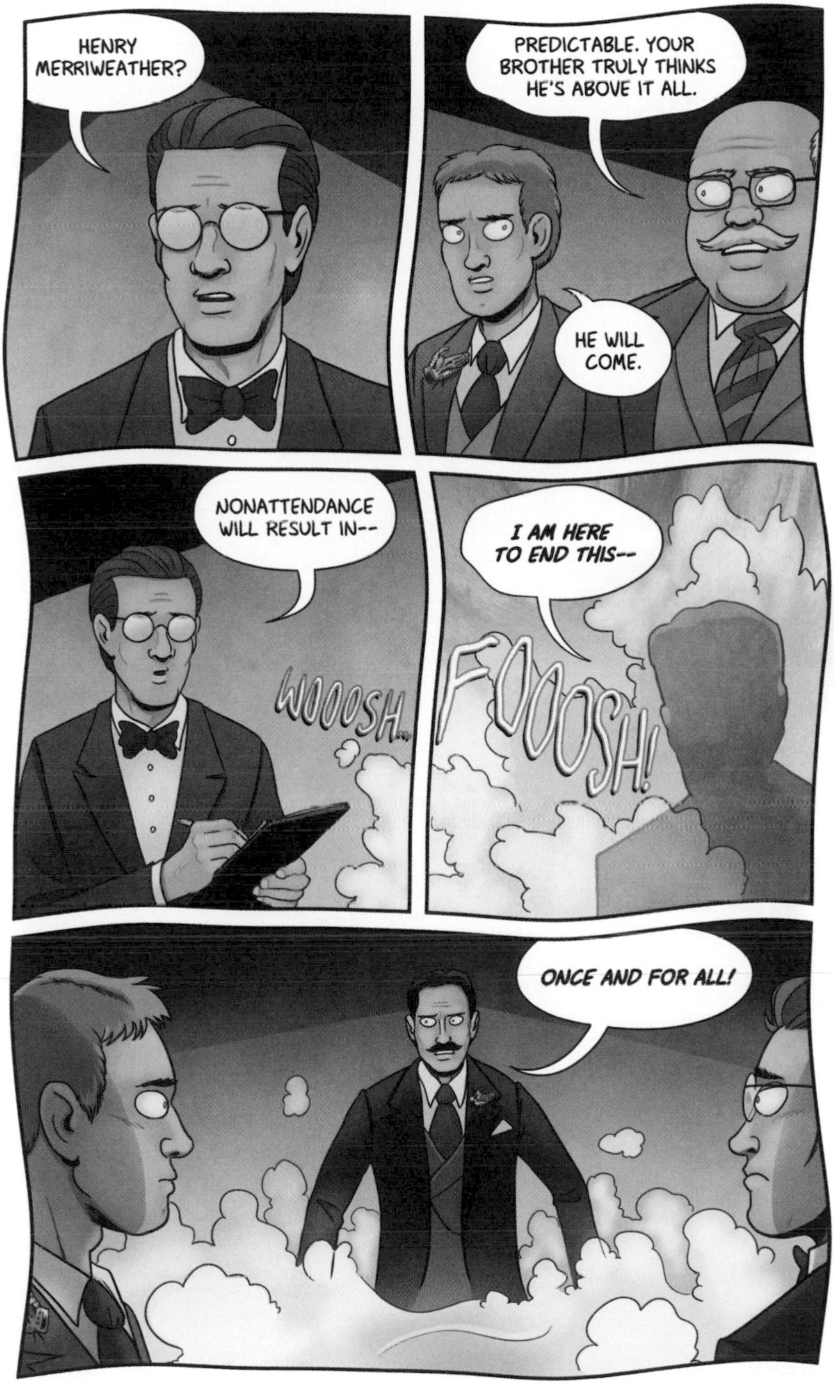
HENRY MERRIWEATHER?
PREDICTABLE. YOUR BROTHER TRULY THINKS HE'S ABOVE IT ALL.
HE WILL COME.
NONATTENDANCE WILL RESULT IN--
WOOOSH...
I AM HERE TO END THIS--
FOOOSH!
ONCE AND FOR ALL!

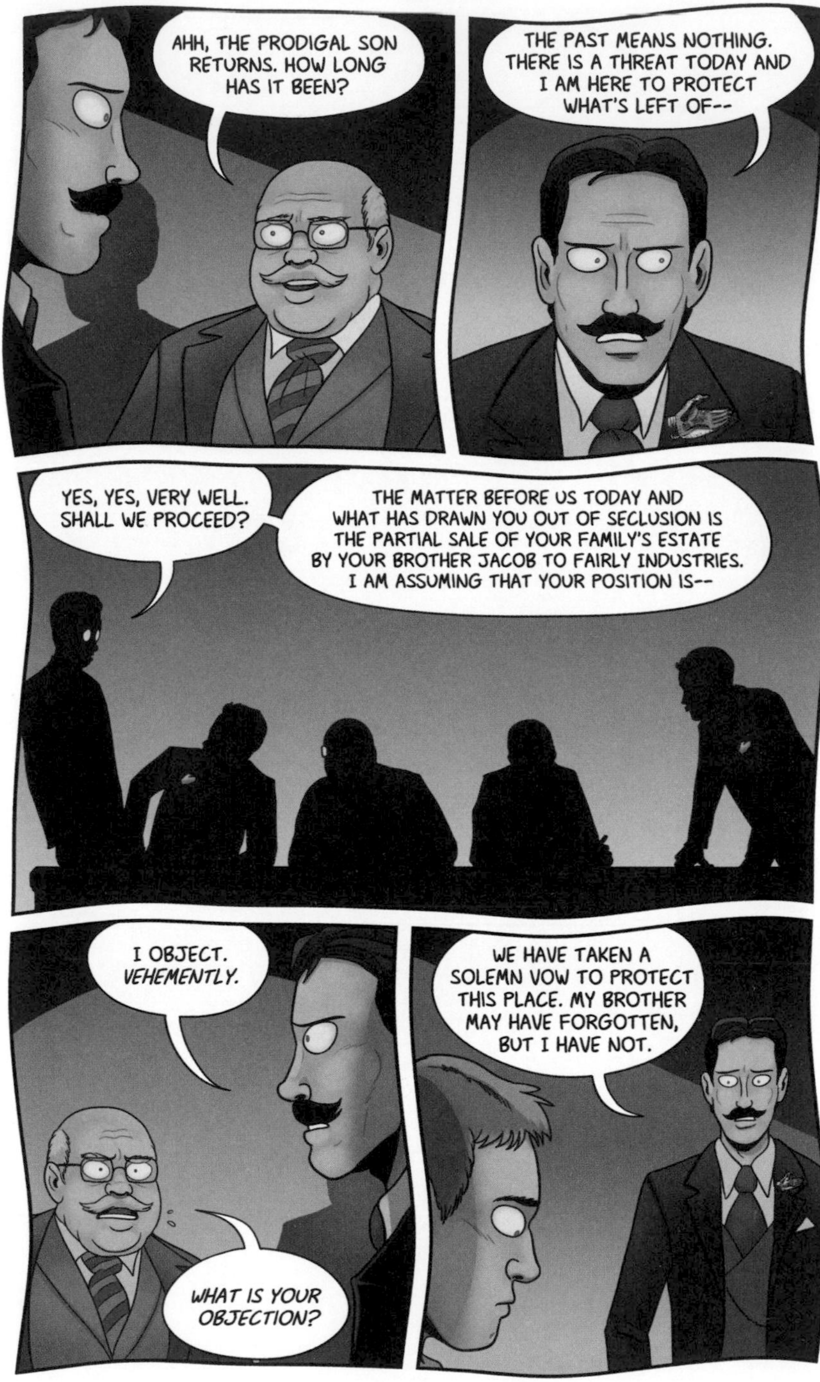
AHH, THE PRODIGAL SON RETURNS. HOW LONG HAS IT BEEN?
THE PAST MEANS NOTHING. THERE IS A THREAT TODAY AND I AM HERE TO PROTECT WHAT'S LEFT OF--
YES, YES, VERY WELL. SHALL WE PROCEED?
THE MATTER BEFORE US TODAY AND WHAT HAS DRAWN YOU OUT OF SECLUSION IS THE PARTIAL SALE OF YOUR FAMILY'S ESTATE BY YOUR BROTHER JACOB TO FAIRLY INDUSTRIES. I AM ASSUMING THAT YOUR POSITION IS--
I OBJECT. *VEHEMENTLY.*
WHAT IS YOUR OBJECTION?
WE HAVE TAKEN A SOLEMN VOW TO PROTECT THIS PLACE. MY BROTHER MAY HAVE FORGOTTEN, BUT I HAVE NOT.

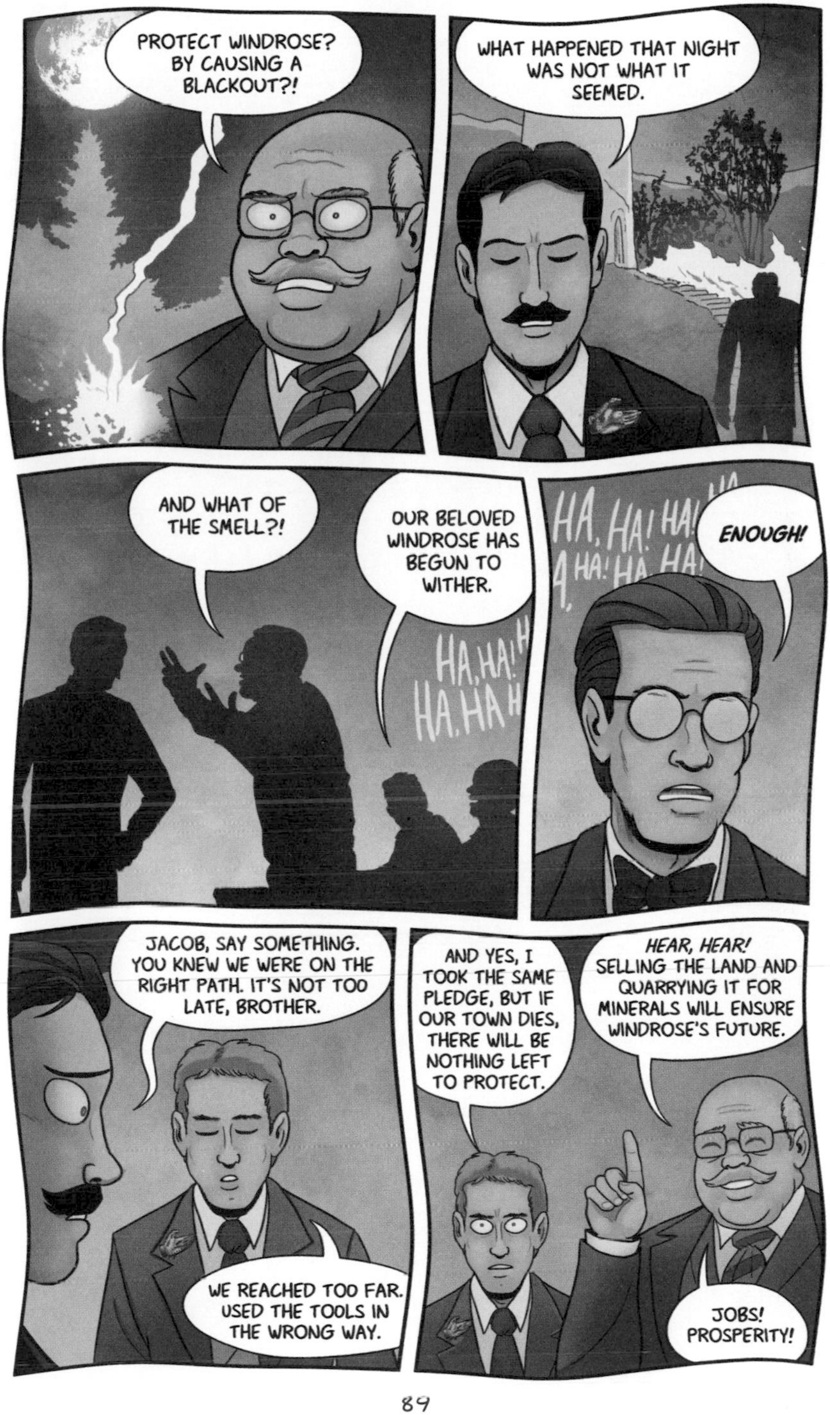
PROTECT WINDROSE? BY CAUSING A BLACKOUT?!
WHAT HAPPENED THAT NIGHT WAS NOT WHAT IT SEEMED.
AND WHAT OF THE SMELL?!
OUR BELOVED WINDROSE HAS BEGUN TO WITHER.
HA, HA! H
HA, HA H
HA, HA! HA! HA
A, HA! HA HA!
ENOUGH!
JACOB, SAY SOMETHING. YOU KNEW WE WERE ON THE RIGHT PATH. IT'S NOT TOO LATE, BROTHER.
WE REACHED TOO FAR. USED THE TOOLS IN THE WRONG WAY.
AND YES, I TOOK THE SAME PLEDGE, BUT IF OUR TOWN DIES, THERE WILL BE NOTHING LEFT TO PROTECT.
HEAR, HEAR! SELLING THE LAND AND QUARRYING IT FOR MINERALS WILL ENSURE WINDROSE'S FUTURE.
JOBS! PROSPERITY!

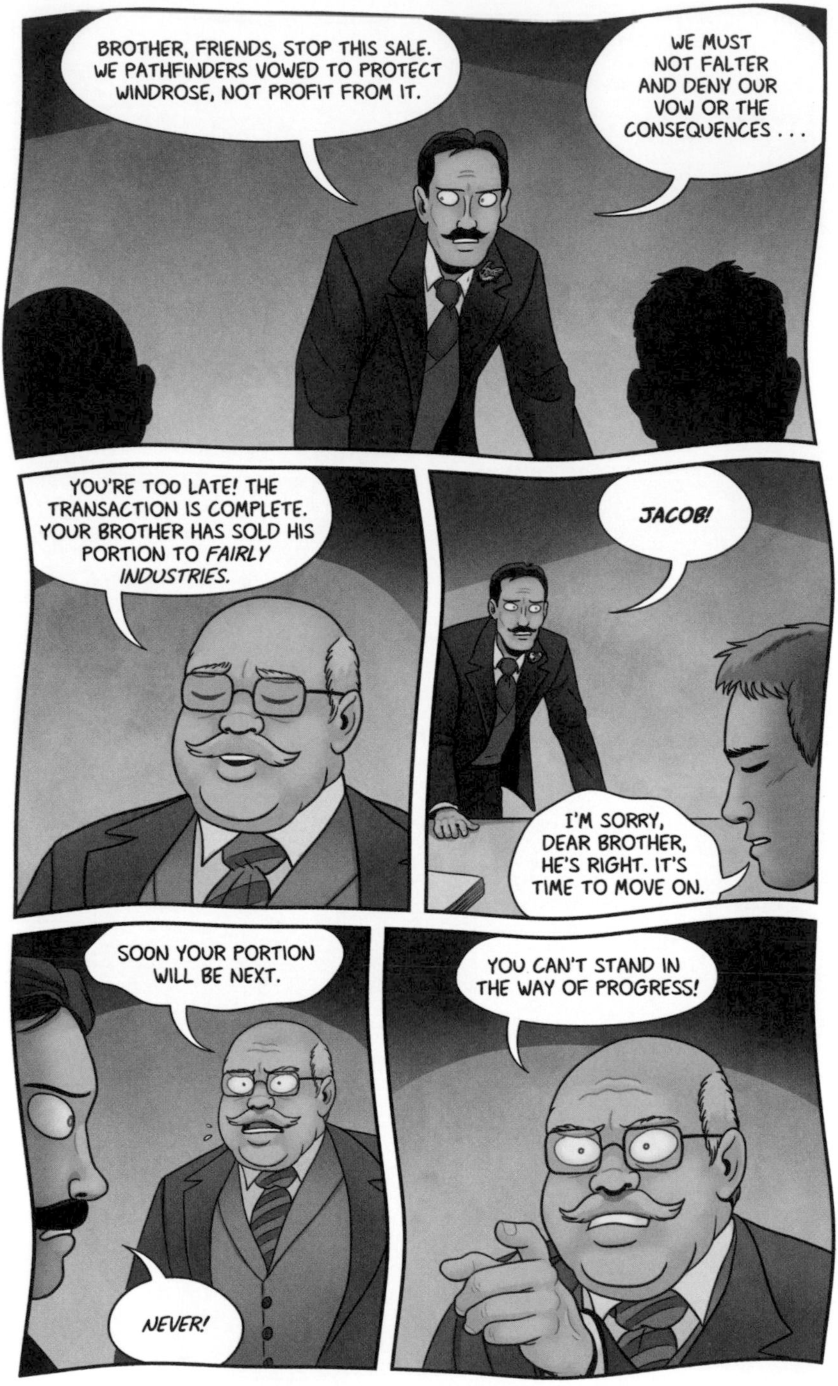
BROTHER, FRIENDS, STOP THIS SALE. WE PATHFINDERS VOWED TO PROTECT WINDROSE, NOT PROFIT FROM IT.
WE MUST NOT FALTER AND DENY OUR VOW OR THE CONSEQUENCES . . .
YOU'RE TOO LATE! THE TRANSACTION IS COMPLETE. YOUR BROTHER HAS SOLD HIS PORTION TO *FAIRLY INDUSTRIES.*
JACOB!
I'M SORRY, DEAR BROTHER, HE'S RIGHT. IT'S TIME TO MOVE ON.
SOON YOUR PORTION WILL BE NEXT.
NEVER!
YOU CAN'T STAND IN THE WAY OF PROGRESS!

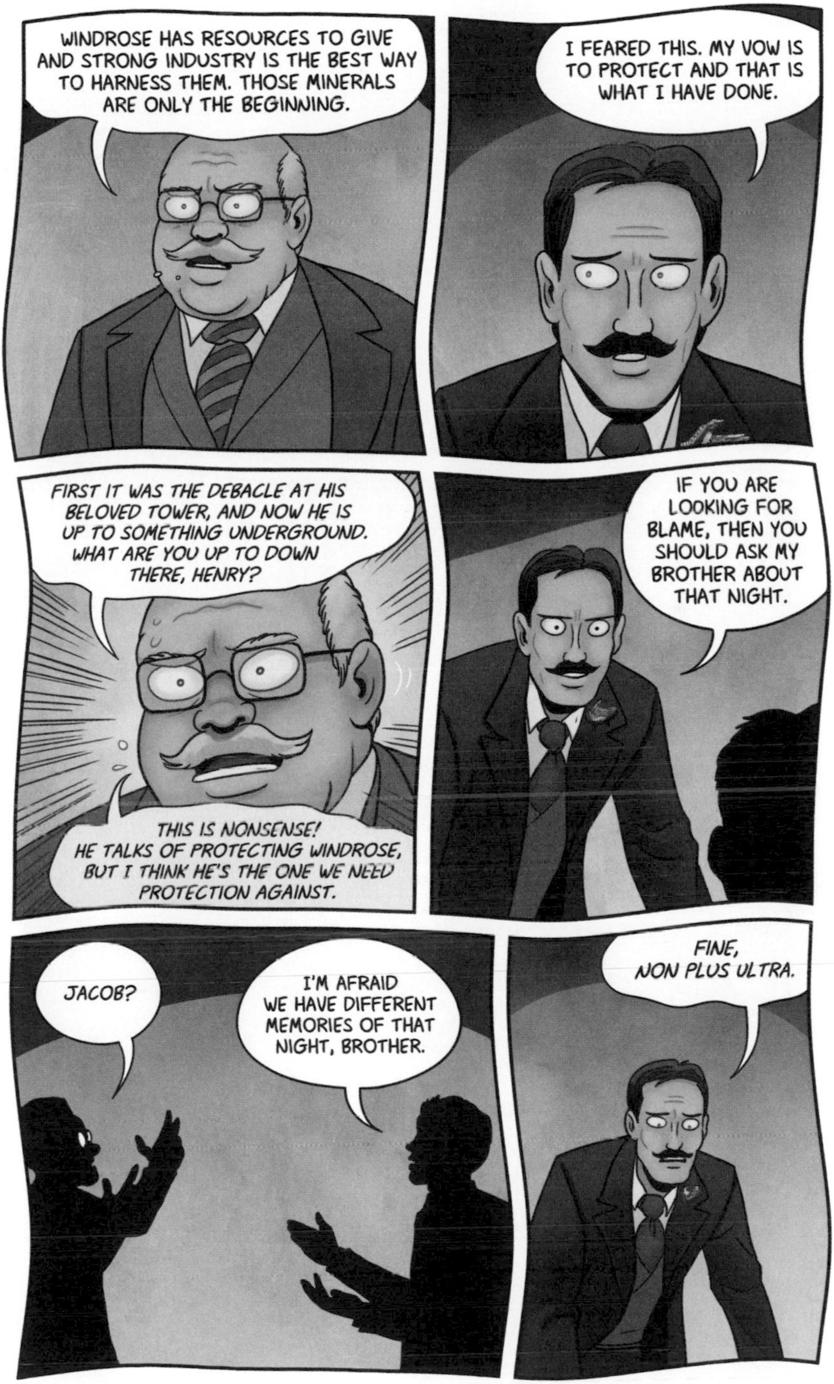
WINDROSE HAS RESOURCES TO GIVE AND STRONG INDUSTRY IS THE BEST WAY TO HARNESS THEM. THOSE MINERALS ARE ONLY THE BEGINNING.
I FEARED THIS. MY VOW IS TO PROTECT AND THAT IS WHAT I HAVE DONE.
FIRST IT WAS THE DEBACLE AT HIS BELOVED TOWER, AND NOW HE IS UP TO SOMETHING UNDERGROUND. WHAT ARE YOU UP TO DOWN THERE, HENRY?
THIS IS NONSENSE! HE TALKS OF PROTECTING WINDROSE, BUT I THINK HE'S THE ONE WE NEED PROTECTION AGAINST.
IF YOU ARE LOOKING FOR BLAME, THEN YOU SHOULD ASK MY BROTHER ABOUT THAT NIGHT.
JACOB?
I'M AFRAID WE HAVE DIFFERENT MEMORIES OF THAT NIGHT, BROTHER.
FINE, NON PLUS ULTRA.

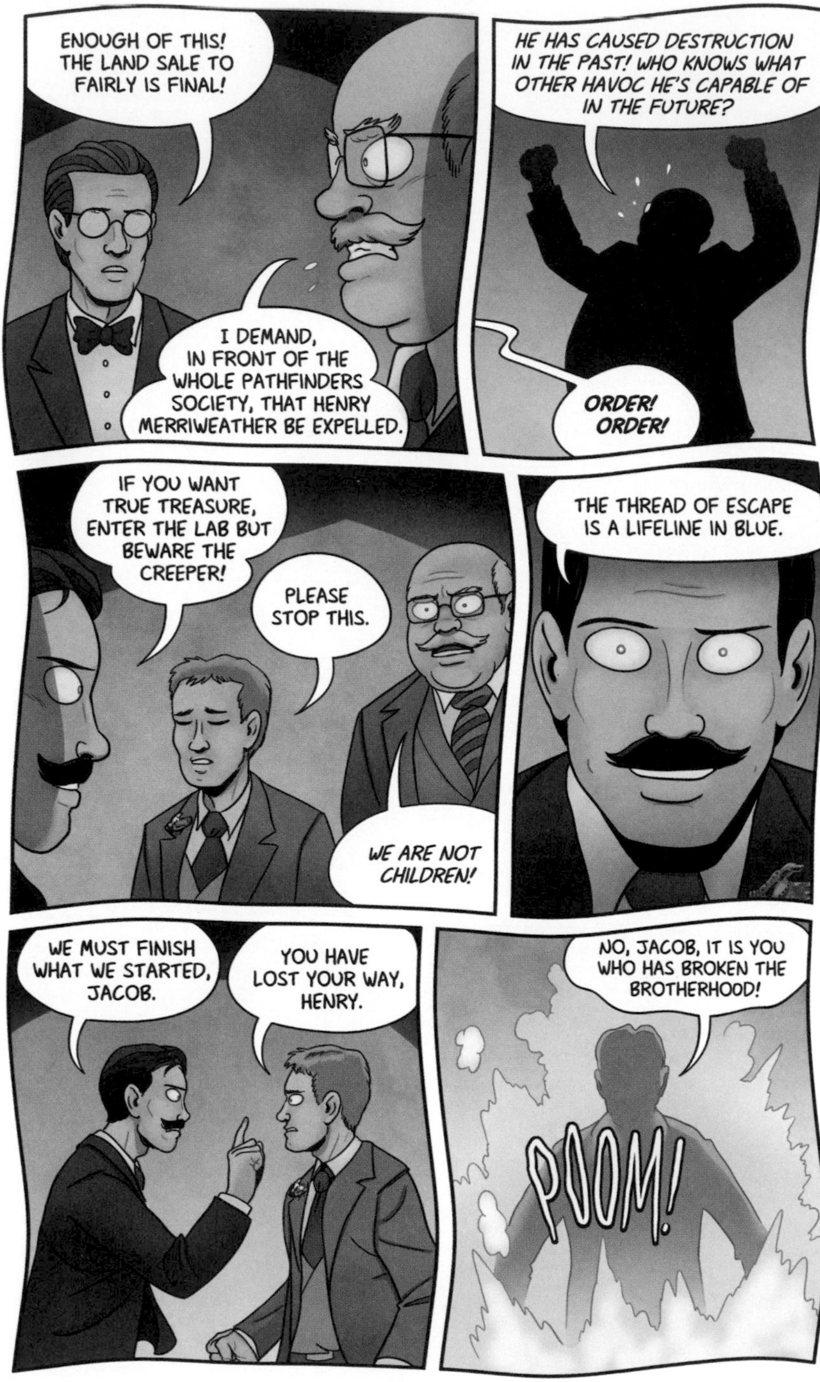
ENOUGH OF THIS! THE LAND SALE TO FAIRLY IS FINAL!
I DEMAND, IN FRONT OF THE WHOLE PATHFINDERS SOCIETY, THAT HENRY MERRIWEATHER BE EXPELLED.
HE HAS CAUSED DESTRUCTION IN THE PAST! WHO KNOWS WHAT OTHER HAVOC HE'S CAPABLE OF IN THE FUTURE?
ORDER! ORDER!
IF YOU WANT TRUE TREASURE, ENTER THE LAB BUT BEWARE THE CREEPER!
PLEASE STOP THIS.
WE ARE NOT CHILDREN!
THE THREAD OF ESCAPE IS A LIFELINE IN BLUE.
WE MUST FINISH WHAT WE STARTED, JACOB.
YOU HAVE LOST YOUR WAY, HENRY.
NO, JACOB, IT IS YOU WHO HAS BROKEN THE BROTHERHOOD!
POOM!

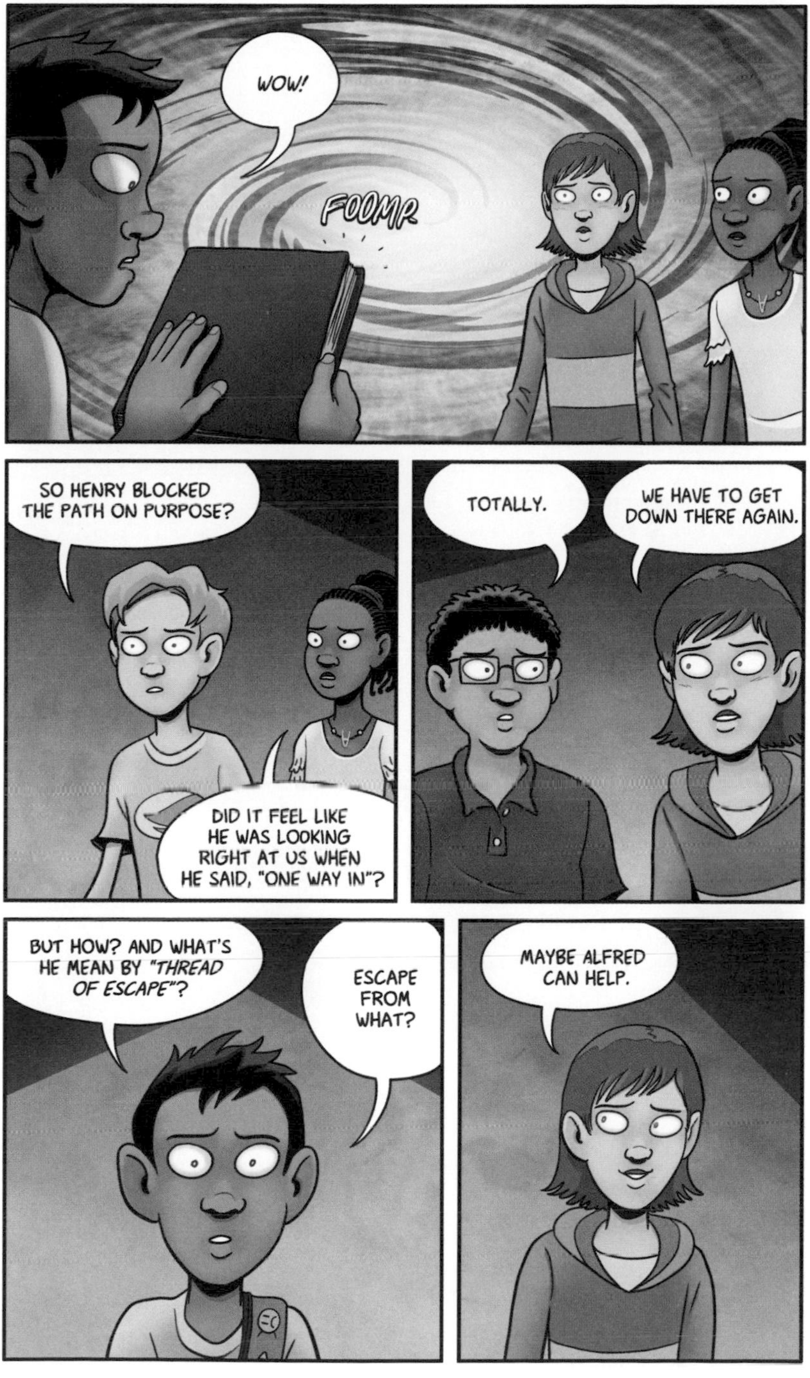
WOW!
FOOMP
SO HENRY BLOCKED THE PATH ON PURPOSE?
DID IT FEEL LIKE HE WAS LOOKING RIGHT AT US WHEN HE SAID, "ONE WAY IN"?
TOTALLY.
WE HAVE TO GET DOWN THERE AGAIN.
BUT HOW? AND WHAT'S HE MEAN BY *"THREAD OF ESCAPE"*?
ESCAPE FROM WHAT?
MAYBE ALFRED CAN HELP.

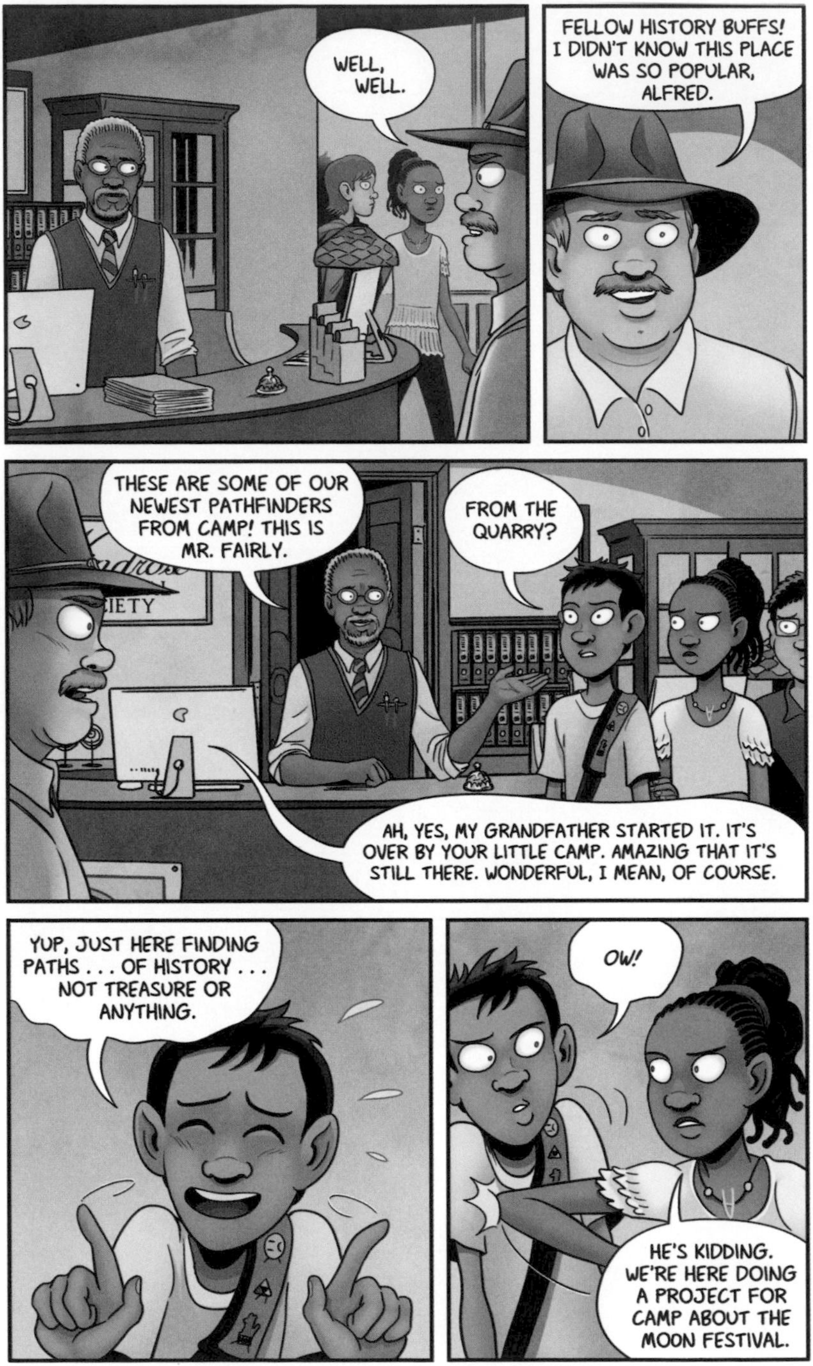
WELL, WELL.
FELLOW HISTORY BUFFS! I DIDN'T KNOW THIS PLACE WAS SO POPULAR, ALFRED.
THESE ARE SOME OF OUR NEWEST PATHFINDERS FROM CAMP! THIS IS MR. FAIRLY.
FROM THE QUARRY?
AH, YES, MY GRANDFATHER STARTED IT. IT'S OVER BY YOUR LITTLE CAMP. AMAZING THAT IT'S STILL THERE. WONDERFUL, I MEAN, OF COURSE.
YUP, JUST HERE FINDING PATHS . . . OF HISTORY . . . NOT TREASURE OR ANYTHING.
OW!
HE'S KIDDING. WE'RE HERE DOING A PROJECT FOR CAMP ABOUT THE MOON FESTIVAL.

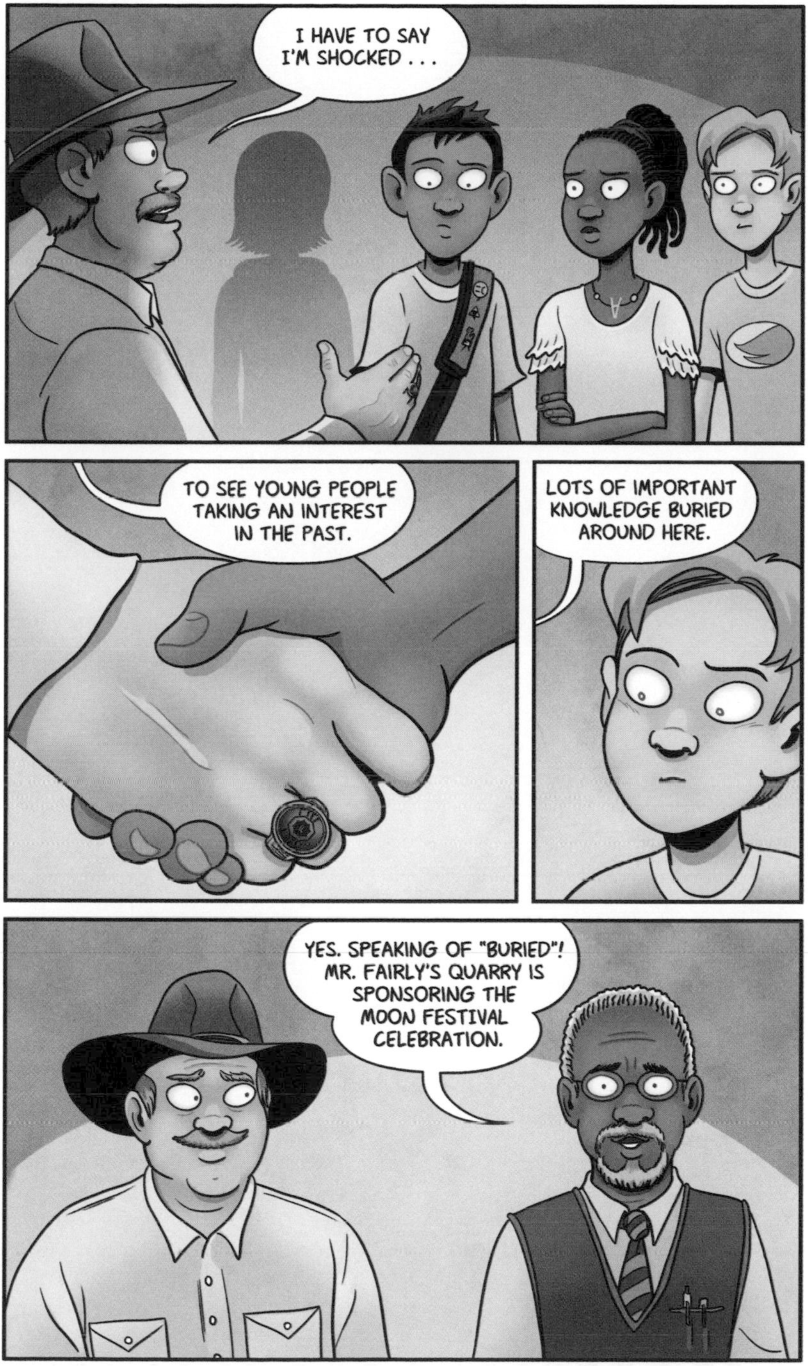
I HAVE TO SAY I'M SHOCKED . . .
TO SEE YOUNG PEOPLE TAKING AN INTEREST IN THE PAST.
LOTS OF IMPORTANT KNOWLEDGE BURIED AROUND HERE.
YES. SPEAKING OF "BURIED"! MR. FAIRLY'S QUARRY IS SPONSORING THE MOON FESTIVAL CELEBRATION.

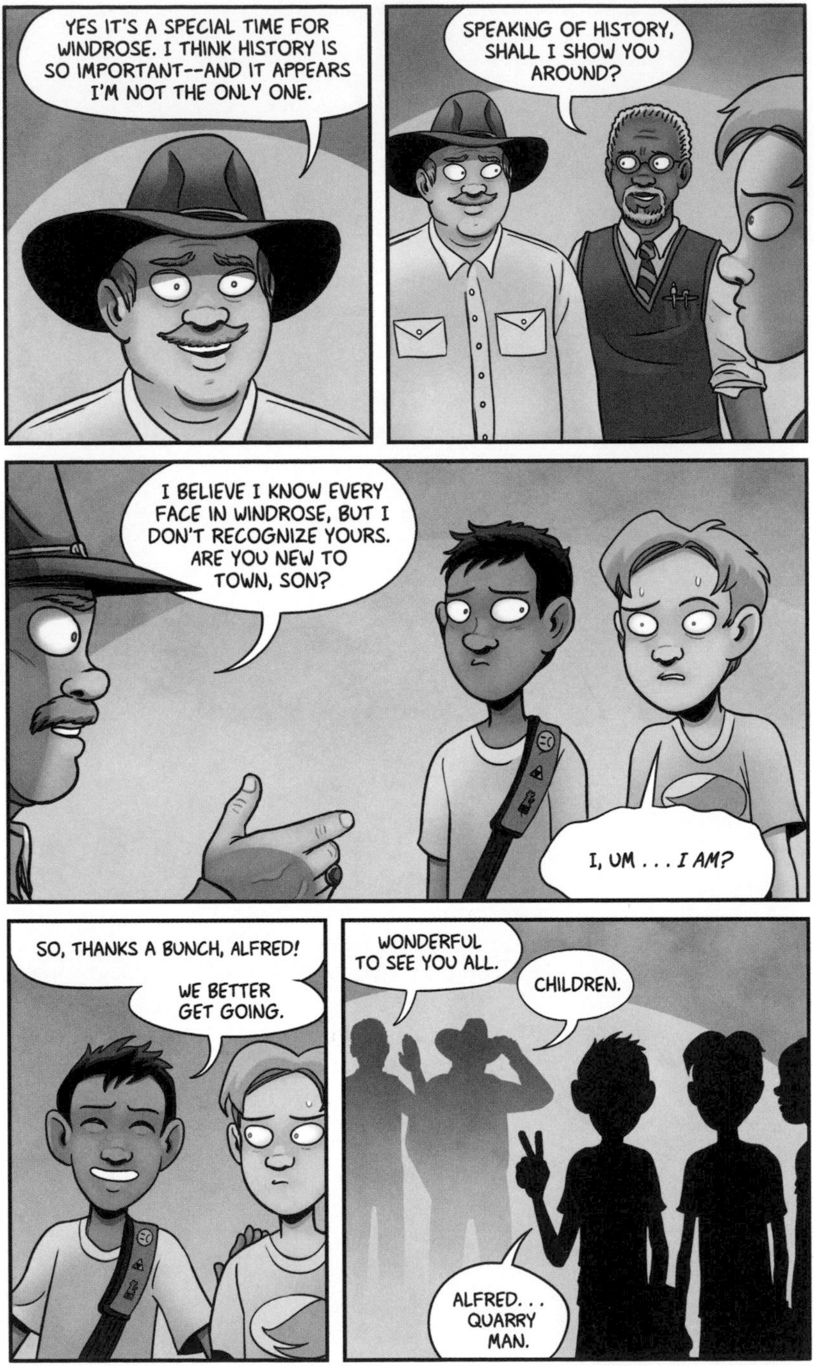
YES IT'S A SPECIAL TIME FOR WINDROSE. I THINK HISTORY IS SO IMPORTANT--AND IT APPEARS I'M NOT THE ONLY ONE.
SPEAKING OF HISTORY, SHALL I SHOW YOU AROUND?
I BELIEVE I KNOW EVERY FACE IN WINDROSE, BUT I DON'T RECOGNIZE YOURS. ARE YOU NEW TO TOWN, SON?
I, UM . . . *I AM?*
SO, THANKS A BUNCH, ALFRED!
WE BETTER GET GOING.
WONDERFUL TO SEE YOU ALL.
CHILDREN.
ALFRED. . . QUARRY MAN.

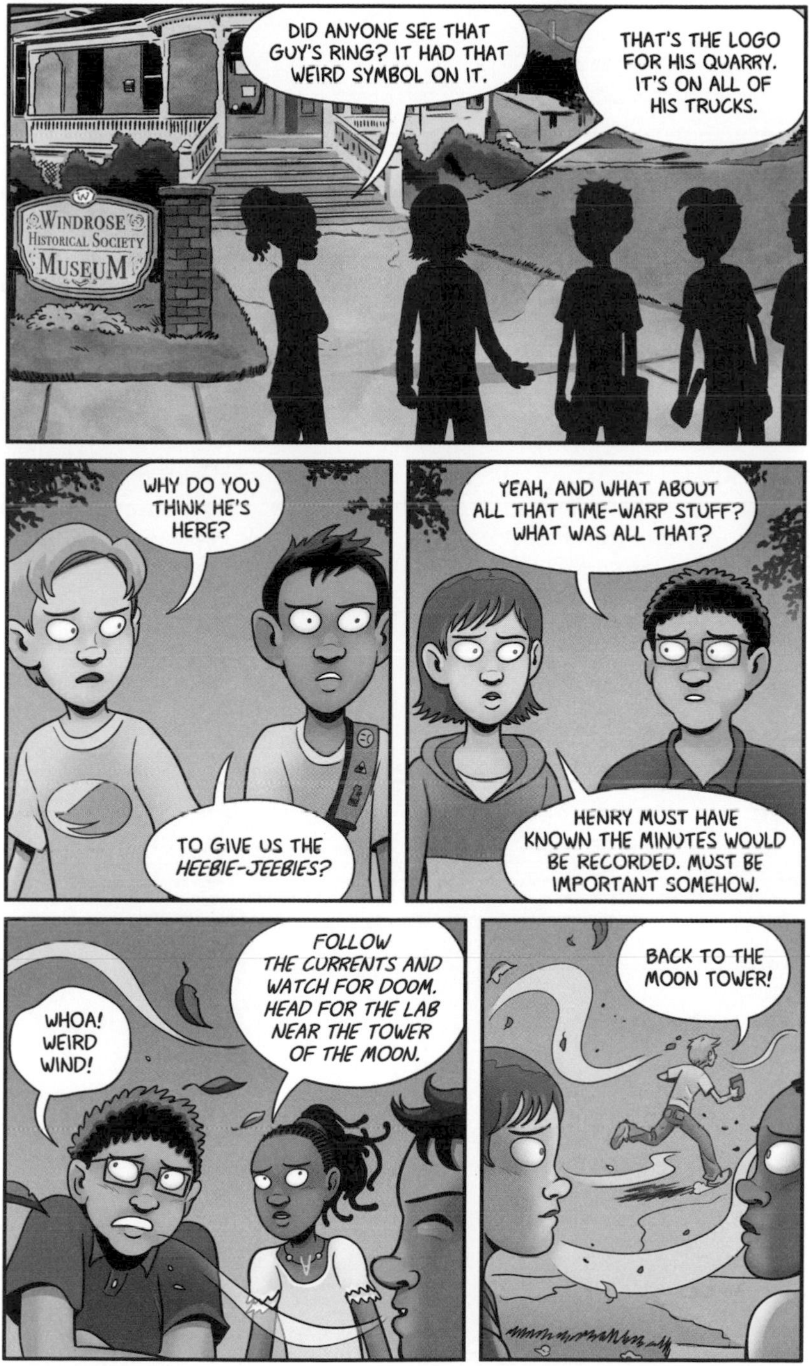
DID ANYONE SEE THAT GUY'S RING? IT HAD THAT WEIRD SYMBOL ON IT.
THAT'S THE LOGO FOR HIS QUARRY. IT'S ON ALL OF HIS TRUCKS.
WINDROSE HISTORICAL SOCIETY MUSEUM
WHY DO YOU THINK HE'S HERE?
TO GIVE US THE *HEEBIE-JEEBIES*?
YEAH, AND WHAT ABOUT ALL THAT TIME-WARP STUFF? WHAT WAS ALL THAT?
HENRY MUST HAVE KNOWN THE MINUTES WOULD BE RECORDED. MUST BE IMPORTANT SOMEHOW.
WHOA! WEIRD WIND!
FOLLOW THE CURRENTS AND WATCH FOR DOOM. HEAD FOR THE LAB NEAR THE TOWER OF THE MOON.
BACK TO THE MOON TOWER!

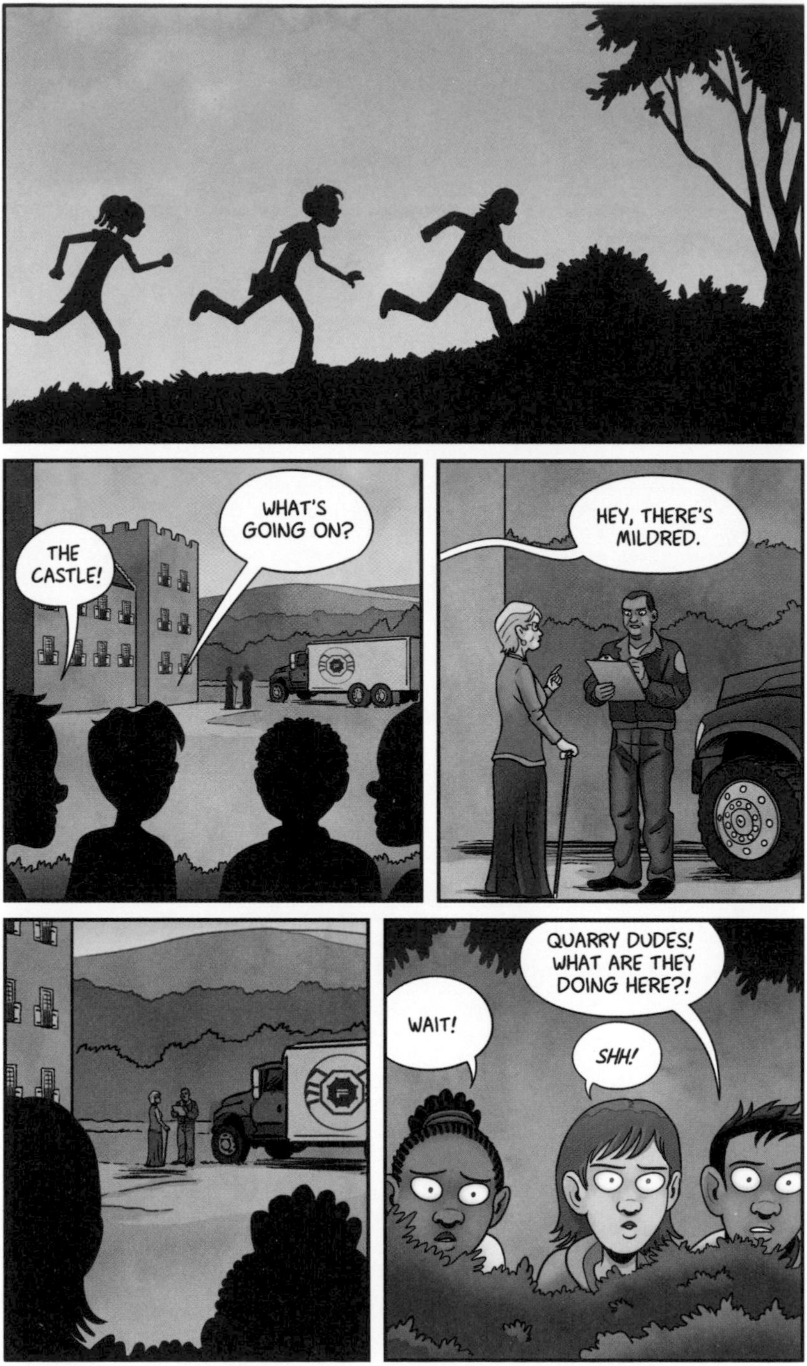
THE CASTLE!
WHAT'S GOING ON?
HEY, THERE'S MILDRED.
WAIT!
QUARRY DUDES! WHAT ARE THEY DOING HERE?!
SHH!

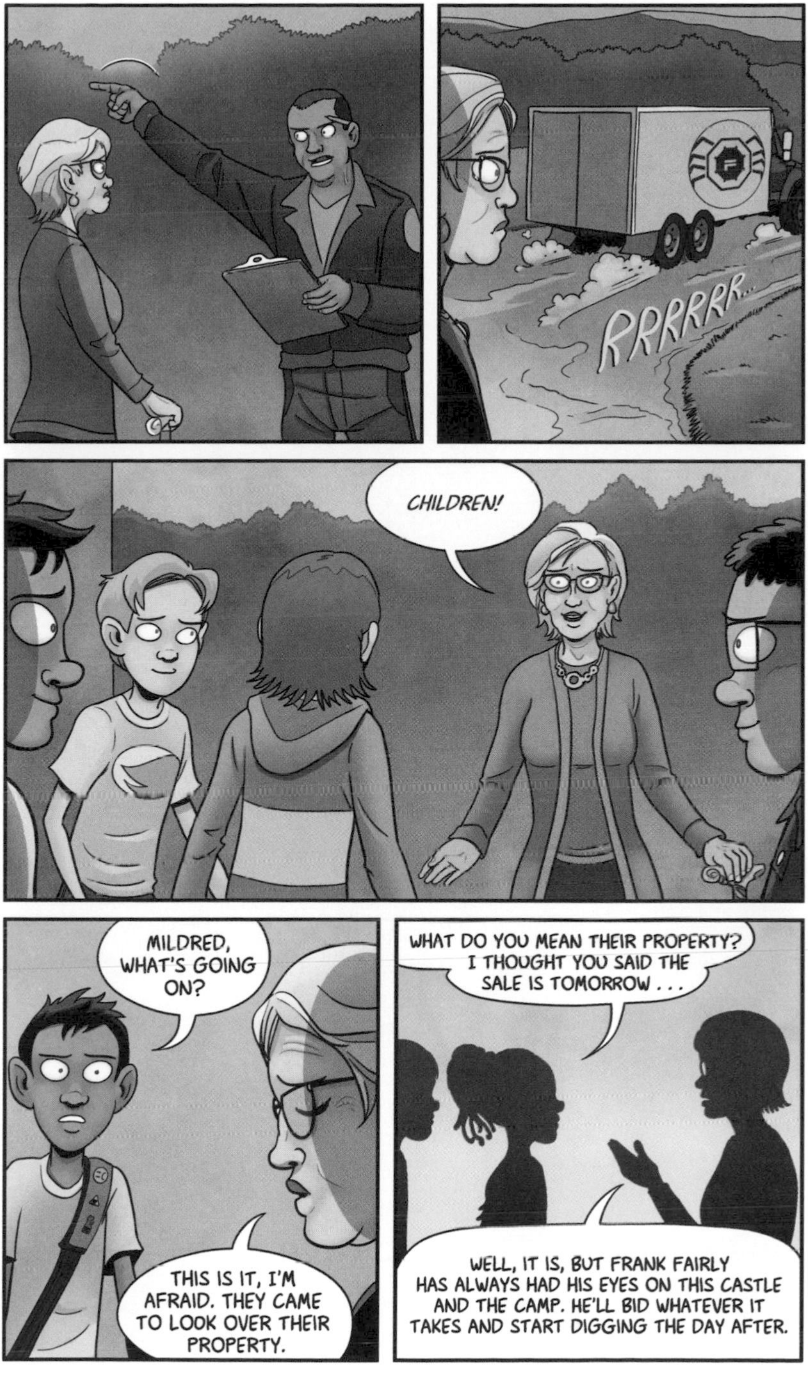
RRRRRR...
CHILDREN!
MILDRED, WHAT'S GOING ON?
THIS IS IT, I'M AFRAID. THEY CAME TO LOOK OVER THEIR PROPERTY.
WHAT DO YOU MEAN THEIR PROPERTY? I THOUGHT YOU SAID THE SALE IS TOMORROW . . .
WELL, IT IS, BUT FRANK FAIRLY HAS ALWAYS HAD HIS EYES ON THIS CASTLE AND THE CAMP. HE'LL BID WHATEVER IT TAKES AND START DIGGING THE DAY AFTER.

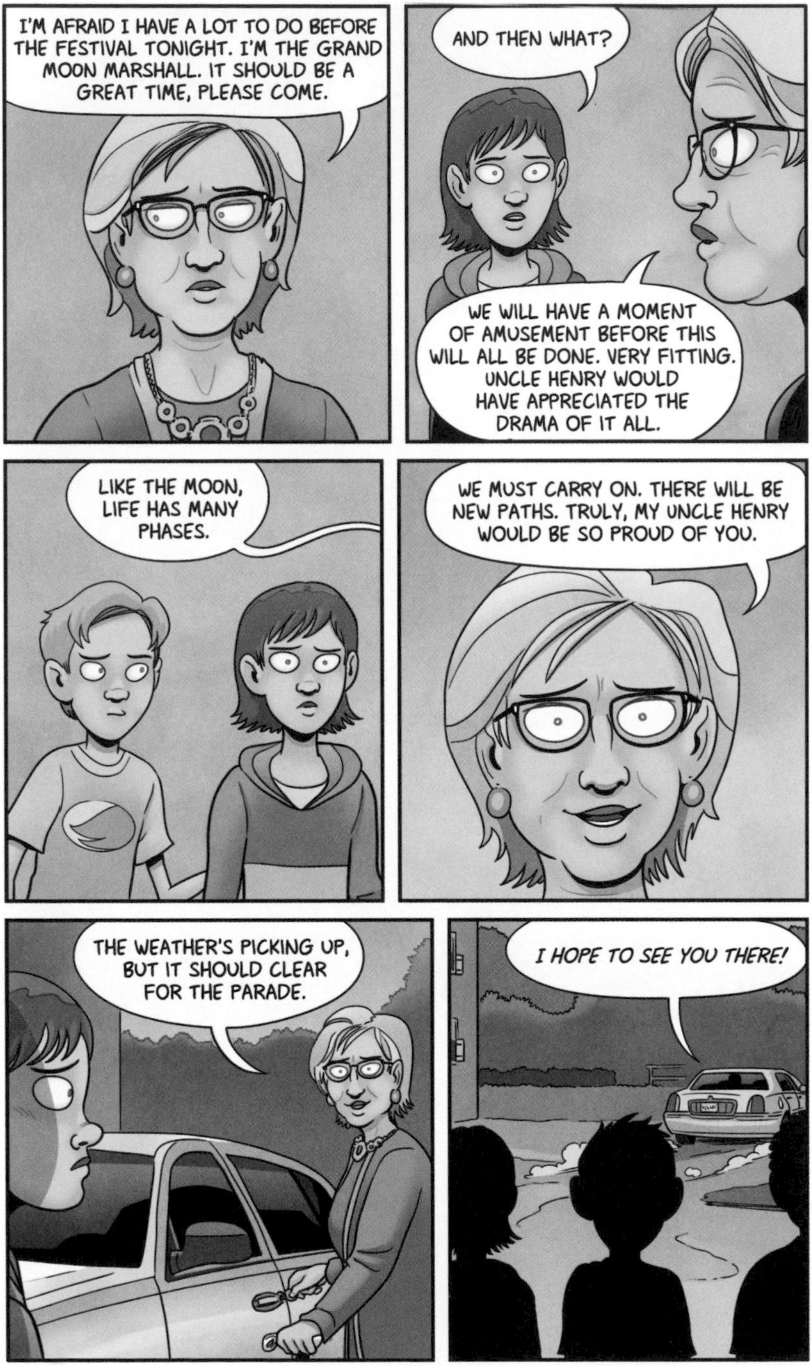
I'M AFRAID I HAVE A LOT TO DO BEFORE THE FESTIVAL TONIGHT. I'M THE GRAND MOON MARSHALL. IT SHOULD BE A GREAT TIME, PLEASE COME.
AND THEN WHAT?
WE WILL HAVE A MOMENT OF AMUSEMENT BEFORE THIS WILL ALL BE DONE. VERY FITTING. UNCLE HENRY WOULD HAVE APPRECIATED THE DRAMA OF IT ALL.
LIKE THE MOON, LIFE HAS MANY PHASES.
WE MUST CARRY ON. THERE WILL BE NEW PATHS. TRULY, MY UNCLE HENRY WOULD BE SO PROUD OF YOU.
THE WEATHER'S PICKING UP, BUT IT SHOULD CLEAR FOR THE PARADE.
I HOPE TO SEE YOU THERE!

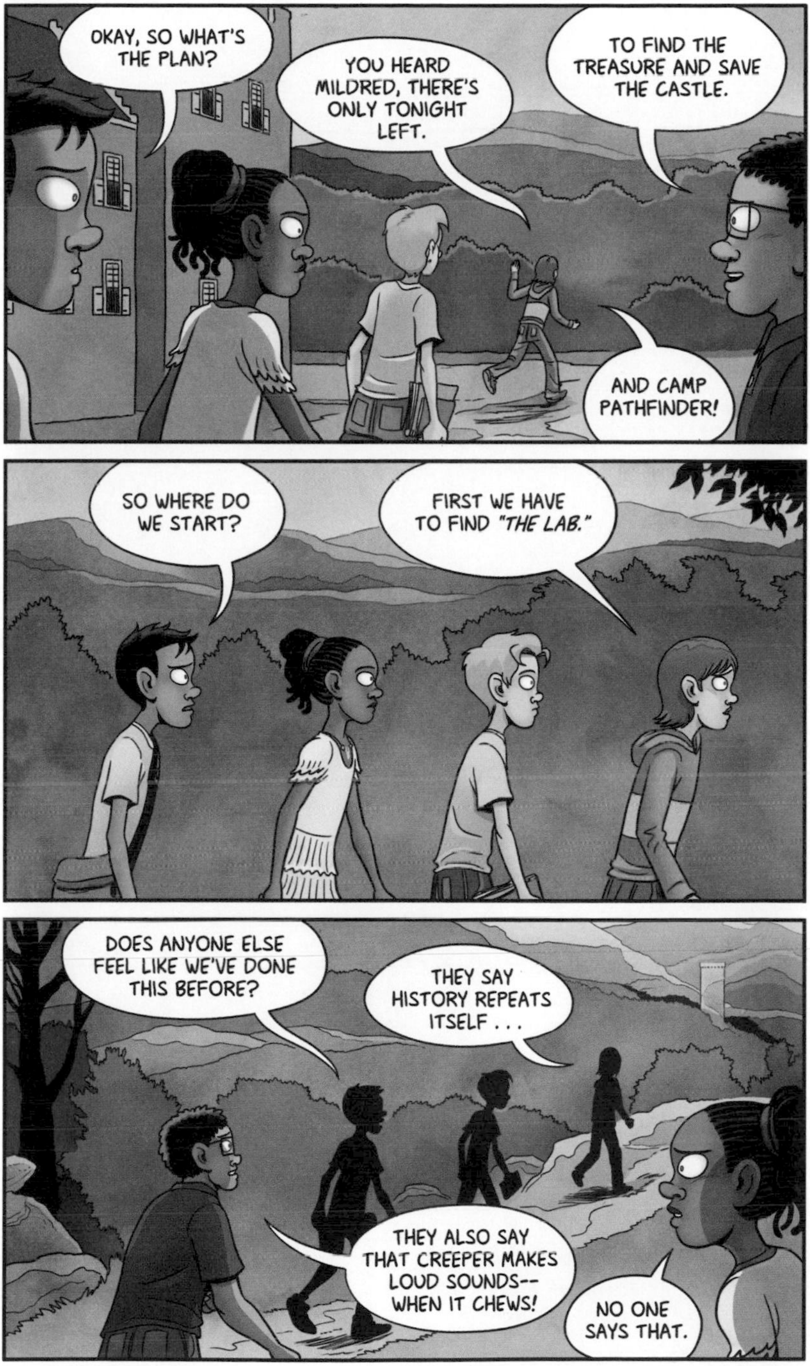
OKAY, SO WHAT'S THE PLAN?
YOU HEARD MILDRED, THERE'S ONLY TONIGHT LEFT.
TO FIND THE TREASURE AND SAVE THE CASTLE.
AND CAMP PATHFINDER!
SO WHERE DO WE START?
FIRST WE HAVE TO FIND *"THE LAB."*
DOES ANYONE ELSE FEEL LIKE WE'VE DONE THIS BEFORE?
THEY SAY HISTORY REPEATS ITSELF . . .
THEY ALSO SAY THAT CREEPER MAKES LOUD SOUNDS-- WHEN IT CHEWS!
NO ONE SAYS THAT.

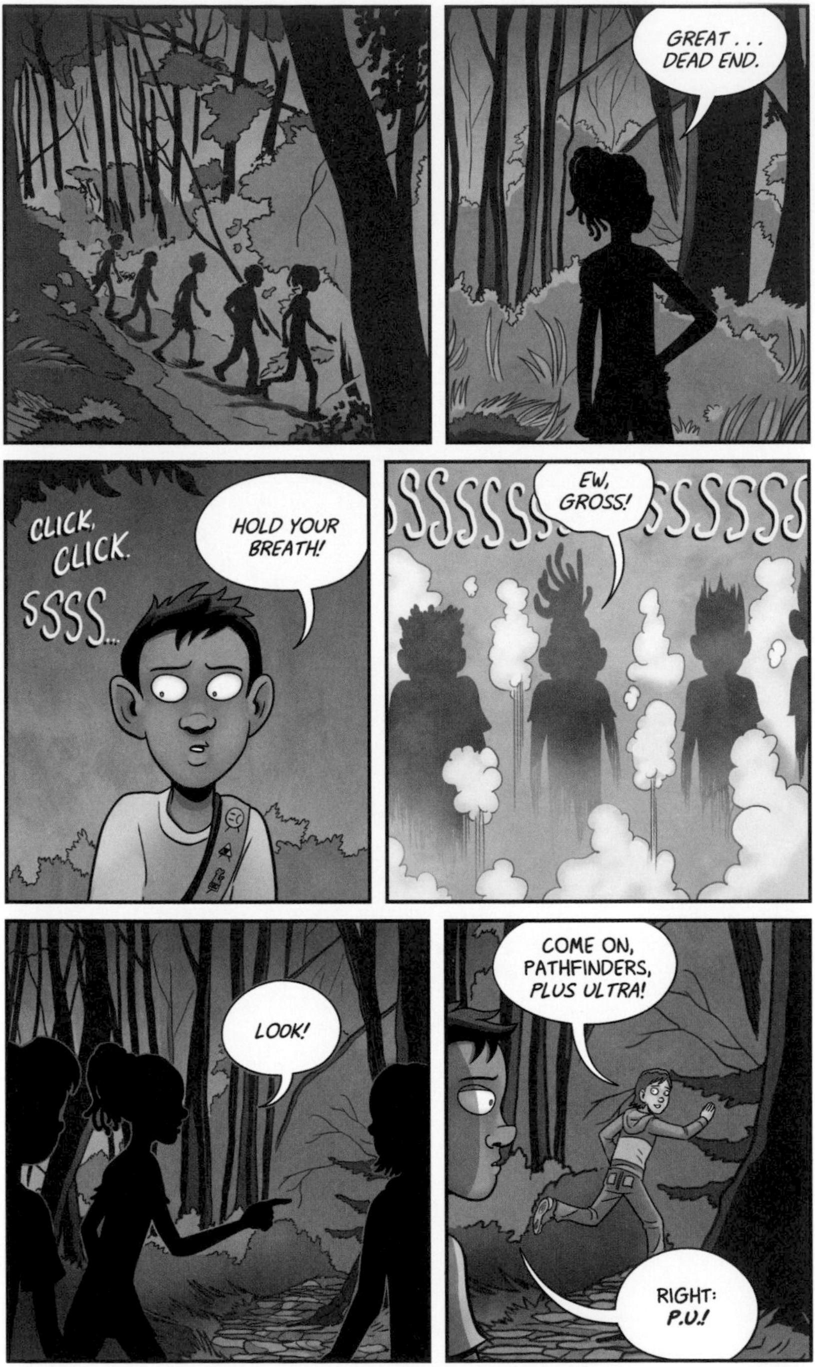
GREAT . . . DEAD END.
CLICK, CLICK.
SSSS...
HOLD YOUR BREATH!
SSSSSSSSSSSSSS
EW, GROSS!
LOOK!
COME ON, PATHFINDERS, PLUS ULTRA!
RIGHT: P.U.!

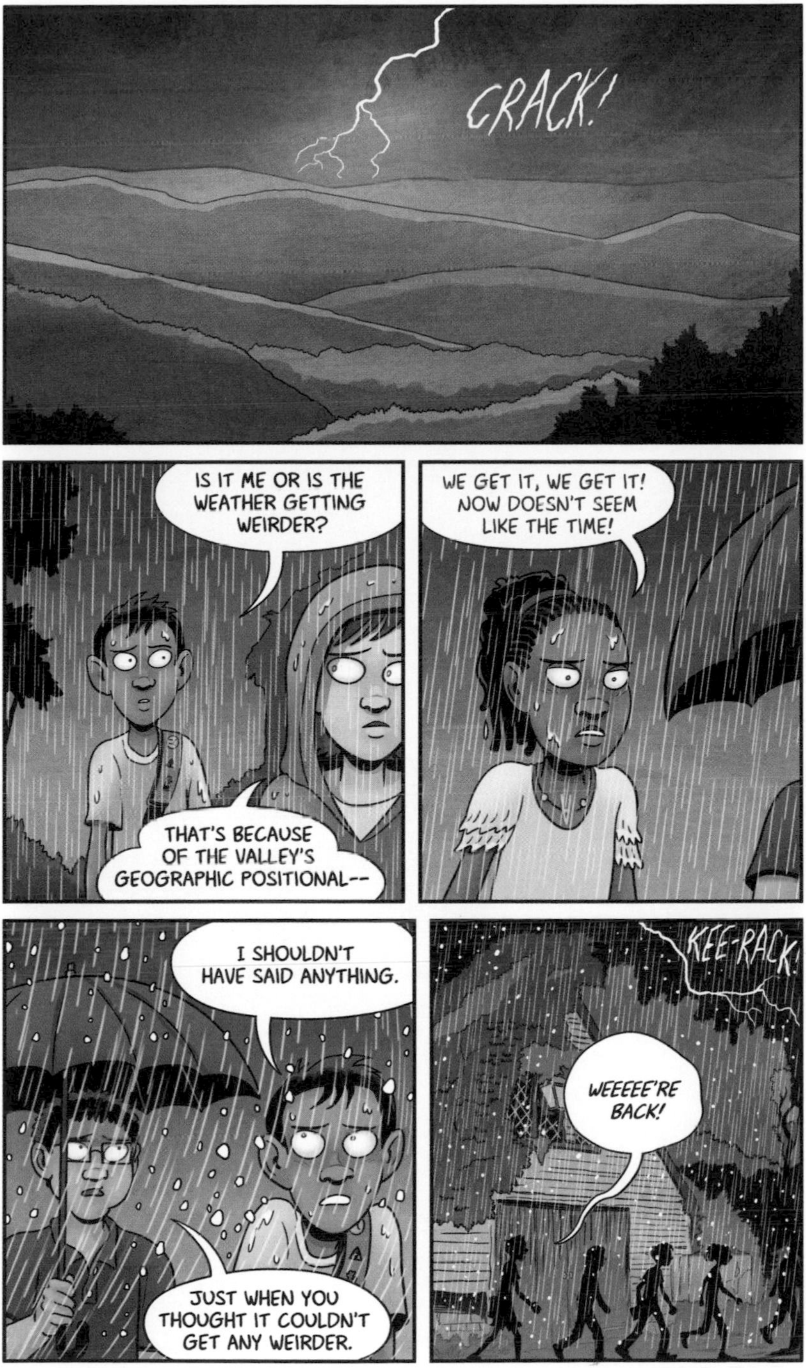
CRACK!
IS IT ME OR IS THE WEATHER GETTING WEIRDER?
THAT'S BECAUSE OF THE VALLEY'S GEOGRAPHIC POSITIONAL--
WE GET IT, WE GET IT! NOW DOESN'T SEEM LIKE THE TIME!
I SHOULDN'T HAVE SAID ANYTHING.
JUST WHEN YOU THOUGHT IT COULDN'T GET ANY WEIRDER.
KEE-RACK!
WEEEEE'RE BACK!

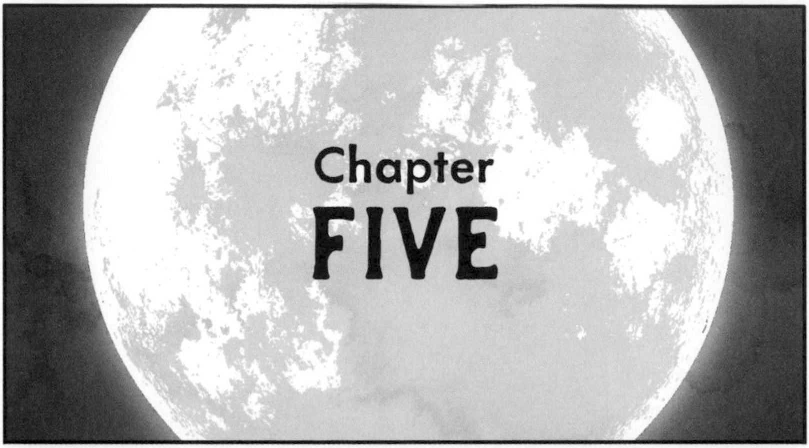
Chapter
FIVE

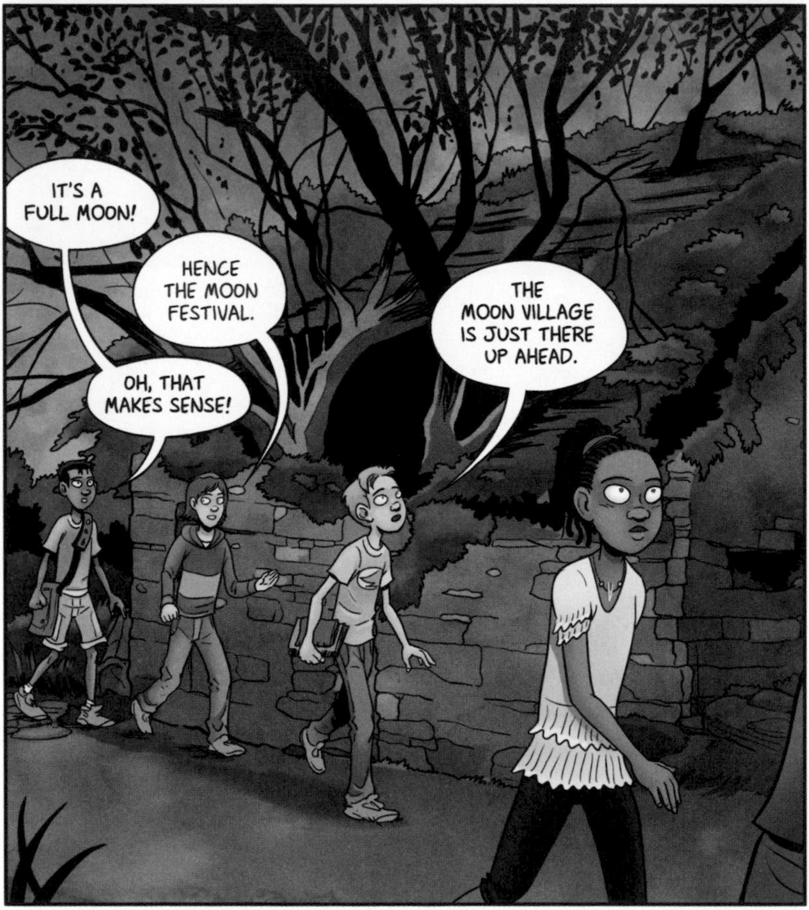
IT'S A FULL MOON!
HENCE THE MOON FESTIVAL.
OH, THAT MAKES SENSE!
THE MOON VILLAGE IS JUST THERE UP AHEAD.

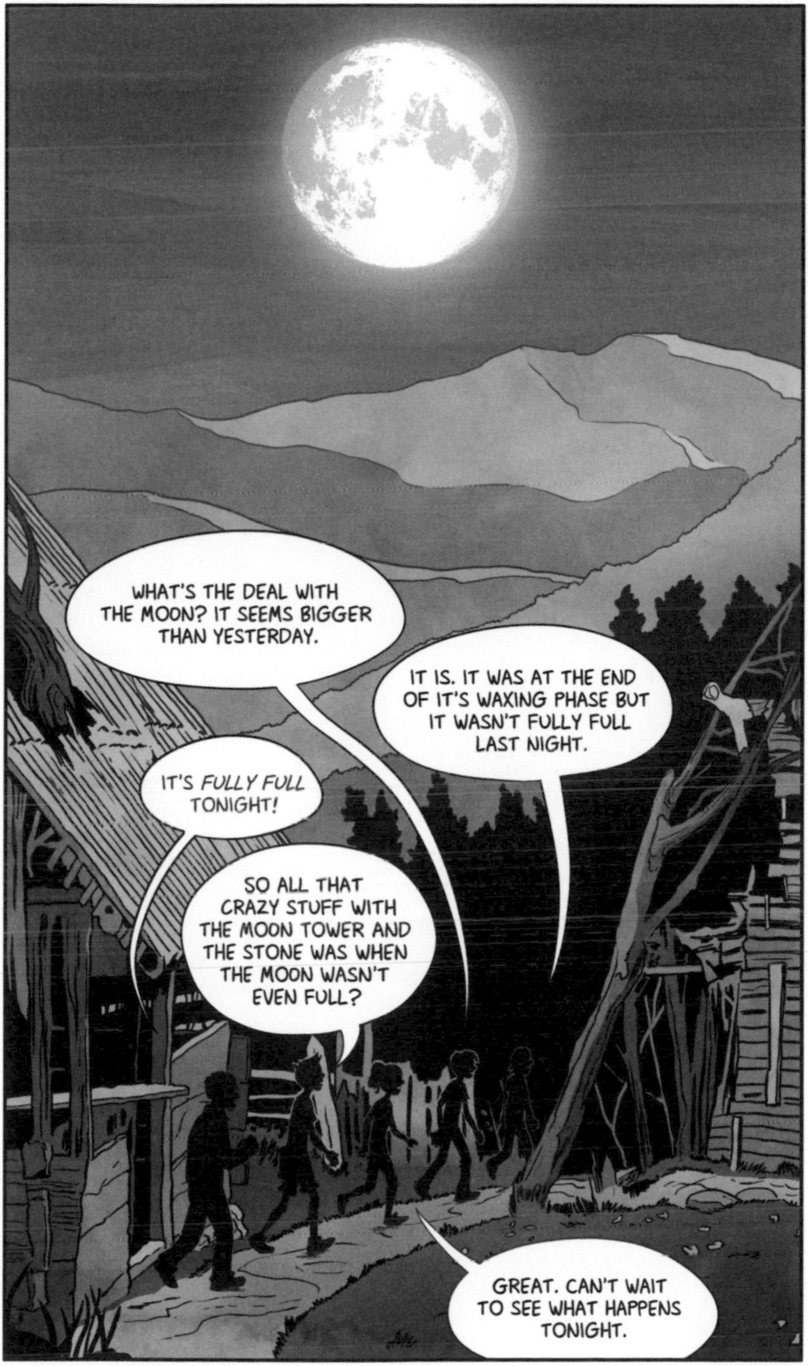
WHAT'S THE DEAL WITH THE MOON? IT SEEMS BIGGER THAN YESTERDAY.
IT IS. IT WAS AT THE END OF IT'S WAXING PHASE BUT IT WASN'T FULLY FULL LAST NIGHT.
IT'S *FULLY FULL* TONIGHT!
SO ALL THAT CRAZY STUFF WITH THE MOON TOWER AND THE STONE WAS WHEN THE MOON WASN'T EVEN FULL?
GREAT. CAN'T WAIT TO SEE WHAT HAPPENS TONIGHT.

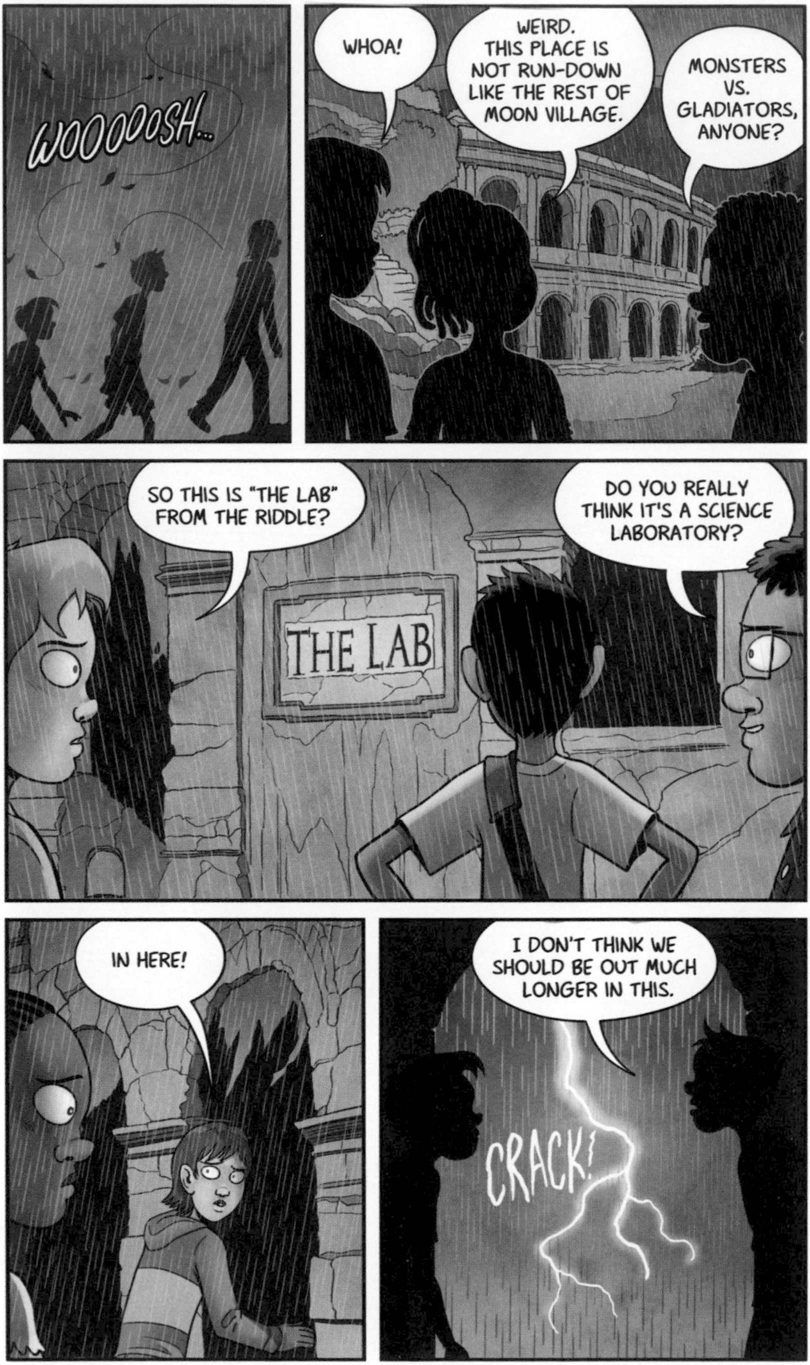
WOOOOOSH...
WHOA!
WEIRD. THIS PLACE IS NOT RUN-DOWN LIKE THE REST OF MOON VILLAGE.
MONSTERS VS. GLADIATORS, ANYONE?
SO THIS IS "THE LAB" FROM THE RIDDLE?
DO YOU REALLY THINK IT'S A SCIENCE LABORATORY?
THE LAB
IN HERE!
I DON'T THINK WE SHOULD BE OUT MUCH LONGER IN THIS.
CRACK!

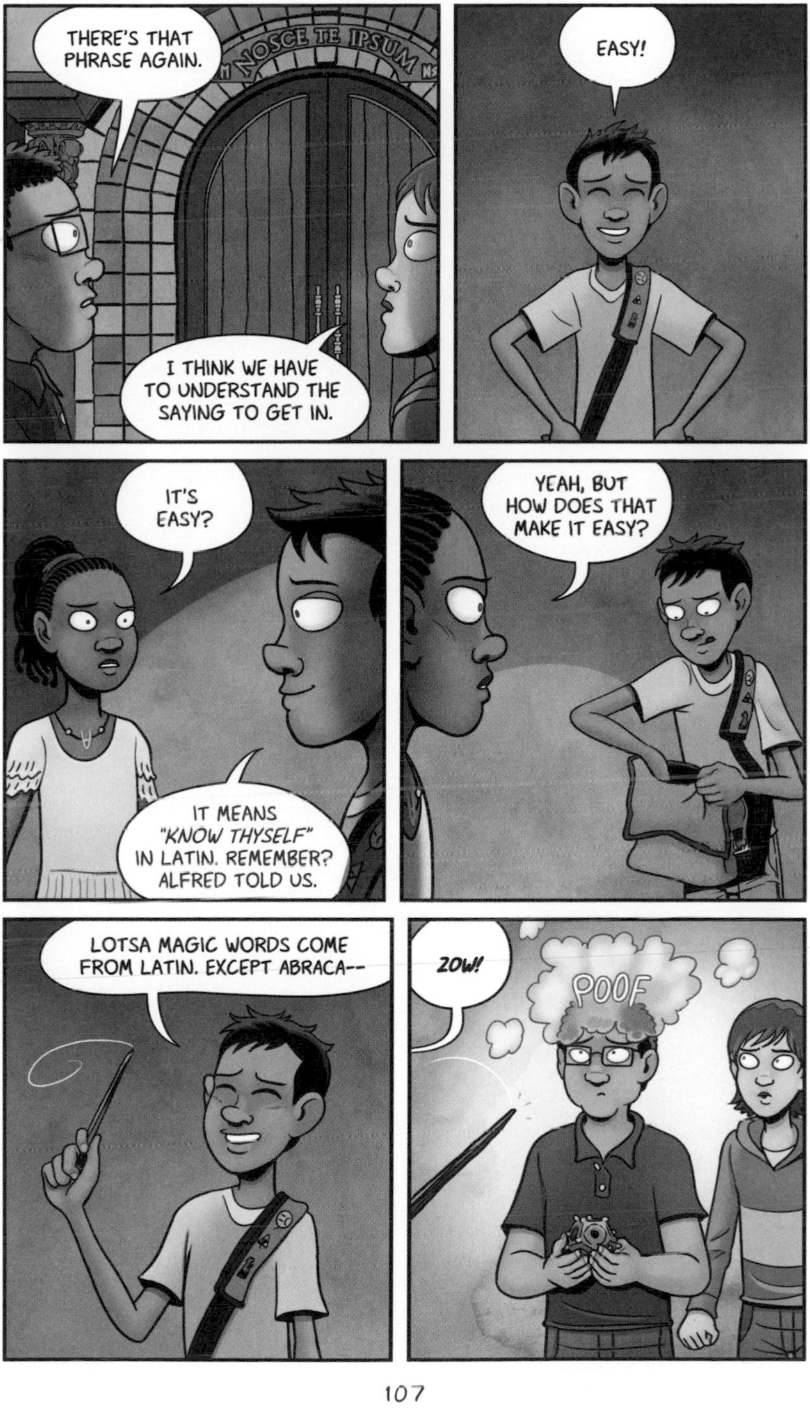
NOSCE TE IPSUM
THERE'S THAT PHRASE AGAIN.
I THINK WE HAVE TO UNDERSTAND THE SAYING TO GET IN.
EASY!
IT'S EASY?
IT MEANS *"KNOW THYSELF"* IN LATIN. REMEMBER? ALFRED TOLD US.
YEAH, BUT HOW DOES THAT MAKE IT EASY?
LOTSA MAGIC WORDS COME FROM LATIN. EXCEPT ABRACA--
ZOW!
POOF

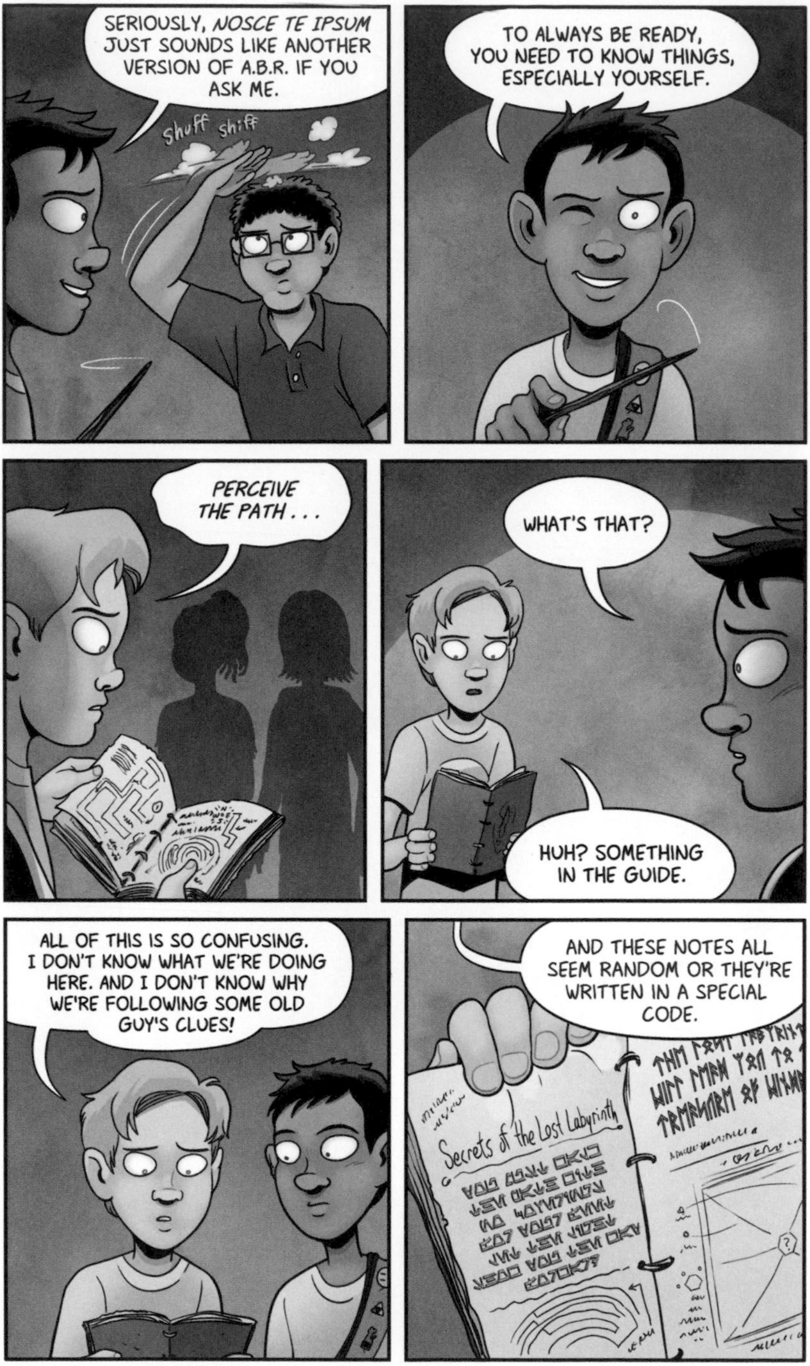

SERIOUSLY, *NOSCE TE IPSUM* JUST SOUNDS LIKE ANOTHER VERSION OF A.B.R. IF YOU ASK ME.
Shuff shiff
TO ALWAYS BE READY, YOU NEED TO KNOW THINGS, ESPECIALLY YOURSELF.
PERCEIVE THE PATH . . .
WHAT'S THAT?
HUH? SOMETHING IN THE GUIDE.
ALL OF THIS IS SO CONFUSING. I DON'T KNOW WHAT WE'RE DOING HERE. AND I DON'T KNOW WHY WE'RE FOLLOWING SOME OLD GUY'S CLUES!
AND THESE NOTES ALL SEEM RANDOM OR THEY'RE WRITTEN IN A SPECIAL CODE.
Secrets of the Lost Labyrinth

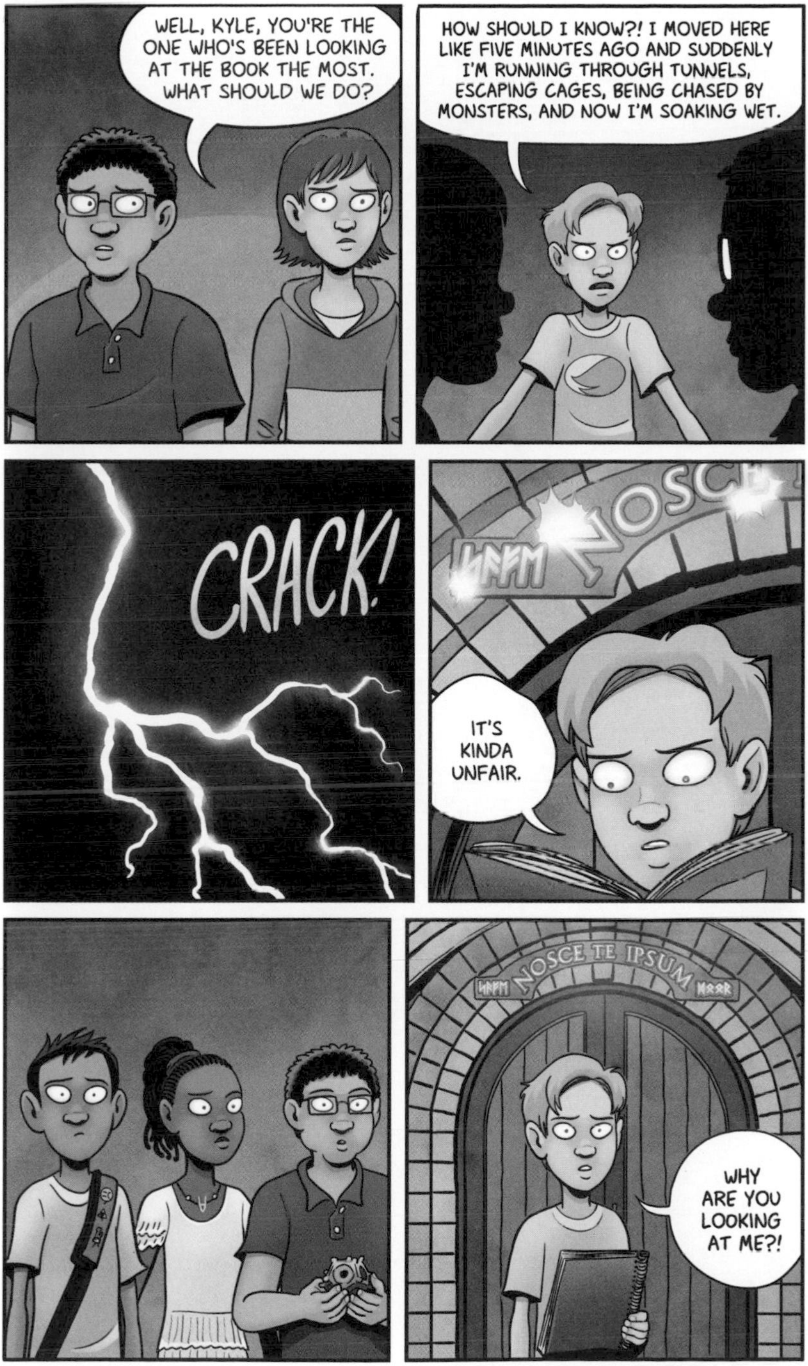
WELL, KYLE, YOU'RE THE ONE WHO'S BEEN LOOKING AT THE BOOK THE MOST. WHAT SHOULD WE DO?
HOW SHOULD I KNOW?! I MOVED HERE LIKE FIVE MINUTES AGO AND SUDDENLY I'M RUNNING THROUGH TUNNELS, ESCAPING CAGES, BEING CHASED BY MONSTERS, AND NOW I'M SOAKING WET.
CRACK!
IT'S KINDA UNFAIR.
NOSCE TE IPSUM
WHY ARE YOU LOOKING AT ME?!

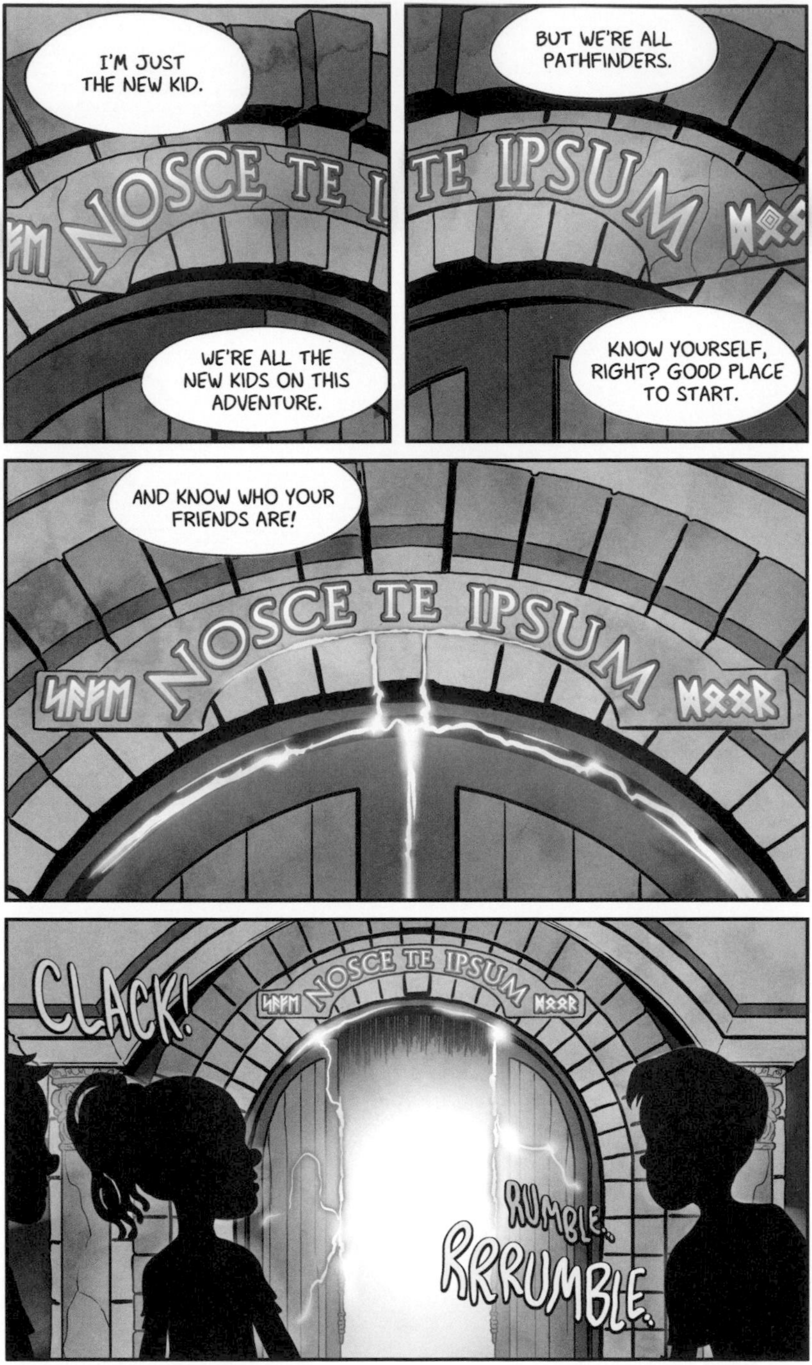
I'M JUST THE NEW KID.
WE'RE ALL THE NEW KIDS ON THIS ADVENTURE.
NOSCE TE I
BUT WE'RE ALL PATHFINDERS.
TE IPSUM
KNOW YOURSELF, RIGHT? GOOD PLACE TO START.
AND KNOW WHO YOUR FRIENDS ARE!
NOSCE TE IPSUM
CLACK!
NOSCE TE IPSUM
RUMBLE..
RRRUMBLE..

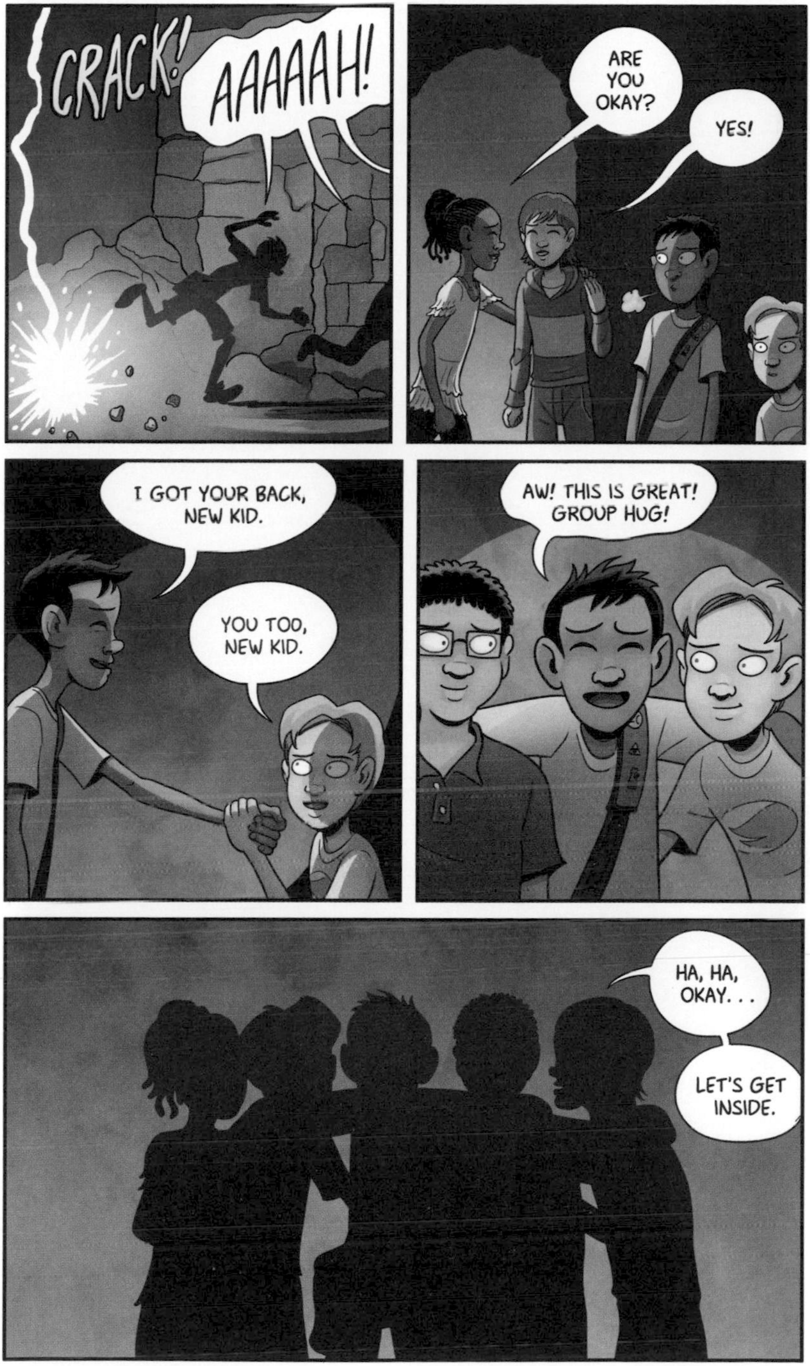
CRACK!
AAAAAH!
ARE YOU OKAY?
YES!
I GOT YOUR BACK, NEW KID.
YOU TOO, NEW KID.
AW! THIS IS GREAT! GROUP HUG!
HA, HA, OKAY. . .
LET'S GET INSIDE.

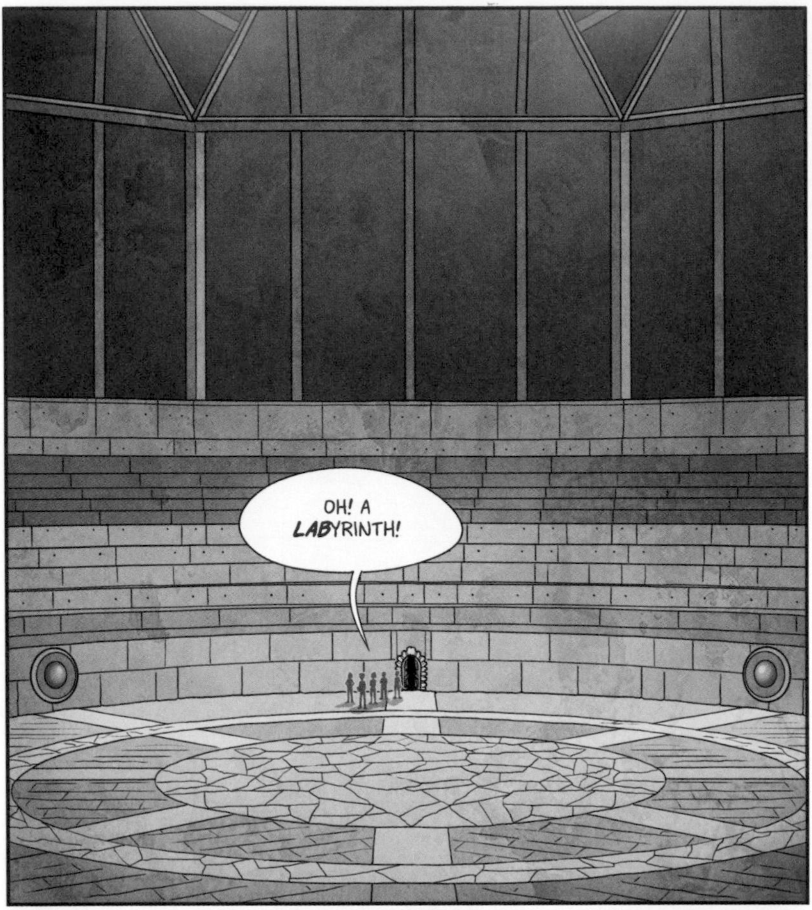
OH! A LABYRINTH!

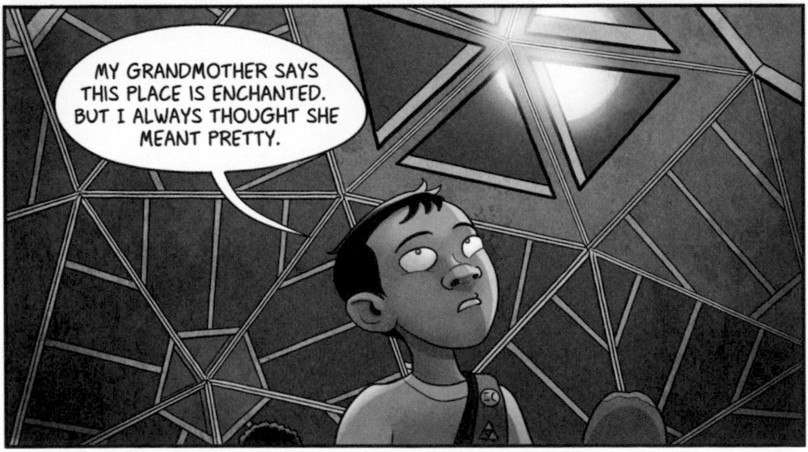
MY GRANDMOTHER SAYS THIS PLACE IS ENCHANTED. BUT I ALWAYS THOUGHT SHE MEANT PRETTY.

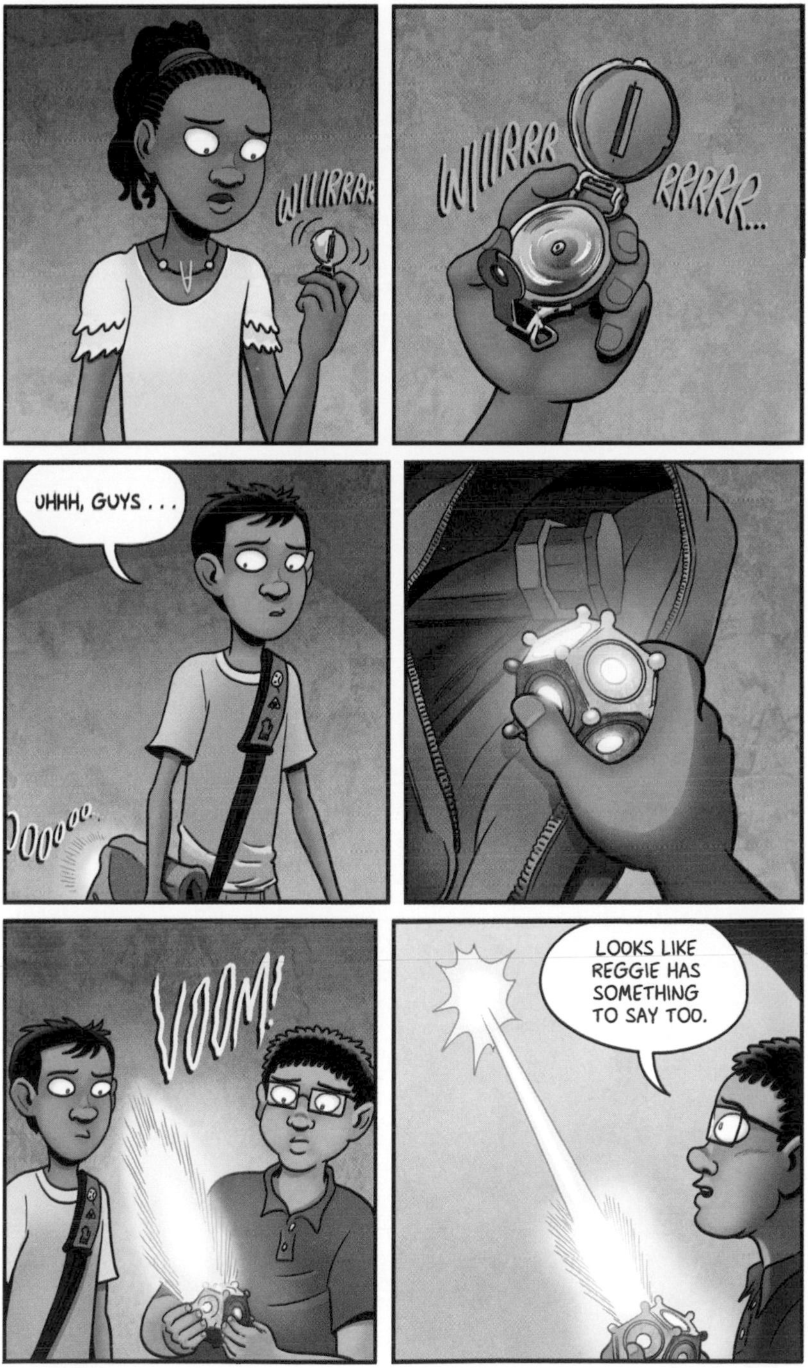
WIIIRRRR
WIIIRRR
RRRRR...
UHHH, GUYS . . .
VOOM!
LOOKS LIKE REGGIE HAS SOMETHING TO SAY TOO.

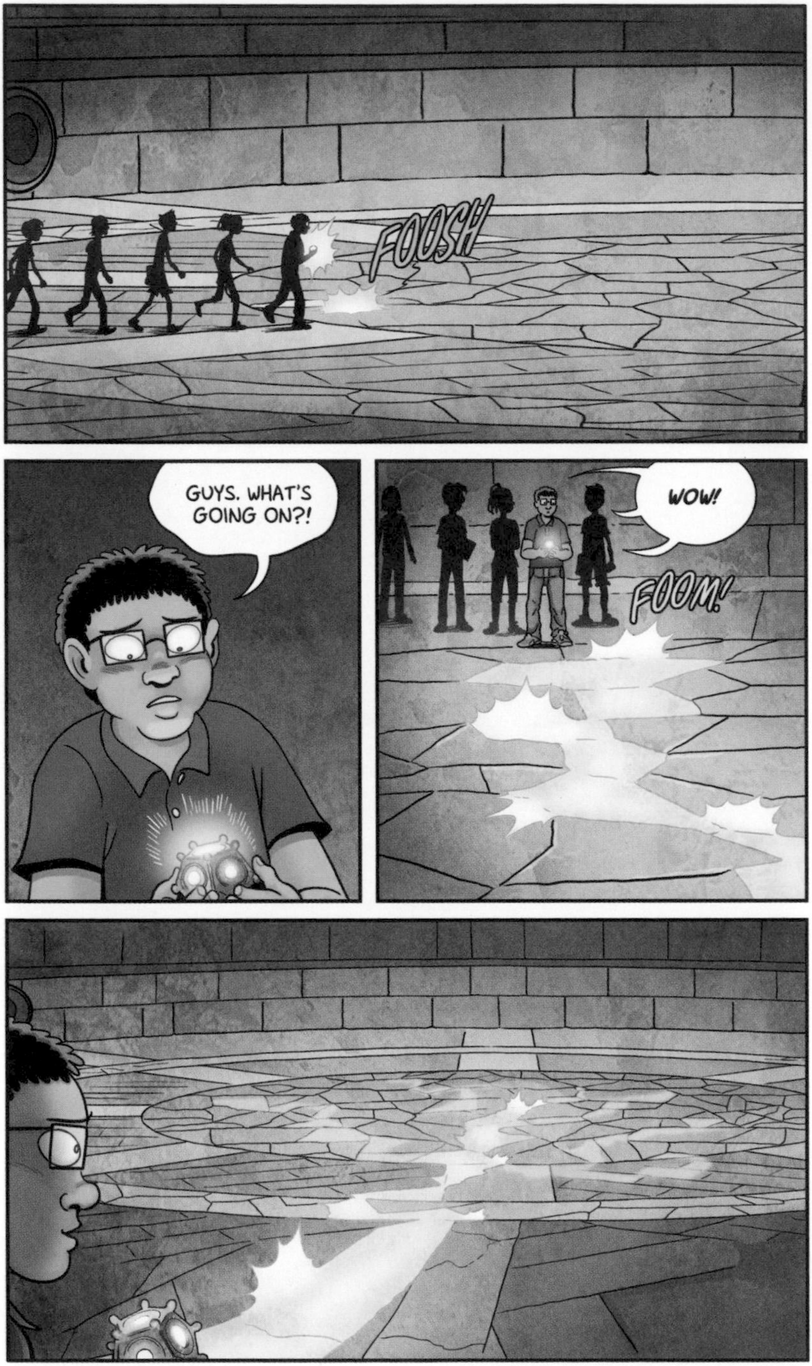
FOOSH
GUYS. WHAT'S GOING ON?!
WOW!
FOOM!

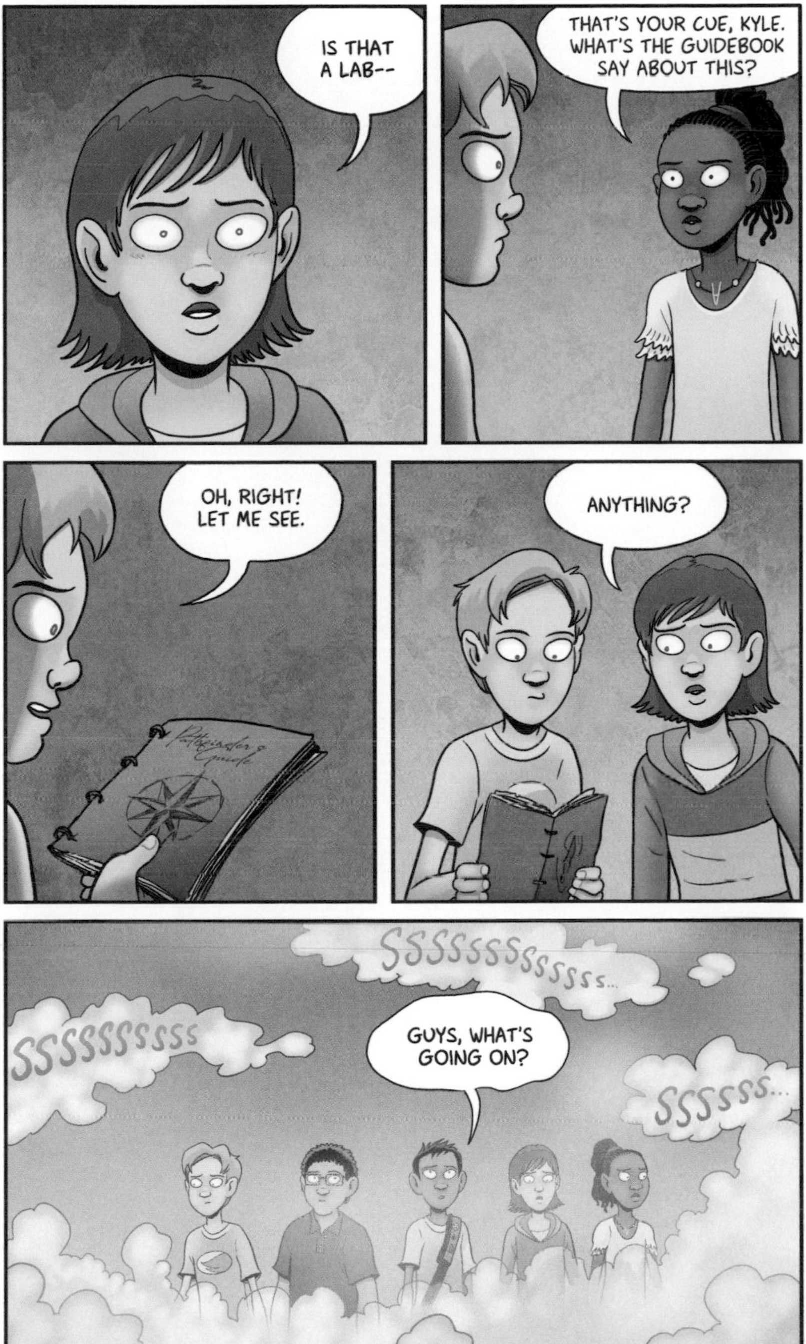
IS THAT A LAB--
THAT'S YOUR CUE, KYLE. WHAT'S THE GUIDEBOOK SAY ABOUT THIS?
OH, RIGHT! LET ME SEE.
Pathfinder's Guide
ANYTHING?
SSSSSSSSSSSSS...
SSSSSSSSSSS
GUYS, WHAT'S GOING ON?
SSSSSS...

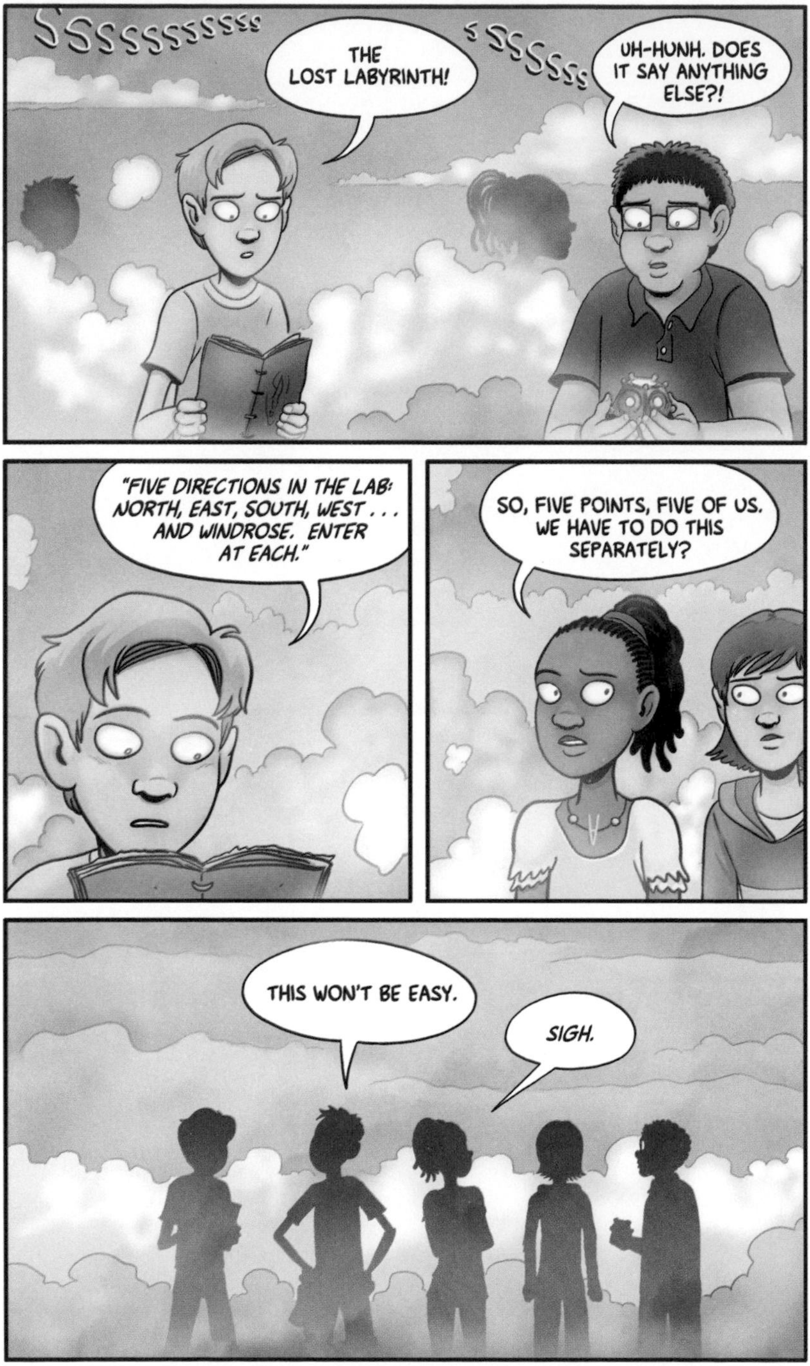
SSSSSSSSSSS
THE LOST LABYRINTH!
SSSSSSS
UH-HUNH. DOES IT SAY ANYTHING ELSE?!
"FIVE DIRECTIONS IN THE LAB: NORTH, EAST, SOUTH, WEST . . . AND WINDROSE. ENTER AT EACH."
SO, FIVE POINTS, FIVE OF US. WE HAVE TO DO THIS SEPARATELY?
THIS WON'T BE EASY.
SIGH.

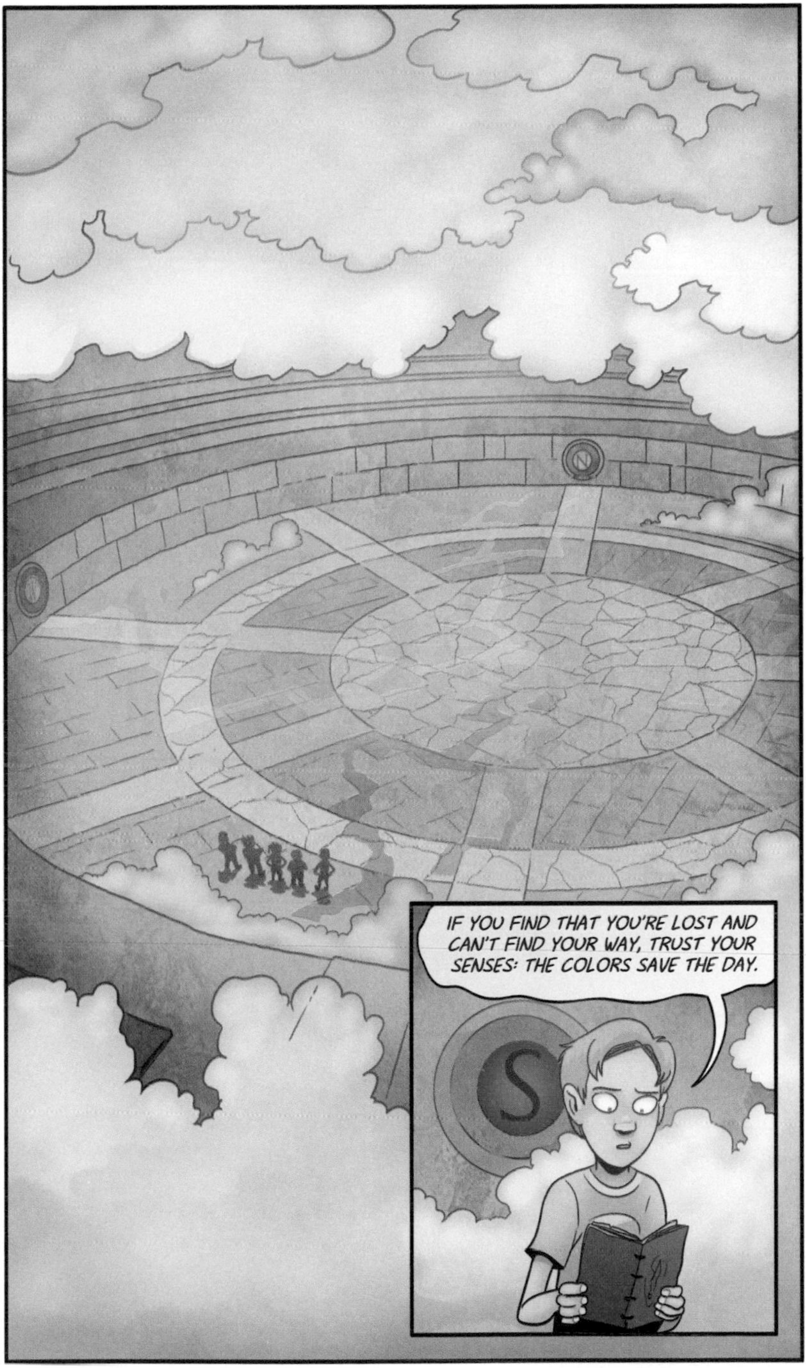
IF YOU FIND THAT YOU'RE LOST AND CAN'T FIND YOUR WAY, TRUST YOUR SENSES: THE COLORS SAVE THE DAY.
S

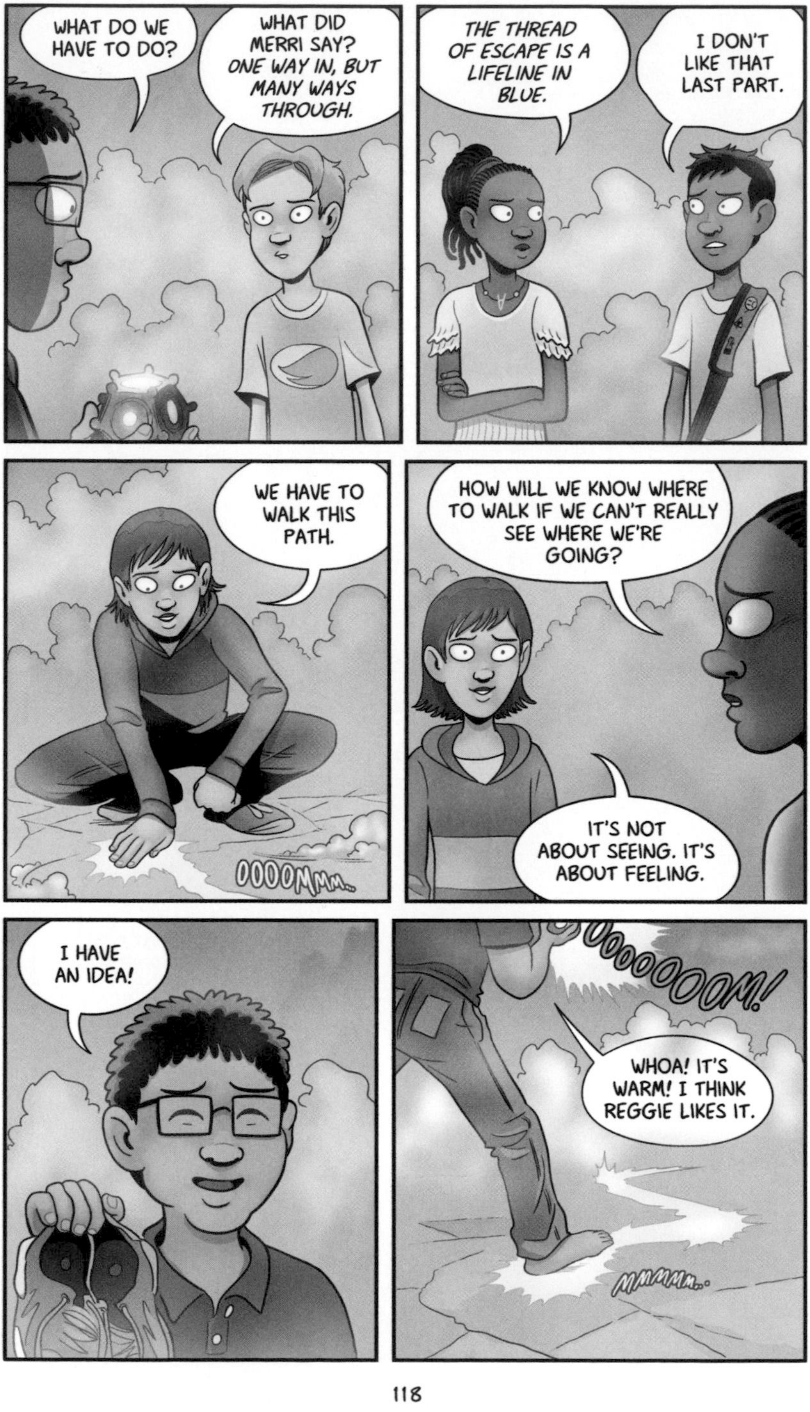
WHAT DO WE HAVE TO DO?
WHAT DID MERRI SAY? ONE WAY IN, BUT MANY WAYS THROUGH.
THE THREAD OF ESCAPE IS A LIFELINE IN BLUE.
I DON'T LIKE THAT LAST PART.
WE HAVE TO WALK THIS PATH.
OOOOMMM...
HOW WILL WE KNOW WHERE TO WALK IF WE CAN'T REALLY SEE WHERE WE'RE GOING?
IT'S NOT ABOUT SEEING. IT'S ABOUT FEELING.
I HAVE AN IDEA!
OOOOOOOOM!
WHOA! IT'S WARM! I THINK REGGIE LIKES IT.
MMMMM...

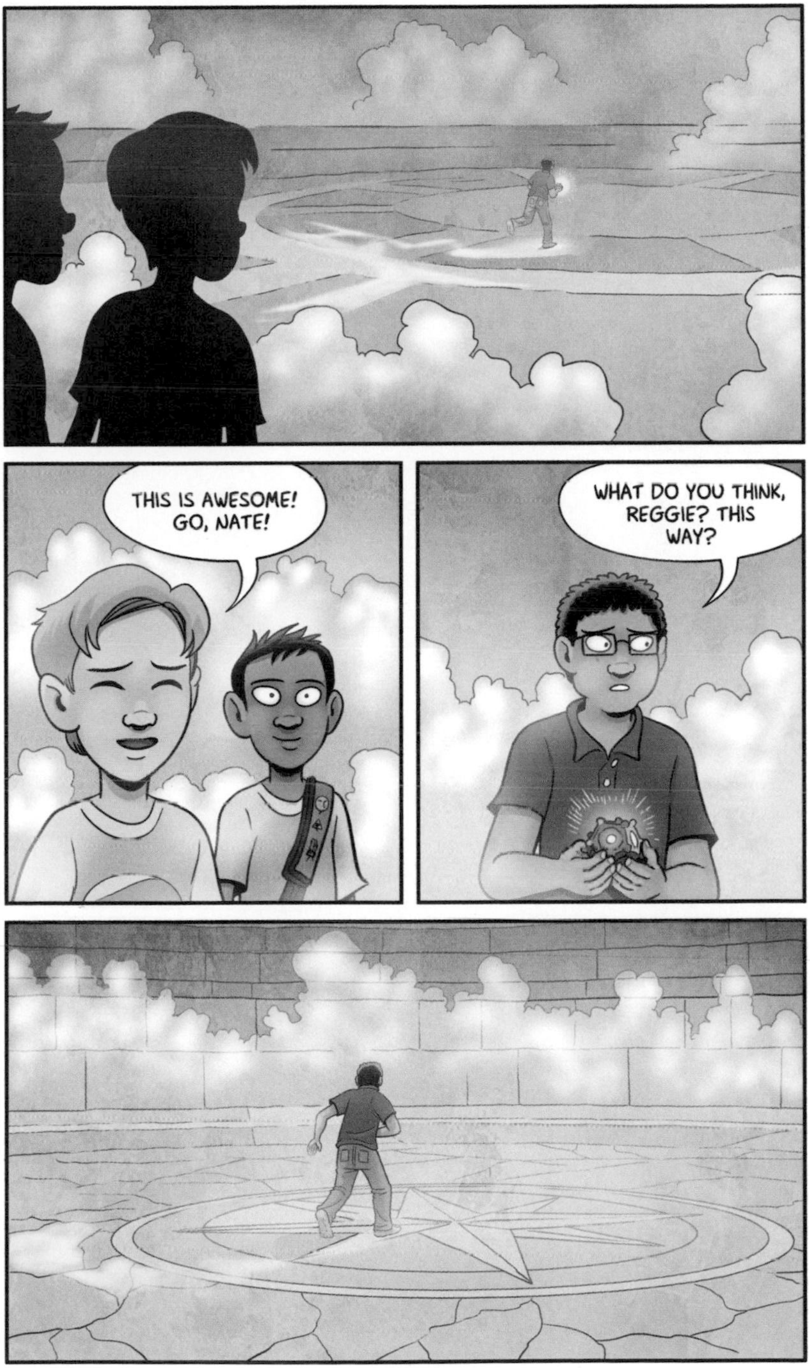
THIS IS AWESOME! GO, NATE!
WHAT DO YOU THINK, REGGIE? THIS WAY?

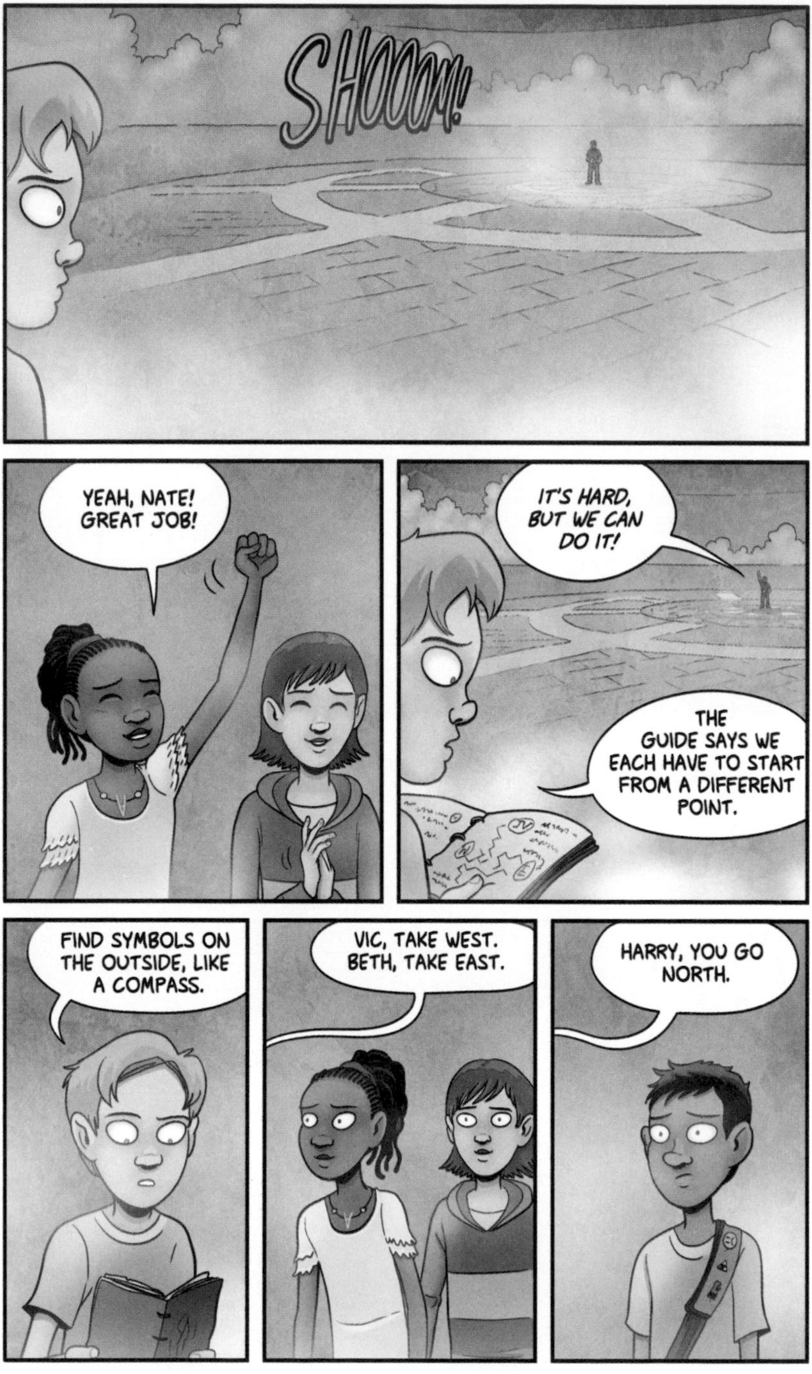
SHOOOM!
YEAH, NATE! GREAT JOB!
IT'S HARD, BUT WE CAN DO IT!
THE GUIDE SAYS WE EACH HAVE TO START FROM A DIFFERENT POINT.
FIND SYMBOLS ON THE OUTSIDE, LIKE A COMPASS.
VIC, TAKE WEST. BETH, TAKE EAST.
HARRY, YOU GO NORTH.

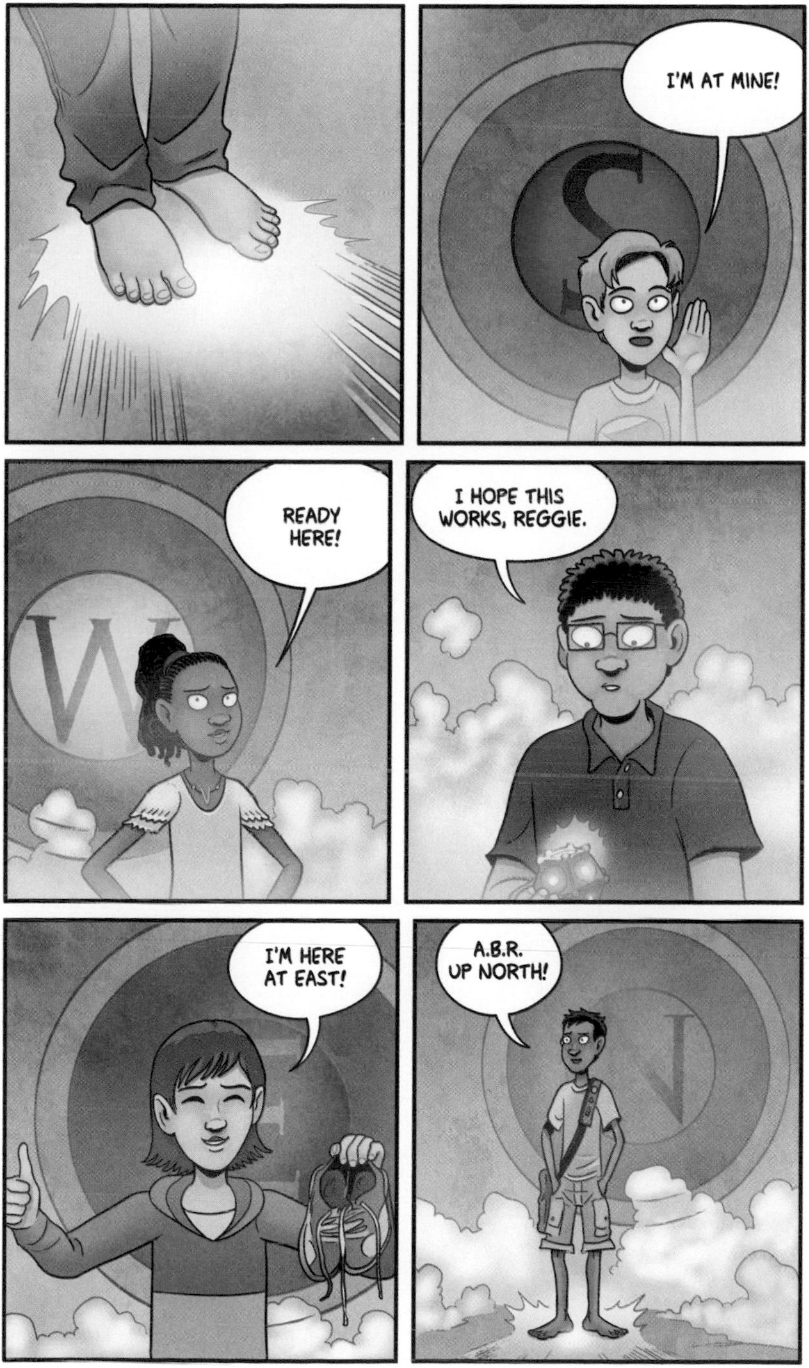
I'M AT MINE!
READY HERE!
I HOPE THIS WORKS, REGGIE.
I'M HERE AT EAST!
A.B.R. UP NORTH!

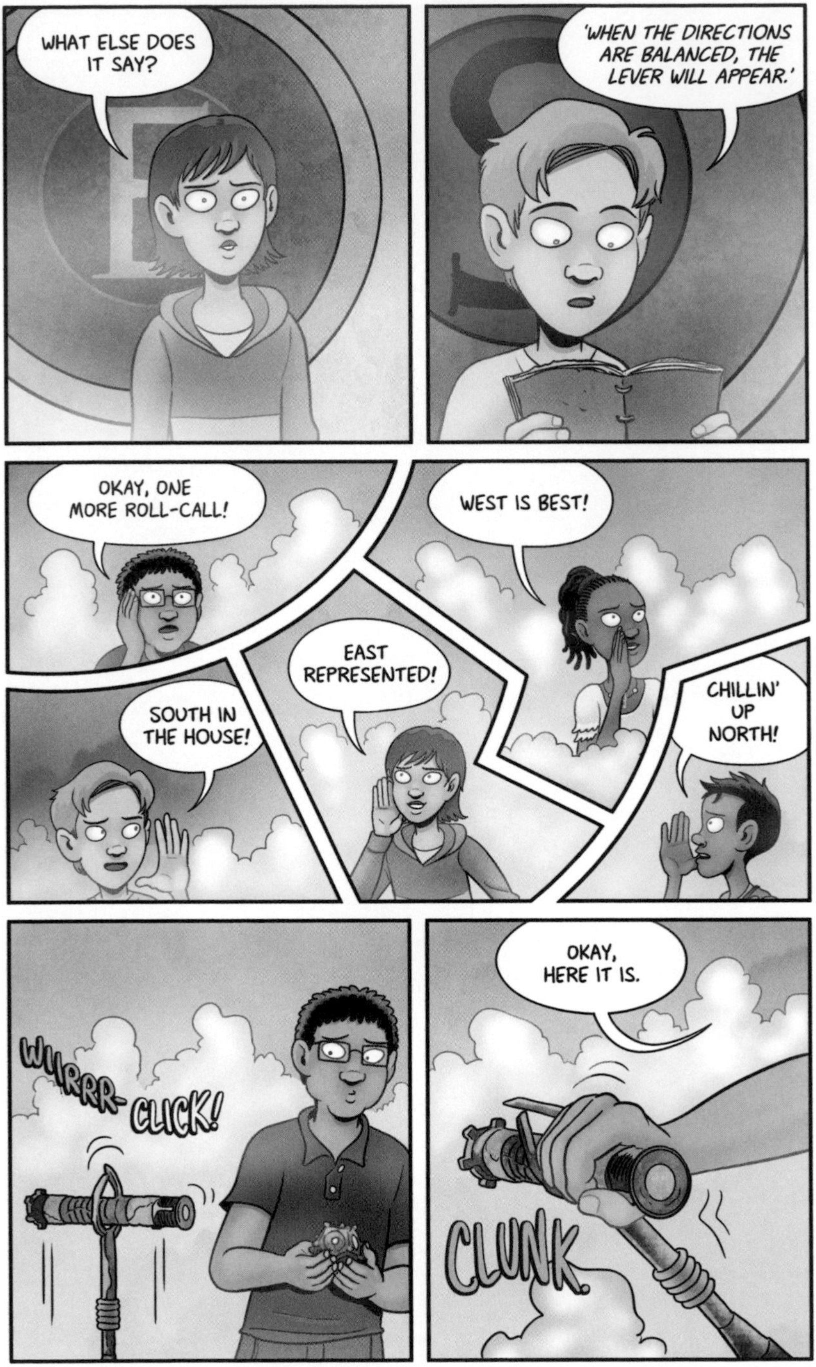
WHAT ELSE DOES IT SAY?
'WHEN THE DIRECTIONS ARE BALANCED, THE LEVER WILL APPEAR.'
OKAY, ONE MORE ROLL-CALL!
WEST IS BEST!
EAST REPRESENTED!
SOUTH IN THE HOUSE!
CHILLIN' UP NORTH!
WHIRRR-CLICK!
OKAY, HERE IT IS.
CLUNK

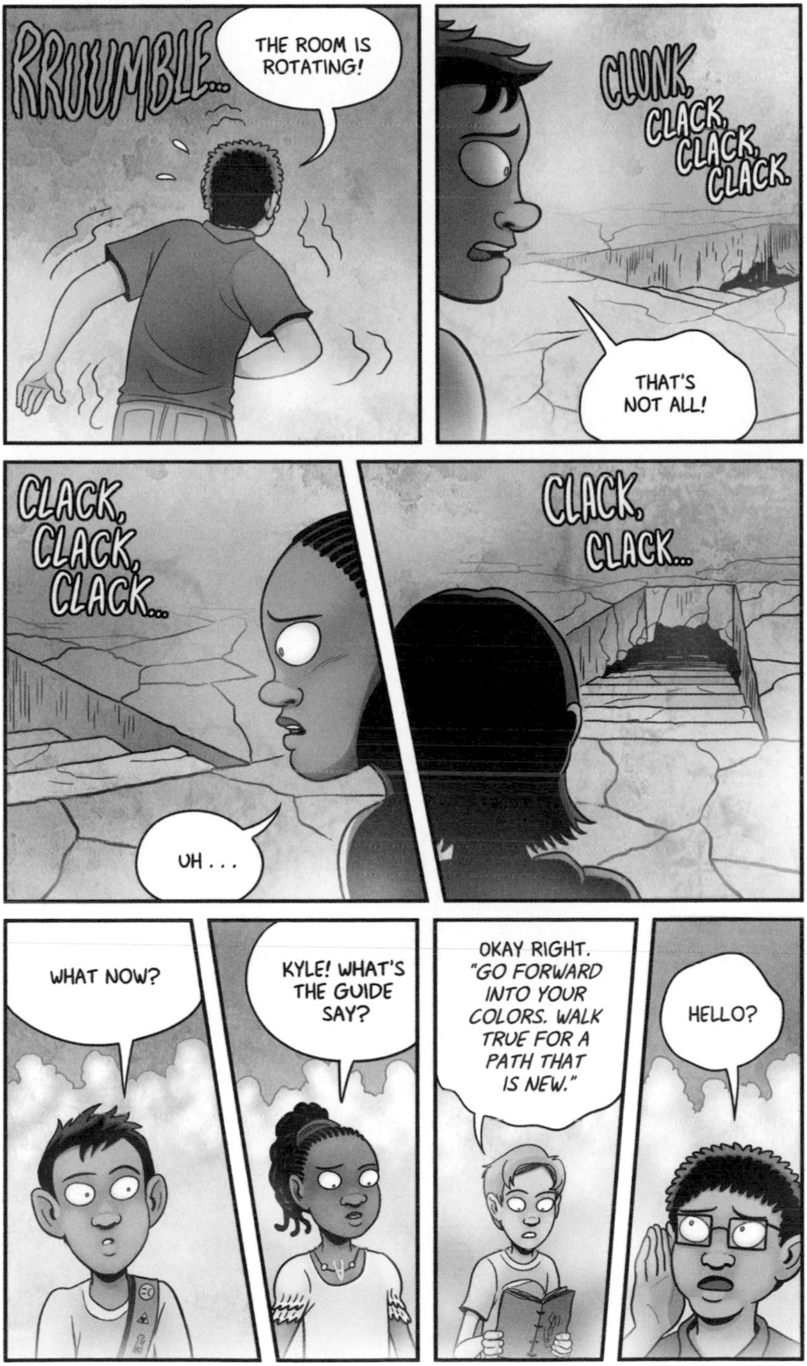
RRUUMBLE...
THE ROOM IS ROTATING!
CLUNK, CLACK, CLACK, CLACK.
THAT'S NOT ALL!
CLACK, CLACK, CLACK...
UH . . .
CLACK, CLACK...
WHAT NOW?
KYLE! WHAT'S THE GUIDE SAY?
OKAY RIGHT. *"GO FORWARD INTO YOUR COLORS. WALK TRUE FOR A PATH THAT IS NEW."*
HELLO?

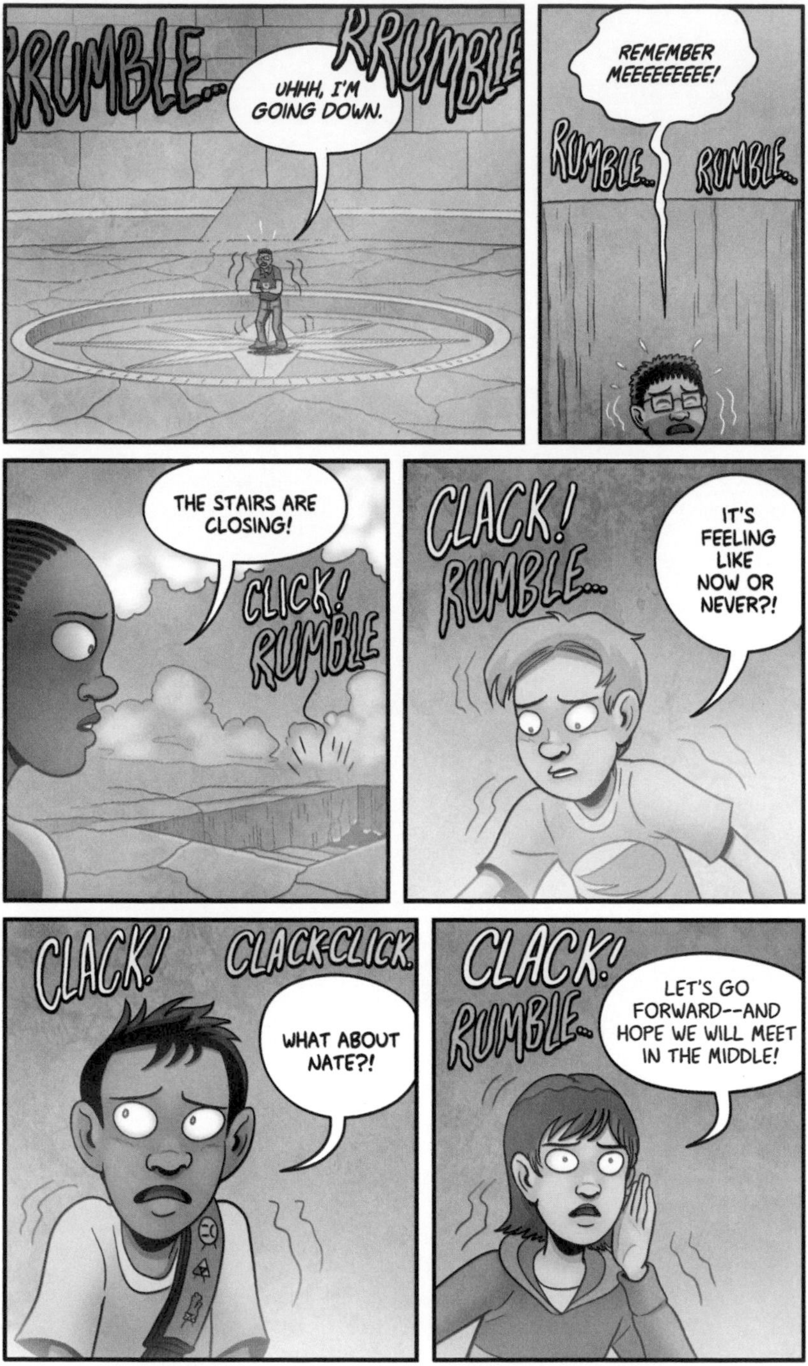
RRUMBLE...
RRUMBLE
UHHH, I'M GOING DOWN.
REMEMBER MEEEEEEEEE!
RUMBLE...
RUMBLE...
THE STAIRS ARE CLOSING!
CLICK!
RUMBLE
CLACK!
RUMBLE...
IT'S FEELING LIKE NOW OR NEVER?!
CLACK!
CLACK-CLICK.
WHAT ABOUT NATE?!
CLACK!
RUMBLE...
LET'S GO FORWARD--AND HOPE WE WILL MEET IN THE MIDDLE!

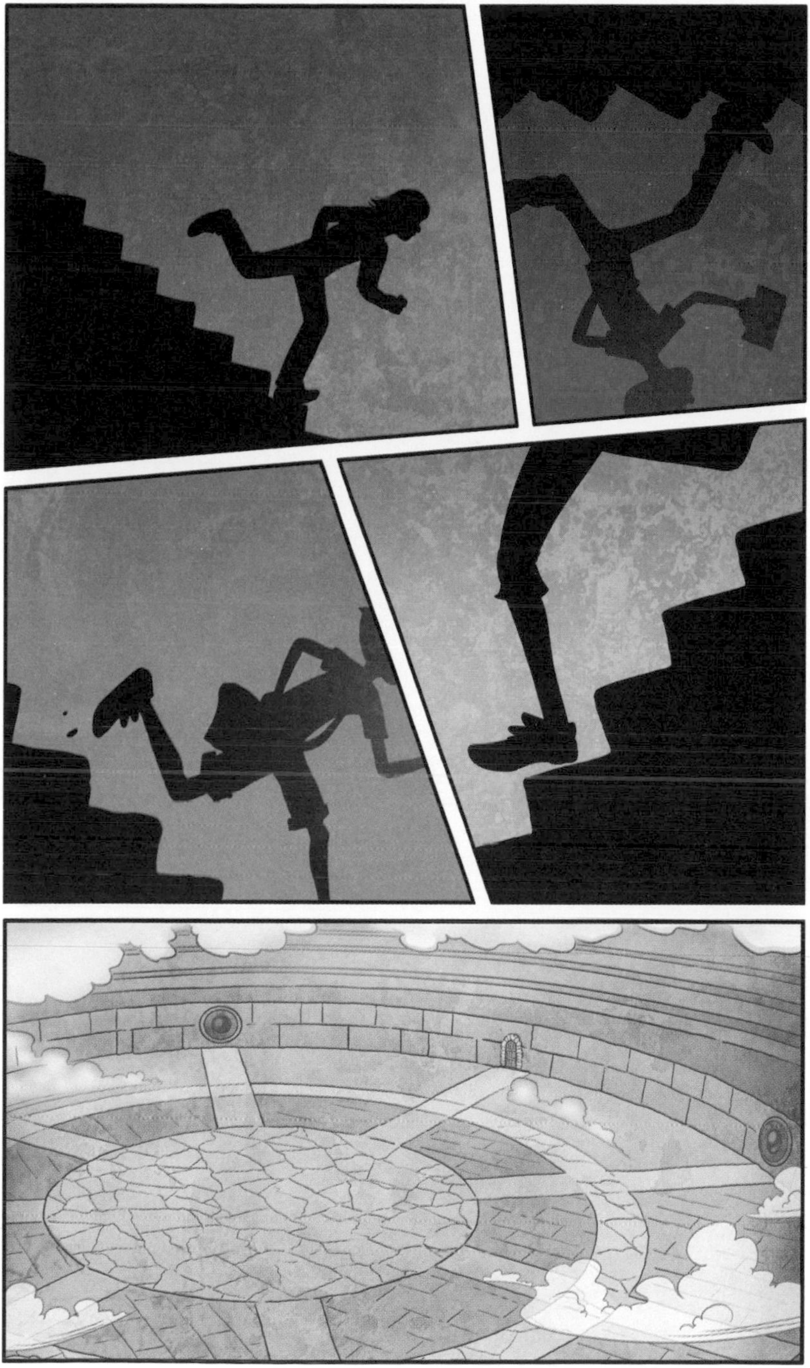

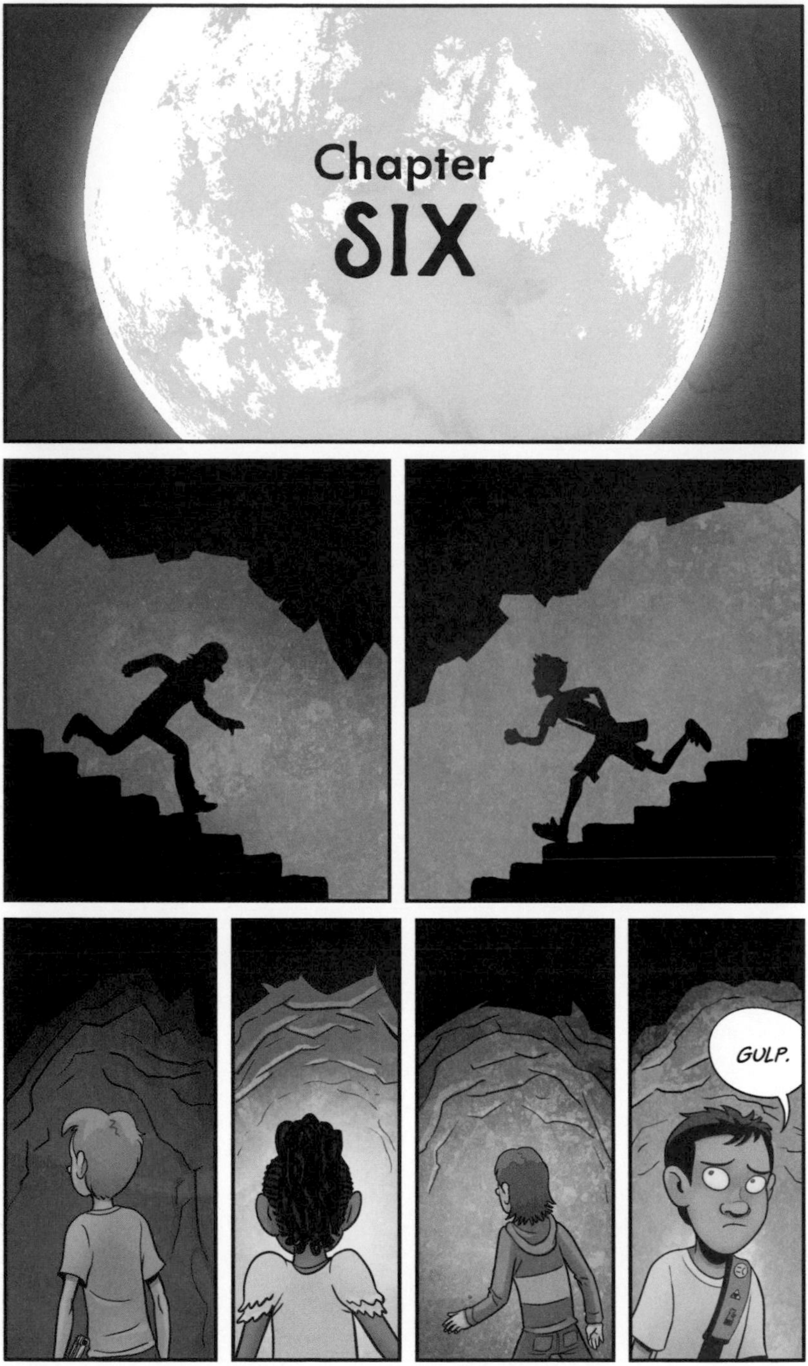
Chapter
SIX
GULP.

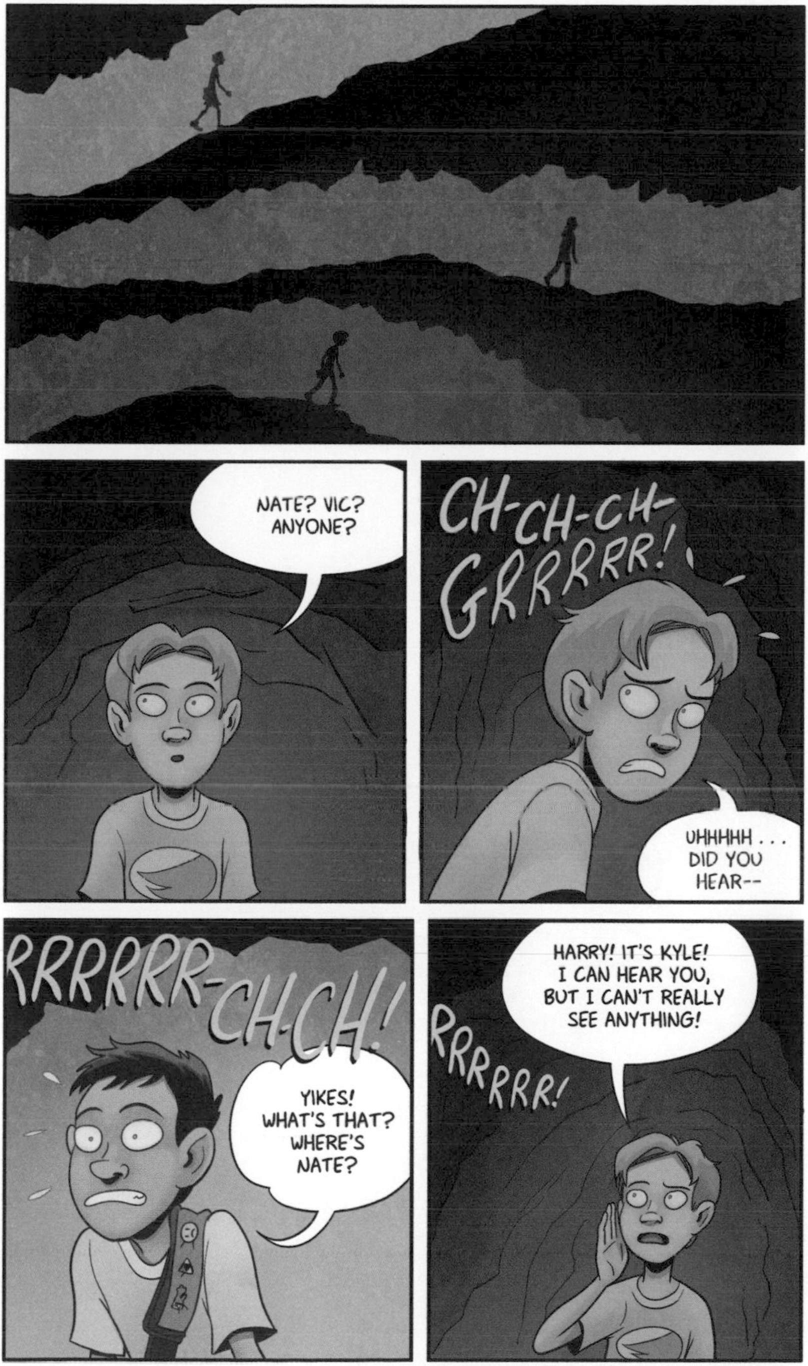
NATE? VIC? ANYONE?
CH-CH-CH-GRRRRR!
UHHHHH . . . DID YOU HEAR--
RRRRRR-CH-CH!
YIKES! WHAT'S THAT? WHERE'S NATE?
HARRY! IT'S KYLE! I CAN HEAR YOU, BUT I CAN'T REALLY SEE ANYTHING!
RRRRRR!

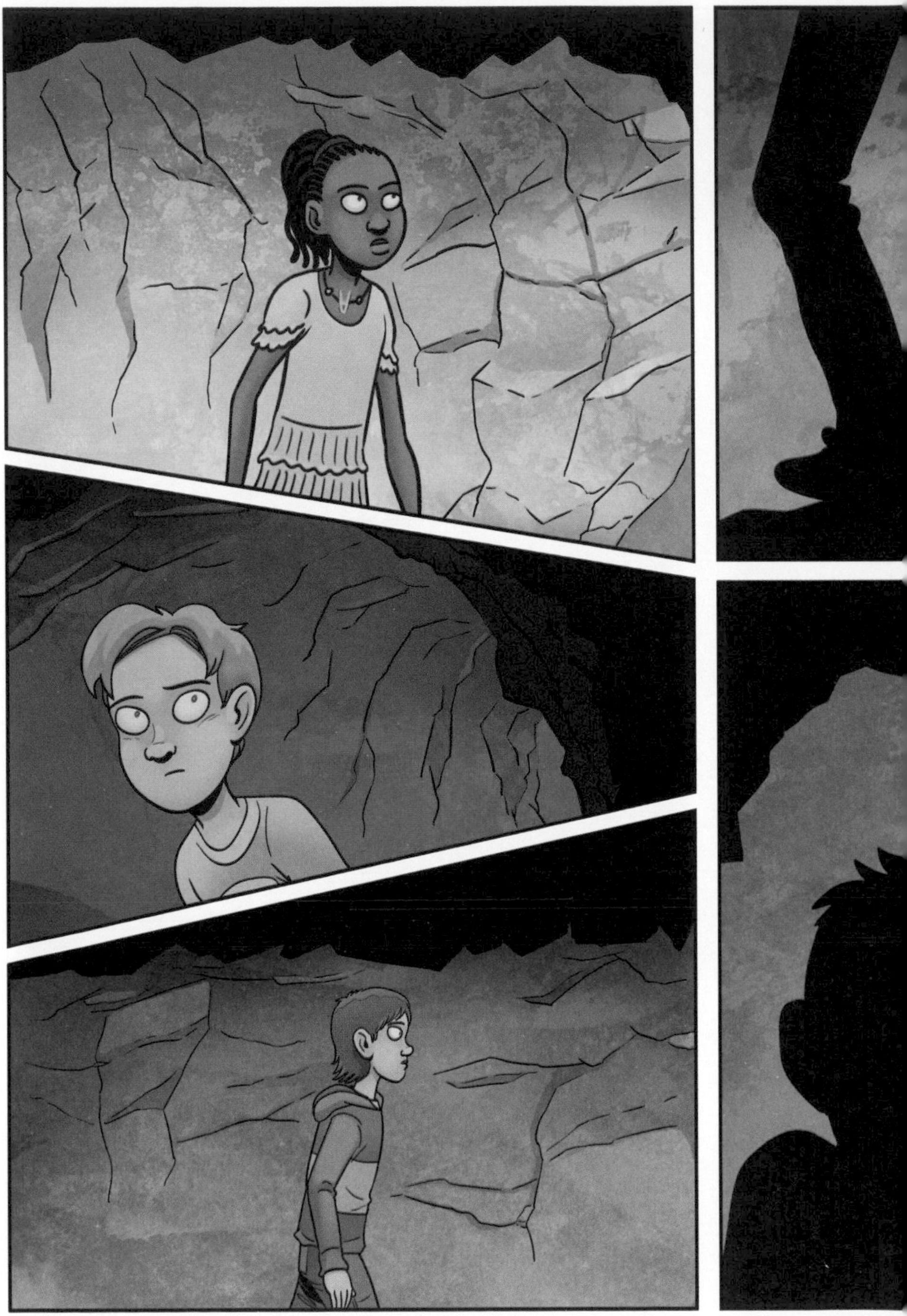

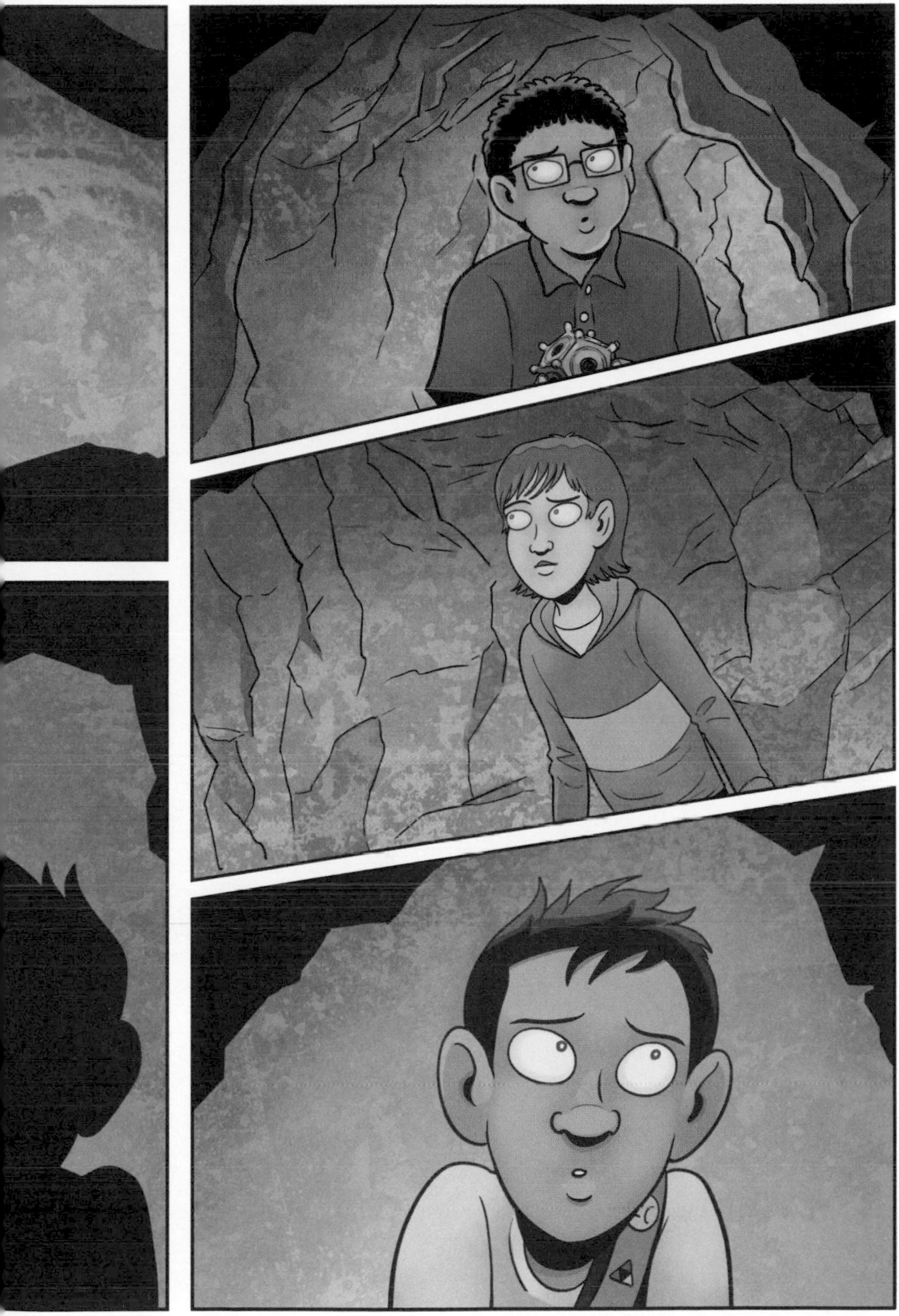

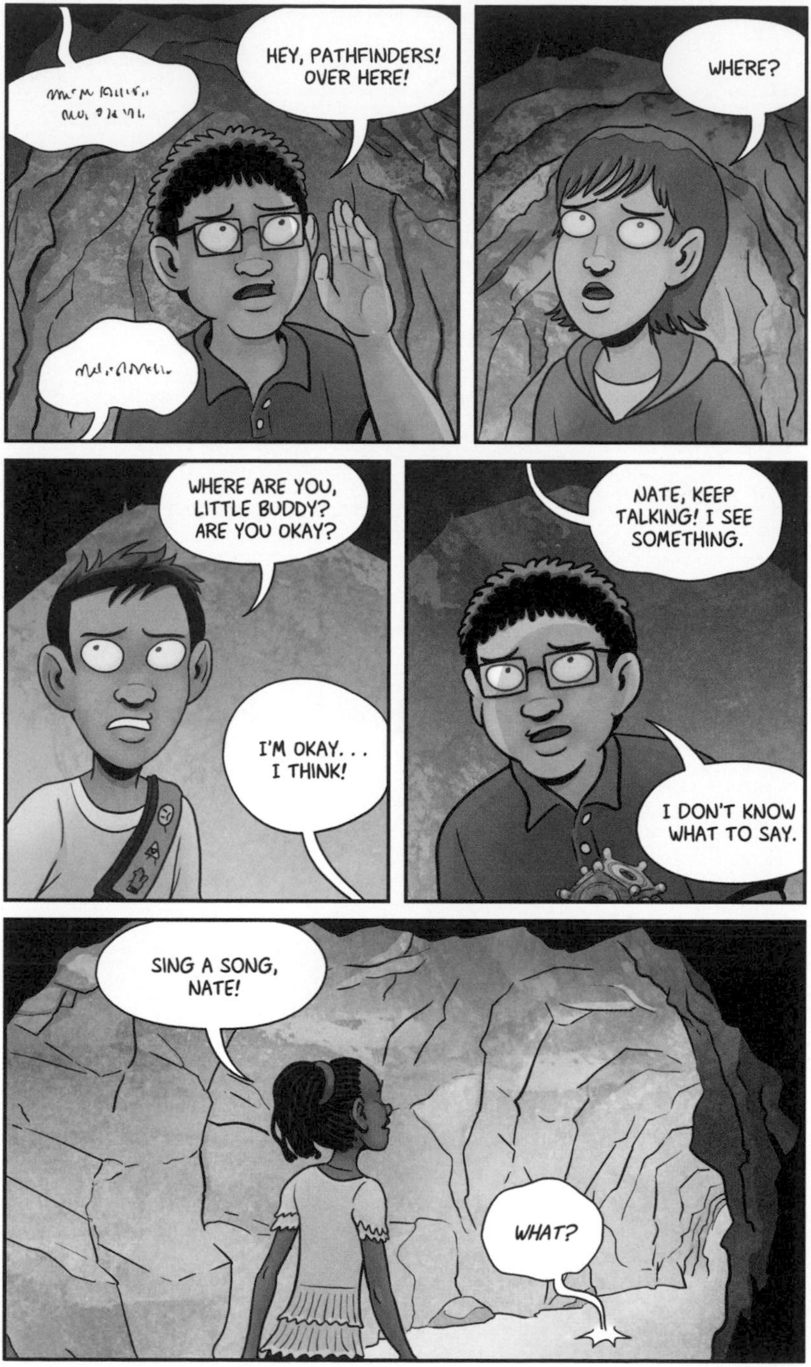
HEY, PATHFINDERS! OVER HERE!
WHERE?
WHERE ARE YOU, LITTLE BUDDY? ARE YOU OKAY?
I'M OKAY. . . I THINK!
NATE, KEEP TALKING! I SEE SOMETHING.
I DON'T KNOW WHAT TO SAY.
SING A SONG, NATE!
WHAT?

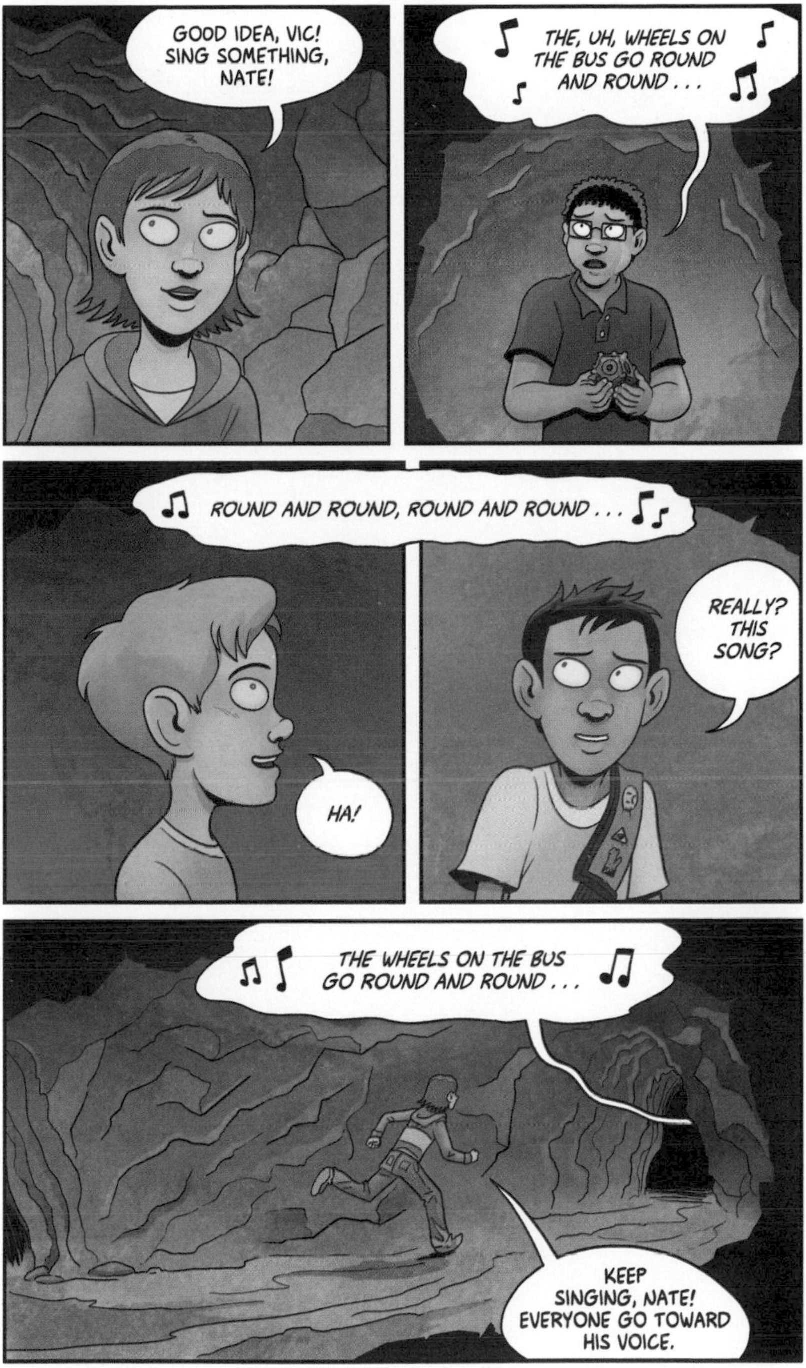
GOOD IDEA, VIC! SING SOMETHING, NATE!
THE, UH, WHEELS ON THE BUS GO ROUND AND ROUND . . .
ROUND AND ROUND, ROUND AND ROUND . . .
HA!
REALLY? THIS SONG?
THE WHEELS ON THE BUS GO ROUND AND ROUND . . .
KEEP SINGING, NATE! EVERYONE GO TOWARD HIS VOICE.

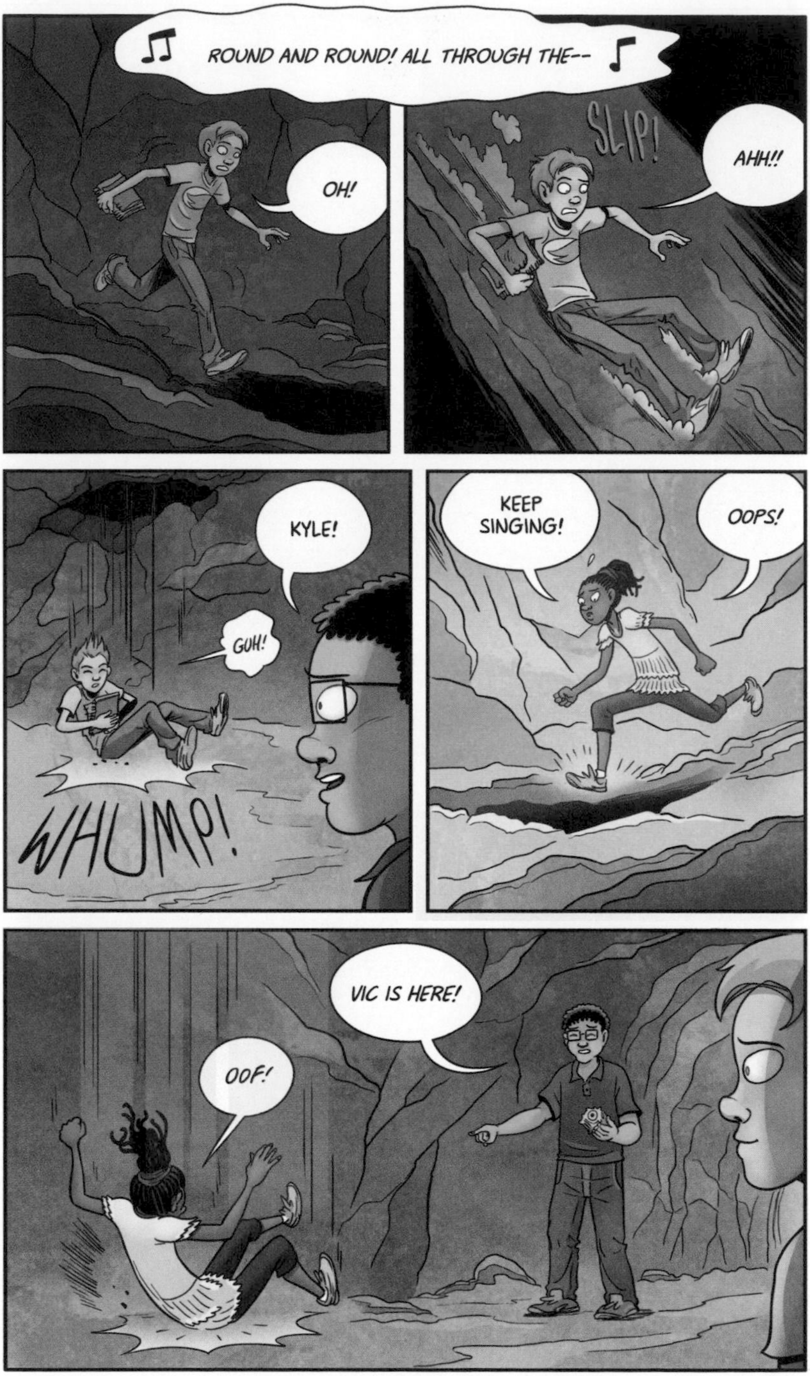
ROUND AND ROUND! ALL THROUGH THE--
OH!
SLIP!
AHH!!
KYLE!
GUH!
WHUMP!
KEEP SINGING!
OOPS!
VIC IS HERE!
OOF!

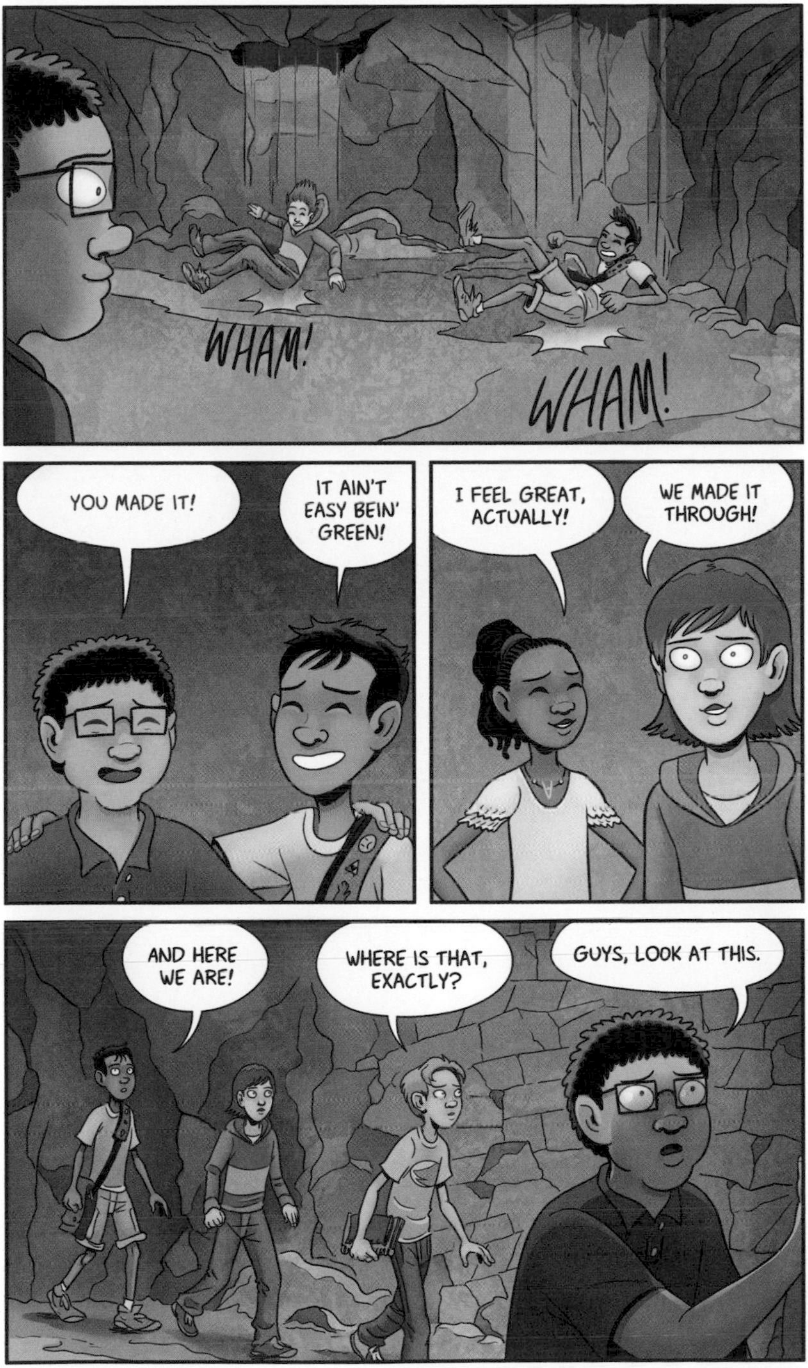
WHAM!
WHAM!
YOU MADE IT!
IT AIN'T EASY BEIN' GREEN!
I FEEL GREAT, ACTUALLY!
WE MADE IT THROUGH!
AND HERE WE ARE!
WHERE IS THAT, EXACTLY?
GUYS, LOOK AT THIS.

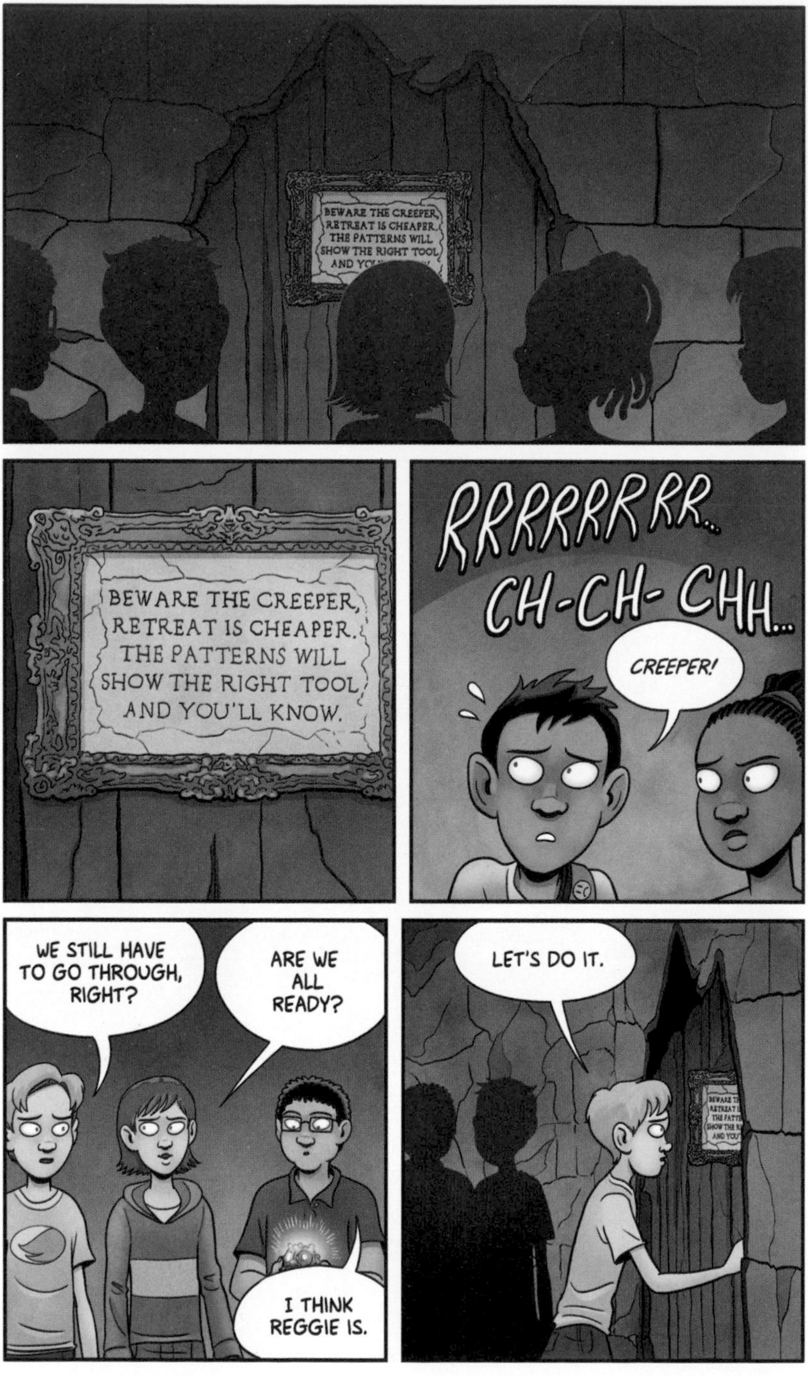
BEWARE THE CREEPER,
RETREAT IS CHEAPER.
THE PATTERNS WILL
SHOW THE RIGHT TOOL
AND YOU'LL KNOW.
RRRRRRRR...
CH-CH- CHH...
CREEPER!
WE STILL HAVE TO GO THROUGH, RIGHT?
ARE WE ALL READY?
I THINK REGGIE IS.
LET'S DO IT.

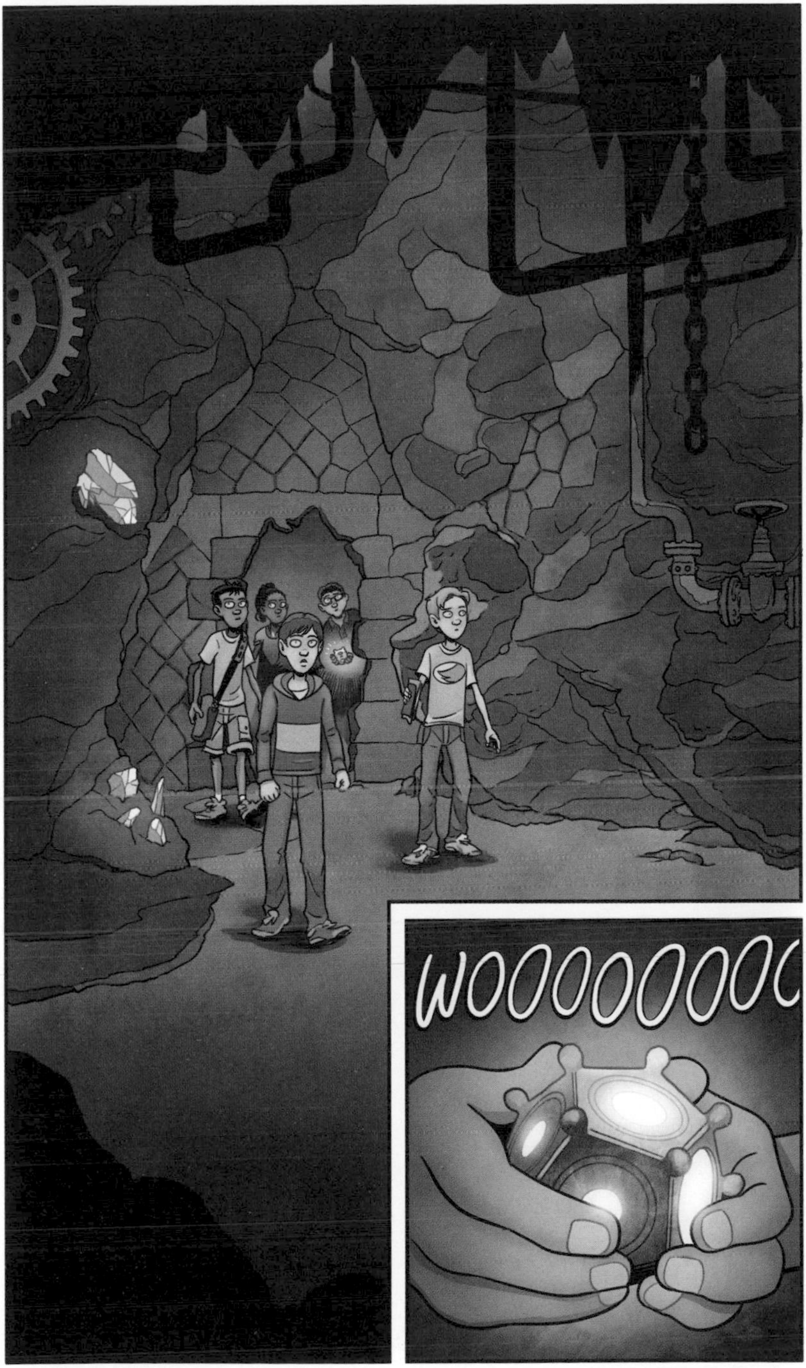
WOOOOOOOO

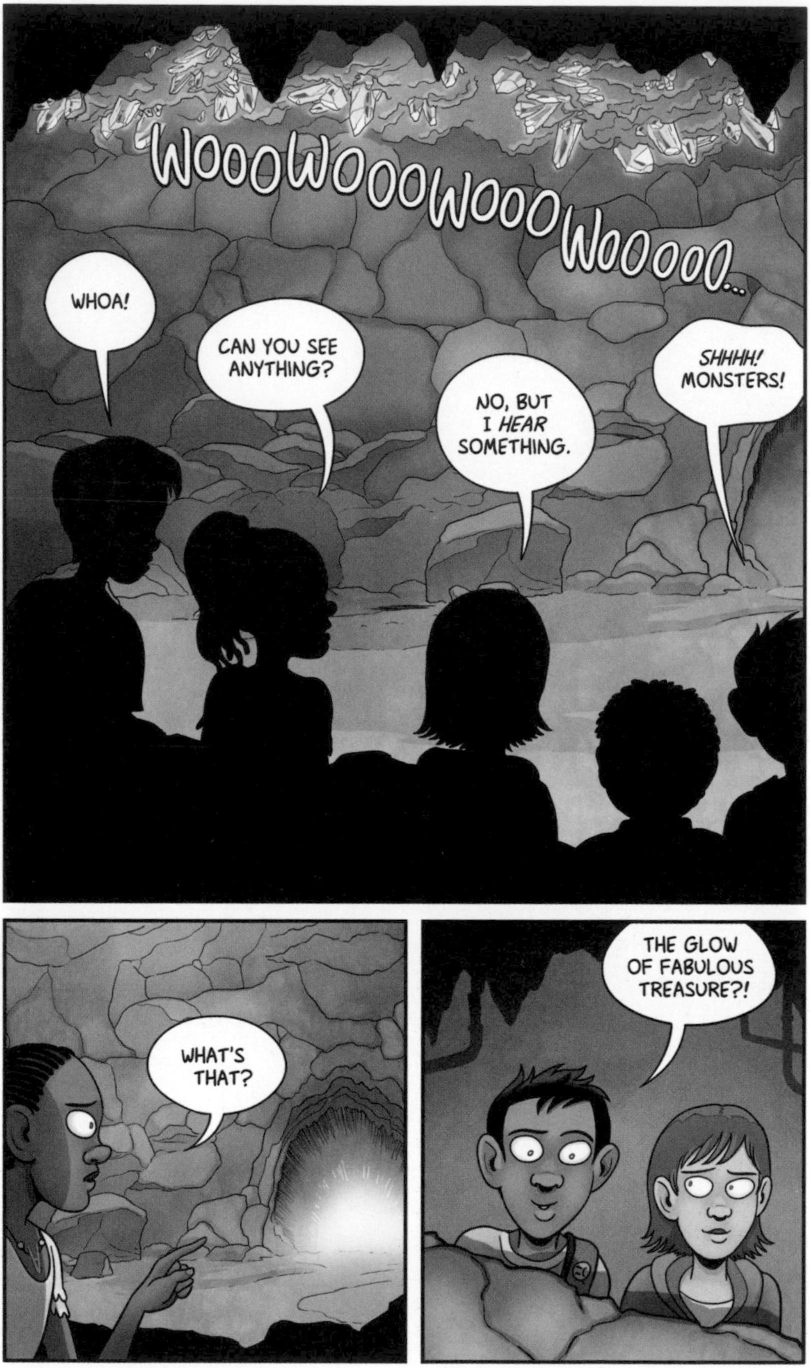
WOOOWOOOWOOOWOOOOO...
WHOA!
CAN YOU SEE ANYTHING?
NO, BUT I *HEAR* SOMETHING.
SHHHH! MONSTERS!
WHAT'S THAT?
THE GLOW OF FABULOUS TREASURE?!

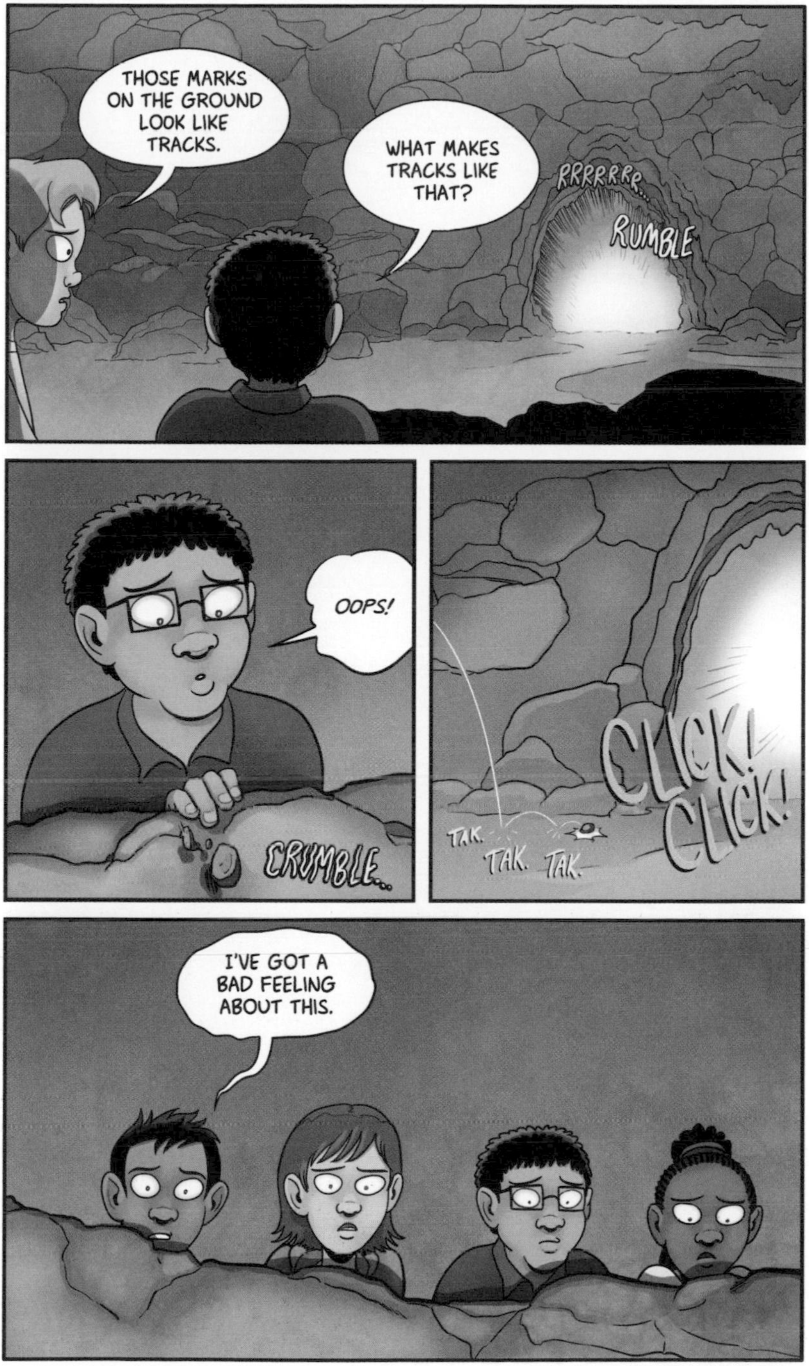
THOSE MARKS ON THE GROUND LOOK LIKE TRACKS.
WHAT MAKES TRACKS LIKE THAT?
RRRRRRR...
RUMBLE
OOPS!
CRUMBLE...
TAK. TAK. TAK.
CLICK! CLICK!
I'VE GOT A BAD FEELING ABOUT THIS.

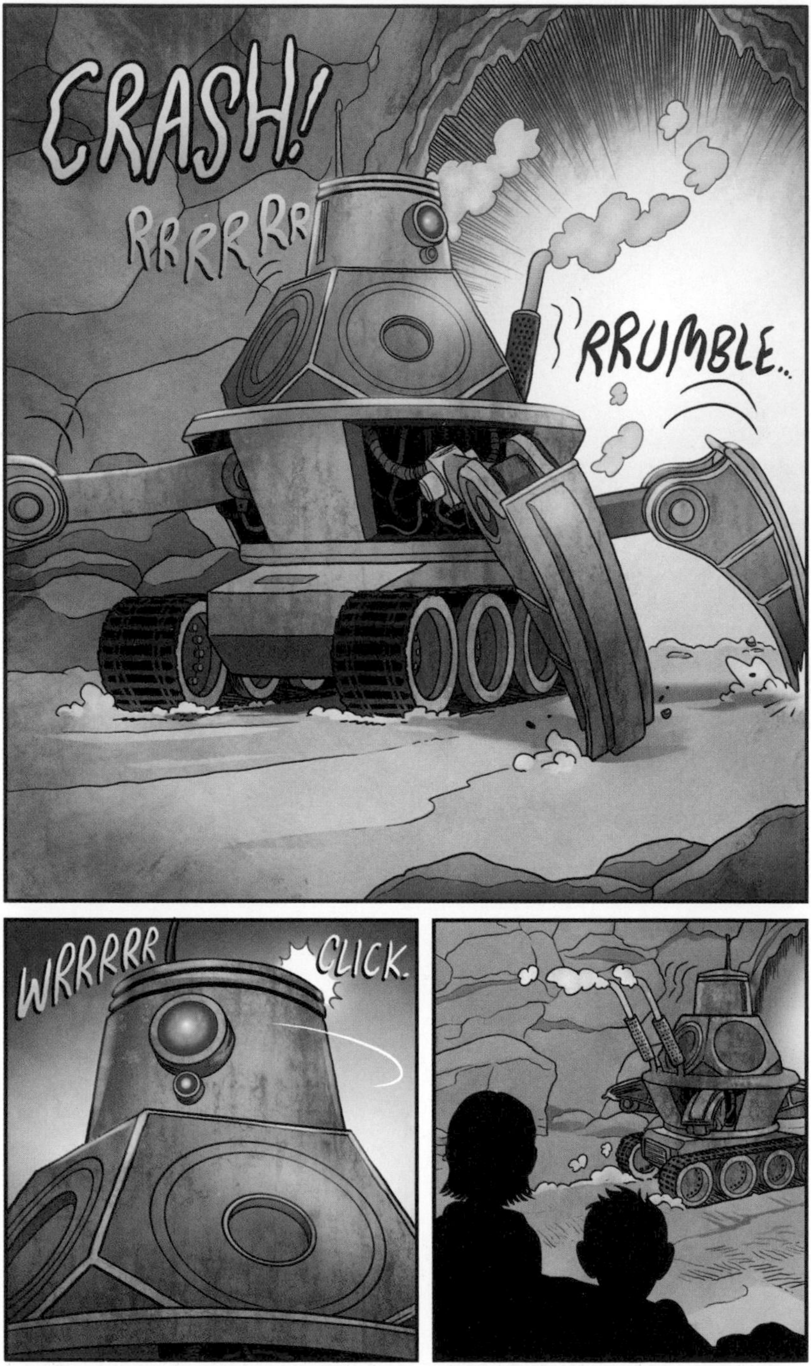
CRASH!
RRRRRR
RRUMBLE...
WRRRRR
CLICK.

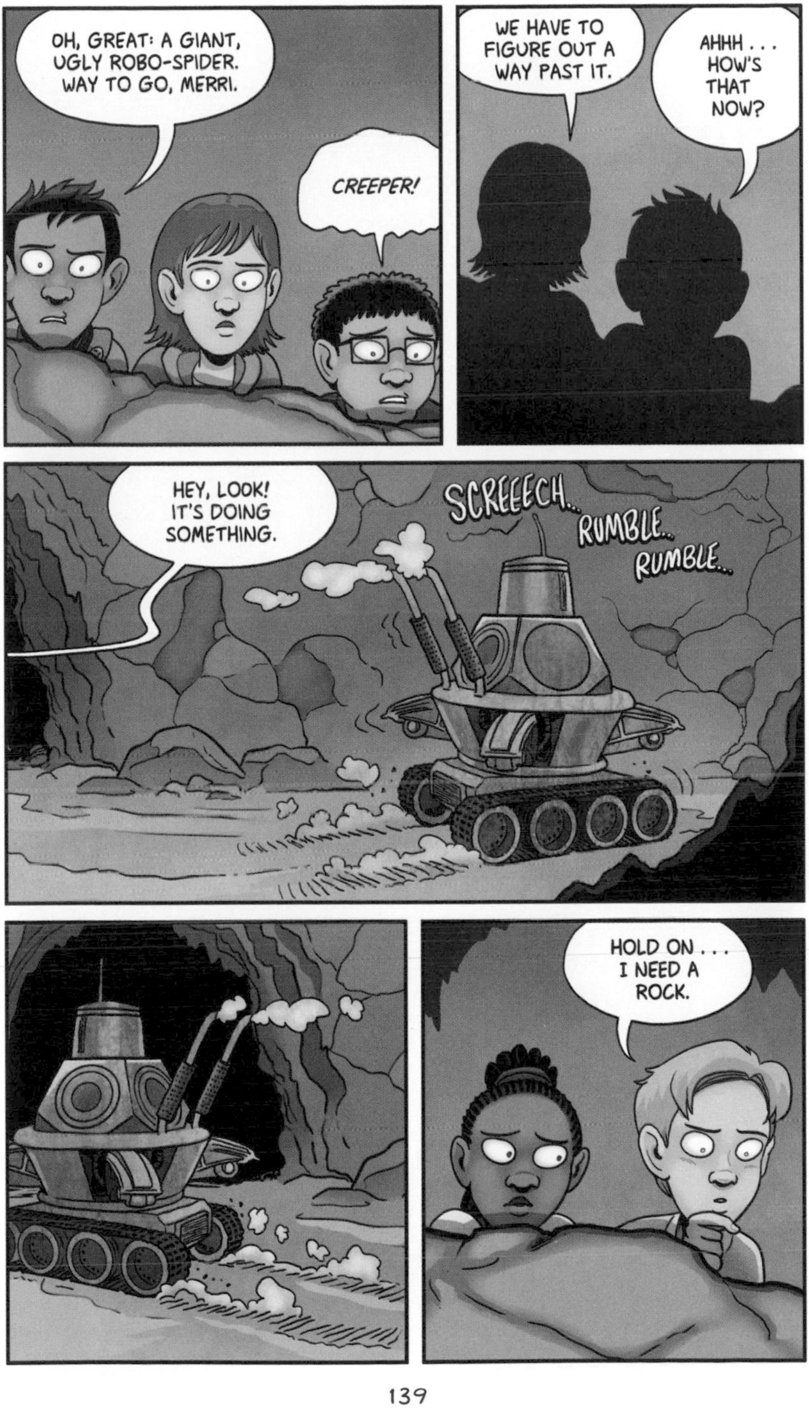
OH, GREAT: A GIANT, UGLY ROBO-SPIDER. WAY TO GO, MERRI.
CREEPER!
WE HAVE TO FIGURE OUT A WAY PAST IT.
AHHH . . . HOW'S THAT NOW?
HEY, LOOK! IT'S DOING SOMETHING.
SCREEECH...
RUMBLE...
RUMBLE...
HOLD ON . . . I NEED A ROCK.

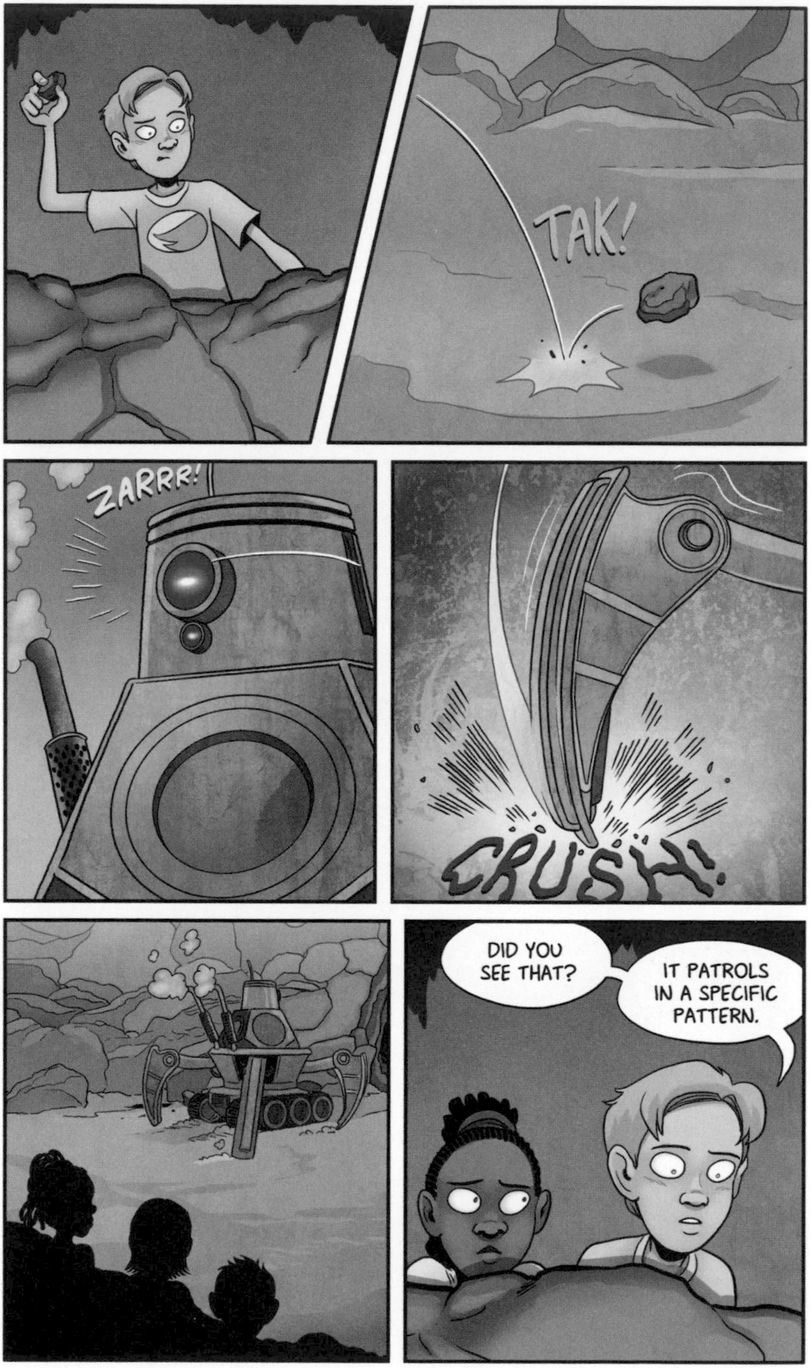
TAK!
ZARRR!
CRUSH!
DID YOU SEE THAT?
IT PATROLS IN A SPECIFIC PATTERN.

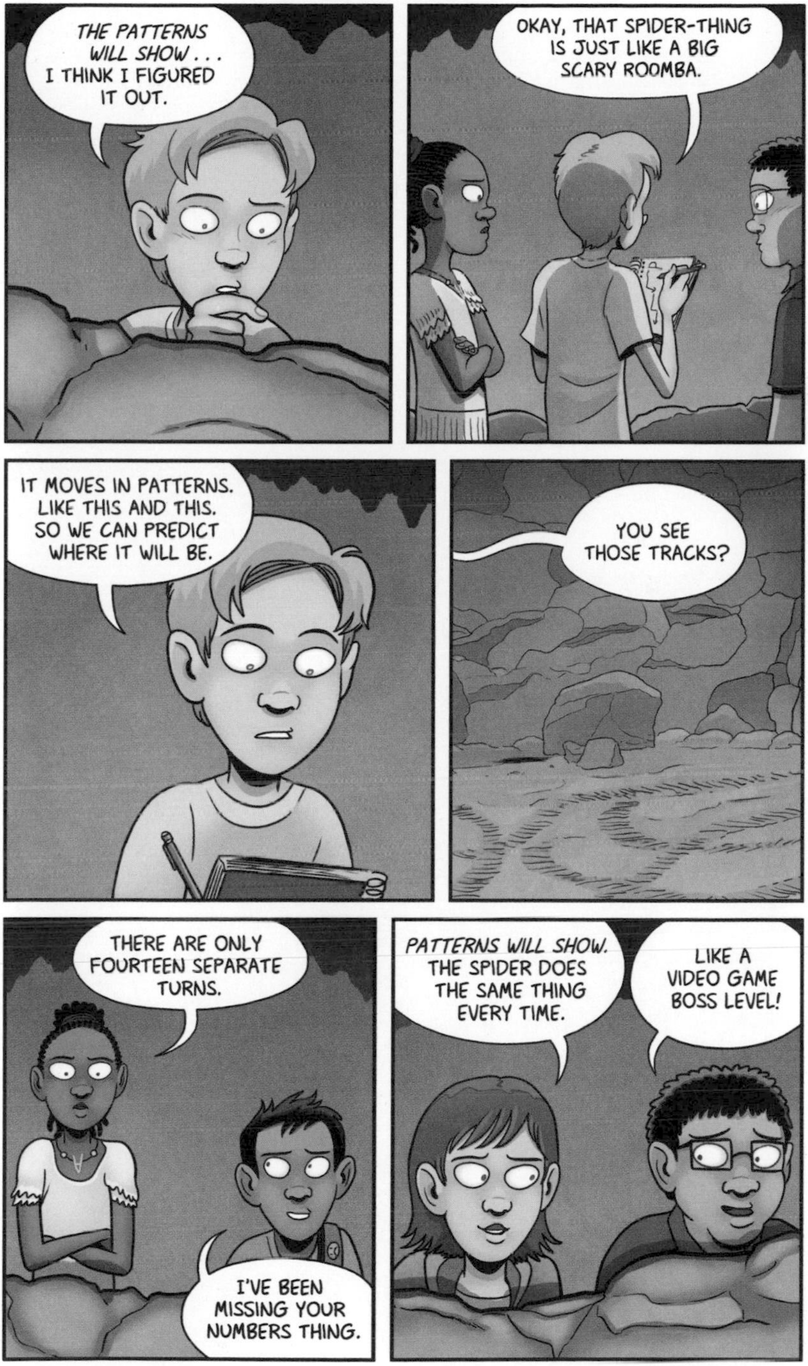
THE PATTERNS WILL SHOW . . . I THINK I FIGURED IT OUT.
OKAY, THAT SPIDER-THING IS JUST LIKE A BIG SCARY ROOMBA.
IT MOVES IN PATTERNS. LIKE THIS AND THIS. SO WE CAN PREDICT WHERE IT WILL BE.
YOU SEE THOSE TRACKS?
THERE ARE ONLY FOURTEEN SEPARATE TURNS.
I'VE BEEN MISSING YOUR NUMBERS THING.
PATTERNS WILL SHOW. THE SPIDER DOES THE SAME THING EVERY TIME.
LIKE A VIDEO GAME BOSS LEVEL!

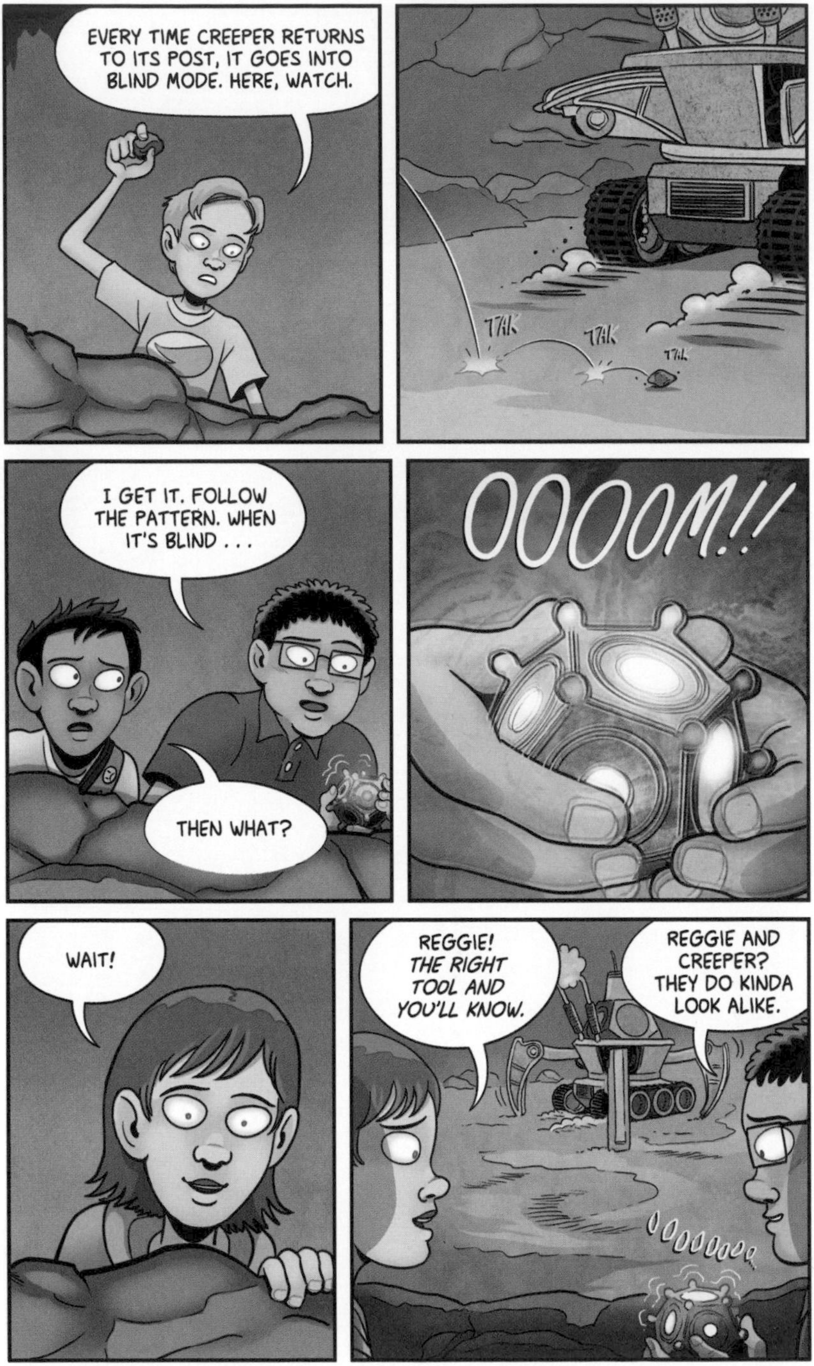
EVERY TIME CREEPER RETURNS TO ITS POST, IT GOES INTO BLIND MODE. HERE, WATCH.
TAK
TAK
TAK
I GET IT. FOLLOW THE PATTERN. WHEN IT'S BLIND . . .
THEN WHAT?
OOOOM!!
WAIT!
REGGIE! *THE RIGHT TOOL AND YOU'LL KNOW.*
REGGIE AND CREEPER? THEY DO KINDA LOOK ALIKE.
OOOOOOOO

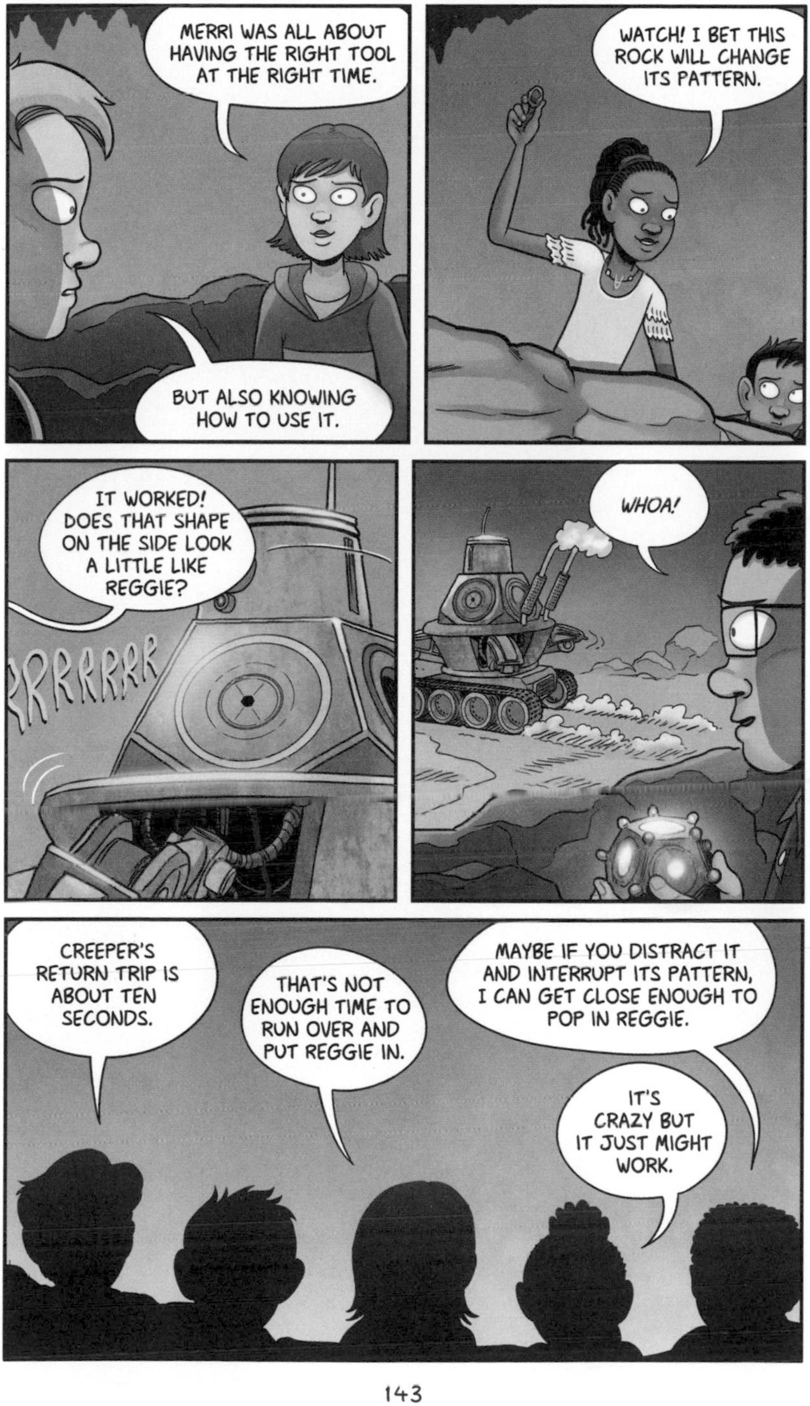
MERRI WAS ALL ABOUT HAVING THE RIGHT TOOL AT THE RIGHT TIME.
BUT ALSO KNOWING HOW TO USE IT.
WATCH! I BET THIS ROCK WILL CHANGE ITS PATTERN.
IT WORKED! DOES THAT SHAPE ON THE SIDE LOOK A LITTLE LIKE REGGIE?
RRRRRRR
WHOA!
CREEPER'S RETURN TRIP IS ABOUT TEN SECONDS.
THAT'S NOT ENOUGH TIME TO RUN OVER AND PUT REGGIE IN.
MAYBE IF YOU DISTRACT IT AND INTERRUPT ITS PATTERN, I CAN GET CLOSE ENOUGH TO POP IN REGGIE.
IT'S CRAZY BUT IT JUST MIGHT WORK.

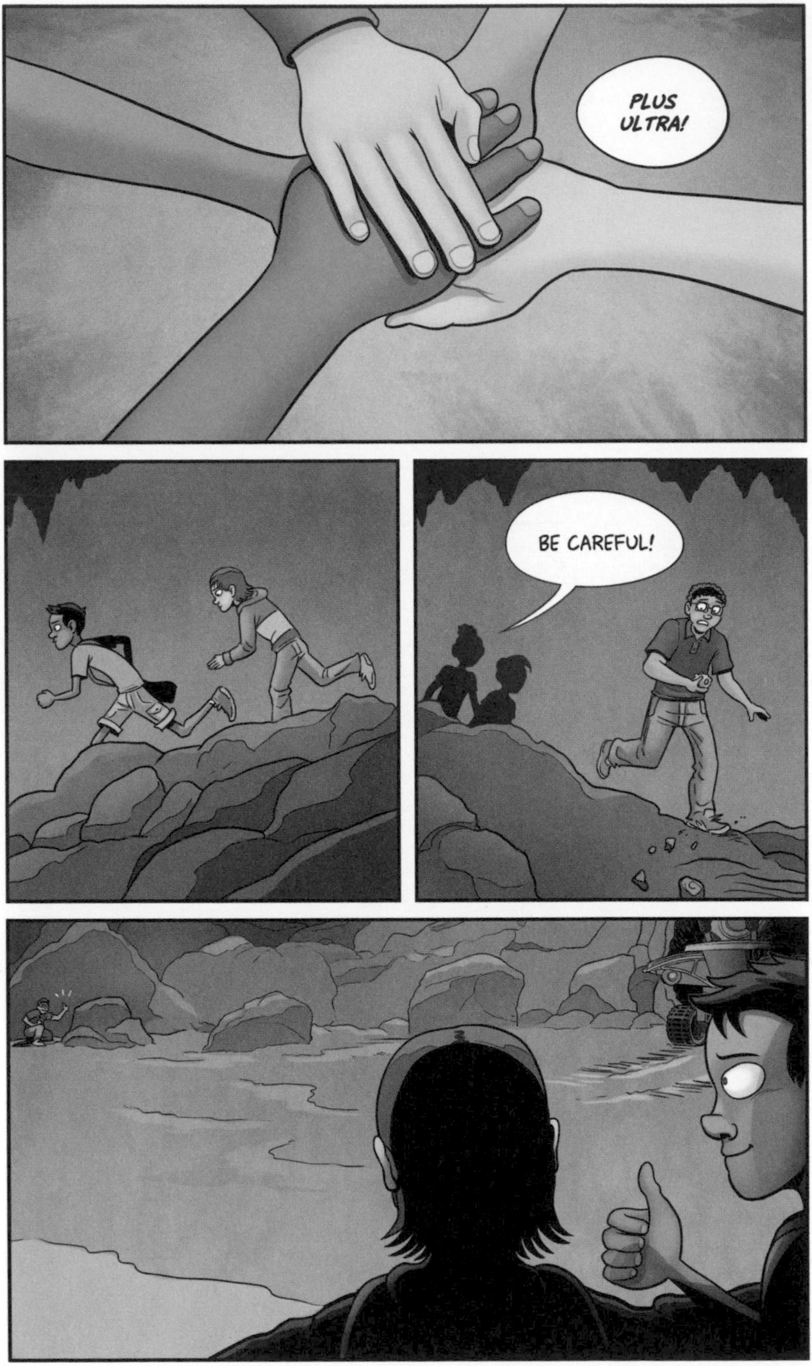
PLUS ULTRA!
BE CAREFUL!

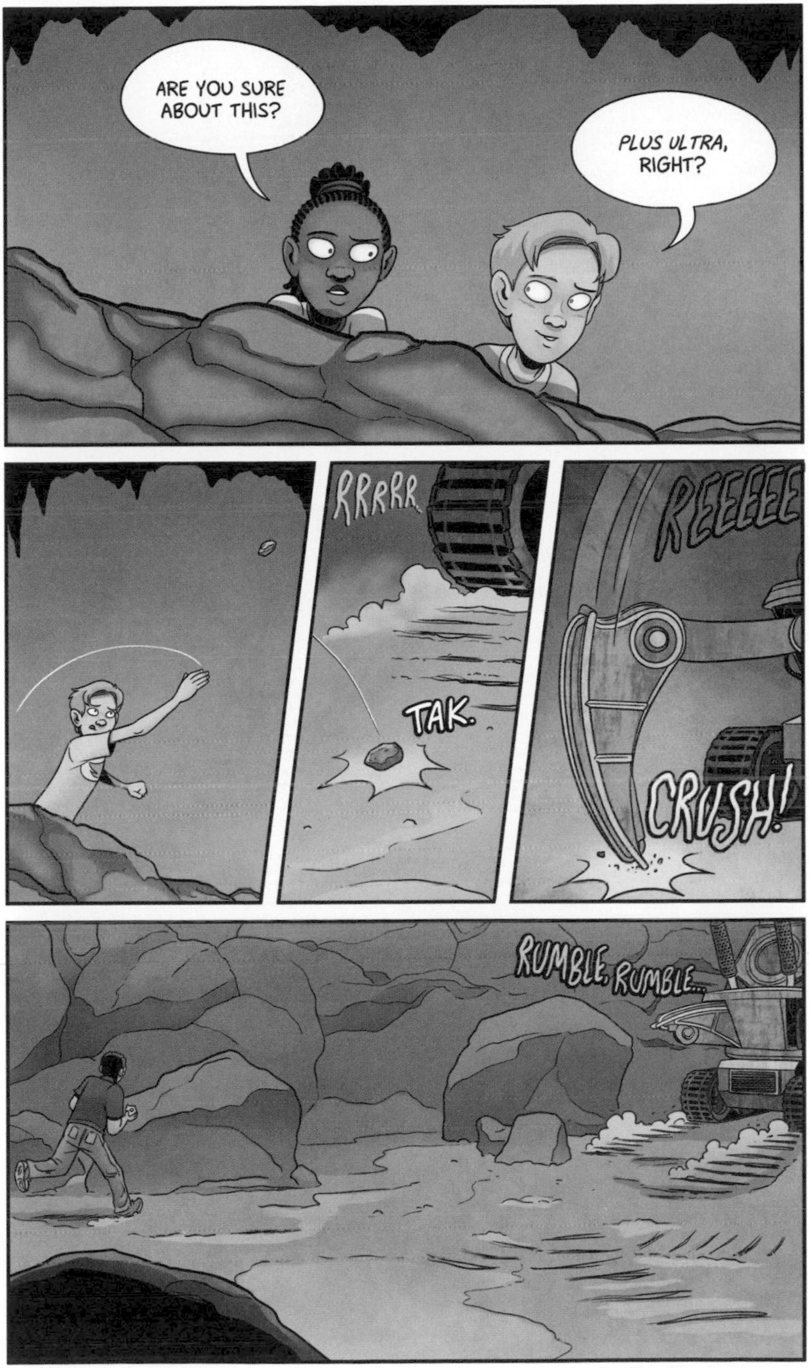
ARE YOU SURE ABOUT THIS?
PLUS ULTRA, RIGHT?
RRRRR
TAK.
REEEEE
CRUSH!
RUMBLE, RUMBLE...

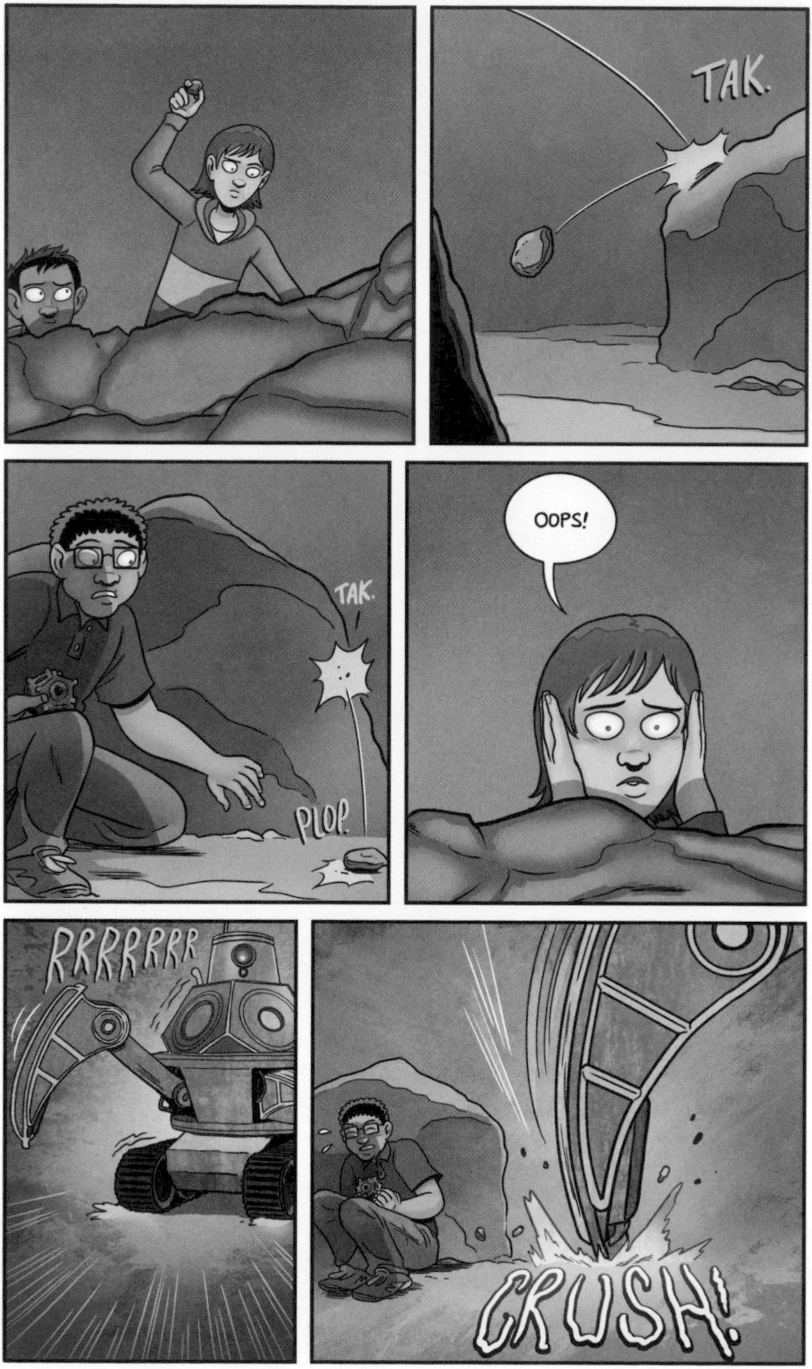
TAK.
TAK.
PLOP.
OOPS!
RRRRRRR
CRUSH!

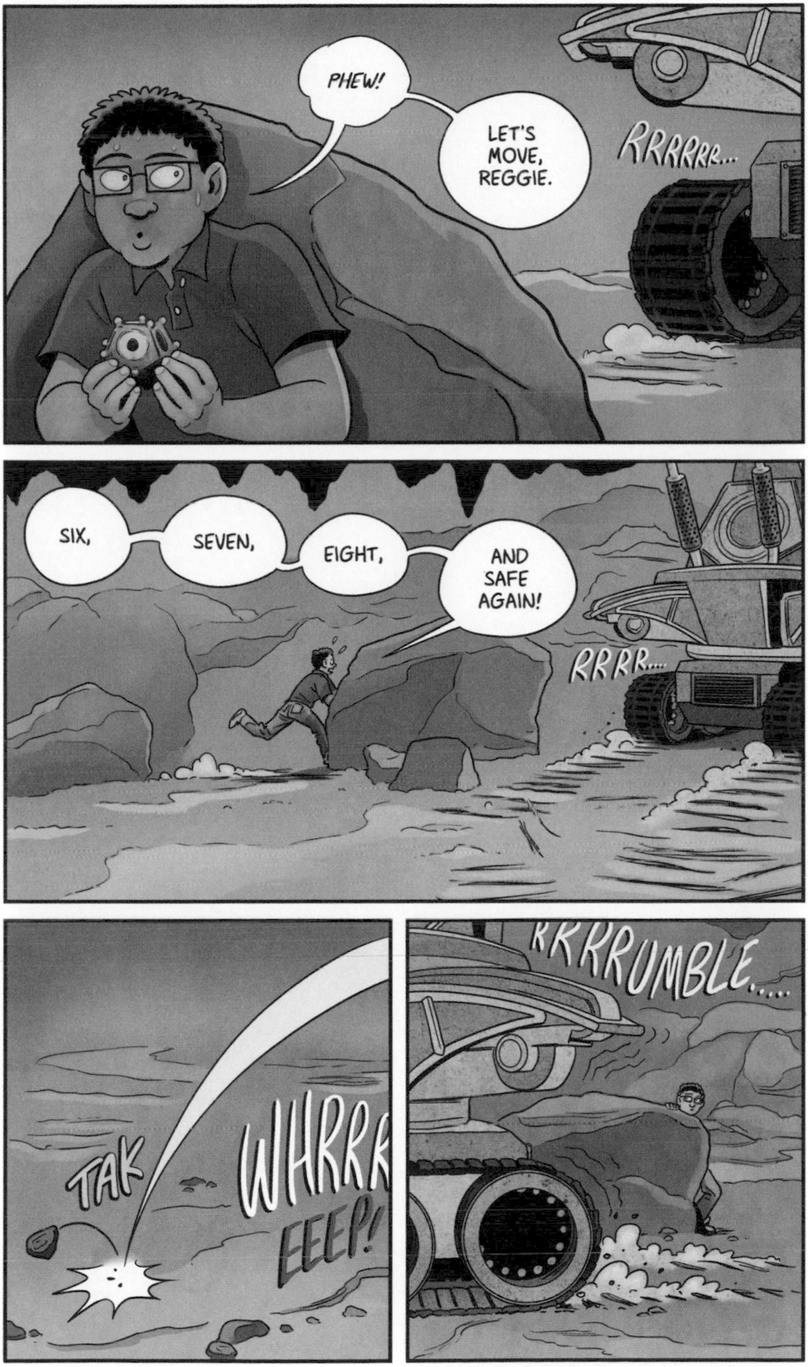
PHEW!
LET'S MOVE, REGGIE.
RRRRRR...
SIX,
SEVEN,
EIGHT,
AND SAFE AGAIN!
RRRR...
TAK
WHRRR
EEEP!
RRRRUMBLE.....

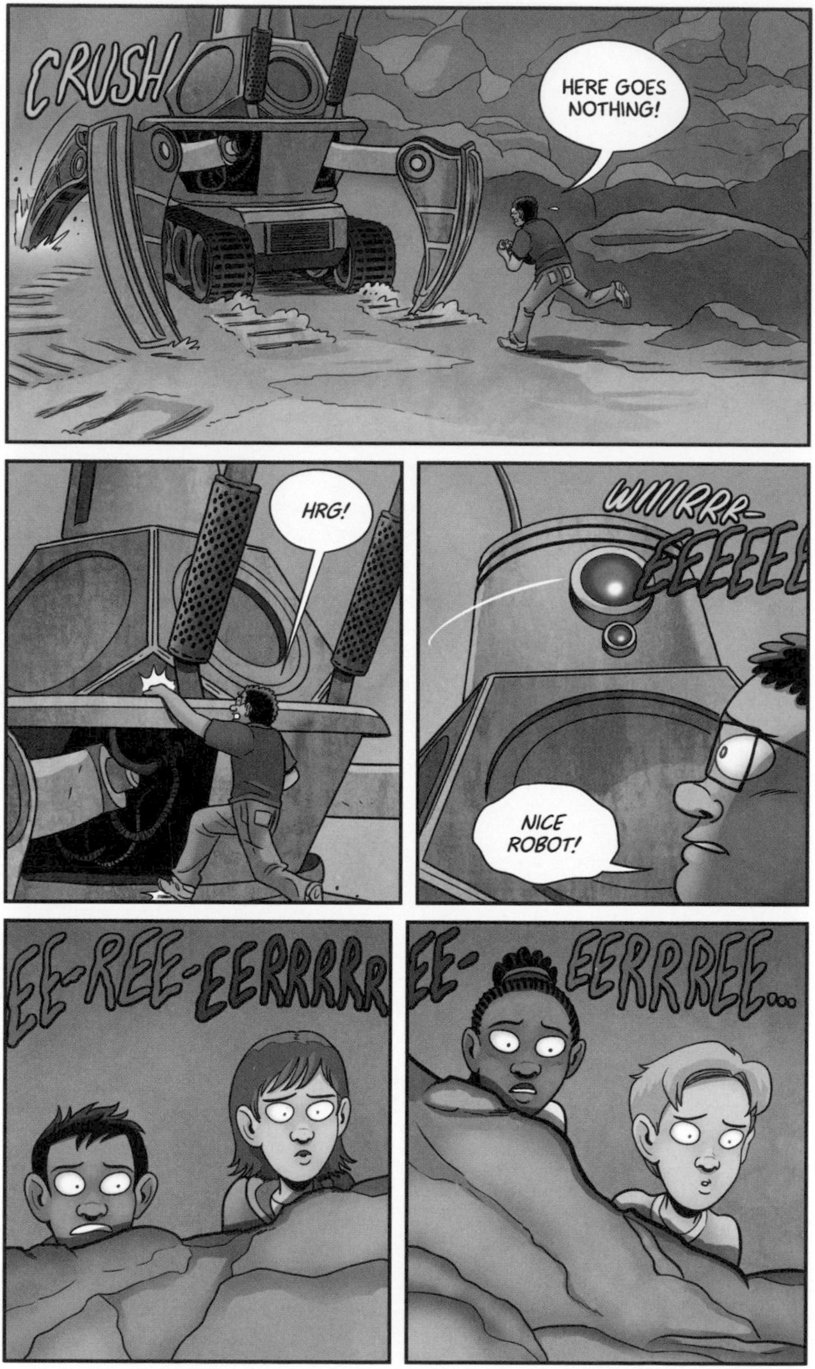
CRUSH
HERE GOES NOTHING!
HRG!
WWIIRRR-
EEEEEE
NICE ROBOT!
EE-REE-EERRRRR
EE-
EERRREE...

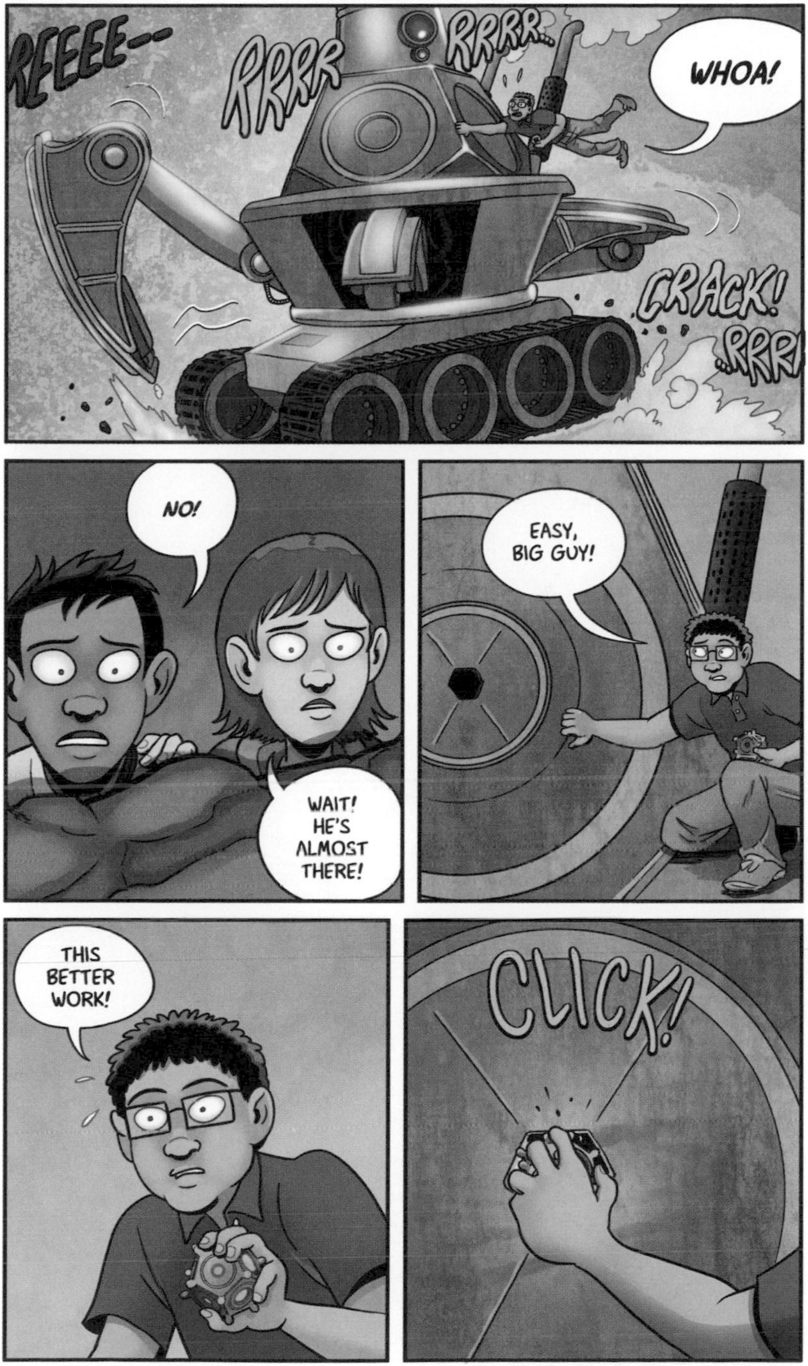
REEEE--
RRRR
RRRR...
WHOA!
CRACK!
...RRR
NO!
WAIT! HE'S ALMOST THERE!
EASY, BIG GUY!
THIS BETTER WORK!
CLICK!

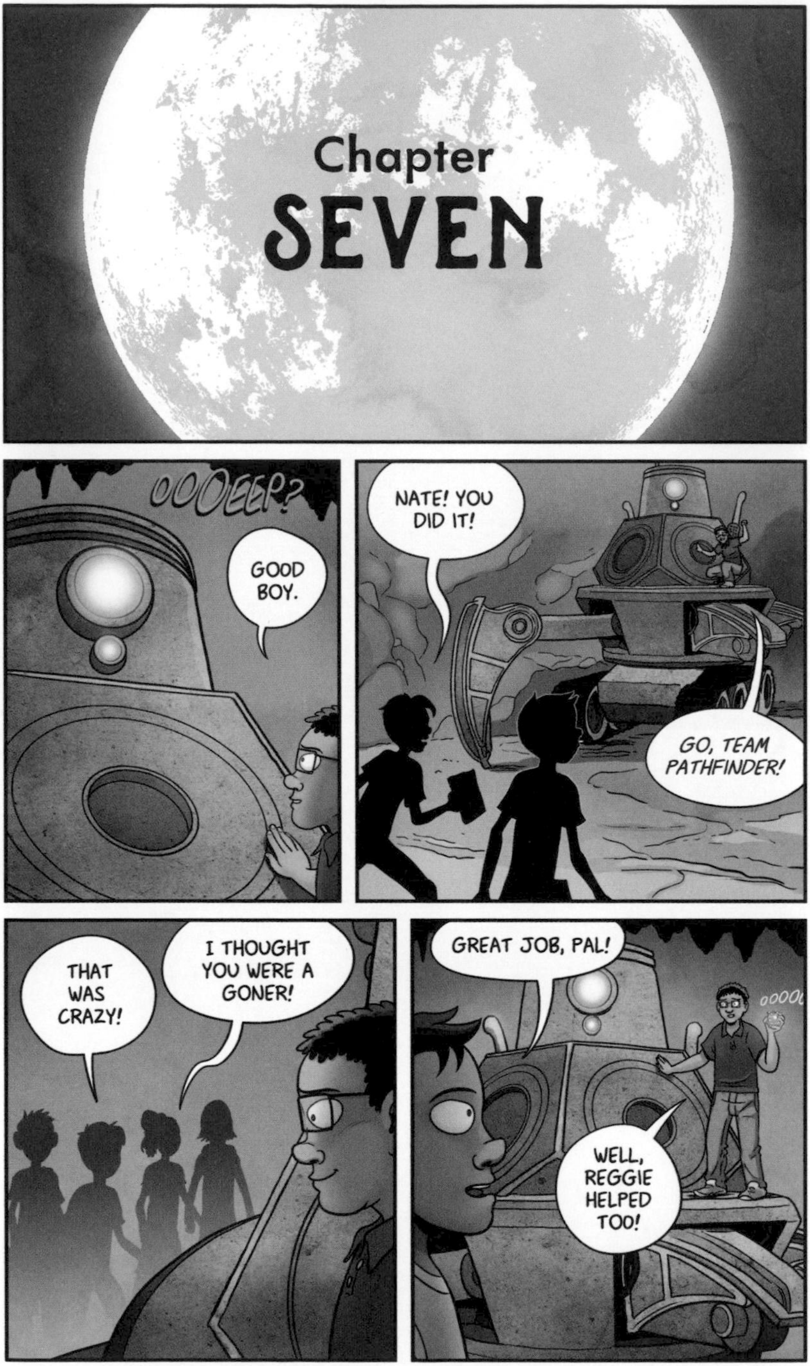
Chapter
SEVEN
OOOEEP?
GOOD BOY.
NATE! YOU DID IT!
GO, TEAM PATHFINDER!
THAT WAS CRAZY!
I THOUGHT YOU WERE A GONER!
GREAT JOB, PAL!
WELL, REGGIE HELPED TOO!

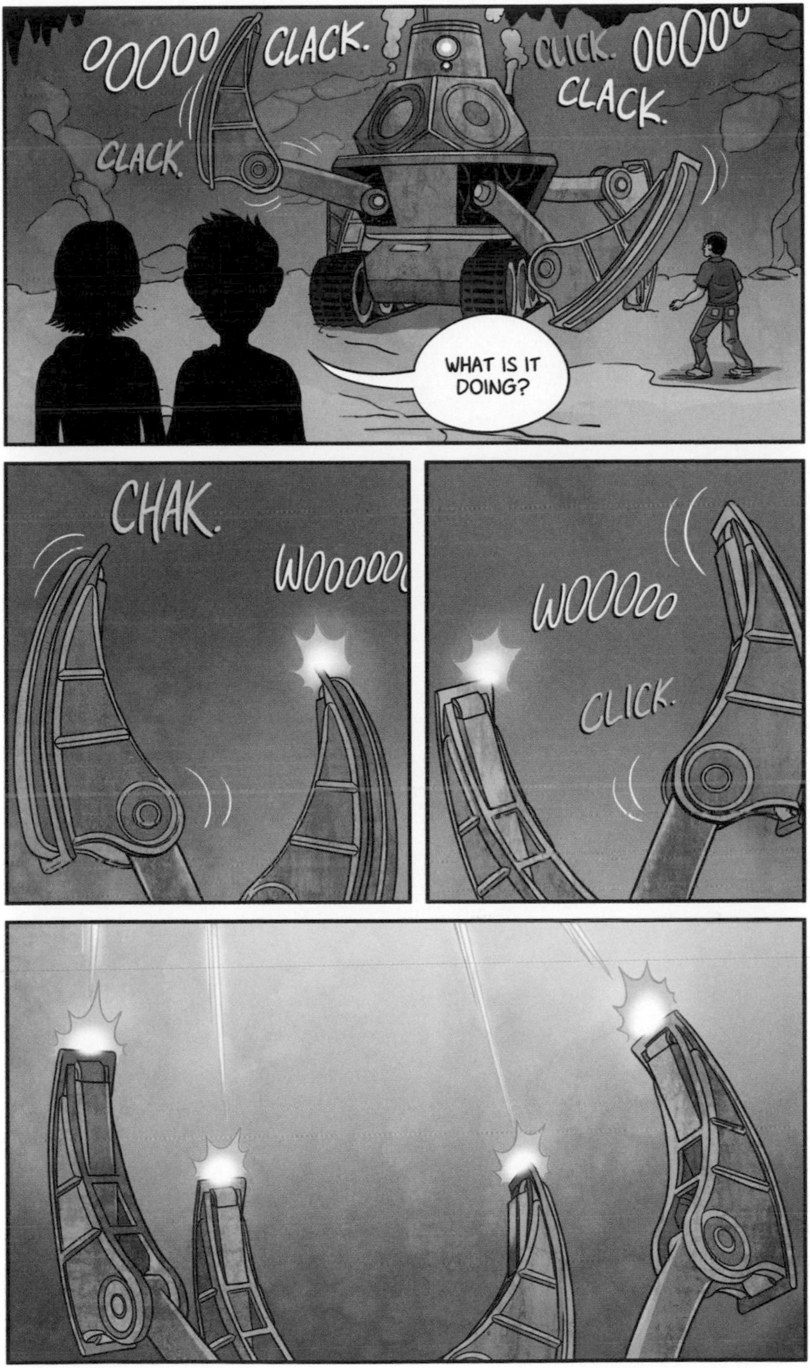
OOOOO
CLACK.
CLACK.
CLICK.
OOOOO
CLACK.
WHAT IS IT DOING?
CHAK.
WOOOOO
WOOOOO
CLICK.

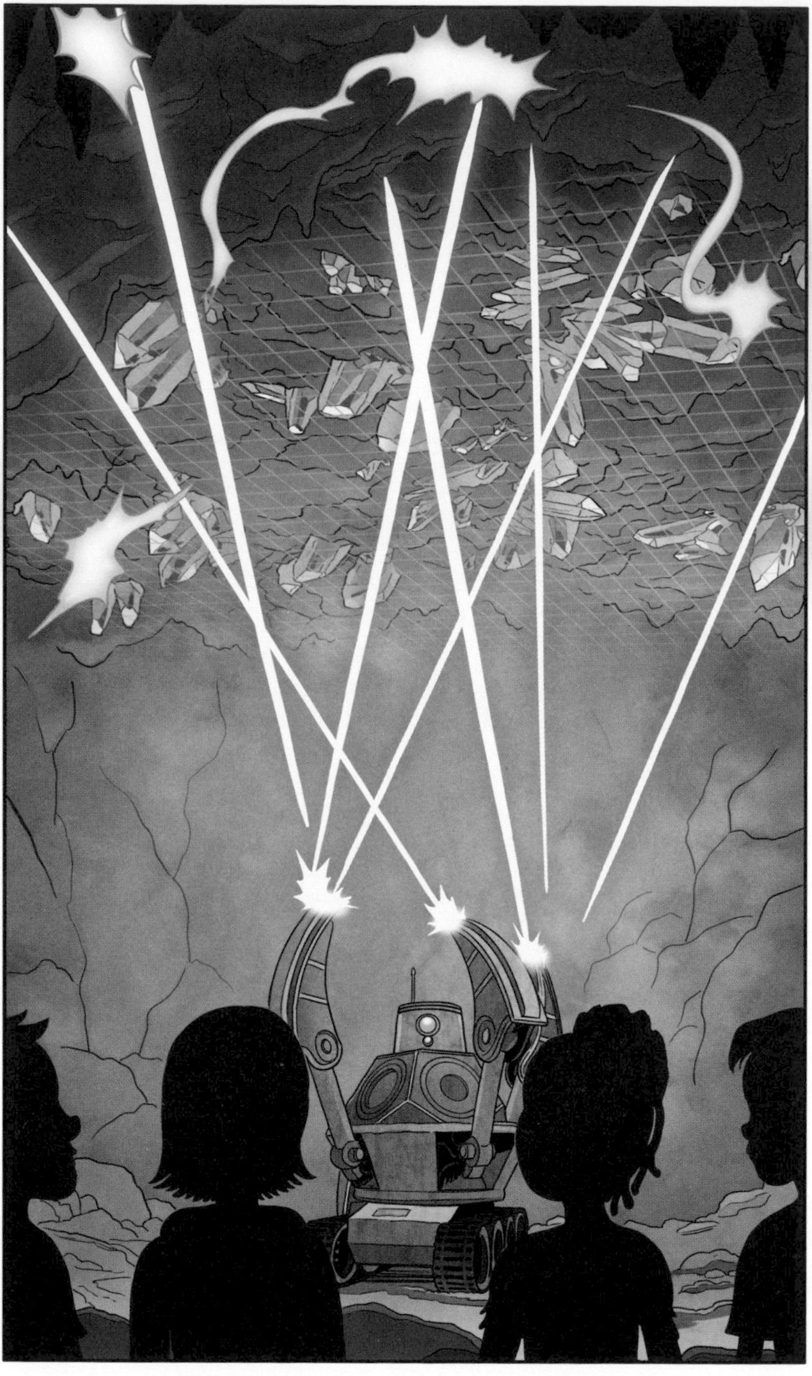

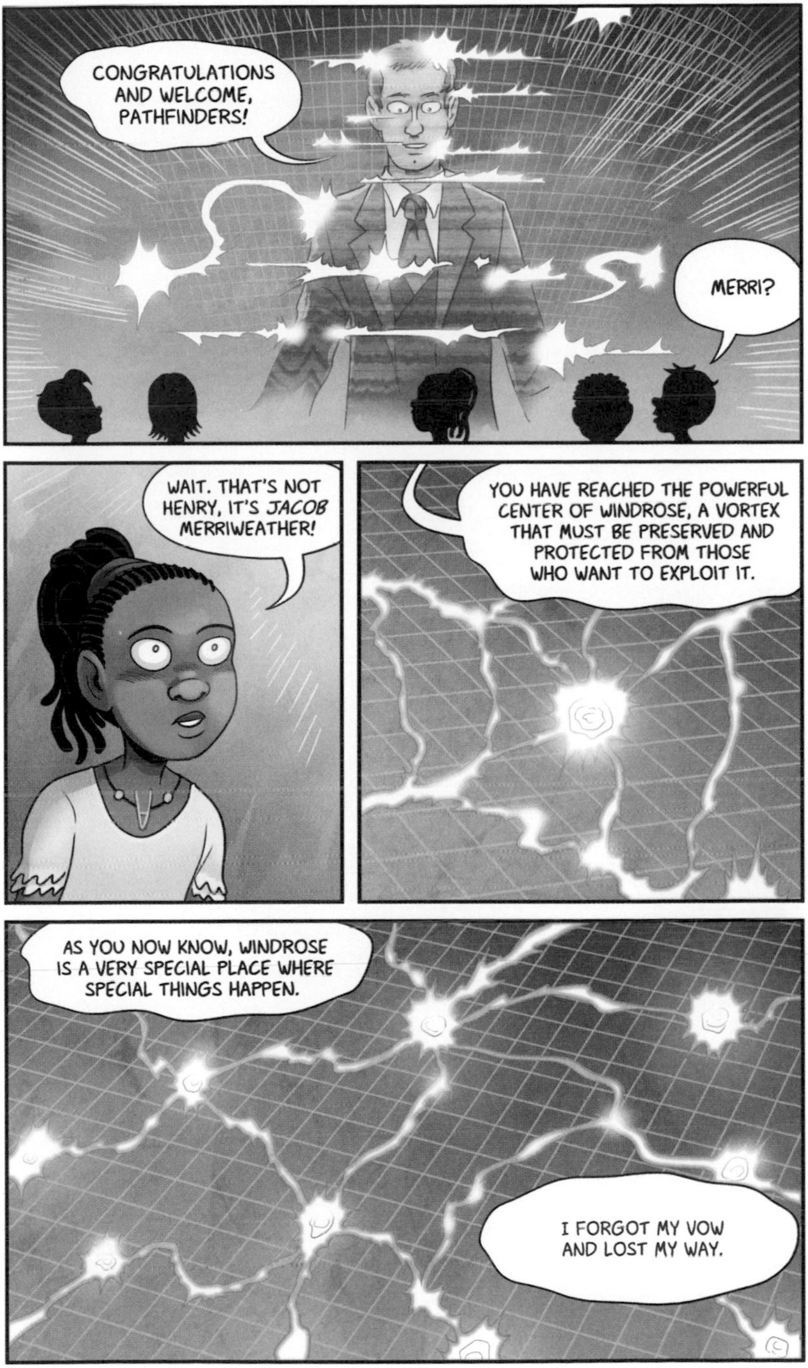
CONGRATULATIONS AND WELCOME, PATHFINDERS!
MERRI?
WAIT. THAT'S NOT HENRY, IT'S *JACOB* MERRIWEATHER!
YOU HAVE REACHED THE POWERFUL CENTER OF WINDROSE, A VORTEX THAT MUST BE PRESERVED AND PROTECTED FROM THOSE WHO WANT TO EXPLOIT IT.
AS YOU NOW KNOW, WINDROSE IS A VERY SPECIAL PLACE WHERE SPECIAL THINGS HAPPEN.
I FORGOT MY VOW AND LOST MY WAY.

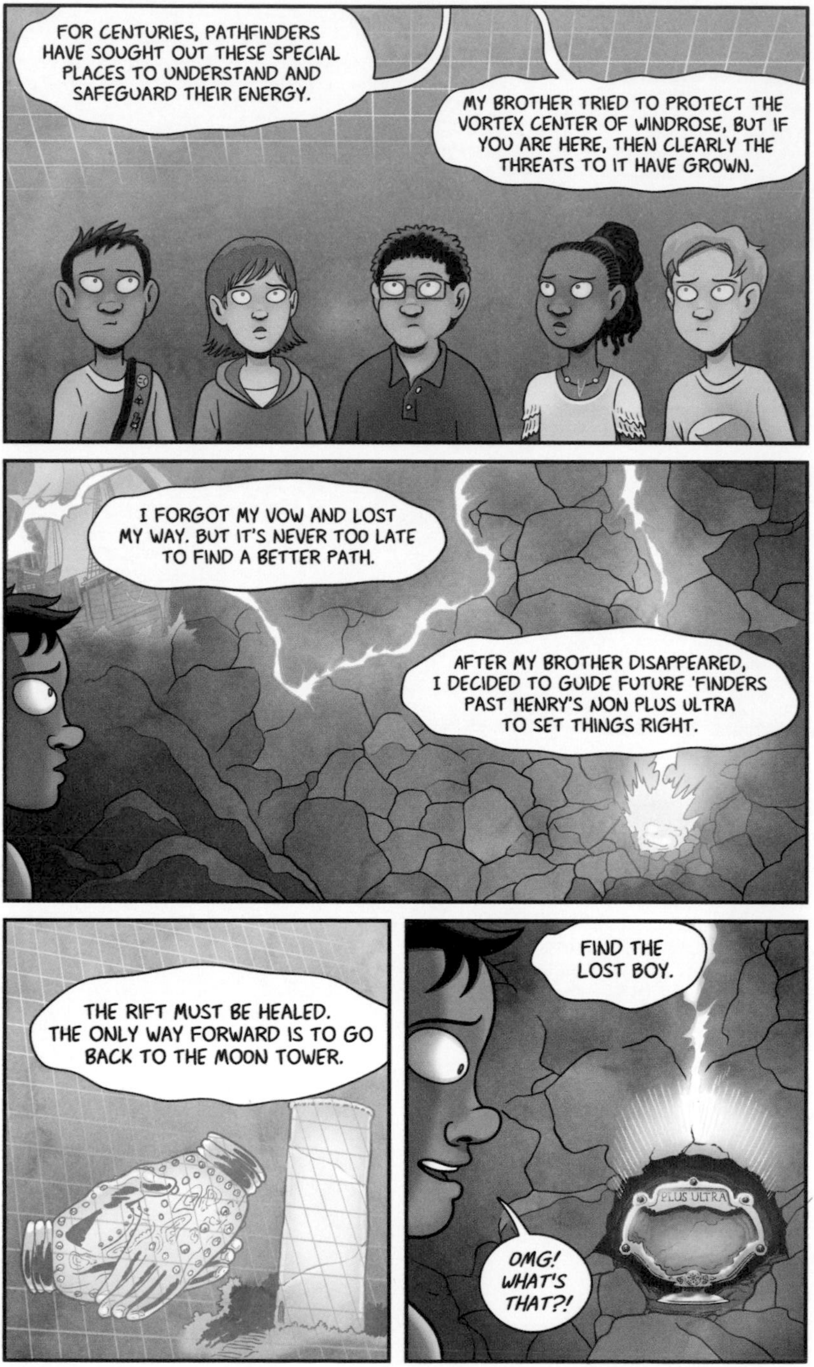
FOR CENTURIES, PATHFINDERS HAVE SOUGHT OUT THESE SPECIAL PLACES TO UNDERSTAND AND SAFEGUARD THEIR ENERGY.
MY BROTHER TRIED TO PROTECT THE VORTEX CENTER OF WINDROSE, BUT IF YOU ARE HERE, THEN CLEARLY THE THREATS TO IT HAVE GROWN.
I FORGOT MY VOW AND LOST MY WAY. BUT IT'S NEVER TOO LATE TO FIND A BETTER PATH.
AFTER MY BROTHER DISAPPEARED, I DECIDED TO GUIDE FUTURE 'FINDERS PAST HENRY'S NON PLUS ULTRA TO SET THINGS RIGHT.
THE RIFT MUST BE HEALED. THE ONLY WAY FORWARD IS TO GO BACK TO THE MOON TOWER.
FIND THE LOST BOY.
PLUS ULTRA
OMG! WHAT'S THAT?!

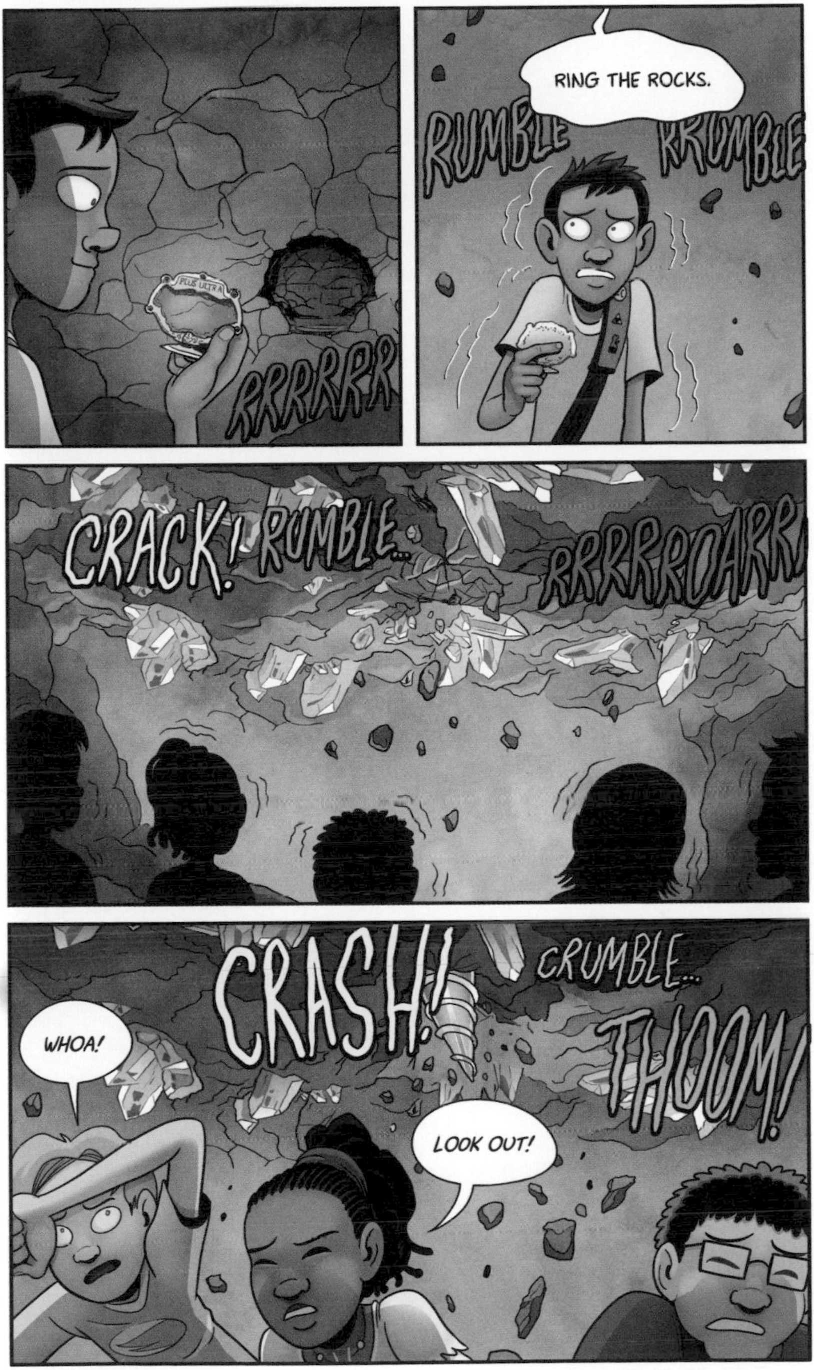
PLUS ULTRA
RRRRRRR
RING THE ROCKS.
RUMBLE
RRUMBLE
CRACK!
RUMBLE...
RRRRROARR
CRASH!
CRUMBLE...
THOOM!
WHOA!
LOOK OUT!

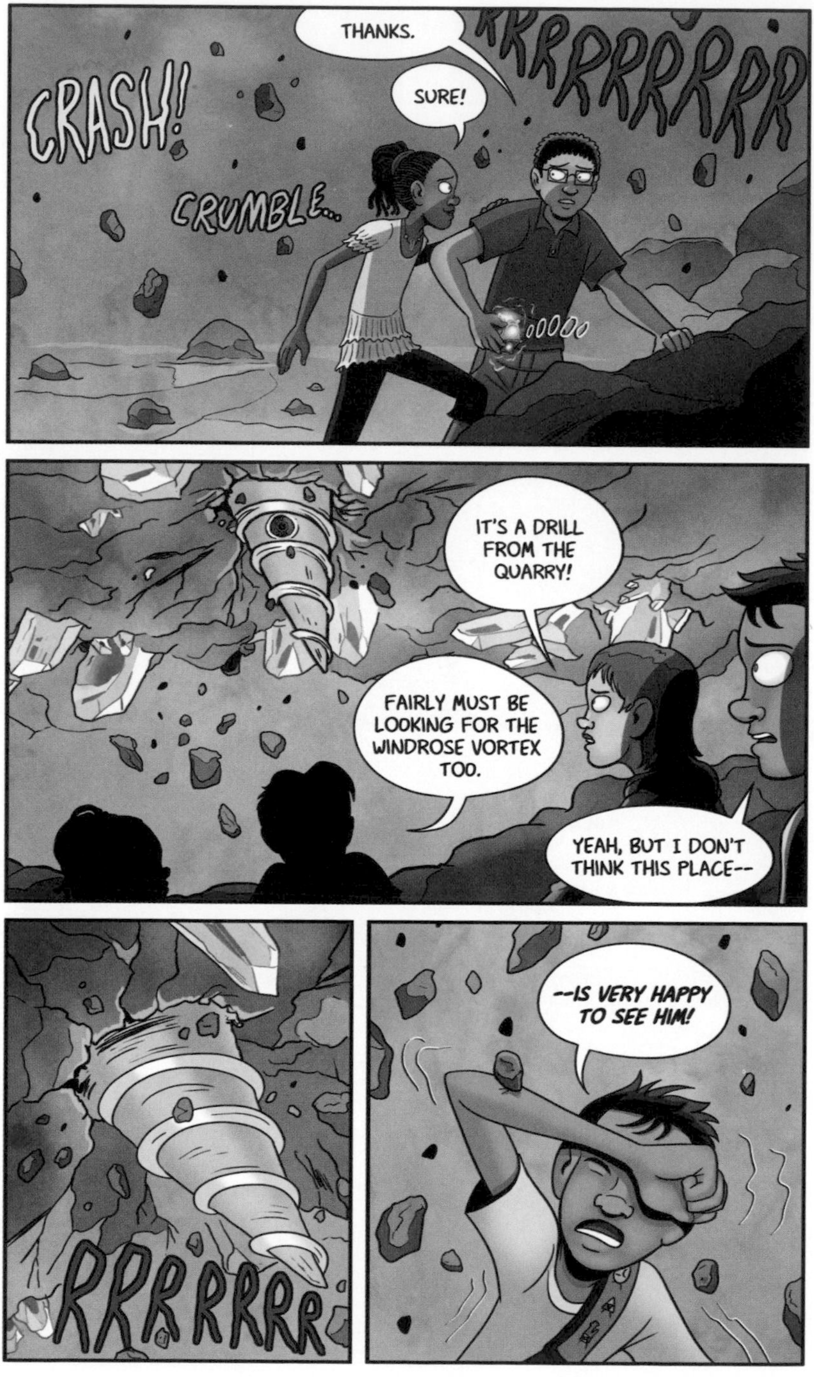
CRASH!
THANKS.
RRRRRRRRRR
SURE!
CRUMBLE...
OOOOO
IT'S A DRILL FROM THE QUARRY!
FAIRLY MUST BE LOOKING FOR THE WINDROSE VORTEX TOO.
YEAH, BUT I DON'T THINK THIS PLACE--
RRRRRRRR
--IS VERY HAPPY TO SEE HIM!

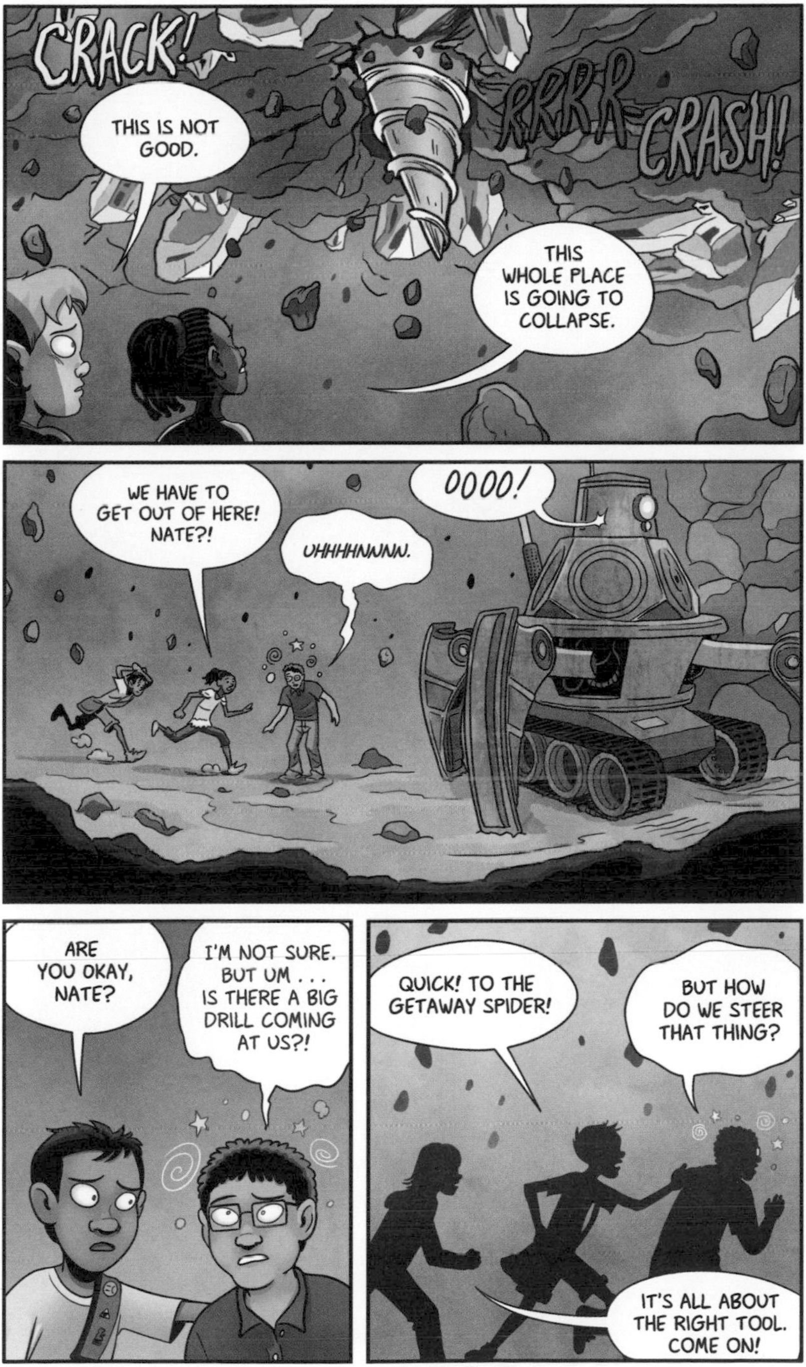
CRACK!
THIS IS NOT GOOD.
RRRR-CRASH!
THIS WHOLE PLACE IS GOING TO COLLAPSE.
WE HAVE TO GET OUT OF HERE! NATE?!
OOOO!
UHHHHNNNN.
ARE YOU OKAY, NATE?
I'M NOT SURE. BUT UM . . . IS THERE A BIG DRILL COMING AT US?!
QUICK! TO THE GETAWAY SPIDER!
BUT HOW DO WE STEER THAT THING?
IT'S ALL ABOUT THE RIGHT TOOL. COME ON!

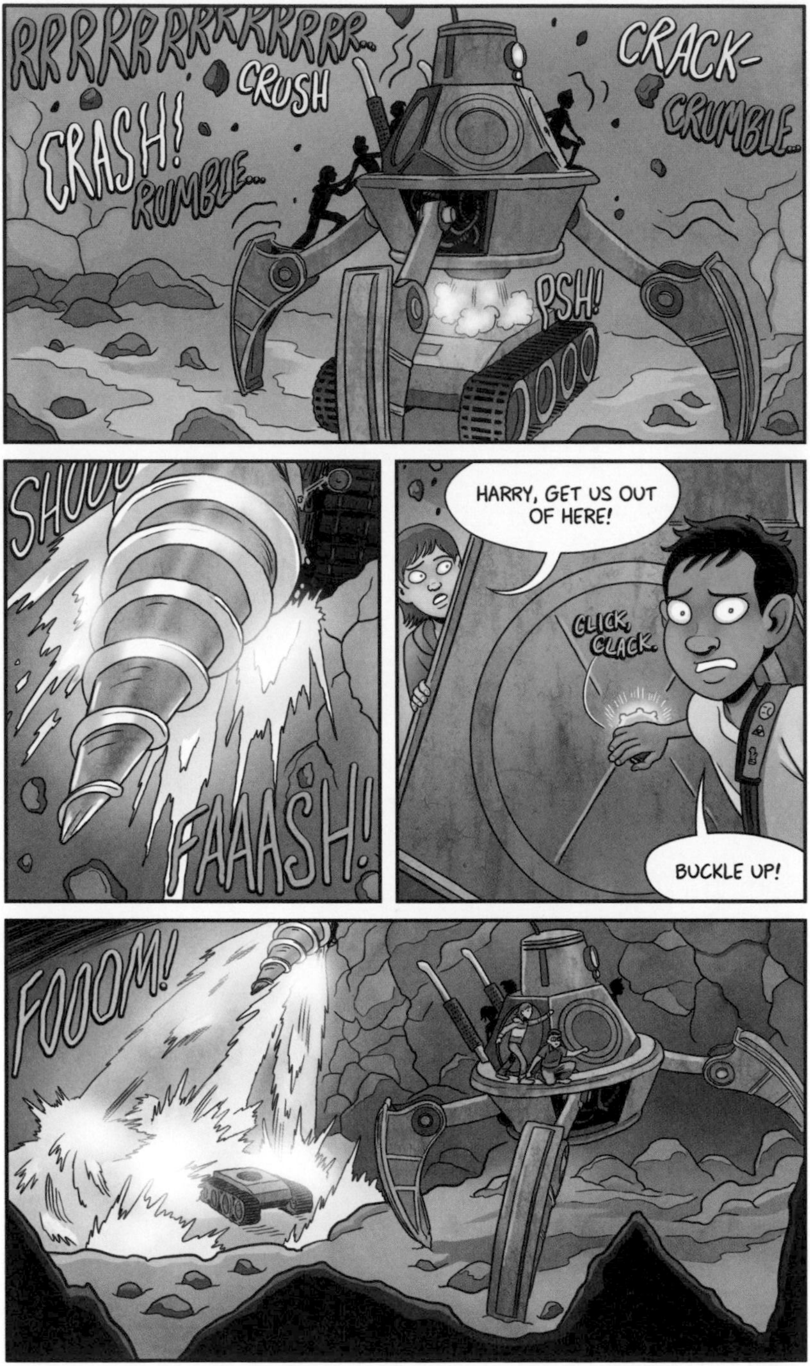
RRRRRRRRRRRRR...
CRUSH
CRASH!
RUMBLE...
CRACK-
CRUMBLE...
PSH!
SHOOO
FAAASH!
HARRY, GET US OUT OF HERE!
CLICK, CLACK.
BUCKLE UP!
FOOOM!

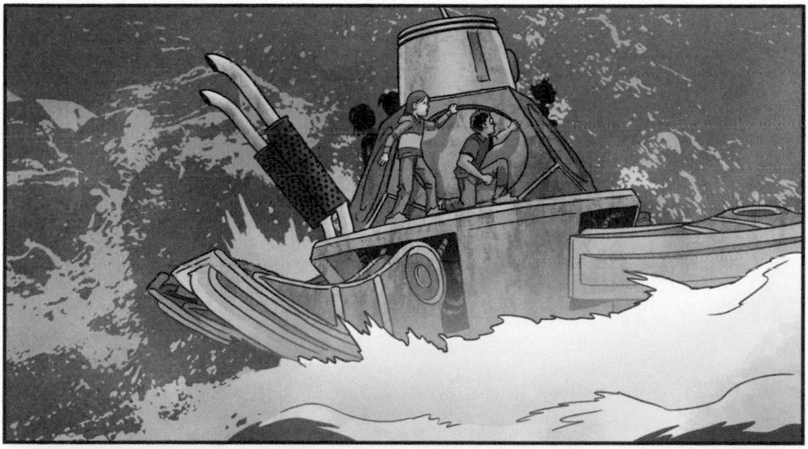

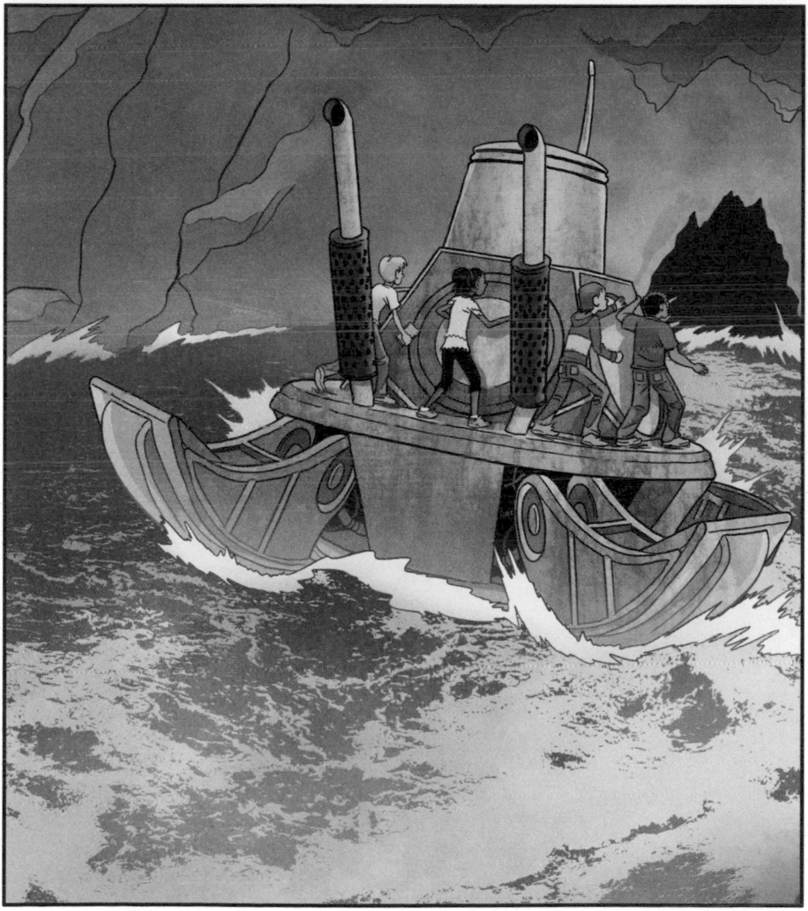

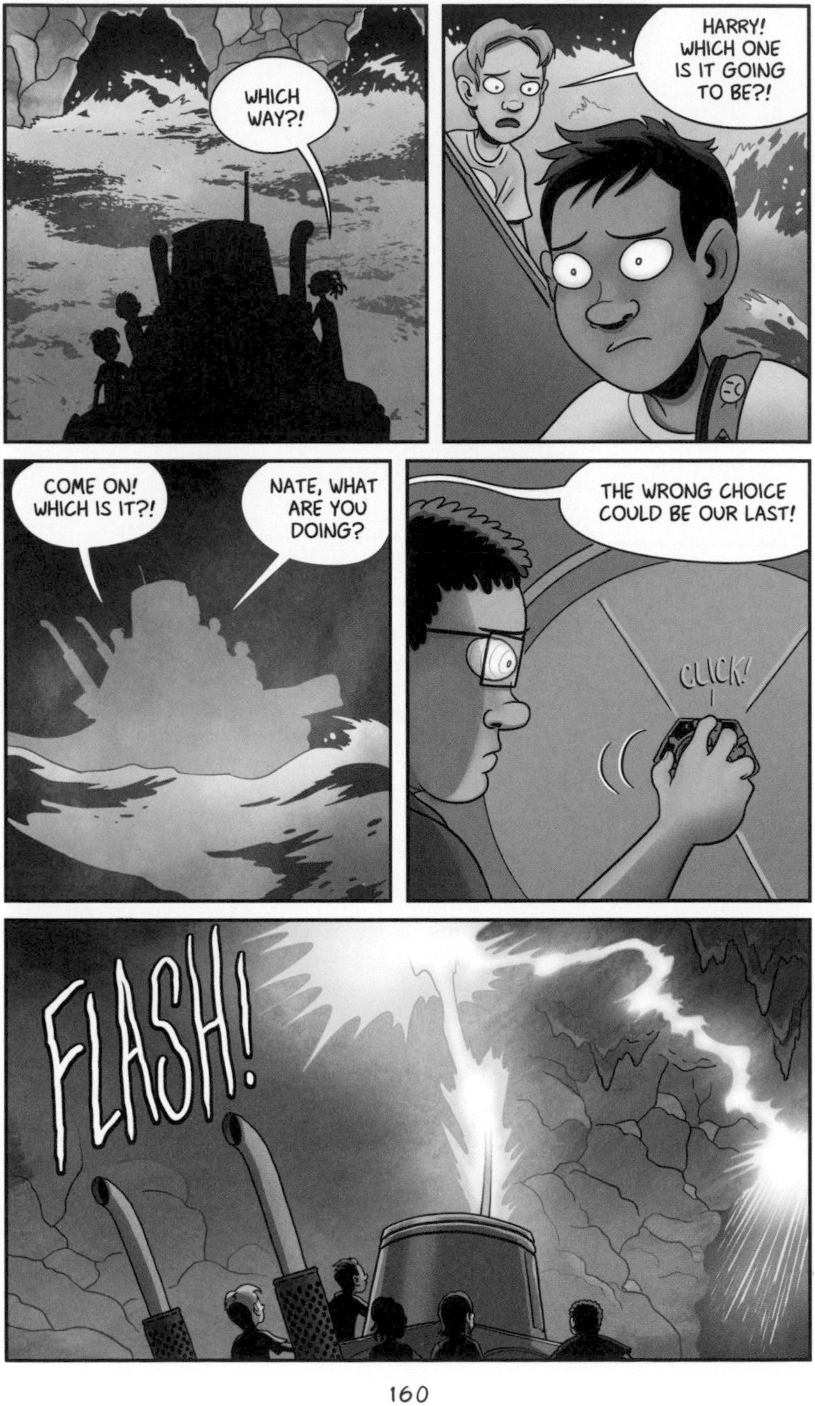
WHICH WAY?!
HARRY! WHICH ONE IS IT GOING TO BE?!
COME ON! WHICH IS IT?!
NATE, WHAT ARE YOU DOING?
THE WRONG CHOICE COULD BE OUR LAST!
CLICK!
FLASH!

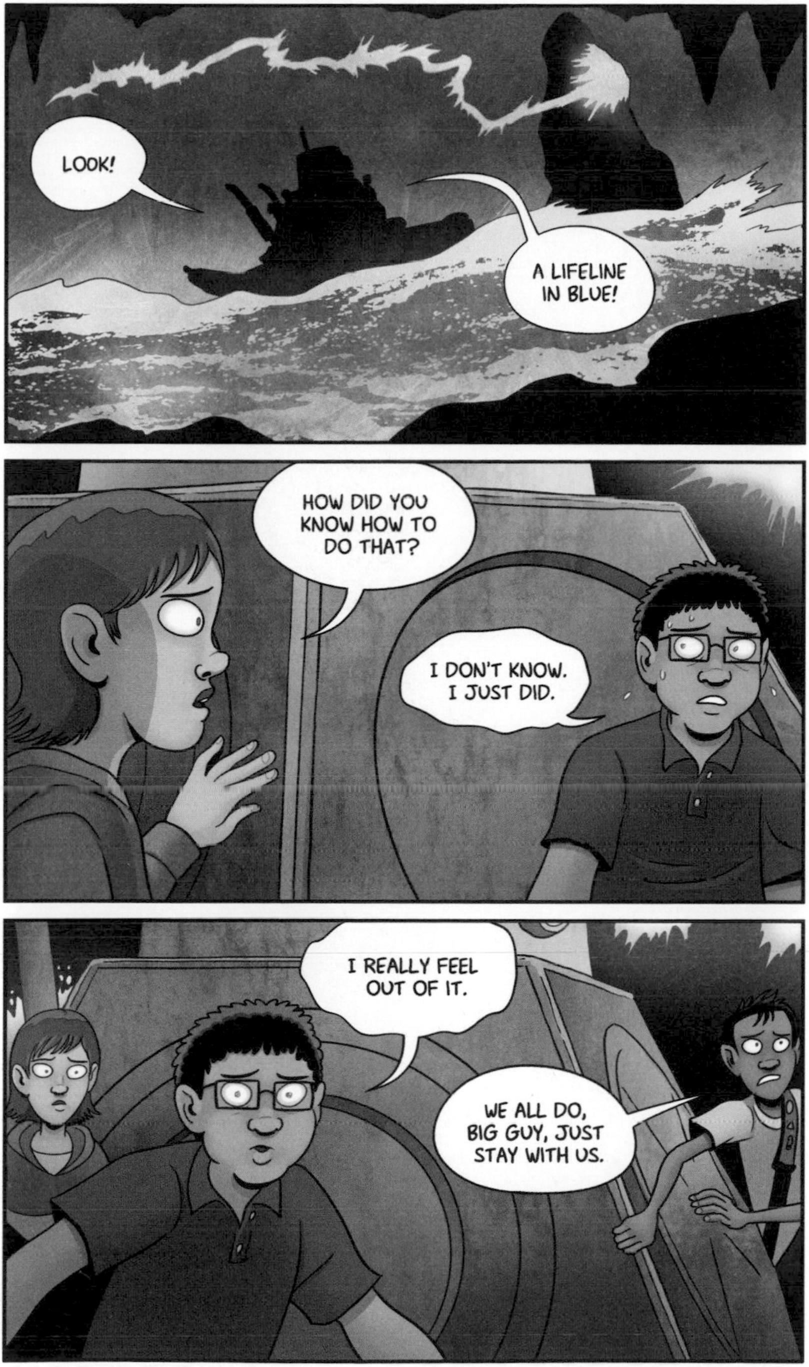
LOOK!
A LIFELINE IN BLUE!
HOW DID YOU KNOW HOW TO DO THAT?
I DON'T KNOW. I JUST DID.
I REALLY FEEL OUT OF IT.
WE ALL DO, BIG GUY, JUST STAY WITH US.

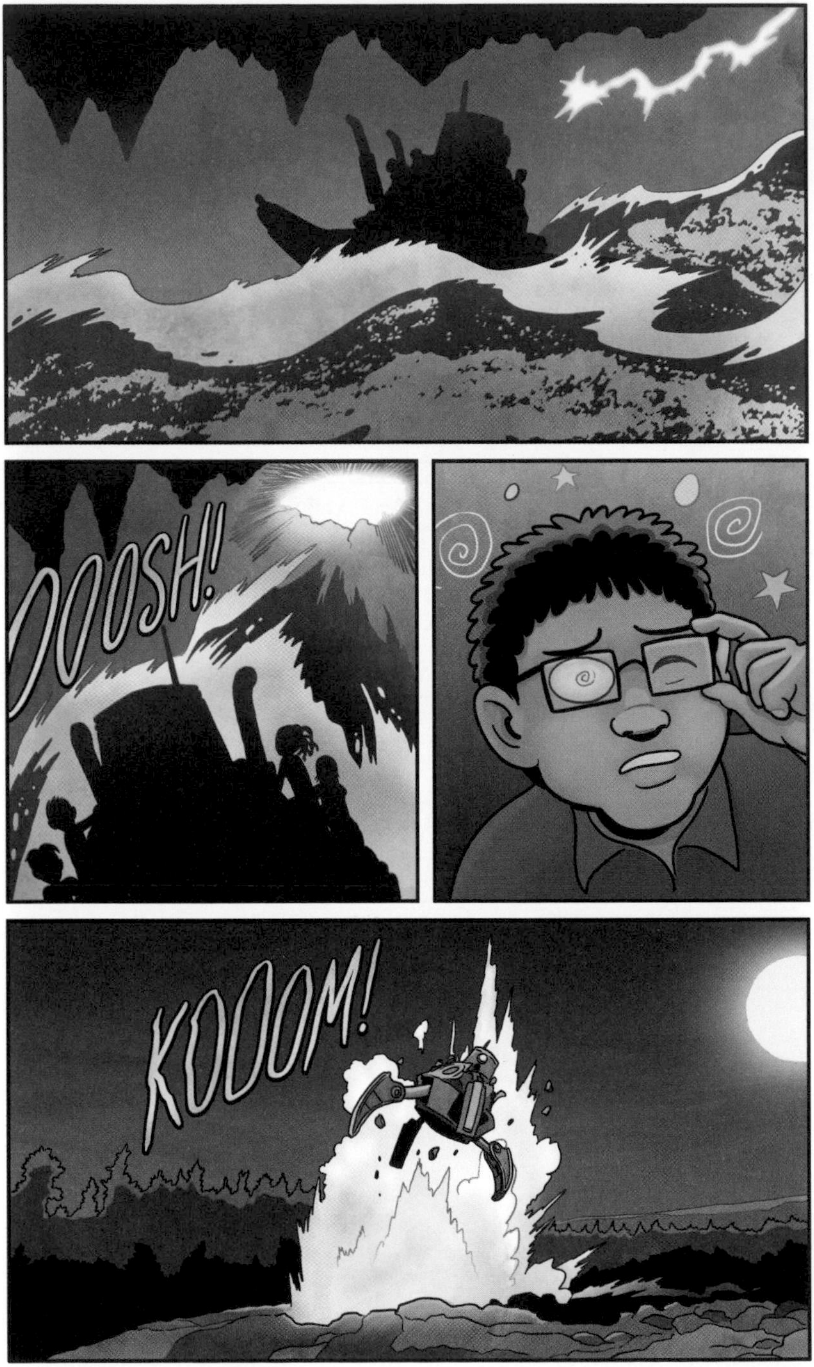
OOOSH!
KOOOM!

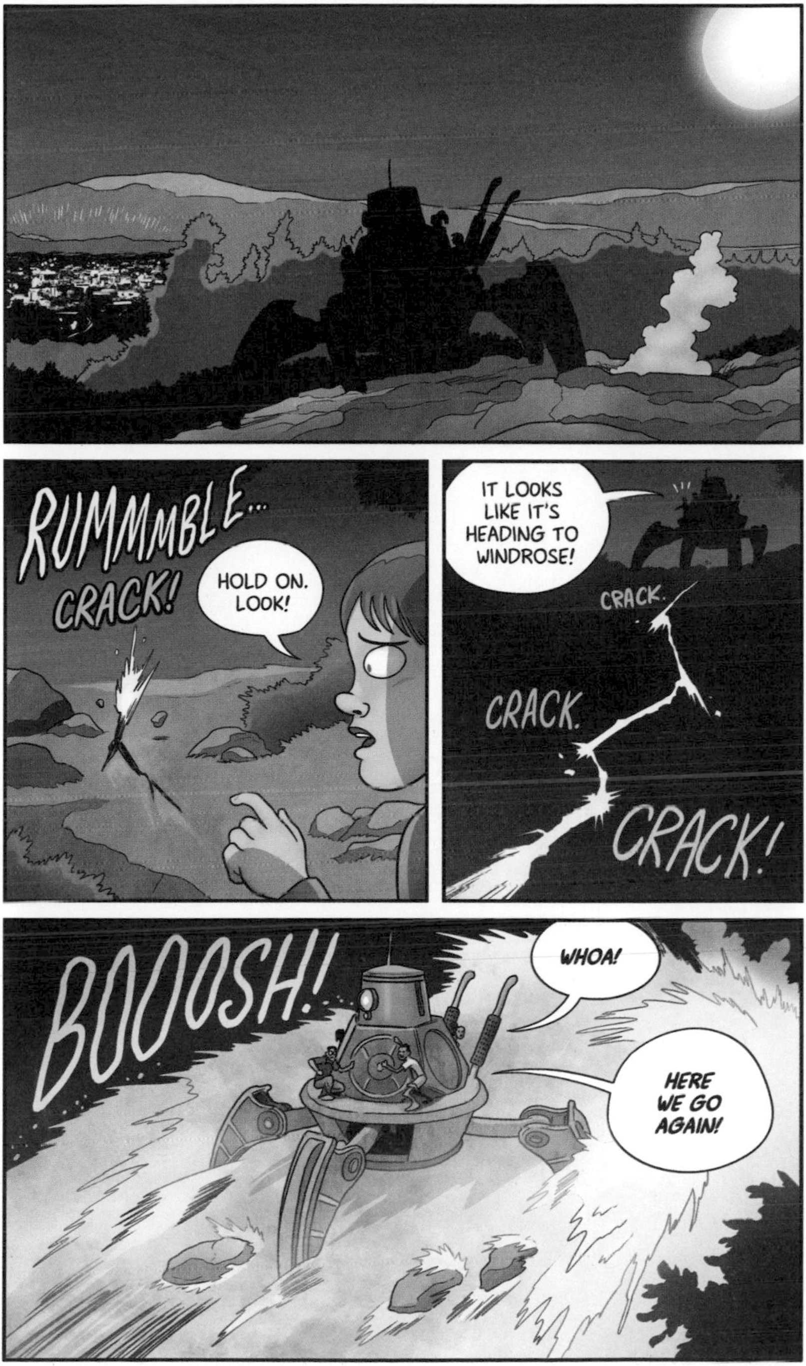
RUMMMBLE...
CRACK!
HOLD ON. LOOK!
IT LOOKS LIKE IT'S HEADING TO WINDROSE!
CRACK.
CRACK.
CRACK!
BOOOSH!
WHOA!
HERE WE GO AGAIN!

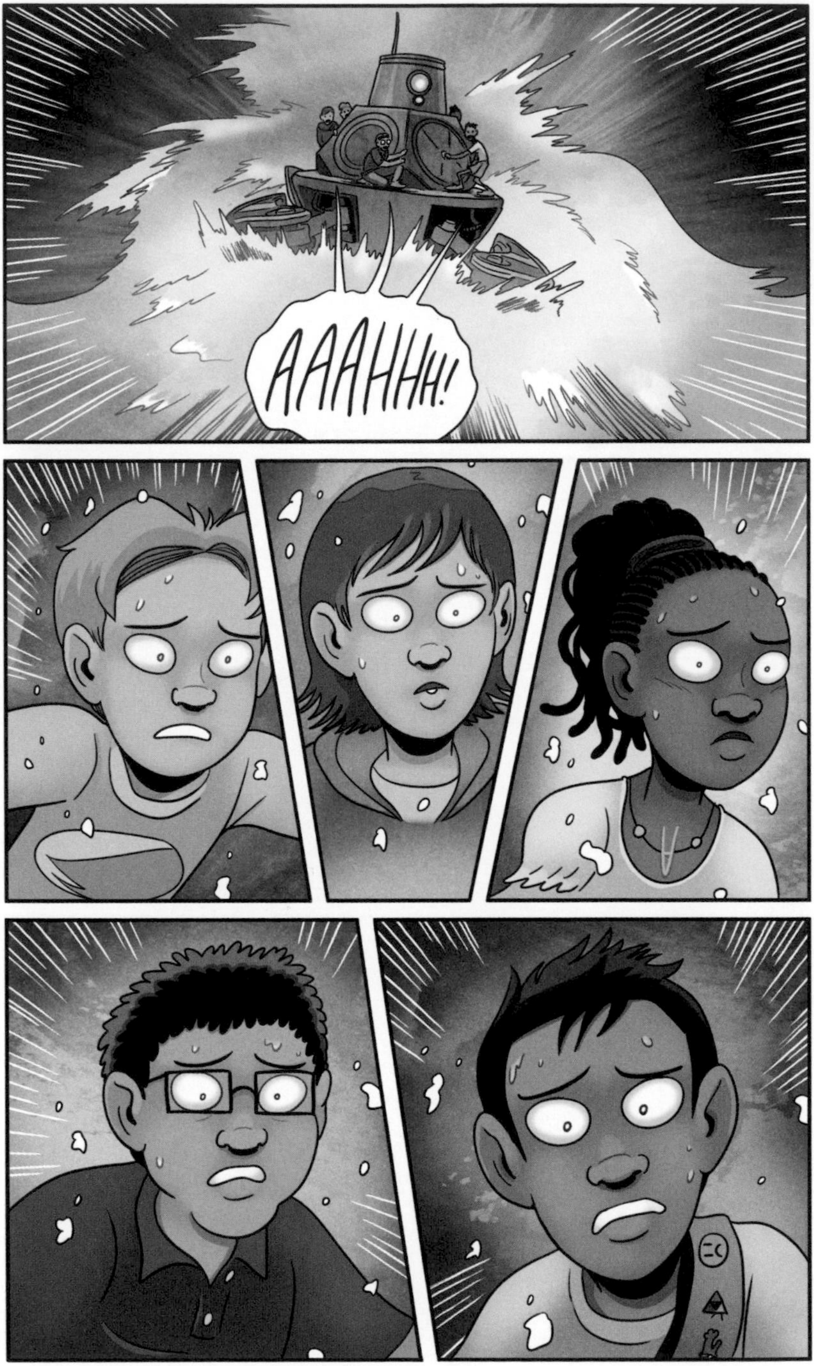
AAAHHH!

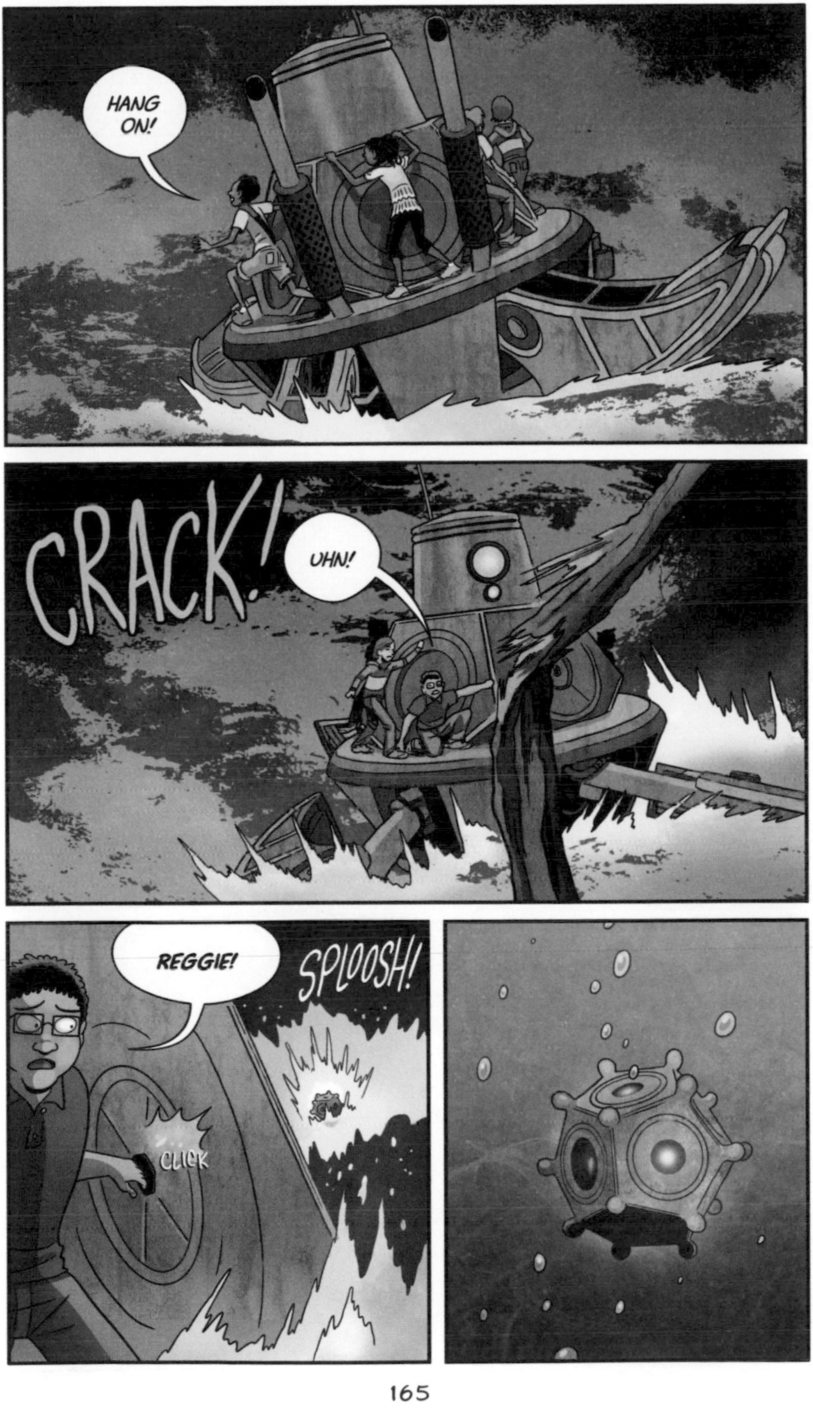
HANG ON!
CRACK!
UHN!
REGGIE!
SPLOOSH!
CLICK

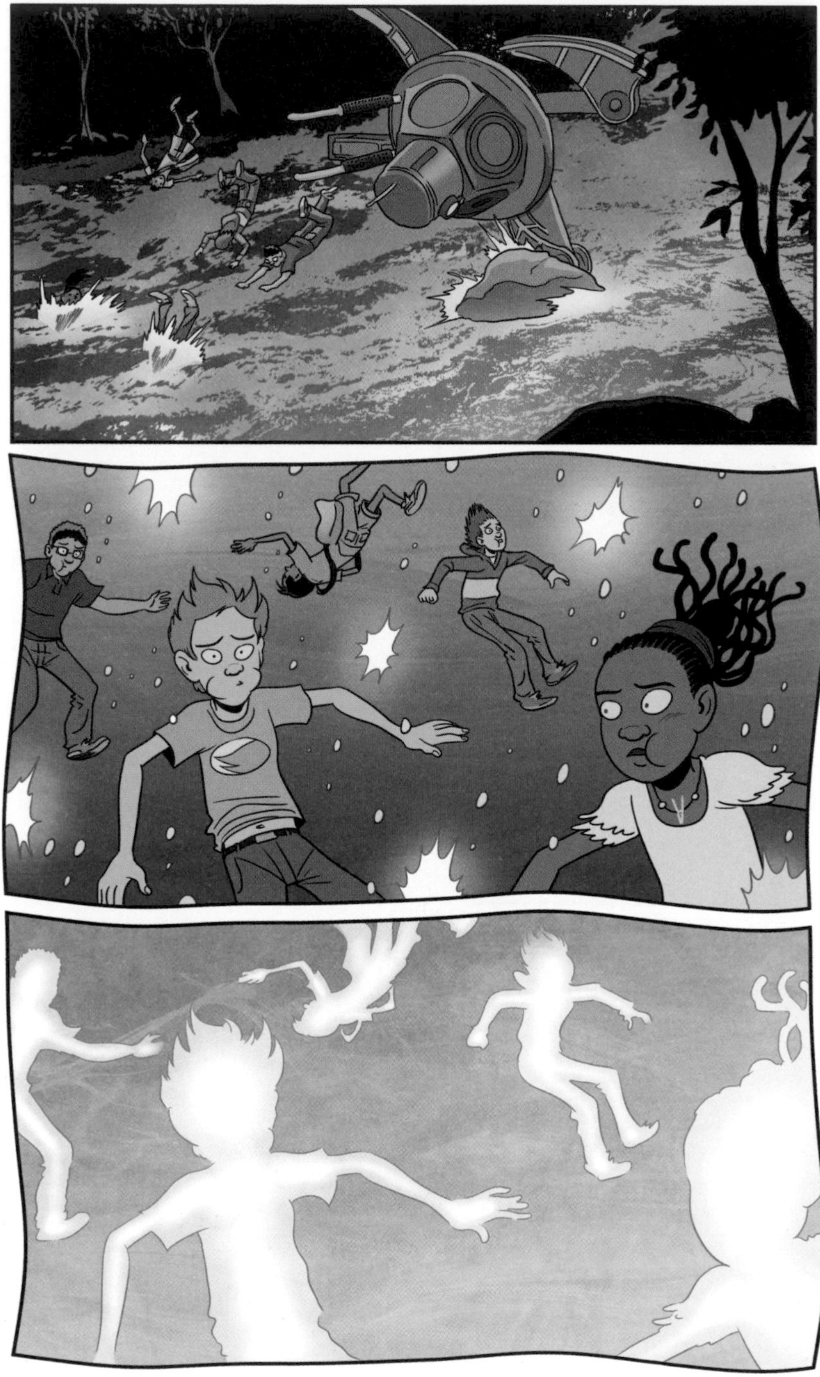

[redacted]

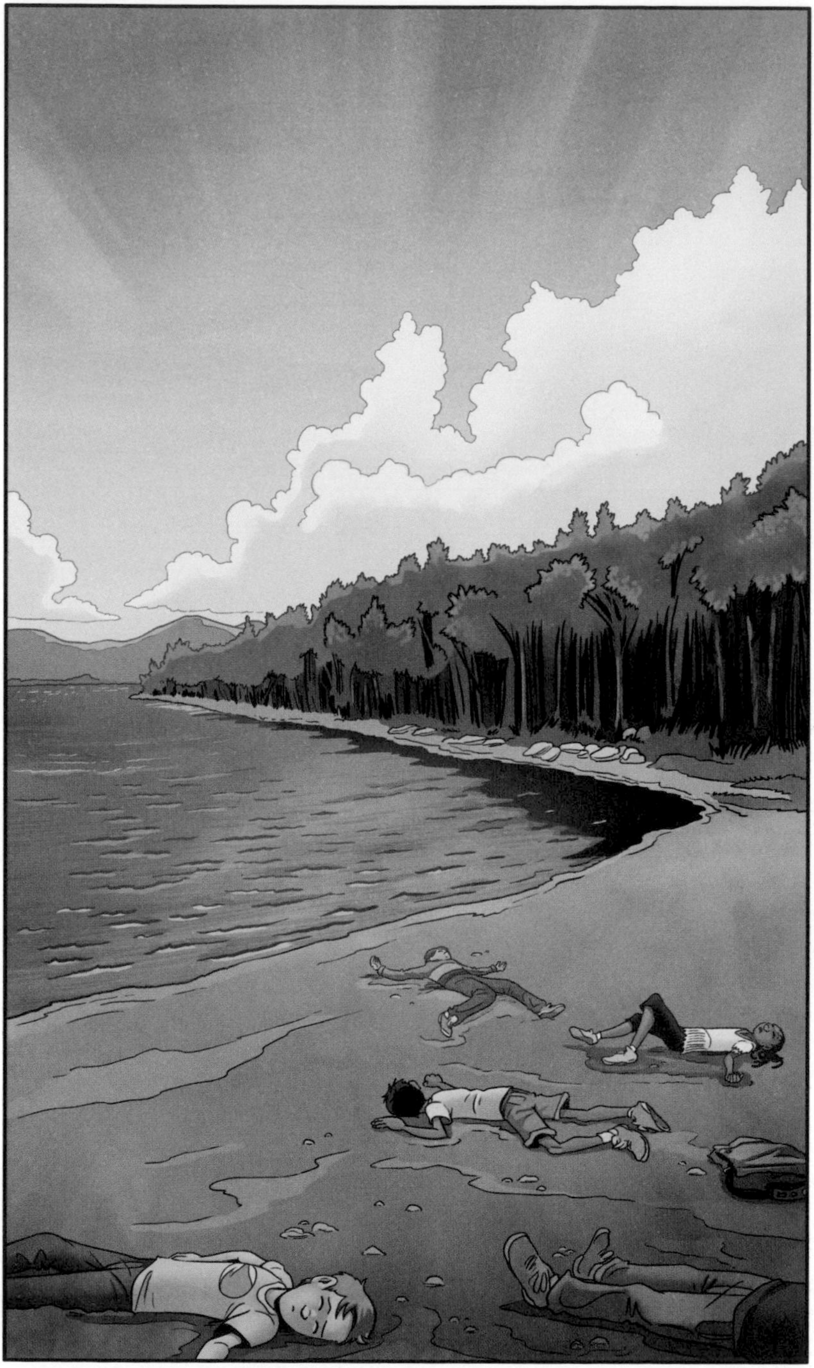

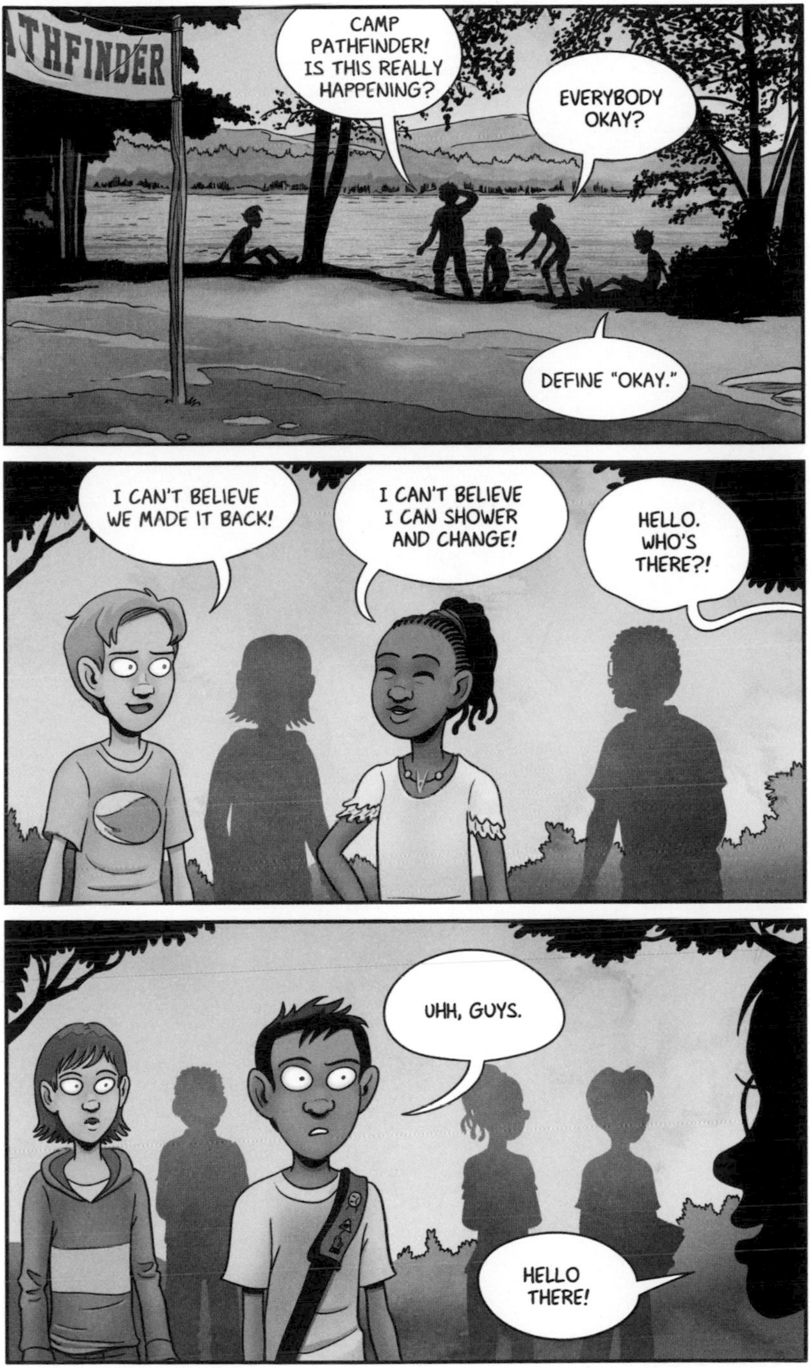
ATHFINDER
CAMP PATHFINDER! IS THIS REALLY HAPPENING?
EVERYBODY OKAY?
DEFINE "OKAY."
I CAN'T BELIEVE WE MADE IT BACK!
I CAN'T BELIEVE I CAN SHOWER AND CHANGE!
HELLO. WHO'S THERE?!
UHH, GUYS.
HELLO THERE!

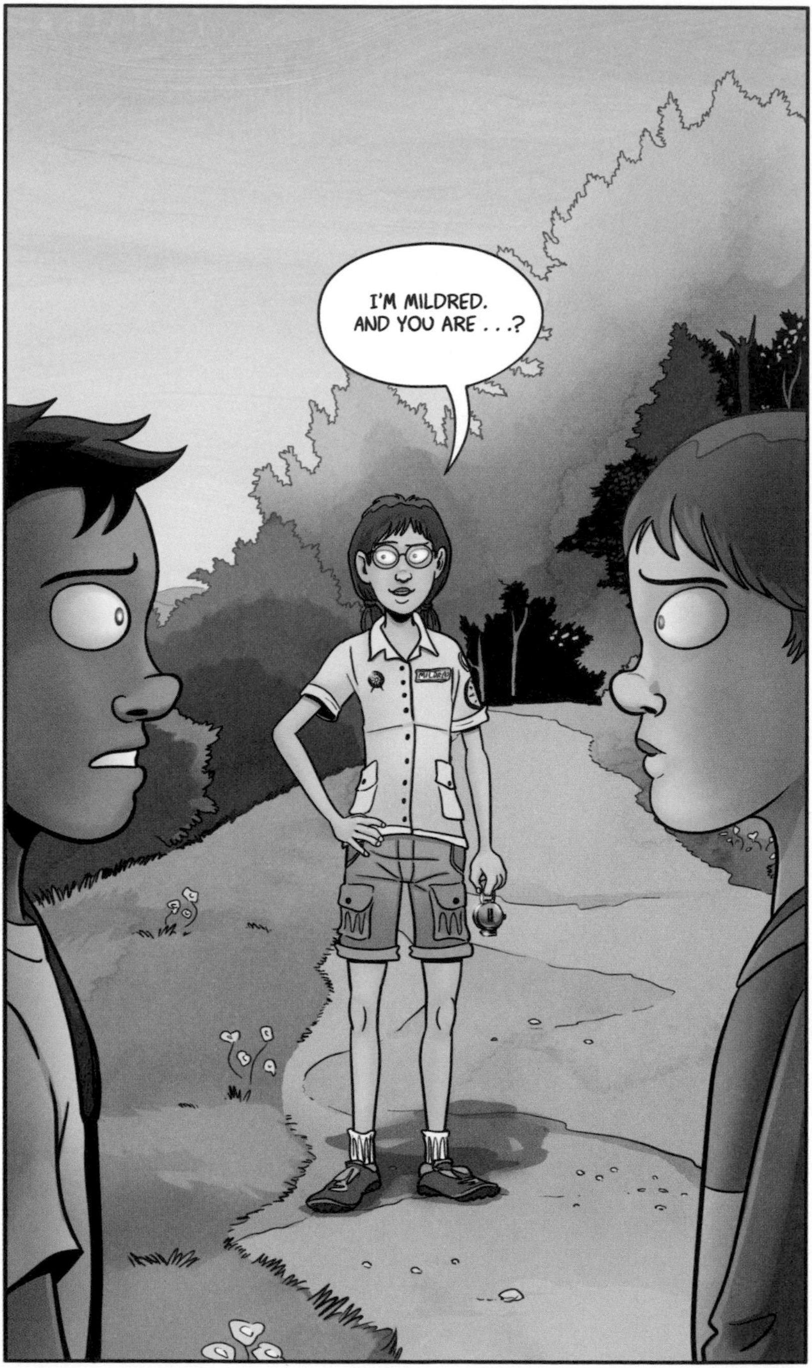
I'M MILDRED.
AND YOU ARE . . .?

To Be
Continued...

Meet the Author

FRANCESCO SEDITA likes to make lots of things, and this book is one of them. Other things he has created are the Miss Popularity book series, the Emmy Award–winning *The Who Was? Show* on Netflix (which he made with his co-author Prescott Seraydarian), as well as lots of other books in his job at Penguin Young Readers, like Mad Libs, WhoHQ bestsellers, and other books with amazing authors like Henry Winkler, Lin Oliver, Giada De Laurentiis, and even Dolly Parton.

When he isn't making stuff, Francesco is cooking in his apartment in New York City or binge-watching a series with his husband or playing with their cute cat, Alfredo. Visit him at francescosedita.com.

Meet the Author

PRESCOTT SERAYDARIAN loves stories and always has. When he was a kid, he wrote stories about himself (and his entire neighborhood!) embarking on endless adventures. That led to *telling* stories as a grown-up with amazing partners like Disney, Penguin, NBC, and Netflix, through his award-winning film company Lunch Productions.

Now he has the best job of all as a film teacher at George School, a Quaker boarding school in Newtown, Pennsylvania. Every day, he gets to teach students (just a little older than the Pathfinders!) skills to share their own stories. Prescott lives at his school with his wife, two daughters, and lovable pup named Asher. Check him out at PrescottSeraydarian.com.

Meet the Artist

STEVE HAMAKER is the Eisner Award–winning colorist of bestselling graphic novel series such as Bone by Jeff Smith and Hilo by Judd Winick. He has also colored online comics series and created his own original web comic, *PLOX*. An avid table-top and video gamer, Steve lives in Columbus, Ohio, with his wife and son. Follow him on Twitter @SteveHamaker.